Seven Years' Travel in Central America

SALZWASSER
VERLAG

Julius Froebel

Seven Years' Travel in Central America

Reprint of the original, first published in 1859.

1st Edition 2022 | ISBN: 978-3-37512-008-5

Verlag (Publisher): Salzwasser Verlag GmbH, Zeilweg 44, 60439 Frankfurt, Deutschland
Vertretungsberechtigt (Authorized to represent): E. Roepke, Zeilweg 44, 60439 Frankfurt, Deutschland
Druck (Print): Books on Demand GmbH, In de Tarpen 42, 22848 Norderstedt, Deutschland

SEVEN YEARS' TRAVEL

IN

CENTRAL AMERICA,

NORTHERN MEXICO, AND THE FAR WEST OF THE UNITED STATES.

BY JULIUS FROEBEL.

WITH NUMEROUS ILLUSTRATIONS.

LONDON:
RICHARD BENTLEY,
Publisher in Ordinary to Her Majesty.

DESERTED M

CONTENTS.

BOOK I.

RAMBLES IN NICARAGUA, &c.

CHAPTER I.

CHAPTER II.

CHAPTER III.

CHAPTER IV.

CHAPTER V.

CHAPTER VI.

CHAPTER VII.

CHAPTER VIII.

CHAPTER IX.

CHAPTER X.

CHAPTER XI.

CHAPTER XII.

BOOK II.

JOURNEY TO THE NORTH OF MEXICO, &c.

CHAPTER I.

CHAPTER II.

CHAPTER III.

CHAPTER IV.

CHAPTER V.

CHAPTER VI.

CHAPTER VII.

CHAPTER VIII.

CHAPTER IX.

CHAPTER X.

CHAPTER XI.

CHAPTER XII.

CHAPTER XIII.

BOOK III.

JOURNEY FROM TEXAS TO CALIFORNIA, &c.

CHAPTER I.

CHAPTER II.

CHAPTER III.

CHAPTER IV.

CHAPTER V.

CHAPTER VI.

CHAPTER VII.

LIST OF ILLUSTRATIONS.

Book I.

RAMBLES AND OBSERVATIONS

IN

NICARAGUA, UPPER MOSQUITIA,

AND ON THE SHORES OF

THE GULF OF HONDURAS.

TRAVELS IN CENTRAL AMERICA,

&c. &c.

CHAPTER I.

Departure from New York — At Sea — Chagres — The American Town and the Town of the Natives — Features of Life — San Juan del Norte — Situation and Vicissitudes in the recent History of the Town — Elements of Population.

In 1850, the project of constructing a ship canal across the Nicaraguan isthmus was generally believed to be near its speedy realization. A corps of engineers had been sent to that country for the execution of the necessary surveys, and a favourable report was expected. Nicaragua appeared to me in the attractive light of a region about to become the theatre of an important movement in civilization, and my interest in the country was excited in a sufficient degree to induce me to visit it.

Accordingly, I took passage in a brig lying in the port of New York, and destined to Chagres and San Juan del Norte. We sailed on the 28th of September. Calms, squalls and thunder-storms made the voyage tedious, though for these annoyances I found a kind of compensation in the various scenes and aspects which nature presented during the time. It is difficult to give an idea of the magic beauty of some of the sunsets I witnessed in the Caribbean Sea on this occasion. One evening the whole western sky was of the deepest vermilion. Golden threads, as if of a metallic web, were spun over its surface. Northward and southward the burning red, with a transition through all gradations of carmine, purple, violet, and indigo, ultimately passed into brown. Here and there, like the unveiled portion of an upper sky, some ethereal region beamed through between the more earthly colours of the lower atmosphere, and appeared in a bluish green of the softest hue. Broad rays of light, of alternating gold and azure, diverging from the sun's place behind the horizon and extending towards the zenith, passed over the whole picture like the transparent radii of a gigantic fan. Fleecy clouds, resembling rose-tinged veils, hung over us, while sails and masts were steeped in the mellow tints of a delicate lilac, which, in different shades, dyed the northern half of the firmament. The next morning exhibited a picture of similar beauty and interest. An arch of flaky clouds of a dark olive colour, with glowing edges of gold, was stretched over a wide clear expanse of the western sky. In the centre of this bright semicircle thick masses of a dark violet, resting on the sharp outline of the ocean, were piled up in strange forms. From west to east, on either side, the horizon passed through every shade of violet and blue, the gradual transition here and there interrupted by dusky piles of a brownish green. A veil of pale lilac was thrown from the zenith towards the east, the form of the moon glimmering through the delicate tissue.

On the 5th of November, towards the evening, the mountains of the Isthmus of Panamá came in sight:—isolated cones of a truncated form. On the next morning a hilly coast extended before us, showing a long line of country covered with forest, and a chain of mountains in the rear. By-and-bye the castle of San Lorenzo, rising above the mouth of the Rio de los Lagardos, became visible; a few hours later we anchored on the roadstead at its base, and on the following morning we succeeded in safely entering the river, where we moored our brig close to the bank, just in front of the frame buildings which constituted the so-called "American" part of *Chagres*. The reader, I suppose, is aware that throughout America the term "*American*" is almost exclusively applied to the people of the United States,—a practice by which the "manifest destiny" of that compound of the most active elements of the present generation of mankind is thoughtlessly recognized even by those who are most immediately threatened by it,—for in all Spanish-American countries "*los Americanos*" means the people of the great northern republic.

This "American town" of Chagres, then, which most likely has ceased to exist since the opening of the Panamá railroad, when Aspinwall has taken its place as the Atlantic terminus of the isthmus route, was situated on the left bank of the river, while on the opposite side, in a nook formed by the hill of San Lorenzo, stood the "*village of the natives*," which, as it existed before the time of Californian travel, may be supposed to have outlived its go-ahead rival, and to be still the home of a few families.

In choosing the place of the American settlement, the exclusive considerations of a reckless love of gain must have decided. In a locality known to be sickly in the highest degree, it was built on the water's edge, on a low and muddy ground. But it stood on the deep-water side of the river, and brigs and schooners could unload a few hundred steps from the houses. These had all been sent ready-made from New York. The most prominent among them was the *Irving House*—the principal "hotel" of the place. At New York I had seen it advertised and recommended as a superior establishment, "in whose spacious halls the traveller was sure to find the comforts and commodities of civilization as it exists in the temperate zone, combined with all the luxuries of the tropics." It was a large barn-like framehouse of two stories, each of them forming one single undivided room. In the lower story a hundred or more travellers, sitting on four long benches of rough boards on both sides of two long tables of the same material, were treated with salt pork and dried beans, while in the upper room several hundred persons, sick with fever, were either shaking from frost or burning in the paroxysm of heat, and those who were able to keep up were sitting on their boxes and trunks in order to secure them from being removed by the numerous thieves and robbers who at that time infested this dangerous highway of travelling adventurers. Between the mud-holes and fetid water-pools of the street in front of the houses stood gambling-tables surrounded by dirty ruffians, and here and there the door of a liquor-shop was left open, and groups of bearded and long-haired, unwashed and uncombed, pale-faced and hollow-eyed men were seen, some of them cautiously holding their hands over their pockets, heavily loaded with the proceeds of a mining season in California, and too heavily altogether for the unsolid condition of their ragged apparel.

None of the foreign residents of Chagres had thought of cultivating the smallest piece of land, or even of making the natural productions of the neighbourhood available to the daily wants of life. For the two or three cows which were kept here, the food was brought from the United States, and so was the fuel for the daily uses of the kitchen, while the trees of the forest stood close to the houses. The most common vegetables or fruits of the tropics, such as plantains, bananas, yams, mandioca, &c., were unknown on the table of the "hotel." The natives did not cultivate more of these articles than they wanted for themselves, and nobody thought of an occupation that would not promise an instantaneous reward.

Such, in 1850, was the North-American settlement at Chagres,—a place where, as Captain B. of our brig observed, no other than an utterly reckless man could be supposed to live of his own free accord. This opinion may have contained too severe a judgment. As to me, however, never more forcibly than at Chagres did the idea strike me, how much the development of many of the noblest qualities of our nature is dependent upon the influence of a home, that is more to us than a fit place for doing business,—to which on the contrary we feel attached, —which we rejoice in improving and adorning, and in which we like to recognize, more or less deeply imprinted, the traces of our taste and character, our thought and action. It is not from men alone that we are entitled to expect a reciprocation of our affections,—nature too, and all the things around us, give us a reward for the interest our heart takes in them, by exerting an ennobling influence upon the mind. Not men alone, but even things cannot be neglected and degraded by us, without the bad consequences of such an offence against the deeper laws of the moral world falling back in just retribution upon our own characters. In neglecting and degrading the things around us, we unavoidably neglect and degrade ourselves. At a place where everybody was but a temporary resident, attracted by no other motive but the lust of gain,—where everybody, from the very day of his arrival, impatiently counted the time to the moment when he would have gained enough to justify his departure, a result for which, at Chagres, a few years were thought rather a long period, —at such a place life must have a mean and debased aspect, without much hope of improvement. I do not know what may have become the character of Aspinwall, to which place many of the inhabitants of Chagres have removed not long after my visit, nor am I informed of the merits of social life in the gold mines of Australia. As to California, however, a considerable number of those, who went there from all parts of the world, have justly found it so desirable a home from the very beginning, that even the mining regions of that country have soon been graced with the charms of home life, and nowhere it has been better understood than in California, that one individual intending to make the country his permanent home, is worth more to the community than a number of temporary residents, however important may be the business they come to transact for a while.

I passed the river to examine the village of the natives. There is a swamp on one side of it, the fetid exhalations of which, mingled with the dew of the evening, were so thick and substantial that, beyond their affecting the olfactory sense, I had the taste of them on the tongue. Nevertheless, this part of Chagres made a far more favourable impression on me than the American town. The habitations, standing on a more or less elevated ground, neatly built of canes, and covered with palm-leaves, were extremely clean. Seen from the opposite side of the river, they represented a very picturesque view. A grove of palm-trees surrounds them in the rear, at the foot of a steep hill covered with a dense forest of exogenous trees, some of them of a gigantic growth, waving their wide-spread umbrella-shaped crowns high over the rest. The inhabitants were a mixed race of Indian, African and Spanish origin, using the Spanish language as a common medium, though some of the negroes or mulattoes living there were from Jamaica; they, too, having been attracted by the expectation of extraordinary gain. I had a conversation with one of these men, an intelligent and fine-looking mulatto, who told me that, indeed, he could make a good deal of money here, but that the climate was too sickly, so that whatever he gained he had to pay to the doctor. It is not without interest to know how such a climate as that of Chagres is looked upon by a coloured native of Jamaica, and at the same time I am touching here upon a fact, unnoticed, as far as I know, in Europe,—the fact of the existence of a moving coloured population, congregating here and there as circumstances may invite them, on the coasts around the Caribbean sea. I shall have to speak more of this fact, which promises to become of importance in the future history of the West Indies, and of Central America, as well as in the development of the coloured races of the new world. Of this class of the coloured population of Chagres, the greater number were from Curaçao and Cartagena. The natives of the place itself seemed to be more of a Hispano-Indian caste, extremely strong and well formed, some of them with very intelligent and pleasing countenances. I found that personal cleanliness and neatness were marked traits in their character, by which they were most favourably distinguished from the inhabitants, and the travelling crowd on the other side of the river. On every morning during the eight days of our stay, men and women, as they passed the river in their small canoes, appeared in a clean suit, although the whole dress of the former consisted only in a straw hat and a pair of white trowsers worn over the skin. Here I had the first opportunity of seeing that peculiar style of half-savage elegance, which characterizes the female dress and deportment of the lower classes of Spanish America. Indeed, these women, with their flounced skirts of striped muslin fastened round their naked waists, their busts loosely covered with the flying *guipil* of white muslin glittering with gold or silver paillettes, or the long striped *reboso* stylishly thrown over the left shoulder, a pair of small white satin shoes, embroidered with silver or gold, on the naked feet, the jet hair tastefully adorned with white, yellow, or crimson flowers just taken from the shrub,—made altogether a coquettish appearance, as they would walk along in assumed dignity with a defying swing of their arms, or would negligently repose in their gently moving hammocks. I observed that a perfect politeness of language prevailed among these people, in whose conversation the address of "*señor*" and "*señora*" was rarely omitted. Only the men who were rowing the canoes on the river, or were occupied in unloading the vessels, mutually addressed themselves in a less formal manner, calling their companions by the simple designation of "*hombre*," (man!)—"*mulato!*"—"*cuadron!*"—"*zambo!*"—according to the gradations of caste.

Between the inhabitants of the two villages a little war had broken out during the time of my visit. The natives had offered to forward the travellers up the river at a lower rate than the Americans would allow; and, as the former neglected the prohibition, one of their canoes, filled with travellers, was fired at from the American side. To these high-handed proceedings the natives responded by similar acts of violence; some wounds were received on both sides, and there was a good deal of excitement for a few days.

Mounting the steep hill on which the castle of San Lorenzo is situated, I saw—as a physician would say—a splendid specimen of *elephantiasis*, in the shape of the monstrous leg of a negro, sitting at the side of the footpath. The castle, which once defended the northern entrance to the passage across the isthmus of Panamá, is one of the most remarkable monuments of Spanish dominion in those parts of the world; though, from the effects of the excessive dampness of the climate, and from want of repair, it is almost a ruin, its material being a variety of sandstone which is unfit for withstanding the attacks of atmospherical influences. In one of the courts stood a wooden building, the residence of a solitary officer styled the "*commandante*;" but I saw no trace of a garrison, not even a single guard to prevent me and my companions from entering a vault which we found to contain I cannot tell how many thousand pounds of moist gunpowder in open boxes, which some of us investigated with a lighted cigar in the mouth before recognizing the dangerous nature of the substance. Old pieces of artillery, some of very heavy calibre, and pyramids of piled-up balls and shells lay about on the ground. Besides a large number of iron guns, I counted ten guns and mortars of bronze. Two of the latter, of beautiful workmanship, reciprocally bore the inscriptions: "*El Escorpion. Sevilla*, 1749;" and "*El Dracon. Sevilla*, 1742."

The view from the castle is grand and beautiful. On one side is the sea, washing the foot of the hill on which it stands, and which is very precipitous in this direction. A line of coast, covered with forest down to the beach, extends from hence in a long sweep. Towards the interior a country of wooded hills unfolds itself, and leaves a passage to the river, which may be traced with the eye for a considerable distance, as it takes its course through the dark shades of the forest.

Behind the castle is a deep ravine, through which a clear brook rushes down to the sea between majestic trees. A crowd of half-naked women were occupied here in washing their linen. As we approached, they made signs that we should not come near—a rare instance of a feeling which in general seems to be almost unknown amongst the lower classes of Spanish America. As we proceeded in our walk we came to a grove of cocoa-nut trees, and on a small square between them saw the remains of a sugar factory, with several large kettles in good condition lying about. The establishment seemed to have never been in a working state, and undoubtedly has been one of the many unfortunate speculations begun in those regions of tropical America without a due appreciation of the difficulties and obstacles inseparably connected with the uncivilized state of a country. I have seen a like result of a similar speculation in British Honduras, where, in the wilderness surrounding the Manatee Lagoon, I found all the improvements and costly machinery of an intended sugar plantation overgrown by the rank vegetation of a forest.

The next day I took a walk along the coast, and after having followed it for two or three miles to a beautiful spot where, near a projecting rock, a little river empties into the sea, I took a footpath leading into the forest. This, after the distance of a mile, brought me to a number of huts constructed of canes and palm leaves. Brown women, in all the finery described above, even the white satin shoes not excepted, were swinging in their hammocks in the open doorways. What might have induced these people to erect their habitations in the midst of the forest I could not learn. Perhaps they wanted to be near enough to the port to profit by the neighbourhood, without having their dwellings exposed to the looks of the passing "Americanos."

Heavy showers of rain, which poured down in torrents every day, prevented me from moving more freely about in the environs, and made the time tedious and unproductive of observation. On the 14th of November, Captain B. having settled his business transactions, our anchor was raised, and our brig towed out into the sea.

It took us four days to reach *San Juan del Norte.* Where first seen by us the coast near that place appeared as a long belt of forest, here and there interrupted by a savana, and extending in a flat country to the foot of a range of hills in the interior. Farther in that direction rose some isolated peaks, indicating, by their pure conical form, the volcanic nature of the region. These, as I learned soon after, were the two cones of the island of *Ometepe*, in the lake of Nicaragua, and some of the nearer peaks of Costarica.

At that time *San Juan* was a little town of about fifty or sixty houses. The place is known by three different names. To designate it in a more general manner, it is called *San Juan de Nicaragua*—to distinguish it from another San Juan, which is situated on the Pacific coast of Nicaragua, it is called *San Juan del Norte:* "mar del norte" and "mar del sur" being old Spanish denominations for the Atlantic and the Pacific ocean,—and to extinguish the memory of the Spanish origin and the former allegiance to Spain as well as to Nicaragua, the English, when they took forcible possession of it in the name of their tutelary kingdom of Mosquitia, in 1848, substituted the name of *Greytown* for the two older appellations.

In spite of the novelty of the latter name, San Juan del Norte is an old Spanish settlement. It is a well known fact that a Spanish garrison was kept here at the beginning of the eighteenth century, and that, from 1796 down to the time of Central American independence, it was one of the official ports of entry for the Spanish dominions in this part of the world. The more recent history of the place, since it has acquired some importance in American politics, is not without interest, intimately connected as it is with the question of the Mosquito Protectorate, with the contended stipulations of the Clayton-Bulwer treaty, with the disputed territorial rights of Nicaragua and Costarica, with the claims of the different transit companies, and the adventurous expeditions of the modern filibusters. At the time of my arrival, the town was governed by the British Consul for the King of Mosquitia. In the name of this sovereign the custom-house duties were collected; in his name the building-lots of the town and divisions of land in the neighbourhood were sold; and this state of things continued until, on the 1st of May of 1851, the inhabitants, with the consent of England, have declared their community to form a free city and independent republic under a constitution of their own, which they adopted in 1852, and which has ever since remained in force. In 1854, after having considerably increased, the place, by an act of the government of the United States, which has been almost universally condemned, was totally destroyed, so that a few houses only remained,—a proceeding which, though produced by no other ostensible cause than a quarrel raised between the town and the Accessory Transit Company, is not without some political signification, in so far as the question of the British Protectorate was thereby put to a decisive test. A consideration of this kind is the only motive which can explain a severity unjustified by the trifling nature of the pretext.

The town of San Juan del Norte, which, since the

catastrophe just mentiomed, has risen again from its ashes, is situated at the mouth of the northern branch of the river by which the basin of the lake of Nicaragua is connected with the ocean. The situation is incomparably better than that of Chagres. The soil upon which it stands is sandy, small black grains of Titanic iron, or *Iserine*, entering largely into its composition. Wherever the ground is touched with a magnet a more or less considerable quantity of that substance will be attracted, and may be taken up. Undoubtedly, it has been carried down from the interior by the river, as it is originally derived from the volcanic eruptions of *Ometepe*, of the *Mombacho* and of the volcano of *Massaya*, some of the lavas and tuffs of these localities containing a very large proportion of the mineral, while on the shores of the lake of Nicaragua it exists, in an almost pure or unmixed state, in banks of the same loose black grains, which may be taken up by the magnet, at San Juan del Norte.

To this sandy condition of the soil undoubtedly is attributable an essential part of the comparative salubrity of the climate of the latter place. I have never seen a soil absorb the water more quickly and dry up in a shorter time than that of San Juan, where, in a quarter of an hour after the heaviest rain, the streets may be passed without soiling your shoes. Such a soil, with the sea on one side, the river on the other, a little lagoon on the third and almost on a level with all, must be impregnated with water, however dry it may be on the surface. Wherever, therefore, an empty barrel is sunk into the ground it speedily fills, and this I observed to be the way of procuring the drinking-water in common use. This I found to be pure and of good taste, and according to the statements of the inhabitants, perfectly healthy. The lagoon just mentioned is in the rear of the town, a few hundred paces from the last houses as they stood at that time. Its water is sweet, as it is connected with the river and shut up towards the sea. It does not appear to have a marked influence in making the situation unhealthy, which may be accounted for by the prevailing sea-breeze driving the exhalations towards the interior.

The water of this lagoon is of a dark brown colour, which contributes to the peculiar character of the scenery. It is surrounded by a thick growth of trees of the most luxuriant vegetation. Heavy masses of foliage, leaving an opening here and there through which the eye is led into the darkest shades of the forest, are resting on the very surface of the lake. These openings are narrow channels, by which the lagoon extends into the woods to a considerable distance, covered, for the most part, with so dense a foliage that no ray of the sun can penetrate. The lagoon is full of alligators, or rather crocodiles, some of them of an extraordinary size for an American species; the peculiar degree of savageness imputed to the alligators of San Juan may be explained by their not being true alligators, but, in fact, a species of crocodile—*Crocodilus Americana*, of which a fine specimen, from this very place, is in the British Museum.

The population of San Juan was by far superior in character to that of Chagres, and ever since has this town represented a very respectable community. The most perfect order and security prevailed at the time of my visit, though hundreds of Californians, who had come through the interior of Nicaragua from Realejo, filled the taverns. The English protectors of the King of Mosquito kept up an excellent police here. A considerable proportion of the inhabitants were coloured people from the interior as well as from the West Indies, but the better class was almost entirely composed of foreigners—Americans, English, Frenchmen, Spaniards, Germans, and Italians; and such the population has remained up to the present time, representing a type of what the population of Central America in general will no doubt in due course become—a mixture of all the elements able to contribute to the development of civilization and prosperity in this beautiful and interesting region.

CHAPTER II.

Journey into the Interior — Scenery on the River — Old Castle of San Juan — San Carlos — Aspect of the Lake of Nicaragua — Adventures of a young German amongst the Indians of the Rio Frio — Science held in high Esteem in Spanish America — Canoe Navigation on the Lake — Arrival at Granada.

THE few days of my stay at Chagres had been sufficient to produce a severe attack of that peculiar form of remittent fever which is known and dreaded under the name of the Chagres or Panamá fever. I think I knew the very moment when the fetid miasmata, rising from the neighbouring swamp and mixing with the air at the fall of night, took effect upon my constitution. A sickening sensation instantaneously pervaded my system; sea-sickness prevented me during the next four days from having a very distinct feeling of the state of my health; but, when I arrived at San Juan, I found that all my energy was gone. For a few days I still kept up, but at last I was subdued by a violent paroxysm. My landlord, an old Frenchman, a political refugee from the time of Charles X., who had passed many years on the island of Hayti, and there had acquired practice in the treatment of this kind of disease, prepared a large bottle of medicine for me, which, trusting more to the experience of this man than to the doubtful science of some questionable member of the profession who may have existed at San Juan at that time, I swallowed without hesitation, and, after having taken a strong dose of quinine on the next morning, I followed his advice to continue my journey into the interior, whatever the state of my health might be, the chances of my recovery being by far better there than on the sea-coast. In this he was right, for, during the twelve days of my passage to Granada, while I slept every night in the open air on board a canoe, several times even exposed without any shelter to the heavy dew, or lying under an india-rubber blanket in a torrent of rain, I recovered, though the consequences of the attack, manifesting themselves in a general want of muscular power and in a high degree of nervous irritability, did not leave me for many months.

At that time steamboats were not yet plying on the San Juan river and the Lake of Nicaragua, and I had to content myself with the accommodations of one of the large canoes of the natives called "*bongos,*" which were then the principal means of transport between the coast and the interior, for passengers as well as for merchandise. In company with two Americans, who, like myself, were anxious to proceed to Granada, I hired one of the largest of these clumsy little crafts, manned with ten boatmen or "*marineros,*" together with their captain or "*patron,*" all of them coloured people from the interior. We laid in provisions for a fortnight, such being the full time of a passage which is now performed by steamers in two days.

We left San Juan on the 23rd of November, and arrived at Granada on the 5th of the following month. In reference to the beauties of nature, the trip is one of the most interesting that can be made, though the state of my health prevented me from enjoying it then, as I did afterwards on two different occasions. At the present time the forest is cleared at several places on the river, where the wood has been cut to provide the river steamers with fuel, and a few plantations have been established. In 1850 an open shed, furnished with a hammock and surrounded by a plantain garden of half an acre, was the only improvement of the kind in an extent of more than a hundred miles. With this single exception, and with that of the site of the old castle of San Juan, more generally known by the popular name of the *Castillo Viejo,* the banks were covered with trees to the water's edge, their branches often bearing a vegetation of vines, climbers, and parasites, so densely interwoven that the whole appeared like a solid wall of leaves and flowers.

I shall never forget the impressions of one night and morning on this river. Our boat had anchored in the midst of the stream. Strange forms of trees, spectre-like in the dark, stood before us, and seemed to move as the eye strove in vain to make out their real shape. From time to time a splash in the water, caused by the movement of an alligator, the bellowing of a manati, the screeching of a night-bird, or the roar of some beast of the forest, broke the silence, and mingled at last with my feverish dream. In the morning, a song our boatmen addressed to the Virgin roused me from my sleep. It was a strain of plaintive notes in a few simple but most expressive modulations. Several years later I heard them again, sung by the Mexcan miners in the subterraneous chapel of the quicksilver mine of New Almaden in California, and I never shall forget the deep emotion felt on both occasions, so widely different in every other respect. In the latter case the scene passed in a narrow excavation before a little altar cut out of the natural rock, on which, before a gilded image of the Virgin, two thin tallow candles were casting their scanty light over the dark forms of fifteen or twenty men calling down the blessing of Heaven upon their day's work in the interior of the mountain—in the former, it was in the brightness and splendour of a morning of which no description can convey a full idea to one who has had no experience in the most favoured regions of a tropical climate. The sun was just rising, and as the first rays, gilding the glossy leaves of the forest, fell upon the bronze-coloured bodies of our men, letting the naked forms of their athletic frame appear in all the contrast of light and shade, while accents, plaintive and imploring, strained forth from their lips, I thought to hear the sacred spell by which, unconscious of its power, these men were subduing their own half-savage nature. At once the same song was repeated from behind a projecting corner of the bank, and other voices joined those of our crew in the sacred notes. Two canoes, covered from our view, had anchored near us during the night. The song at last died away in the wilderness. A silent prayer—our anchor was raised, and, with a wild shout of the crew, twelve oars simultaneously struck the water. The sun was glittering in the river. The tops of the trees were steeped in light—monkeys were swinging in the branches—splendid macaws flew in pairs from bank to bank—all around exhibited the glory and brightness of superabundant nature.

Near the mouth of the river, as far up as the higher end of its delta, the banks are almost on the water's level, overgrown with reeds, mangroves, and a low species of palm-tree, the latter forming extensive thickets in the swamps. After a distance of fourteen or fifteen miles, the land gradually becomes a little higher, and steep embankments of a brown or reddish clay rise to some ten or twenty feet above the water. The low palm thickets of the swampy region disappear, and a vegetation of splendid trees, mostly exogenous, overhung with blooming vines, takes their place. Flowery garlands, swung from branch to branch, hang over the stream, while now and then the slender shafts of one of the tallest species of the palm tribe wafts its little crown of feathery leaves high over the gorgeous masses of the heavier foliage.

Eight or ten miles higher up, the region of the "*raudales*," or rapids, begins. Here the river, locked in between wooded hills, presents a new character of scenery. The trees, covering the hill-sides with an almost impenetrable forest, exhibit an extraordinary variety of forms in striking contrast. The most interesting situation in this region is that of the *Castillo Viejo*. Here, where the river foams over a bed of rocks, stands the old Spanish castle of *San Juan*. Since 1780 it has remained a ruin, though Nicaragua has always kept a few soldiers here, occupying a shed at the foot of the hill on which the remains of the fort are seen. In the civil wars of the last years this place has repeatedly been occupied and evacuated by the contending powers. In 1854 the Leonese party held it with a small force, when the Granadinos under Chamorro took it, and spared the lives of none of their adversaries who fell into their hands.

Amongst the rapids, that of the Castillo Viejo is the only one which forms a real impediment in the navigation of the river. With the necessary caution canoes may descend, and I myself have passed over it on my way back to the coast in a bongo carrying forty passengers;—upwards, however, all classes of boats must be towed, after having been unloaded, and the continuity of steam navigation is interrupted here. The steamboats from the mouth of the river proceed as high up as the foot of this rapid, while those from the Lake come as far down as the end of the still water above it. Not long before the time of my arrival the two first steamboats destined to ply on the river and Lake had been sent from New York by the Canal Company; one of them, however, lay at the Castillo waiting for the means of being towed over this rapid; the other had grounded in the rapid of Machuca, and never got afloat again. When I passed down the river some years later the wreck had given origin to a little island, and, though the structure still kept together, trees were growing on the deck.

After the opening of the steam navigation on the river, several houses have been erected at the Castillo, and the place promised to become a little town. In 1855 several hotels stood here, in which two or three thousand dollars were spent every fortnight by passing travellers, detained for a few hours by the change of steamer. The total interruption of the transit, in consequence of the high-handed proceedings of William Walker, the filibuster, soon after checked the progress of this dawning settlement.

Above the region of the rapids the river is almost stagnant, and the designation of the "*aguas muertas*," or dead waters, is not inappropriately applied to it. It is a deep and still water, full of fish, with low and swampy banks, on which the palm thickets of the delta reappear.

Beyond this latter portion of the river the lake of Nicaragua opens to the view. On the little promontory formed by the lake and the inlet of the river, the customhouse of Nicaragua, designated by the high-sounding name of the *fort of San Carlos*, has been established. There are a few houses at this place, and a small military force is kept up to protect the establishment and, in case of necessity, enforce the payment of the duties. The ruins of an old Spanish castle still exist here, but they are hidden among the trees and shrubs with which they are overgrown.

The view from this elevation has a peculiar character of grandeur. At the foot of the hill a broad sheet of water is spread, studded, in the immediate neighbourhood, with some green islands of diminutive dimensions, and extending, in a north-westerly direction, as far as the eye can reach. To the left, a low wooded shore begins at the outlet of the lake, and continues in that direction till it is lost in the distance of the western horizon. A chain of high mountains, cast in a shroud of dark forests, rises in its rear, covering an unknown region of Costarica. It comprises several active volcanoes, which on late occasions, as in 1854, have illumined the surface of the lake by their flames and red-hot streams of lava. To the right, the view does not extend beyond the nearest hills; but, at a short distance on the lake, it ranges over a long line of broken eminences, with the mountain chain of Chontales in their rear, bordering like a wall the table-land of Upper Mosquitia. Hill and dale, forests and savanas, appear in endless variety in this direction. On the distant horizon in the centre of the view the two cones of the island of Ometepe are seen, faintly traced, and as their forms are lifted up by refraction, they seem to swim over the water.

At the very spot where the San Juan river leaves the lake, the Rio Frio enters it. This is a river coming down from the mountains of Costarica, through an absol wilderness which, it is asserted, has never been trodden by the foot of a civilized man. The dense forests of this region are inhabited by a warlike tribe of Indians who refuse to have any intercourse with the rest of the world. They are said to be of very fair complexion, a statement which has caused the appellation of *Indios blancos*, or *Guatusos*—the latter name being that of an animal of reddish-brown colour, and intended to designate the colour of their hair. It is stated that not only do they not allow a foreigner to enter their territory, but that they are even in the habit of killing those of their own people who again fall in their hands after having been away amongst the civilized inhabitants of the neighbouring settlements. Nevertheless, some of them—if really belonging to that tribe—are occasionally seen at Tortugas, a small Nicaraguan place on the western shore of the lake, and eight or ten miles to the south-east of Virgin Bay. A Nicaraguan gentleman who had lived at Tortugas and had collected information there concerning these Indians, asserted that amongst them men very often take their own daughters for wives. While in California, I heard of a young German, living in the neighbourhood of San Francisco, who recounts a little romance of adventures he met with amongst this people. Though the story was not told to me by the man himself, still, as it was repeated by a trustworthy friend who had derived it from the original source, I may be allowed to introduce it here. The young man was on his way to California. When at San Carlos, he had some difference or quarrel with his travelling companions, and being afraid of a pistol-ball or a bowie-knife, took the desperate resolution of swimming to the opposite side of the river, where he soon fell into the hands of a body of these Indians. He was tied to a tree, and they then held a council as to the manner—so at least he believed—of putting him to death. Suddenly, however, as it has happened before in similar cases, a young girl, the daughter of the chief, hurried forth, clasped her arms round the neck of my blue-eyed countryman, and gave a favourable turn to his fate. Of course, he married the girl, and, as the consort of this Indian princess, he spent a few months in the forest, till he was ungrateful enough to forsake his generous bride, and avail himself of an opportunity to swim back to San Carlos, continuing, after this romantic episode, his journey to California. According to his statements, he would have remained with the Indians had he been able to endure the life in the wilderness, which he found rather too ill-provided with accommodations for enjoying his honey-moon. During the rainy season the tribe lived almost exclusively on the trees, and he speaks in very high terms of the dexterity with which they would leap from branch to branch, a mode of travelling in which he often found it too difficult to follow his nimble spouse. At the time of each full moon the whole tribe met in council, for which the place was designated from one meeting to the next by the chief, and whatever was done by common agreement was regulated according to the phases of the moon.

Some years before the period of my first arrival in Nicaragua, the officer then in command of the fort of San Carlos fitted out an expedition for the purpose of exploring the country on the Rio Frio, which is known to be rich in gold. This little corps, having hit upon a deserted village of the Indians on the bank of the river, and resting in the shade of some trees on the outskirts of the forest, was suddenly assailed by a shower of arrows, and with the exception of the commanding officer, who was severely wounded, but succeeded in hiding himself between the reeds till a boat from the fort came to his rescue, every man of the expeditionary force was killed.[1]

At San Carlos my luggage had to pass the custom-house visitation. When the first of my boxes was opened, and a botanical work, lying uppermost, and being recognisable as such by its plates, came to view, all further

[1] Mr. Squier, in his recent work on the 'Central American States,' has given some very valuable information in reference to the *Guatusos*.

investigation was dispensed with. "Este cavaliero es botanista"—this gentleman is a botanist—cried the director, giving an order to leave my things unmolested. As far as I know the Spanish-American nations, scientific occupations are held in very high esteem amongst them—a trait of character worthy of a better fate than to be effaced by the brutalizing influences of continued revolutions and civil wars. It may be fairly said that this feature, originally belonging to the Spanish nationality, has been greatly developed and generalised, as to the colonial populations, by the travels and highly scientific researches of Baron Humboldt.

Our passage up the river had taken us nine days, making an average progress of about twelve miles per day. Three days more were spent in crossing the lake. With the native boatmen it seems to be a rule to abstain from using oars, even when they are becalmed. Before we left the "aguas muertas" a small tree had been cut. This was now erected as a mast, a sail was spread, and slowly we began to move in the direction to Granada. Our navigation was of a very primitive kind. At night, while every soul on board slept soundly, our bongo was left to find its own way, which, however, it refused to do, for when I awoke at dawn, I saw that we were heading to the place we had come from. By-and-bye, nevertheless, we drew nearer to our point of destination. When we had left the two peaks of Ometepe on one side, the summit of the Mombacho, designating the site of Granada, gradually rose from the water. We passed the island of Zapotera, celebrated for its idols, which have been discovered and described by my friend, Mr. Squier. It is uninhabited, and may be said to be a mountain covered with a forest, here and there interrupted by a patch of savana. Like other islands in this lake, it contains numerous wild animals, such as deer, pecaris, monkeys, and panthers. The name is generally written *Zapatero*, a word which, translated into English, means "the shoemaker." But I never heard it pronounced otherwise than *Zapatera*, and I have no doubt that its correct form is *Zapotera*, meaning the *Zapote Island*. According to this derivation, the name is formed analogous to that of the island of *Formentera*, in the group of the Baleares. *Zapote* is the name of a well-known fruit of the tropics, very common in Nicaragua. In its original Aztec this latter name is *Zapotl*. In a similar manner a cluster of small coral islands in the gulf of Honduras is called the *Zapodilla Keys*, from the Zapodilla trees growing on them. According to Mr. Squier, the old Aztec name of the island of Zapotera was *Chomitl-Tenamitl*, a compound, the second part of which occurs again in the name of another island in this lake—that of *Solentenami*. According to Mr. Buschmann, *tenamitl*, in the Aztec language, means a stone wall.

On the evening of the 5th of December we doubled the outermost rock of the *Corrales* or *Isletas*,—a cluster of more than a hundred diminutive islands at the foot of the Mombacho, and a few hours after dark landed on the "playa" or beach of Granada.

CHAPTER III.

Granada and its Environs — Geological Character of the Soil — Volcanic Fissures — Habitations of the Lower Classes — Indian Population — Excursions in the Neighbourhood — The Playa — Los Corrales — La Joya — Lake Songozana of Oviedo — Laguna de Salinas — Home Life of the Author — Tame Animals kept in the House — Slaveholding Ants — Nicaraguan Scholars, and Reputation of German Philosophers.

As, during the whole time of my residence in Nicaragua, Granada has been my standing quarters to which I have returned from all my excursions, I will unite in this chapter what I have to say of it. My remarks in reference to the town itself must be very restricted. Since that time Granada has been reduced to ruins by William Walker, and my statements, if they were to go too deeply into the particulars of a description, would most likely be antiquated. Only those features, therefore, which have a more lasting character shall be dwelt upon.

At the time of my visit Granada was a town of thirteen or fourteen thousand inhabitants, built in the usual style of Spanish-American cities under the tropics. It stands half a mile distant from the lake, on the northern foot of an extinguished volcano called *Mombacho*, on a soil of volcanic tuff of a very friable and sandy nature. During the dry season, when an almost continual fresh breeze—which, in fact, is the north-easterly trade-wind—is blowing over the country, and sweeping the streets of the city, the fine sand fills the air and enters through the doors and windows of the houses, covering every piece of furniture and every article exposed to it so rapidly and copiously that to dust your table every quarter of an hour will prove insufficient, and you cannot finish one page of a letter without feeling the accumulating grains under your fingers. Glass windows being unknown in Nicaragua, no protection is possible against this annoying effect of a climate which in other respects is a most delightful one. I may state in connexion with this subject, that mosquitos are scarcely seen at Granada, and that in general I do not remember having been troubled by them anywhere in the interior of Nicaragua. The sand I am speaking of contains such a number of grains of titanic iron, already mentioned in reference to the soil of San Juan del Norte, that you may collect this substance anywhere in your room—from its floor, from the material of its walls, from the surface of the furniture—by a magnet. During the rainy season, when heavy showers are of frequent occurrence, torrents are often rushing through the streets, but as they have a sufficient slope to let the water flow off without delay, while the sand washed out of the loamy soil remains covering the surface, the streets of Granada may be called very clean even after a rain.

These showers are sometimes exceedingly violent. I have known an instance when, at the beginning of a rainfall at Granada, a little parrot, whose wings had been clipped to prevent it from flying away, was drowned in our court before it had had time to take refuge under a shelter not distant beyond twelve or fifteen paces, and after the rain had continued for an hour, the court was laid completely under water to a considerable depth, though it had a drain of not less than one foot in diameter.

The soil in the neighbourhood of Granada is intersected by deep ravines, which have been enlarged and otherwise modified in their character by the recurring effect of such violent and copious rains; but which, without any doubt, are fissures caused originally by earthquake. They are rather an interesting feature in the site of the city, which, on each of its two sides, is lined by one of these formations beginning in its rear and running down to the lake. By one of them the city is entirely separated from one of its suburbs, which from that very circumstance is not inappropriately called *Otrabanda*,—"the other side." There are only a few places where this deep ravine can be crossed, and some of these crossings can only be effected by passing through side branches of the main fissure so narrow that there is scarcely room for one man, the walls being quite perpendicular. The bottom of the principal trunk of this long cleft has been filled up by the material washed or crumbling down from the perpendicular walls of tuff, and now forms a horizontal floor through the whole length of the cleft, which extends for several miles, with a width nowhere exceeding a few paces, and an average height of the walls —if I judge right from memory—of twenty to thirty feet. The whole, for a certain distance upwards, forms a cool alley under the shade of shrubs and trees that grow above the banks, uniting their branches over it. The walls, always perpendicular, are distinguished by a variety of delicate ferns and lycopodiaceous plants, and by the rich violet flowers of a Gesnera growing on them. They are full of holes and cavities. Some of the latter, even large enough for men to enter, seem to be the abode of different kinds of animals, while the former are occupied by numerous owls, and by the nests of some birds of brilliant plumage of the family of the kingfishers, as well as of a peculiar bird called *Guarda-barranca*, of a light greenish blue, with two long feathers in its tail.[1] Near its upper extremity

[1] This bird seems to be the Hylomanes superciliaris, of the family of the Todidae.

this curious fissure becomes so narrow that, at some places, a man finds it difficult to pass, and the whole formation, without having become less deep, abruptly terminates by a kind of perpendicular shaft, just wide enough for a man to stand at the bottom of it, and look up through a narrow opening, over which he perceives nothing but a little patch of sky.

The huts of the outskirts and environs of Granada are scattered between thickets of shrubs and fruit trees, or hidden in the woods, which in most directions close immediately upon the city. A few hundred steps from the last houses of *Jalteva*, which, though it is called a suburb, and is always in a decided political opposition with Granada, yet in fact forms an essential part of the city, I have seen a deer crossing my way, which I did not shoot, because I could not imagine that it was not a tame one belonging to the next habitation; and when, on another occasion, on my return from an excursion which I had been making in company with some friends, we all were under the impression of having lost our way, we found ourselves immediately in front of the first houses of Granada.

The huts of the lower classes, scattered, as I have said, over the outskirts and environs of the city, are often distinguished by their charming sites, in which the peculiar taste of their Indian or half-Indian inmates is recognisable. For weeks the stranger may stroll about in the neighbourhood, and daily he will discover new gems of beauty in the situation of some humble dwellings, built of reeds and thatched with palm leaves;—here, in idyllic retirement hidden from the world, the footpath leading to the place scarcely visible—there boldly on a hill, under a group of trees, or standing on an open patch of savana, with a look over the lake and its islands and distant shores. As he passes close by, tawny children in the costume of nature, are playing in intimate fellowship with pigs, dogs, and chickens, under the shade of some orange or mango trees, between shrubs covered with flowers; while brown women, busy in their domestic occupations, are seen through the open door.

In the population of the suburbs and of the scattered habitations of the environs of Granada, the Indian element is predominant—in part even exclusive. Amongst the lower classes of the town, a considerable proportion of African blood is mixed with it. But to what an extent the Indian element, even as a pure unmixed race, predominates, may be seen every morning on the market-place of Granada. Without the Indians, it would be empty. Early in the morning they are seen arriving in long files, one after the other, men, women and children, bringing fruits and vegetables, chickens and eggs, venison and fish, wild honey, starch prepared from the yucca or mandioca root, maize and rice, hammocs, water-jars, drinking-cups made from the *jicara* or fruit of the calabash tree, and with other productions of their small plantations and of their industry. It is altogether an erroneous opinion, which, however, seems to be very general, that this people is naturally lazy. Whatever may be said of the descendants of the Spaniards in this, or in any other American country, and however unwilling the free negro may be to work, the Central-American Indian is naturally industrious, and is, without any doubt, the most useful and the most respectable component in the Central-American population. He is of a short frame, stout and robust, well-built, with an intelligent and agreeable countenance. His mouth is well-formed, with a beautiful set of teeth. His eyes are jet black, with a peculiar want of transparency or superficial lustre, but often with a strange interrogatory expression, which, in young persons, looks like a mischievous coyness, while in old individuals it is more or less expressive of diffidence and caution.

In speaking of the great features presented by the situation and the popular life of Granada, I have to mention the beach of the Lake, next to the town. Never have I seen a brighter scene than the "*playa*" of Granada. The way down from the city passes through thickets of shrubbery covered with the most splendid flowers, amongst which the *Poinciana*, with scarlet panicles, is most prominent. With the exception of the noon-time, there is always considerable life on this road. Clumsy carts drawn by oxen move awkwardly along, hauling goods up and down from and to the landing-place. Groups of mischievous girls, boldly balancing their red water-jars on their heads, laugh and chatter as they walk between gay flowers and swarms of splendid butterflies. Swarthy women, always in good humour, with baskets filled with linen on their heads, move down in files in the morning and return in the evening. For more than half a mile the beach is occupied by them, as, more than half undressed and kneeling in the water up to their hips, they beat their linen on a stone, rub it and wash it, or, moving about, spread it on the clean sand of the beach, where it dries almost instantaneously from the heat of the bottom and the powerful rays of a perpendicular sun. Every morning and evening hundreds of persons of both sexes and of every age are bathing here promiscuously. That this is no place for modesty, as the civilised nations of a colder zone understand it, is a matter of course; but I may add that the ladies of the higher classes observe a stricter decorum. They go early in the morning when the playa is less frequented, and select their place at some distance from absolute publicity. I have observed, as a general rule at this public place, that young and beautiful women were more modest than others who were not in possession of sufficient charms to attract the eyes of men, and in some cases of shocking ugliness no reason for modesty at all seemed to exist in the opinion of those most immediately concerned in the question. This observation, which contradicts a remark made by Goethe, is not without its moral interest. It is merely justice to add that, however slightly the common people of Nicaragua may think of chastity and external modesty, I have never witnessed any coarseness or vulgarity of behaviour in the promiscuous crowd of this public bathing-place of both sexes.

During the season of the trade-winds a heavy surf is generally breaking over the beach, and I have often heard its roaring in my bedroom in the centre of the city. By the action of the waves on the sand a separation of its constituent parts, according to their specific gravity, is effected, and by this process whole banks of black sand, composed of grains of titanic iron, or iserine, have been formed at some places, mixed only with a few grains of olivine, spinell, ryakolite, and other minerals of volcanic origin. These substances are derived from the different masses ejected from the crater of the Mombacho, either in the form of lava or in that of ashes, which have made, or contributed to make, the volcanic tuff of this region. Everywhere in the neighbourhood blocks of lava are found imbedded in this tuff. The lava is sometimes of a basaltic character, including particles of titanic iron, of spinell, and of trichromatic olivine (red, blue, green, according to the three axes)— sometimes it is of a trachytic nature, including various minerals of the felspar family, such as ryakolite and others. The basaltic lava not seldom takes the form of a very heavy black scoriaceous rock, the high specific gravity of which, no doubt, is caused by the large proportion of the titanic iron it contains. The trachytic lava, on the other hand, occasionally appears in the condition of pumice, which it is quite common to see swimming in the Lake.

A ride on horseback along the shore, either north or south of the landing-place, is full of interest and enjoyment. Trees and bushes follow the line of the sand beach some twenty paces distant from the water's edge, so that the greater part of the ride can be made in the shade, while the eye passes over the Lake, resting there on the long chain of mountains separating Nicaragua from Upper Mosquitia; here, on the twin cones of Ometepe, on the wooded hill of Zapotera, or on the eastern slope of the Mombacho and the group of the *Corrales*, situated at its base.

This cluster of several hundreds of little islands, separated from the mainland as well as from each other by a most intricate system of narrow channels, is apparently the production of a stream of lava ejected from the crater of the Mombacho, and which, flowing down its eastern side and reaching the Lake, has been violently burst and cracked into so many islands by sudden cooling in the water, by which it was only half covered. The rock of which they are composed is a basaltic lava, of a somewhat scoriaceous character, at least in some sections of the whole mass. These little rocky islands are overgrown with the most magnificent trees; the branches often meeting over the narrow channels between them, forming dark vaults through which the canoes of the Indian inhabitants of this diminutive archipelago find their way in a labyrinth of passages. Many of the islands are inhabited, each of them, in general, only by one family. But they are so near to each other that the respective occupiers, without any difficulty, can have a conversation with their neighbours across the separating channel. Monkeys pass from one island to the other by leaping from branch to branch. The inhabitants have a few banana plantations and some fruit-trees; they keep pigs and chickens; besides which they are fishermen, who provide the market of Granada. Mr. Squier has visited one of the outer islands of the group, and has given a description of its idols. But the interior has never been examined by any one capable of observing and describing what objects of interest it may hide, and I am greatly mistaken if it does not offer a rich harvest, alike to the naturalist and the antiquary. From Granada, the nearest portion of the group is not distant more than two or three miles. Here the foot of the Mombacho advances to the shore of the lake, and the *Corrales* form its immediate continuation. The path along the beach is interrupted at this place, the communication with the southern side of the mountain being connected with considerable difficulties in that direction. The narrow channel by which the little archipelago is separated from the mainland at this spot is a still water, overgrown with floating leaves, on which the copper-coloured *jacana*, with armed wings and yellow front-plate, is seen to alight. Splendid kingfishers shoot over the surface, and disappear in some dark vault formed by the thick masses of foliage on the opposite shore. There the white heron stands in silent contemplation, as if looking at its own reflected image, while from the reeds a *cancroma*, a large brown bittern, or some other huge water-bird, suddenly flies up with startling noise.

The whole region to the south of the city is occupied by the Mombacho, the sides and summit of which are covered with almost impenetrable forests. Connected with it is a little group of hills, partly covered with savanas, standing in the rear of the city, at a few miles' distance in a south-westerly direction. I have been on the summit of one of them, and was recompensed for my trouble by a beautiful view over the plain and lake. But there is another interest connected with these hills which causes me to mention them. It is generally believed, as I have often heard at Granada, that they are slowly and continually growing higher. Such a fact is by no means impossible in a region of powerful volcanic activity such as this; but I could not learn by what means it had been ascertained by the inhabitants.

On the way to the hills just mentioned, and about a mile from the city, a deep circular chasm is seen, sunk into the general level of the surrounding country, which, at that place, may have reached an elevation of one or two hundred feet above the level of the lake. There is little doubt that it once must have been a volcanic crater. An entrance into this chasm exists on one side, where the wall is split and the general level of the land has a depression. At the bottom of it is a "platanar" or plantain garden, which seemed to be in a most luxuriant condition. Trees are growing at the foot of the perpendicular wall of rocks by which this locality is surrounded, their tops reaching up beyond the edge of the circular precipice, so as to make it difficult to get a glimpse at the enchanted garden below. The place is called *La Joya*—"the gem."

A few miles north of Granada a swampy lagoon begins, following the shore of the lake in that direction as far as the neighbourhood of the Estero de Fanaloya, or Rio de Tipitapa, which is the connexion of the lake of Nicaragua with that of Managua. During the dry season it is an extensive morass, with deep waterholes half overgrown with reeds; when the rains prevail it fills with water, which by one or more outlets empties into the lake. At that period numbers of fish pass through these channels from the lake into the lagoon. I have not the slightest doubt that this is the lake *Songozana* of which Oviedo speaks in his history of Nicaragua. Mr. Squier, who, in his interesting work on Nicaragua, gives the translation of a passage from Oviedo in reference to this item of Nicaraguan geography, seems to have misunderstood an expression of that author. When Oviedo says: "from the lake *Cocibolca* (*i.e.* the lake of Nicaragua) towards the south is the little lake *Songozana*" —this seems to be in utter contradiction to the situation of the lagoon, but "towards the south"—"*al sur*"—with reference to this passage, means towards the South Sea, just as "*San Juan del Sur*" means San Juan on the South Sea, or on the Pacific; and by this interpretation every difficulty as to the meaning of Oviedo disappears. In Oviedo's time this lagoon was full of alligators, or rather crocodiles, and the country around was infested by black panthers and other savage animals, which greatly annoyed the first Spanish settlers. At present the panthers have disappeared, and the crocodiles have become more scarce; but the sportsman will always find an almost incredible variety and number of the most interesting waterfowl, such as ducks, teal, a most beautiful species of small brown geese, waterhens, jacanas, snipes, plovers, herons, spoonbills, flamingoes, a gigantic species of tantalus, and many others.

On one of my excursions to this locality, turning my horse from the shore of the lake towards the swamp, I hit upon a boa snake, which after I had killed it proved to be only nine feet in length, but unusually thick in proportion, and so heavy that I found it difficult to take it home with me behind the saddle. My horse, too, was very much frightened when I first tried to lay the reptile on his back. I cannot tell the exact species of the animal, but it had a complete resemblance to some boa snakes I have seen in menageries; and a Nicaraguan, who passed by while I was occupied in opening its body, called it *bova*. In the abdomen I found ten or twelve young ones of eight or nine inches in length, on which I noticed the fact that their brains lay entirely bare under a most delicate and transparent membrane. When I entered the city with my unusual game I produced quite an excitement,—not that the snake was thought to be a dragon and I a second St. George, but because nobody imagined that I could have taken it home for another purpose than to eat it. When, on another occasion, I caught a large toad and put it in alcohol, some fellow, who saw me do so, asked his companion: "What can these foreigners do with the toads?" —"*Comen*"—"they eat them"—answered the other with an indescribable expression of contempt. To save the honour of the European nations, I pretended to catch toads for the purpose of preparing medicine. "*Para remedio*" —"for making medicine"—was my answer to similar questions from that time.

In company with some friends I made an excursion to the *Laguna de Salinas*, which lies four or five miles to the west of Granada. It is a formation similar to that of the locality described above, called *La Joya*. In an elevated and thickly-wooded region a wide circular chasm is sunk, the bottom of which is occupied by a lake. The surrounding wall is not quite perpendicular, and a path leads down to the cauldron—as the formation may appropriately be designated; but the descent is very steep, and we had to leave our horses above. Numerous cattle, however, belonging to some farm in the neighbourhood, and roaming about in the woods, descend daily down to drink at the lake. The latter may be two or three miles in circumference. Its water, according to the statement of Dr. B——, then resident in Granada, contains a considerable proportion of *iodine*, and has been effectually made use of in the cure of the wen, a disease so frequent in the neighbouring town of Masaya. It has a disagreeable saltish taste, and Dr. B—— himself, who was of our party, had a violent attack of vomiting produced by drinking it.

My time between these and the more extended excursions, which will be related in the following chapters, was spent in town, in what I may call my home life at Granada. It was always an interval of recovery from fatigues, and under this plea I may venture to claim the kind reader's attention for a few minor remarks.

I lived in the house of a German physician, at that time practising at Granada. Our life was rather of a sybaritic kind for a country like Nicaragua. When the dinner was ready, the dishes were carried in procession from the kitchen through the courtyard to the dining-room, which was an open verandah, by the servants, who, on that occasion, represented the dignity of the household by a strictly-observed hierarchical order. At the head of the procession the cook—a withered beauty with fresh yellow flowers in her black hair, her naked feet in a pair of dirty white satin shoes embroidered with gold, the *reboso* thrown over her left shoulder, and a cigar in her mouth; carrying a plate on each hand, spread out at the side of the head in a horizontal line with the ears. In a manner equally studied, though a little less pretending, the others, male and female, followed, and the rear was brought up by a boy carrying an earthen jar filled with drinking water, who, according to his humble station in this domestic hierarchy, was clad in a straw hat and a shirt reaching from his neck down to his waist. We kept a number of the little parrots called *chocollitos* in our court. At one time we had twenty of them. As soon as we sat down to our meal they would assemble to receive the sweets we threw to them, and would fight clamorously for the largest piece. These chocollitos are very beautiful and amusing little birds, which become tame almost instantaneously, and readily attach themselves to man, as they are in general of an amiable disposition. This temperament was shown in a touching manner by a sad catastrophe that carried away one of the little creatures. Most of them were young ones, and had not yet formed their alliances, which they generally keep with the strictest monogamic fidelity. There was, however, one male amongst them unconscientious enough to disturb the matrimonial peace of a united couple by seducing the mate of a fellow-parrot. When the latter understood the whole extent of his misfortune, and after he had made the last unsuccessful attempts to bring his faithless companion back to the path of duty, the unhappy creature, heartbroken by his wrongs, took his lonely seat on the perch on which he had passed happier nights closely pressed to the side of his partner,—refused to eat and drink, and one morning was found dead on the floor below.

By another startling event the number of our little chocollitos was diminished. We kept a tame deer in our courtyard, which suddenly became transformed into a carnivorous beast. There is no doubt that this animal had been demoralised by the society of man. At our dinner-table it first learned to eat meat,—thoroughly cooked, it is true—but whether its nature was more and more perverted by this unnatural diet, or that the green colour of the chocollitos contributed to the result, one day our deer seized one of the little birds in his mouth, and before rescue was possible, ate it alive. From that time the deer followed the savage instincts of a beast of prey, feeding on parrots, ducks, and chickens, till at last we found ourselves under the necessity of parting with its dangerous company.

We had another mischievous animal in our house, called *pisote*. A recent author on Central America has identified the pisote with the racoon, but this is a mistake. The pisote is the *Nasua fusca.* This animal becomes perfectly tame, but neither precaution nor chastisement will prevent it from doing mischief. Just now it had killed a chicken, and was chained up in consequence. Suddenly, while we were sitting at breakfast, it came from some unexpected quarter, dragging its chain after it, leaping on the table, overturning the sugar-bowl and scattering the sugar around, dipping its long bushy tail in our cups and whisking it in our faces. The offender was chastised most unmercifully and closely confined, but a few minutes after it appeared again quite contented, with a young chicken in its mouth. The criminal was threatened with instantaneous death, but escaped over the roof of the house, and soon after the cook discovered him committing ravages in the pantry.

I had several opportunities of observing the manners of several kinds of ants living in the houses. All of them are very inoffensive and even useful creatures. On one occasion I witnessed a remarkable instance of the concerted and organised action of a crowd of them. They were of a minute species, but by the wonderful order and expediency in which they worked together, and which it would have been difficult to realise with men, they succeeded in performing a task apparently quite beyond their capability. They carried a dead scorpion of full-grown size up the wall of our room from the floor to the ceiling, and thence along the under surface of a beam to a considerable distance, where at last they brought it safely into their nest in the interior of the wood. During the latter part of this achievement they had to bear the whole weight of the scorpion together with their own in their inverted position, and in this way to move along the beam. The order was so perfect that not the slightest deviation from an absolute symmetry and equality of distances and arrangement in the manner of taking hold of the body of the scorpion and in the movement of the little army of workmen was observable. No corps of engineers could be drilled to a more absolute perfection in the performance of a mechanical task. According to a rough calculation there must have been from five to six hundred of these intelligent little creatures at work. Besides those engaged in this transport no others were seen. A single one was sitting on the sting at the end of the scorpion's tail, as if placed there to overlook and direct the whole movement; all the rest, without any exception, were at work. The whole operation may have lasted about an hour.

At another time I witnessed the transmigration of a whole state or commonwealth of ants, from a hole in the wall, across our verandah, into another hole in the opposite wall. Two facts struck my attention in this case. The first was that the marching army of these insects, all moving in one direction, consisted of individuals of such a difference in size and shape, that to consider them as belonging to one species seemed very difficult, and the idea of a commonwealth of different insect nationalities was strongly suggested; the second that some little beetles of the family of *Coccinellidae* marched along with the ants from one hole into the other, not quite of their own will, for I observed that several times one of them tried to deviate from the line, but was quickly brought back to the ranks by some of the ants placing themselves at its side. The fact of little beetles of the very family just mentioned existing in the nests of ants is well known, but it is of considerable interest to see the fact repeated in distinct climates, with different species of insects of both tribes, and under opposite circumstances.

My intercourse with the native inhabitants of Granada has not been very extended. The unfortunate Ponciano Corral, a man of an excellent character, who was then the military commandant of the place, but who, a few years later, was shot by order of William Walker, accompanied me one day to see the Padre Vigil, a distinguished member of the Nicaraguan clergy, who was afterwards sent by the Walker government as a diplomatic agent to Washington. The conversation, in which other eminent persons participated, turned upon that favourite topic of Hispano-Americans—the mines; all the gentlemen present having some interest in a certain mine in the province of Chontales which yielded a yellow substance respecting which a doubt existed as to whether it was gold or not. In the course of the conversation I was asked by which of the planets the gold was produced and by which the silver. The Padre Vigil is a man of enlightened views in religious matters, who has always belonged to the liberal party of the country, and has ever been favourable to foreigners. Religious toleration and hospitality towards them were the constant theme of his sermons delivered in the cathedral of Granada during the time of my residence.

It was not without interest to me, to make the

acquaintance of two brothers, young gentlemen belonging to one of the more distinguished families of the country. One of them filled a government office at the capital; the other had studied medicine at the University of Leon and had commenced following his profession at Granada. Both were distinguished by their scientific and literary pursuits. The doctor, however, seemed to be stronger in philosophy than in the medical art and science. The people of Granada, who are much in the habit of showing their interest for a public character by giving him a nickname, called him *Doctor Matagente*,—i. e. Doctor Menkiller. But he was of a metaphysical turn of mind, feeling himself greatly attracted by the mysteries of German philosophy, into which he had been initiated by some French books that had found their way to Nicaragua. "The Germans," he observed, "have a great philosopher named Schlegel, who has written a book bearing the title of 'Philosophy of Life.' They have another great philosopher called Hegel, but this one is too difficult to be understood." "Los Alemanes," he continued in an enthusiastic strain, "son la nacion la mas cientifica, la mas filosofica, la mas profunda!" a compliment I was not prepared to hear paid to the German nation in these quarters of the world; but which, considering that we had no man like Mr. Chatfield to make us respected in Central America, I thought a great consolation. The doctor's brother, the politician, is the author of several pamphlets printed in Nicaragua. In reading one of them, it struck me how schools and systems of philosophy, even without being understood, extend their influence over the world, and how even the most abstract metaphysician of Germany should never forget—and especially if he should have the misfortune of being translated into French—that he may cause some mischief in Nicaragua. The Nicaraguan writer I am speaking of, the brother of the admirer of Schlegel and Hegel, is the author of an essay on the Nicaraguan revolution in which he quotes Tacitus and Puffendorf, Ancillon and Vattel, Guizot and Louis Blanc, Madame de Staël and Montesquieu, Droz and Matter, Necker and Mirabeau; and speaks of idealism and antagonism, aspirantism and dualism, proselytism, anachronism, and several other equally dangerous principles.

CHAPTER IV.

Indian village of Jinotépet — Columnar Cactus and Yucca-trees — Dividing Ridge between the Pacific and the Atlantic — Climate of this Region — Cultivation of Sugar and Coffee — Boundary-line between different Indian Races — Indian Languages of Nicaragua — Aztec Words in the Spanish Idiom of the Country — Geographical Names of Aztec Origin — Pretended Gold Mines — Indian Hospitality.

Towards the end of December I made an excursion to a large Indian village called *Jinotépet*, situated about twenty miles from Granada, in a west-southwesterly direction. I wished to examine a vein of silver-ore, which was said to exist in the neighbourhood. The samples which I had seen presented a considerable proportion of the red silver-ore, accompanying a mass of sulphuret of antimony.

The road to Jinotépet crosses a range of hills extending from Mount Mombacho, in the direction towards the volcano of Masaya. There is a spring on the road-side at the eastern foot of the pass, which, from that circumstance, is called *La Fuente*, the fountain. Springs are of rare occurrence in this country.

On the other side of the ridge a hilly country extends, in which the scenery is agreeably varied. Here and there a hut with a small plantation of bananas is seen in the woods. I passed the village of *Diriá*, where I saw for the first time the columnar cactus, and a species of Yucca, of high tree-like growth, which the inhabitants call *espadillo*, while to the columnar cactus they give the name of *órgano*. Both plants belong to the drier and more western region of Nicaragua, to which they communicate something of the character of the Mexican table-land. This kind of cactus is planted in some villages for enclosures of gardens and courtyards, to which such a fence affords the most effective protection. It may be called a living vegetable wall, which has no fault, but that it grows too high if allowed to do so; the columns frequently reaching fifteen or twenty feet. Nothing is more easy than to plant such a fence. Old trunks are divided into stumps of a certain length, and these, taking care not to invert them by mistake, are placed side by side vertically in the ground, where they soon begin to strike root and thrive. In the more eastern, the lower and moister regions of the country, the *piñuela* —a kind of Bromelia or wild pine-apple—is used for fences.

The western half of the road passes over a plain occupied by a savana without trees or shrubs, called the *Llano de Jinotépet.* This is the central part of a flat swell of country separating the slope to the Atlantic from that to the Pacific. To the north of this plain the volcano of Masaya is seen, with which a short ridge, called the *Sierra de Masatépet,* is connected. On a hill of the latter, marked by a group of high palm-trees, stands the village of Masatépet. To the north-east is the Mombacho, and round its southern foot, passing the village of *Diriomo,* the plain slopes gradually down to the lake, changing at the same time the character of the vegetation by its transition into a park-like country with groups of trees and bushes. This change seems to be the effect of the greater moisture of the local climate of the south-western side of the mountain. As is the case with other high peaks of this region, the lee or south-western side of the Mombacho is moistened, even during the dry season, when the country around is parched, by an almost daily atmospheric exudation of a very restricted local character, extending scarcely beyond the base of the mountain. While riding over the plain, the *fata morgana* produced the aspect of an extended lake with numerous wooded islands,—a charming and unexpected view.

The situation of Jinotépet, at the western extremity of the plain, and separated from it only by a little valley where trees re-appear, is on the highest elevation of the flat swell above-mentioned. At a little distance only from the village are the springs of several brooks flowing to the Pacific. They have a rapid fall, passing through narrow gorges, overgrown with forests of mighty trees. The distance from Jinotépet to the Pacific, however, is about the same as that to Granada. Some maps, which place this village close to the sea-coast, are defective in this respect. By its elevation above the sea Jinotépet has a cool and bracing climate. Early in the morning I found the air so sharp, that I regretted to have no gloves with me. This place, most likely, is as healthy as any on the face of the globe. The census made in 1847 gives 4650 inhabitants, with 255 births, and 83 deaths; and reports a mean temperature of 15° Réaumur, from which, according to the general equality of the climate of Central-America, the extremes can be but slightly deviating. The inhabitants of the village, who are almost exclusively Indians, are a very industrious race. They are the principal sugar-growers in Nicaragua, and all around, during my visit, I heard the rattling noise of their *trapiches*, or primitive sugar-mills, turned by mules. The cultivation of the coffee, too, had been lately introduced at Jinotépet, and there is no doubt that the situation and climate are well adapted for the purpose. A considerable stock of cattle is kept on some farms of this neighbourhood. The census of the above-named year shows an export of 400 arrobas of cheese, and several thousand hides.

I found the people of this village very intelligent and polite. Two of the principal men took me between them, and proceeded to show me the sights of the place. This I found very neat and clean. The public square before the church, a building of some pretensions, which, however, remains in an unfinished state, had a fresh green sward, producing quite a northern impression, with which, however, the purity and brightness of the dark-blue sky, the balmy softness of the air, the erect trunks of the columnar cactus, the lily-trees of the yucca, and the plantations of *pulcre*—a small species of agave,—were in strong contradiction.

I am not sure to which of the two adjoining races of Nicaraguan Indians—the Aztecs and the Dirians—the population of Jinotépet is to be referred. They have given up their Indian language. Some old men, I was told, still retain it, but when I was at the place I could get no information on the subject. In their physiognomy and manners, the Indian type could not be mistaken. As I passed through the streets, I saw young women, with the upper part of their body uncovered, but with flowers in their hair, standing in some of the doorways, only withdrawing a little as I came near. In the name of the village, the two last syllables, "*tépet*," are derived from the Aztec language, in which *tepetl*[1] means *a mountain*. The whole name was translated to me by "*wind-mountain.*"

[1] The original termination in *tl* is either omitted entirely, or loses the *l*, or changes into *c* in the remnants of the Aztec language in Nicaragua, and it appears that the same is the case in other parts of Central America and in Mexico. In Nicaragua, for instance, we have the names *Jinotépe*, *Jinotépec*, *Jinotépet*,—*Masatépe*, *Masatépec*, *Masatépet*,—instead of the original *Jinotépetl* and *Masatépetl*.

The derivation of the two first syllables is uncertain. From several circumstances, it appears that the village of Jinotépet is just on the old boundary line between the territories of a fragment of the Aztec race settled in Nicaragua, and of another tribe of Indians called the Dirians or Chorotegans. According to the statements of Oviedo and some other early historians, there were five different languages spoken in Nicaragua at the time of the first arrival of the Spaniards. One of those languages was that of the *Chontales*, or inhabitants of the mountainous regions to the north-east of the lake of Nicaragua. Of that language and race I shall speak in another chapter, when I relate my excursion to the province of Chontales and to the plateau of Upper Mosquitia. Amongst the four remaining Indian languages of the country, the Aztec is the most important. The islands of the lake of Nicaragua and the isthmus of Rivas seem to be the most southern country inhabited by the Aztec race, and it is a fragment of the nation, separated from the main stock, which has occupied this small region placed between other Indian tribes. Mr. Squier was the first to elucidate the fact, that the language of the present inhabitants of the island of Ometépe is the Aztec. The name of that island itself is a compound of the two Aztec words *ome*—which means *two*—and *tepetl*, the whole corresponding to the nature of the island, which is composed of two volcanic peaks with a low neck of land between them. The region inhabited by this fragment of the Aztec nation, or Nahuatlac race—if this latter designation should appear preferable—is *Nicaragua Proper*, the district to which the name now given to the whole country was exclusively applied at the time of the discovery; and even now the residents of Granada or other parts of the republic, when they visit Rivas, San Jorge, or other places of that district, say that they are going to Nicaragua. Mr. Squier, following, if I am not mistaken, Oviedo, reapplies the old name of *Niquirans* to these Nicaraguan Aztecs. At the time of the discovery, another nation, called the *Orotinans,* lived south of them on the gulf of Nicoyo or Orotina, while to the north—in the districts of Granada, Masaya, Tipitapa, Managua, Diriomo, Diriá, Diriamba, &c.—were the *Dirians.* Still farther on to the northwest were the *Nagrandans,* in the district of Leon, and beyond them on the gulf of Fonseca, a nation called the *Cholutecans* had their seats.

These four nations,—the Dirians, Orotinans, Nagrandans, and Cholutecans,—taken together, must have spoken *three* languages, to make up the five Indian dialects mentioned by the old Spanish historians of Nicaragua; and accordingly it remains to be investigated which two of them have had one language in common. Two of these three languages—that of the Dirians and that of the Nagrandans—are still in existence, and vocabularies, together with the outlines of their grammatical structure, have been published by Mr. Squier; the Dirian collected from the Indians of Masaya, the Nagrandan from those of Subtiaba, near Leon. Nothing, however, has come to our knowledge of the language of the two remaining nations, the Orotinans and the Cholutecans. Mr. Squier is inclined to suppose that the Orotinans belonged to the Nagrandans. Amongst the geographical names of the country inhabited by the former, we meet with that of the volcano of *Orosi,* in Costarica; while one of the volcanos of the chain of the Maribios, near Leon, in the old country of the Nagrandans, is called *Orota.* It is very likely that both names have the same derivation, and may be considered as a trace of affinity between the two tribes. The question may still be solved, in case some remnants of the old language of the

Orotinans should be found to exist in the government of Guanacaste, disputed between Nicaragua and Costarica. Another supposition, however, may be made to distribute the three languages amongst the four nations. The Cholutecans may have spoken an Aztec dialect, and thus have had their language in common with the Niquirans. According to Sahagun, one of the seven tribes of the Nahuatlacs, who all spoke the Aztec language, were called the *Chololtecas*, a word which, in its original Aztec form, was *Chololtecatl*, meaning a native of Cholola. If, then, the Cholutecans of the region around the Gulf of Fonseca should have been a branch or fragment of the Chololtecas of Mexico, the name being merely modified by the vicious pronunciation of the other Nicaraguan tribes, they must have spoken the Aztec language; which is to say that they spoke the same language with the Niquirans or true Nicaraguans. The wide distribution of geographical names derived from the Aztec language, which are found spread over the northern section of Nicaragua, seems to corroborate this opinion. There is, however, a circumstance contradictory to it. The old historians have a third form of what is apparently the same word. It is the name of the *Chorotegans.* According to Herrera, the "Cholutecans" were a noble caste of the "Chorotegans." The latter word, therefore, was a more comprehensive denomination than the former, and it was sometimes used for all the four nations above mentioned. Oviedo, on the other hand, uses the two names of Dirians and Chorotegans indiscriminately for the same nation, whose language is sufficiently known to prove that it has no affinity with the Aztec. From these facts it would appear that the name of the Chorotegans must have been used in more than one sense, but which had nothing to do with the affinity of races, and most likely expressed some old political connexion of the Cholutecans with nations who spoke a different language from that of the latter. In this extended historical application the name was vulgarised, while the caste of "nobles" (*i. e.*, the *real* Cholutecans), who may have been a fragment of the Chololtecas of Mexico, retained the purer form of the denomination. Whatever may be the true explanation of these difficulties, the question as to the language of the Cholutecans of Nicaragua may still be decided by the study of the Indian idioms still existing in the district of Honduras called Choluteca, on the Gulf of Fonseca, and in the Nicaraguan provinces of Nuevo Segovia and Matagalpa.

As to the village of Jinotépet, Mr. Buschmann, of Berlin, who is deeply engaged in the investigation of American languages, and who has published a paper on the geographical names derived from the Aztec,[1] could not translate the two first syllables; but, the whole name being translated to me as signifying "wind-mountain," *Jino* may be a contraction or mutilation of the word *Chiquinau*, which, according to Oviedo, was one of the two names the inhabitants of Nicaragua gave to the god of the wind. The other name was *Hecact*, which is the Aztec *Ehecatl*, signifying *wind*. *Chiquinau*, then, must have been the name of that deity, or of the element of the air, in the Dirian language, and the name of Jinotépet appears as a compound of two words derived from two languages. The same seems to be the case with the name of the neighbouring village of *Masatépet*, though Mr. Buschmann translates it by *deer-mountain*, from the Aztec *mazatl*, deer. That village, however, is quite close to the town of *Masaya*,

---

[1] Ueber die Aztekischen Ortsnamen. Von Joh. Carl Ed. Buschmann. Berlin, 1853.

and, like Jinotépet, was situated on the boundary-line between the two languages—the Aztec and the Dirian. In the latter, according to Oviedo, the word *masaya* means "the burning mountain." By the Aztec neighbours of the Dirians, the volcano at the foot of which the town of Masaya is situated was called *Popogatepec*—"the smoking mountain"—a name synonymous with that of the celebrated *Popocatepetl*, of Mexico. Thus, the name of the village of Masatépet likewise seems to be a compound of two words belonging to two languages, as the first part is apparently connected with that of the town and volcano of Masaya.

The encroachments of the Aztec language on the other idioms of Central America are an interesting fact which may contribute to throw light on the migrations of the American aboriginal races and the history of their civilization. In Nicaragua, where, as far as we know, only a fragment of the Aztec race existed at the time of the conquest, still a considerable number of Aztec words have been admitted in the Spanish idiom of the country; as, for instance: *moyote*, the mosquito; Aztec *moyotl*;—*sacate*, grass; Aztec *sacatl*;—*mecate*, thread; Aztec *mecatl*;—*metate*, the stone on which mais is ground; Aztec *metatl*. The latter three words, like many others, are in common use in the Spanish idiom of Mexico. A beautiful little bird, of red colour, frequently seen in Nicaragua, is called *cicitote*. The name, no doubt, is a compound of the two Aztec words, *chichiltic*, red, and *tototl*, bird. One circumstance, however, is particularly striking, as an instance of the adoption of Aztec words in the Spanish dialect of Nicaragua. In the social life of Granada the word "*pipe*" (pronounced *peepey*) is used as an address or title of honour and affection granted to any superior or more distinguished and cherished person of the male sex. A younger brother addresses the older one with this title. I heard the word first during a surgical operation, throughout which the patient, a young girl, continued to exclaim, "Ay doctorcito!—ay mi hermano!—ay *pipe!*"—*i. e.*, oh my dear doctor!—oh my brother!—oh *pipe!* On asking, I received the above explanation. At this moment, an Aztec tribe, living in the State of Salvador, is called the *Pipiles*. According to Mr. Buschmann, this name is an Aztec word. *Pipilli*, as he states, and a reduplication of *pilli*, which has the double meaning of *child* and *nobleman* (like the German word *junker*), and which, in the compound meaning of *noble child*, is used as the name of the tribe in Salvador, and as an expression of tenderness and respect in the social life of Granada. The latter town, however, stands on the site of an old city of the Choroteguans or Dirians, *not* of the Niquirans, and the Aztec element in its society, therefore, must have been introduced from Nicaragua Proper and the islands of the lake; while its Indian suburb of Jalteva has remained purely Dirian in its population. It is of considerabe interest to see that in the political dissensions of the country the inhabitants of Jalteva have always been on the side of the city of Leon against Granada, while the latter has invariably been supported by the whole Aztec population of Nicaragua Proper. The fact shows how the old animosities of different Indian nations are still at the root of the civil wars of Central America.

But I have almost forgotten my visit to Jinotépet.

The information that a foreign "cavallero" had arrived for the purpose of examining the mines of Jinotépet, had spread through the village and produced a considerable excitement. People of both sexes and of all ages came to see me. Foremost amongst them was a number of old women, who crowded around me, all the time speaking of gold-mines and silver mines, of yellow metals and white metals, and of certain lights or flames seen at night, called *carbunculos*, by which those metals are indicated. As they became more and more excited by their recitals, their imaginations grew heated, their statements extravagant, and their gesticulations violent. A crowd of naked children, with mouths and eyes wide-open, were standing or sitting around. One little boy in particular struck my attention. Sitting on the floor, his monstrous globular belly resting on his crossed legs, the soles of his feet turned upwards, each of his hands holding one of his great toes, while all the time he was staring in my face; he resembled more an idol formed of brown clay, than a living human being.

As the result of my inquiries into the situation of the silver mine of which I had heard at Granada, I learned that a complete mistake had prevailed; the metallic vein which it had been my intention to inspect being farther distant from Jinotépet than from Granada. The *cura* of the place, however, to whom I had a letter of recommendation, in explaining the error, took pains to convince me that I had no cause to repent my visit to Jinotépet, as he had discovered two gold-mines on his own land which would be equally worth examination. One of them he called the "mina del Salto," the other the "mina de la Conquista." Being here, I consented to visit the two places. The alcalde of Jinotépet provided me with a fresh horse and a guide; several boys of the village volunteered to accompany me, and I rode out in the direction to the Pacific.

The road, after we had left the sugar-plantations of the village behind us, passed through a charming landscape of hills partially wooded. Towards the Pacific, the country assumes gradually a wild and romantic character. Narrow gorges began, rapidly descending towards the coast. Little streams of transparent water rush over coloured pebbles, and hastening from cascade to cascade, enter a belt of forest separating the open region of the higher country from the sea-shore. We passed several deserted indigo estates, where extensive buildings were left to decay in the wilderness. The rocks of this region seemed to belong to a metamorphic tertiary formation, somewhat of a chloritic and schisteous character. "*Aqui está la mina!*"—here is the mine!—cried the guide, pointing to the bank of a brook. The rock, of the character just described, contained numerous little crystals of iron pyrites. Of course, it is not impossible that some particles of gold may accompany the pyrites, but the priest who was the owner of the locality and designated it as a gold mine, had no other reasons for his extravagant opinion than the yellow colour and metallic appearance of the pyrites.

When my guide and the boys who had followed me saw me break off a few samples of the rock and put them in my pocket, they began most eagerly to do the same. To tell them that the yellow specks in the rock were not gold would have been absolutely fruitless. The poor horses were chiefly to be pitied, as, besides their riders, they had to bear their newly acquired wealth. On our way home the guide came up to my side asking me in a confidential manner how many *pesos* the pound of gold was worth. In the village the excitement grew so high, that I felt induced to throw away the samples I had collected. This again the others imitated. A crowd of little boys ran after the stones, throwing them farther and farther off in a spiteful manner, and I am confident the village has been purged of the last particle of the delusive yellow substance.

There was, however, a gentleman in the room in which I had been received, a priest from a neighbouring village, who, with an expression in his countenance which seemed to say: "I know better," looked doubtfully and seriously at these proceedings. After he had remained silent for a time, he drew a sheet of the official gazette of Leon from his pocket. It contained a proclamation from the Nicaraguan minister for the interior, stating that in the neighbourhood of the capital a most important discovery had been made. A bed of gold dust had been found, richer than the richest "*placer*" of California. "In consequence of this discovery"—thus the proclamation concluded—"our beloved Nicaragua will soon take the honourable position assigned to it amongst the nations of the globe. This country, favoured with the predilection of divine providence, will reach its glorious and happy destiny." This proclamation the gentleman read aloud. My sceptical remarks were received with contempt, and I perceived that I was looked at as a man who, from selfish motives, tried to dissuade the people from believing in the treasures hidden in the ground of their country. When I returned to Granada, however, it was already discovered that the authorities of Leon had been deceived—nobody knew for what exact purpose—by some Yankees returning from California, who buried a small quantity of gold-dust and then announced their pretended discovery to the government.

The place described above was what the owner called the "mina del Salto." The "mina de la Conquista" proved to be of the same description: the same rock, the same little cubes of iron pyrites disseminated through it. But I had no cause to repent my ride of twenty-four miles. The country had some spots of incomparable beauty. At noon I rested at the habitation of an Indian family. Their little hut in the woods was surrounded by a selection of the rarest and most distinguished flowering shrubs of the country. This, as I have already observed, is a characteristic taste of the Indian population of Nicaragua. Near their habitations I have seen some plants and flowers of extraordinary beauty, which I observed nowhere else, neither in a wild nor in a cultivated state, and which it might even be of some historical interest to study as to their native region. I was very politely received by the female inhabitants, no men being present, a dinner of eggs, chocolate, plantains, and oranges was served up in a clean and decent manner, and when, on taking leave, I proposed payment, I was told that it had been given "*de cariño*," out of hospitality.

CHAPTER V.

A Trip to Leon — Tipitapa — Connexion between the two Lakes interrupted — Decreasing Level of the Lake of Managua — Hot Sulphur Springs — A Saint's Day — Adam and Eve — Theatrical Entertainment — Managua and Mateares — Silver Ore and Lignite — Amber found in Nicaragua — Nagarote — The Volcanic Chain of the Maribios — Pueblo Nuevo — The Chachalagua — Leon — General Muñoz — The Cathedral — Proletarians of Leon — A French Colonization Project — Gold-Mines of Matagalpa — Extensive Gold Region.

On the 12th of January, 1851, I left Granada on a visit to *Leon*, the capital of Nicaragua. The direct road leads to Masaya, but intending to pass there on my way back, I took the direction to *Tipitapa*, a village thirty miles to the north of Granada, situated on the channel connecting the lake of Nicaragua with that of Managua, but which had been dried up by an earthquake in 1844.

I crossed a plain overgrown with shrubs and trees, where I saw or heard numerous monkeys, parrots, macaws, curassows, pigeons, and other birds that I did not recognize. In passing I shot a pair of beautiful pigeons, of a species called *morena*, for my supper. This is the largest of seven different species which I have observed in Nicaragua, being of the size of our common domestic pigeon, and of a brownish rose-colour. In the evening I arrived at Tipitapa and took up my abode in the house of a man of distinction in the village, where I found such accommodations for the night as a traveller has a right to expect in Central America.

The next morning I went to see what is called the river and falls of Tipitapa, but which I found to be the dry channel once occupied by a river, with a perpendicular rock from twelve to fifteen feet high, crossing it, which would form a cascade if there was water to fall over it. This is the present condition of the *Rio* and *Salto de Tipitapa*—or rather was its condition when I visited the place. I was afterwards informed, as I have already stated, that the river ceased to flow in consequence of an earthquake which happened in 1844. This, however, must not be understood in the absolute sense of the word. A little streamlet may run over the "salto" in the rainy season, and the more probably as there are several springs of hot water in the bed of the river. At the time of my visit they filled only some stagnant pools, but they may contribute to produce a rivulet during the rainy season. The lower section of the old river channel is now to be considered as a narrow branch of the lake of Nicaragua, extending upwards to the neighbourhood of the "salto," and called the *Estero Panaloya*, of which I shall have to speak hereafter. To study the changes in the hydrographic system of this region produced by the earthquake mentioned above, more time would have been necessary than it was my intention to spend in my visit to Tipitapa; but the principal cause of my inability to give a more exact account is that the fact of the earthquake was only communicated to me after my return to Granada, none of the inhabitants of Tipitapa mentioning the matter. While travelling along the shore of the lake of Managua I afterwards saw indubitable traces of the lake having had a higher level in former times and having decreased gradually, or in intervals, as indicated by the repetition of watermarks on the rocks. If the sudden sinking of the lake was produced by earthquake, the slow and gradual diminution of its water, which I suppose is still going on, may have been caused by the combined influence of subterranean drainage and of evaporation; and perhaps the latter alone may be sufficient to explain the fact. This lake, with the exception of its middle section, is very shallow. While bathing near Mateares, I observed that you may walk into it for a great distance from the shore, and I was even told at the latter place that a man on horseback might cross over to Momotombito, a distance of twelve or fifteen miles. Whether this is true or not, I cannot tell, but from my observation of the nature of the bottom of the lake I should think it very possible. As far as I could observe, the lake rests on a horizontal sheet of lava.

Much has been said respecting the former navigation of the San Juan river. Vessels coming directly from Spain, it has been stated, have formerly ascended that river, passed through the lake of Nicaragua and anchored at Granada. Such a thing being now utterly impossible, as the reader is aware from my statements in reference to the rapids at the Castillo Viejo, a question has been raised as to the cause by which the change has been produced. The Castillo rapids, it has been maintained, have been purposely rendered impassable by the Spaniards throwing rocks into the river. This may be true. But, at the same time, may not a general diminution of water in the hydrographic system of the San Juan river, including the lake of Managua, be the principal and original cause of so important a change in the natural facilities of communication existing in Nicaragua? I do not know whether these considerations have ever been brought to bear on the question of the inter-oceanic canal.

To return to Tipitapa, I have to state that the copious hot spring which bursts from the ground on the bank of the old river-bed is strongly sulphurous, with excellent medical qualities. The whole place has the smell of sulphuretted hydrogen, and the mineral incrustations around the spring are impregnated with sulphur. The taste of the water, which is boiling, corresponds to this chemical character; but the sulphurous element is less strong than might be expected. Besides this, the taste is sweet, and has much the savour of broth, so general in a certain class of hot mineral waters. I drank from this spring copiously before my breakfast, and experienced a very pleasant sensation from it, as if I had taken a plate of soup or a good cup of coffee. Close to this hot sulphur spring is another of pure cold water, and cold and hot springs seem to exist close together in the old river-bed. I shot a cormorant, which fell into a pool of cold water filling a basin in the channel. When I sent my servant in to fetch the bird, his feet suddenly encountered a hot spring in the midst of the cold water, and were nearly scalded. Below the step of rock which had formed the fall was a deep basin filled with warm water, in which I intended to bathe, when I saw some small alligators rise from the bottom and then disappear again. On a rock in the midst of this pool sat an *iguana* of the size of a boy ten years old, the largest specimen of this repulsive kind of lizard I have ever seen. I was previously unaware of the fact that these animals can swim.

Strolling about at this interesting locality, I spent a day at Tipitapa. The following day was to be the festival of "our Lord of Esquipulas," who has a sanctuary at this place, and from all directions the inhabitants of the neighbouring country arrived, until in the evening Tipitapa had the aspect of a gay and crowded fair. After dark the people were amused by a theatrical entertainment in which priests were the actors. The subject was a clownish reproduction of a character similar to the *Tartuffe*—a hypocrite who tries to seduce the virtuous wife of his friend. The female part, too, was represented by a priest. Coarse jests and morals were mixed up in the play, by which the crowd appeared to be mightily amused and edified.

The immense congregation of people who had arrived on the eve of the celebration deprived me of the accommodations I had enjoyed for the first night. I had to give up my "cama" or bedstead, in which I had rested, after the fashion of the country, on a skin or sheet of parchment stretched on a frame, and was reduced to sleep on a rough and stiff hide spread on the floor of a large room, in which the bed of the landlord and his pretty young wife, decently surrounded with curtains, held a conspicuous place. When I opened my eyes at dawn, I saw my landlord and his wife up. The young woman was singing, in a low voice, the "Versos de la Viuda," or Song of the Widow—a favourite air of the country—and she afterwards took a jar filled with water, which she poured over the head of her husband, then dried his back carefully with a towel, after which the happy couple dressed in joyful mood.

During the morning I spent half an hour in the room, finishing a sketch I had made of the scenery near the hot springs. Several women stood around me, looking at my occupation, and making their remarks as if I did not understand their language. "Look!" said one of them, "he is only writing a little, and yet he is perspiring as if he was doing hard work." "Es cavallero tan delicato—he is such a delicate gentleman," replied the other.

On the 14th I continued my journey, and in the evening reached Mateares, a little village situated on the shore of the Lake of Managua, and distant about forty miles from Tipitapa. From the latter place to Managua the road leads through the woods close to the Lake, but without an opening to allow a view of it. *Managua*, the seat of the Nicaraguan legislature, is a town of twelve or thirteen thousand inhabitants, in a splendid situation, on an elevated portion of the shore. Between this place and Mateares a peninsula projects into the Lake. It is formed of steep and wooded hills. The road takes the straight line, by passing over the neck by which the peninsula is joined to the mainland. This is a pass of considerable importance in a military point of view. On the south-eastern side of it the traveller, between magnificent trees on the edge of a precipice, looks down on the lake at his feet, while beyond it his eye is arrested by the high volcanic cones in the vicinity of Leon, or by the more distant chain of Matagalpa. The road descends gradually towards Mateares, passing through an open forest of scattered trees, with an undergrowth of piñuela and a variety of shrubs. Many of the trees and shrubs were in full blossom, entirely covered with yellow, pink, or violet flowers.

At *Mateares* I found lodgings in the hut of a good-natured thick mulatto woman, where I passed the night in a hammock. Doña Juana was famous for preparing the best chocolate on the road, and I found she merited her reputation. She liked to have a talk with the travellers who entered her dwelling, and I was soon such a favourite with her that with her own lips she lit a cigar and put it in my mouth. After I had taken my meal, some of the more distinguished personages of the village assembled around me, and we were soon engaged in a lively conversation, during which I was asked whether I was a Christian, and whether the Jews were not very bad men. As long as they were of opinion that I was a native of the United States, they spoke in terms of admiration of that people; but when they learned that I was born in Germany, one of them asked me, quite in a confidential manner, whether I did not think "que los Americanos son bestias." Upon my objecting to this expression it was revoked; but the man, having once given vent to his feelings, could not abstain from expressing them in a milder form, by adding that, at least, the Americans were devils. "Pe o son demonios!" he exclaimed; "demonios son estos hombres!"

At Mateares I had a conversation with a young man of one of the more distinguished families of the country living at Managua. He stated that on the hacienda of San Lorenzo, thirty miles from Mateares, on the coast of the Pacific, he had discovered a quicksilver mine. But the specimen he communicated to me, instead of being cinnabar, proved to be *red silver ore.* This metallic vein must be in the vicinity of that which I intended to examine when I went to Jinotépet, and the ore is probably of the same nature as that of the latter. In the region between Mateares and the Pacific strata of *lignite* are found, and the young Nicaraguan said that he could show me the locality of a coal mine. This, however, is a more general feature in the geology of the Pacific side of Central America, and even of other Pacific regions of the continent; as, for instance, of California, where small layers of tertiary coal are very general in the coast-range. In Central America, lignite, including *amber*, occasionally occurs from Costarica to Salvador, and, in all probability, farther south as well as farther north. Pieces of amber, some with insects in them, derived from the tertiary coal formation of the Bay of Tamarinda, I saw at Leon in possession of Dr.

Gregorio Juares, and of the American consul, Dr. Livingston. The latter showed me some samples of coal from the neighbourhood of Leon. They were of a greyish black colour, rather hard, with the texture of wood clearly visible. On being burnt, a considerable quantity of ashes were left, in some cases of a white, in others of a red colour. In the state of Salvador this tertiary coal formation seems to have a sufficient development to promise a certain degree of future importance.

On the following day I proceeded to *Pueblo Nuevo*, where I passed the night. From Mateares this is only a distance of thirty miles or a little more. The road, between Mateares and Nagarote, a village halfway to Pueblo Nuevo, is most interesting and has some charming sections. For a time it leads along under the shade of gigantic trees, while the eye passes over the lake and rests on the mountains of Matagalpa and the peaks of the Maribios, beginning with the island of *Momotombito* visited by Mr. Squier, who has described its idols. Next comes the noble cone of the *Momotombo*, about 7000 feet high. From its summit a thin cloud of steam rises, scarcely traceable in the pure atmosphere. Farther on, the *Asososca*, or, more correctly spelled, the *Axosco*, is seen. Mr. Buschmann thinks that this name can be derived from the Aztec *ak*, meaning *water*, and *xotla*, signifying *to kindle* or *burn*, the whole word *Axochco* having the signification of a "volcano of water," like the "volcan de agua" of Guatemala. Then follow the *Pilas*, the *Orota*, and the *Telica*, the *Santa Clara* and the *Viejo*, which complete the enumeration of the whole system, but are concealed from the view. At certain places the road, still following the shore of the lake, passes over small tracts of loose sand, overgrown with shrubs of the mimosa, with yellow catkins of a most exquisite odour, from which the shrub, which yields a gum like the gum arabic, bears the name of *aroma.*

Nagarote is a village of bad reputation. I arrived there at noon and spent an hour at dinner. After I had left, my servant rode up to my side and said: "El señor de la casa es capitan de ladrones;" "the landlord of the house where we stopped is the chief of a band of robbers." On both sides of Nagarote the road passes through a forest, and this neighbourhood was deemed among the unsafest parts of Nicaragua.

I left *Pueblo Nuevo* early in the morning. The streets of this village, which is a place of some consideration, are between rows of the columnar cactus or *órgano*, the houses standing back in the courtyards formed by these natural walls. The first part of the road from hence to Leon leads again through the woods. The sun had not yet risen when I entered them, and in all directions I heard the call of the *chachalagua*, a kind of wild chicken or pheasant, common throughout the hot regions of Central America and Mexico. I could never succeed in shooting this bird, of which I was told in Honduras that it crosses with the tame chicken, producing hybrids of which the males are highly valued as fighting cocks.

When the road approaches to within a few leagues of *Leon* the country opens, and a beautiful plain, well cultivated with maize, expands before the sight. To the left a ridge of wooded hills, bordering the sea-coast, discovers itself; to the right is the chain of volcanic peaks enumerated above. "There is Leon!" cried my servant, a boy of fourteen, with all the pride of a patriotic Nicaraguan. But remembering that he was a native of Granada, his jealousy was roused, and he added: "Leon is larger, but Granada surpasses it in civilization!"

I hastened to call on General *Muñoz*, at that time the chief personage in Nicaragua, to whom I brought a letter of introduction. He received me in complete undress, throwing, however, in the moment of my entering the room, a little cape or diminutive cloak, outside yellow and inside blue, over his shoulders, in which he reminded me strongly of Leporello in the opera. The effect of the letter surpassed my expectations. The general assured me of his sincerest friendship, and, as far as my interest with him has gone, I have had no reason to doubt his sincerity. In another chapter I shall have to say more of this distinguished individual, who has since perished in the civil wars of Central America. Another letter introduced me to Señor Ramirez, then the President, or as the Nicaraguan title runs, the "*Director Supremo*" of the republic.

Having made the acquaintance of these and other prominent men of the capital, I went lounging about to see the city. From the effects of long and desperate struggles, of which Leon has been the theatre during the civil wars of the country, the greater number of the houses were in ruins, and I have no reason to suppose that these have since diminished. Nevertheless, Leon is still one of the largest cities of Central America. At the time of my visit it was stated to have 30,000 inhabitants. This may be a gross exaggeration. But it is very difficult to form an opinion of the matter, as even from the roof of the cathedral the suburbs cannot be seen in their whole extent. The scattered houses of the outer parts hide themselves in a forest of trees and between thickets of shrubbery. The cathedral—a large and well-constructed stone building with a massive cupola and roof—is one of the most distinguished works of architecture in Spanish America. The view from the roof is magnificent, and ranges over the most beautiful scenes of this kind I have ever seen. Round a large area the red roofs of the houses are seen here and there peeping out between trees of the most luxuriant growth, while the plain beyond is occupied by an immense forest, occasionally broken by fields of maize more extensively and carefully cultivated than I have seen elsewhere in Nicaragua. In a westerly and north-westerly direction the plain slopes gradually down to the coast of the Pacific, without any intervening hills. This is not the case towards the south, where the north-western termination of a range of hills running close to the sea-coast is seen. Towards the north and the east the whole line of volcanic cones enumerated above, from the Viejo to the Momotombo, rise in strange regularity of form so as to appear more like gigantic works of art than natural mountains.

The population of the suburbs of Leon is mostly Indian; that of *Subtiaba*, which is considered a suburb but is more a town by itself, is entirely so, and has even preserved its Indian language. In some respects my servant was right when he said that Granada was more civilized than Leon, as apparently the latter city has preserved more of the original Central American life than Granada, where the influence of foreigners and foreign mercantile connexions has been much greater. Granada, moreover, is chiefly a commercial town, and in its population the "*bourgeois*" character predominates; while Leon represents the allied interests of a landed aristocracy and a very active and determined democracy.

While I passed through the streets, a young fellow, whom I may call a true type of this latter, element, accosted me, requesting that I would allow him to light his cigar. "Your Grace," he said, after I had complied, "is a stranger, but a very polite gentleman. When I left the house of my father, he told me: My son, you must be polite towards the high as well as towards the low, and when a gentleman wants to light his cigar, you must be quick to serve him: in this my father was right. But I say that the gentleman should not be less polite than the common man of the people, and when I want fire for lighting my cigar he should show himself obliging in turn. Don't you think so, sir?"

One evening I took a sketch of a street of *Saragosa*, which is a suburb of Leon, and while thus occupied, a whole crowd of people gathered around me. Some gentlemen on horseback, accidentally passing, stopped their horses and looked at the operation with apparent dislike. "I have no patience to look on," said one of them; "after the *mapa* is finished, I will inspect it." "Better to know how to make it than to inspect it," replied a man standing next to me. He seemed to be a military character, something like a veteran from the war of independence. After the gentlemen on horseback, disgusted, I suppose, by the pointed remark of the proletarian, had taken their departure, the latter turned to the crowd, "Look at this man," he said, in a patronising manner, "he comes from afar, takes his place here at this corner, and sketches our street with all its little houses and cocoa-nut trees, and makes a map of it. The first man who ever made a map of this country had come, with many followers. But as they carried contraband goods, they were attacked, and five and twenty of them were killed, after which he conquered Realejo and then made the map." . . . . The reader does not expect me to explain the dark meaning of this speech, with which I was introduced to the good people of Saragosa.

Amongst the more distinguished men whose acquaintance I made at Leon, was the military governor of the city, Colonel Don Francisco Diaz Zapata, who formerly had been prefect of the department of Nuevo Segovia. The colonel, I was informed, was a great musical composer, and one of his symphonies was executed at a public concert during my stay at Leon. At the colonel's house I saw a Frenchman, M. Méyonnet, who had entered into a contract with the Nicaraguan government for the establishment of a French colony on the *Rio Cocos*. On the maps which had appeared up to that time, this river has been laid down as being identical with the Bluefield river. From the information, however, which Colonel Zapata gave me, and which was corroborated by another gentleman of Leon well acquainted with those regions, it results that the river of New Segovia, or Ocotal, under the different names of Rio Cangrejal, Cocos, Segovia, Oro, Yaré, Herbias, Wanks, and Cape River, runs to Cape Gracias á Dios, where it empties itself into the sea, while the Bluefield river, under the names of the Escondido and Boswas, has its source in Matagalpa and Upper Mosquitia or Chontales, and in this manner the latest maps have placed it. Of the French colonization project no farther notice has reached me.

General Muñoz introduced me to a distinguished citizen of Leon, the owner of extensive lands in the farthest north-eastern part of Matagalpa; but having incurred the ill-feelings of the Indians of that region, had been obliged to retire from it. This circumstance Don Nazario Escoto had just reason to lament, as he had to leave some rich gold mines behind; while speaking of these mines, he went to an adjoining room and returned with a little basket full of gold bars from that locality, which seems to form part of an extensive gold region, reaching from the sources of the Bluefield river northward to the valleys of the Upper Patook or Guayape, in Honduras. In the chapter containing the narrative of my trip to Chontales and Upper Mosquitia I shall return to this subject.

CHAPTER VI.

Excursions in the Neighbourhood of Leon, and return to Granada — The Mud Volcanoes of San Jazinto and Tisate — The Volcano of Telica — Village of Telica — A Drama represented by the Inhabitants — Musical Instrument of pretended Indian Origin — Ascent of the Mountain — The Crater — View from the Summit — Remarks concerning the Orthography of Nicaragua — Nindiri — Old Stream of Lava — Masaya.

From Leon I made an excursion to the *hervideros*[1] or mud volcanoes of *San Jazinto* and *Tisate*, situated at the foot of one of the volcanic cones to the north of Leon.[2]

The plain, which extends from the city towards the mountains, is partly cultivated in extensive fields of maize, and partly overgrown with shrubs and trees. These, as I rode through the country at an early hour of the morning, were literally covered with thousands of pigeons, of a species called the *ala blanca*, i. e. the white wing.

After a ride of eight or nine miles I came to the first of the two interesting localities just mentioned. The *hervidero of San Jazinto* is a kind of solfatara—a smooth, horizontal plain of considerable extent, in the bottom of which, formed of red, brown, yellow, green, blue, black, and white clay, are numerous holes filled with a thick red water in a boiling state, from which steam and various gases, principally sulphuretted hydrogen and sulphurous acid escape; while sublimations and incrustations of sulphur and various salts

[1] *Hervidero* means a boiler, from *hervir*, to boil.

[2] From an omission in my notes I am unable to give a more exact description of the locality.

are formed around them. The whole place is heated in different degrees at various spots.

A few miles distant, on another side of the same mountain, is the *hervidero de Tisate.* This is a small crater filled with a thick mud, kept in violent commotion by the steam and gases that escape through the boiling paste. In large flakes and voluminous masses the stiff mud is thrown into the air, and, falling down at the edge, where it quickly dries from the heat prevailing throughout the locality, it forms a circular wall of clay of an ashy colour with portions of various other colours similar to the clay of San Jazinto. In the flakes which had just fallen down while I stood near, and were still hot and in a pasty state, I observed innumerable bright little cubes of iron pyrites, which appear to be continually forming in this natural laboratory. Hereafter this paste will consolidate into a rock, with these cubes interspersed throughout its substance. It is not without scientific interest to observe this instance of the formation of a rock produced by the combined agency of fire and water,—a class of rocks and mineral productions generally neglected in the speculations of exclusive geological schools, but to which some of the rocks now called *plutonic* may one day be referred. Here and there considerable efflorescences of a white salt were seen. That it was a salt of iron was manifested on the spot by a characteristic reaction. My guide, seeing that I collected a portion of the salt, took the fresh bark from the branch of a tree and rubbed its inside with the salt, by which a deep black colour was instantly produced. "That's the way we make our ink here," added the man, as a commentary on his chemical demonstration.

I spent the night in a house on the hacienda de San Jazinto. For the hospitality which I enjoyed at this place I paid a full equivalent to the fleas of the house, though, to speak the truth, they were neither more numerous nor more bloodthirsty than I have found them in some of the huts of the herdsmen of the Alps. The men with whom I passed the night at San Jazinto were nothing better, but they were more polite and animated than most European peasants would have been. Before going to bed, the company, sitting in front of the door of the house, amused themselves by telling stories, the obligation to contribute by this means to the general entertainment of the company passing round the circle. I have observed the same pastime amongst the herdsmen and muleteers of Mexico. In the present case the stories were all of one stamp. An Indian has a pretty wife, whom the priest tries to seduce. But the Indian is too sharp for the priest, and the latter is caught in a trap. "*Otro Indio*"—another Indian!—was the call inviting the next in the circle to come forward with his narrative.

A few days later I set out from Leon to visit the volcano of Telica. The village of Telica, at the foot of the mountain, is six or seven miles from the city. There I went to pass the night, take a guide and start very early in the morning to ascend the summit of the mountain. I had a letter to the curate, in whose house I found the necessary accommodations. It happened that I had an opportunity of spending the evening in a very interesting and instructive manner at this village. Its inhabitants, who are Indians, though perfect *ladinos*, i. e. thoroughly romanised, represented what is called "*un baïle*," a ball, meaning, however, a play with songs and dances, a performance uniting the requisites of the drama, the opera, and the ballet. The piece was called "*El juramento ante Dios*," the oath before God. Its fable was this: a Moorish king and a Christian king are neighbours. After continued wars they make peace. The Christian had fallen into the hands of the Moor, but the latter is a noble, high-minded man, who becomes the friend of his captive enemy, and under a solemn oath a treaty of friendship and alliance is concluded between them. The Christian goes back to his kingdom. As soon, however, as he has arrived, he breaks his oath, treacherously attacks his neighbour and friend, and becomes his prisoner for the second time. Now the faithless neighbour it is expected will receive the punishment of his perjury. But here the moral of the piece comes to light. The Christian succeeds in converting the heathen by arguing that even virtue without true faith is worthless. The Moor is baptized, amidst universal rejoicings, and with a solemn chorus, "*infinida gloria damos*," which the old Indians executed in a masterly manner, the play ends. With the exception of the introduced part of a buffoon, the whole passes on and was performed in the most serious style.

I am not well enough acquainted with Spanish literature to know whether this piece may not be the production of one of the more distinguished Spanish dramatists, changed so as to suit the intelligence of the Nicaraguan Indians. The metre was trochaical and the language noble and high-sounding, which, from the lips of Indian peasants, produced rather a comical effect, as in the case of the Christian king addressing his knights and lords as

"*Condes, duques y marqueses* . . . ."

The play was divided into several acts, marked by the performance of dances connected with the progress of the action. They were executed in a serious style by a slow movement of different figures to the music of a peculiar instrument called *marimba*. In its present structure, improved upon the old Indian design, this instrument is composed of twenty-five narrow steel plates of increasing length, laid side by side like the keys of a piano, and each of them resting on the open upper end of a wide vertical wooden tube. The length of these tubes increases in proportion to the length of the plates. Each tube, closed at its lower end, has a side opening which, being made wider or narrower by a piece of wax, regulates the pitch of the sound produced by the steel plate on being struck with a small hammer constructed for the purpose. The whole is kept together by a wooden frame, and rests on a stick which the musician, who is in a sitting posture, keeps between his knees; while a strap, fixed on the frame, passes round his shoulders. To produce the music, he holds a little stick of elastic wood in each hand, and with them strikes the steel plates. For this purpose one of the sticks has one, the other two, leather buttons at its end, one of them thus forming a single, the other a double hammer. The two buttons of the latter are placed at such a distance that two keys can be touched at once. In the original Indian[1] construction of the instrument the keys are made of wood instead of steel, and calabash shells

[1] Since the above was written I have read the following passage in Livingstone's 'Travels in Africa,' from which it appears that the marimba is of *African* origin, though in Nicaragua it was called an old *Indian* instrument. The passage, from the xvi[th] chapter of Livingstone, is as follows:—"The piano, named *marimba*, consists of two bars of wood placed side by side; here quite straight, but farther north, bent round, so as to resemble half the tire of a carriage-wheel; across these are placed about fifteen wooden keys, each of which is two or three inches broad, and fifteen or eighteen inches long; their thickness is regulated according to the deepness of the note required: each of the keys has a calabash beneath it; from the upper part of each a portion is cut off to enable them to en[illegible] the bars, and form hollow sounding-boards to the keys, which also are of different sizes, according to the note required; and little drumsticks elicit the music. Rapidity of execution seems much admired among them, and the music is pleasant to the ear. In Angola the Portuguese use the marimba in their dances."—Dr. Livingstone gives a drawing of the instrument as used amongst the *Balonda*.

of different sizes are made use of instead of the wooden tubes.

When, after the dramatic performance was over, the marimba-player observed the interest I took in his instrument, he felt induced to show himself as a *virtuoso*. With not less coquetry than could be exhibited by one of our lionised originals on the piano, he produced a *fantasia* on the marimba. By degrees his genius carried him away, till at last he fell into a kind of musical frenzy. His little sticks of elastic wood with their little buttons of leather moved quicker than the eye could follow. They flew from the left hand over the right and from the right over the left. Sometimes he would dwell upon an idea so as to give the hearer time to digest it, when suddenly a change came over the spirit of his dream, and following the impulse of a new conception, he rushed on to some unknown region of harmony. In this manner he continued, until, by a present which I made him, he was convinced of my satisfaction.

The curate told me that a much more interesting *baile*, called "*La Conquista de America*," was sometimes performed, in which Hernan Cortez and Montezuma appeared on the stage.

After the entertainments of the evening I suddenly felt very ill during the night, and for a short time I thought it impossible to prosecute my intention of ascending the mountain. Nevertheless when, at three o'clock in the morning, the guide came with the horses, I decided to make the attempt.

The path soon led into the woods, and by the light of the moon we followed it through the thicket. At several places it was very difficult to penetrate. A kind of weed, reaching above the saddle and covered with rough spiny burrs, which grappled over horse and rider, formed a most annoying obstacle from below, while, above, the ropes of climbers and twiners hanging from tree to tree across the way, threatened the traveller with the fate of Absalom. From time to time, while thus toiling along in the dim light of the moon shining through some open spaces of the forest, I was seized with violent vomiting. During one of these attacks, having alighted from my horse and resting my head upon a low branch, the latter gave way and I fell into the bushes. At the same moment a large body leaped from the thicket, bending and breaking the branches where it fell, and passed on, till the cracking noise became lost in the distance. I asked my guide what it was. "Un tigre," a tiger, answered the man, this being the name by which the *jaguar* is designated in this part of Spanish America. This is the solitary instance in which I have come in contact with one of these animals during my travels in Central America. It strikes me as an interesting fact in natural history that the temper of the same species of animals is different in different regions. The jaguar exists in Nicaragua in individuals of monstrous size, though as I believe, it does not occur very frequently. Here, however, it is not at all looked upon as the dangerous and ferocious animal it seems to be considered in other South American countries, as I have read in reference to Paraguay and the Pampas of the Rio de la Plata.

By-and-bye the path became steeper and rougher. With the first light of day I had reached the end of the forest which surrounds the lower part of the mountain. Here savanas began. Where the old grass had been burned they had the appearance of fields of young wheat. Various shrubs and trees, some of them without leaves, but covered with splendid flowers, were distributed in groups over the mountain prairie, so as to give to the whole scene the appearance of a park of the grandest dimensions and the boldest design. A little valley, not very distant from the summit, but still surrounded by higher portions of the mountain, was a particularly charming spot. The bottom, watered by a spring, was occupied by a group of shrubs with pink and yellow blossoms, while rich festoons of large bell-shaped flowers of a lilac colour hung down from a cluster of trees in the midst of it. Here and there in the savana stood a few *coyol palms*, from which a kind of wine, called *chicha coyol*, is made in the country. The whole scenery, the pure mountain air, and the freshness of the morning, together with the aspect of a spotless sky of saturated blue, produced a feeling of enjoyment which made me forget the weakness produced by the sickness of the night.

At the last trees we left our horses, the remaining portion of the mountain being too steep and rough for them. In this upper region its sides are covered with fragments and detached masses of scoriæ, which cannot be considered as portions of a stream of lava, but must have been thrown up from the crater into the air in portions of a semi-fluid melted matter, which, when falling down in the condition of a stiff paste, formed those flat cakes now seen lying loosely on the ground; or, in the case of larger masses that took more time in cooling, rolled or glided down for a short distance on the steep mountain side, producing bulky lumps of a cylindrical shape or irregular forms and of a spongy texture, with large cavities or oven-shaped vaults in them. These detached masses of scoriæ are half overgrown by grass several feet high, concealing their points and edges and the interstices between them, so that it is impossible to avoid hurting the feet, and advancing onwards, if not with great caution, is even dangerous.

The view from the summit is very grand, and, though of quite a different character, may well be compared with that from the top of Mount Righi. In the vicinity are the summits of the other cones of the Maribios, from the Momotombo to the Viejo. Behind the former a portion of the Lake of Managua appears. The country farther to the east was lost in the indistinct colour of distance. To the west the eye found no horizon to rest upon—no line of demarcation between the Pacific ocean and the atmosphere being discernible. It was a view into empty space. The line of the sea-coast, however, was well defined in this direction. The eye could follow its course as far as the plain of Leon is not separated from the sea by intervening hills. Several small rivers, emptying themselves into the ocean, and bright little bays are seen shining between dark-wooded headlands. Along the northern side of the panorama runs the mountain chain, or rather terrace, of Matagalpa and New Segovia, separating the low-lands of Nicaragua from the table-lands to the north and north-east. Along the line of its foot, in the plain of the *Estero Real*—that long, narrow branch of the Gulf of Fonseca which extends in a south-easterly direction towards the north-western corner of the Lake of Managua—a number of diminutive cones are seen, leaving the impression of a row of mole-hills. The country around the south-western base of the mountain appears as one single forest, interrupted by nothing but a few bright spots where some streamlet expands sufficiently to produce a reflection of light from its surface. A few red specks marked the tile-roofs of Leon.

Though the summit of the mountain is now bare of trees, there is no doubt that in a former time pines have grown on it. The forest of the lower region, with the exception of a few palm-trees, is entirely composed of exogens. As far as I have been informed, coniferous trees are not found in the interior section of Nicaragua, while in Mosquitia, Honduras, and Yucatan pines grow from the table-lands down to the sea-shore. A few hundred feet below the summit I saw a young pine—the only specimen I could discover on the mountain. But an old stump of a tree of this class, and of considerable size, stood at the brink of the crater. To this stump a rope, which we had brought for the purpose, was fastened, and by it I climbed down the perpendicular wall which, in a circle, forms the upper part of the crater. At the place where I descended it may have had an elevation of forty or fifty feet. It is the place where the edge of the crater is lowest, and where the slope in the interior comes highest up—while, on the opposite side, the wall rises many hundred feet in perpendicular elevation from the centre of the one-sided funnel, a vertical cut of the crater representing this figure:—

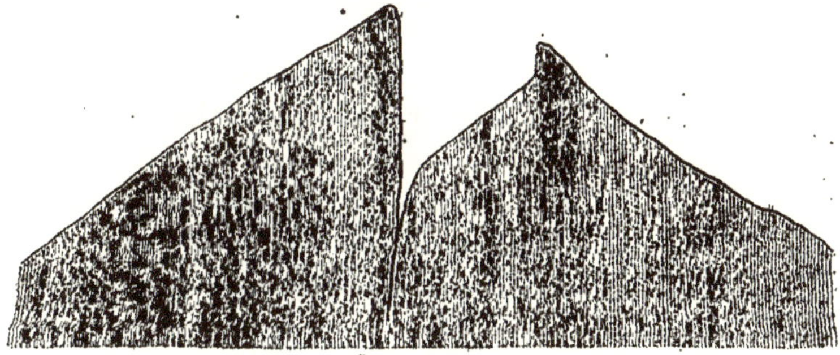

At the foot of the wall I began to descend the slope towards the centre. It is very steep, but not without vegetation, consisting of some tufts of grass, some weeds, and a few shrubs. Amongst the latter there was one kind of the dimensions of a common whortle-berry shrub, with clusters of white bell-shaped flowers. I descended on a ground formed by a loose agglomeration of tuffaceous or clayey parts, lapilli, scoriæ, and fragments of rocks, with efflorescences of various salts, and loose crystals of sulphur scattered about over the surface, in such a manner as to admit of no other opinion but that they must have fallen down from an ascending column of hot steam and gases, by which they were either carried up already formed, or in which they were formed during its passage from the interior of the mountain into the atmosphere. Several of these crystals were even lying on the grass. Amongst the rocks scattered about, or half imbedded in the tuff, I saw some large fragments of white crystalline marble, and others of an augitic rock of great hardness and tenacity. The remaining fragments were of the same nature as the loose masses of scoriæ covering the outer sides of the summit. The vertical wall, on the opposite side of the crater, shows strata of different colour, indicating the various nature of the matter ejected during successive eruptions of the mountain: for I have little doubt that the cone has been formed by the accumulated material fallen down after having been ejected into the air from the crater.

I regret that these few remarks comprise all the information I am able to give in reference to the crater of the volcano of Telica. The state of my health continued to be very weak. I descended the slope towards the centre of the funnel for a few hundred steps, when suddenly my feet broke through the hard crust of the clayey soil and entered into a hot mud from which sulphurous vapours rose. I had just time and strength left to fall back on the ground, and to crawl up a few steps, where I remained for some minutes in an exhausted state, produced, no doubt, by the inhalation of the gases which emanated from the bottom. The guide, who had descended after me, was nowhere to be seen, nor did he answer my repeated calls. With the utmost exertion I succeeded in reaching the foot of the wall where the rope hung down from the old stump, and when I looked up I despaired of ever emerging from the crater again. After a while, however, I resumed confidence. The guide, who had been collecting sulphur, reappeared. We reascended by the rope, and in the pure atmosphere beyond the crater I soon acquired new strength. At the edge of the woods we found our horses. By four o'clock in the afternoon we were again in the village, and before night I had returned to Leon.

The main features of the orography of Nicaragua have been well established by Mr. Squier's map of the country. On the maps that existed before the publication of his work, the volcanoes of the plain of Leon, for which he has reclaimed the old Indian denomination of the Maribios,[1] were represented as being in connexion with the mountains of New Segovia on one side, and with the Nicaraguan coast range of hills on the other. This was a double error.

Three lines of mountains or hills, parallel to each other and to the coast of the Pacific, pass through Nicaragua, and they are *not* connected by transverse yokes, which do *not* exist.

From the narrows and rapids of the San Juan river, which, at that place, passes through an interruption in the chain, the main ridge of the country takes the general north-westerly course as far as the department of Choluteca,

[1] Being the name of a tribe of Indians formerly inhabiting this mountain region, which, as a district, was called *Maribichoa*.

in Honduras. All this way it leaves the low region of the Nicaraguan lakes, and of the gulf of Fonseca to the south-west, and the table-land of Upper Mosquitia, Matagalpa, and New Segovia to the north-east. This ridge, strictly speaking, is more the edge of a table-land than a central chain of mountains, though the table-land, of course, has a decided slope to the east and north-east.

A second range of hills runs along the coast. It has occasional depressions, and at several places is entirely interrupted. The first depression is between the Rio Sapoa and the bay of Salinas, the second between Virgin Bay and San Juan del Sur, the third between the lake of Managua, near Nagarote, and the little bay of Tamarinda. South of Leon it is interrupted by the little river which, from the plain around the capital, passes to the sea-coast; and around the port of Realejo the broad plain of the interior is entirely open towards the Pacific. North-west of Realejo, however, the hills of the coast begin again, the range becoming higher and higher, till, at the entrance of the gulf of Fonseca, it terminates abruptly with the famous volcano of Coseguina.

Between these two lines of elevations there is a third one, consisting of a series of isolated volcanic cones and hills. Beginning in the south-east, the first of these detached elevations is the island Solentenami, in the lake of Nicaragua. Then come the two cones of the island of Ometépe, the island of Zapotera, the Mombacho, the volcano of Masaya, the hills of the peninsula between Managua and Mateares, the island Momotombito in the lake of Managua, the Momotombo, which, I think, is the highest peak among the chain of the Maribios, and the highest mountain in Nicaragua, reaching an altitude of 7000 feet, the Axosco, the Pilas, the Orota, the Telica, the Santa Clara, the Viejo, and some smaller cones of this chain; and the islands of Tigre and Sacate Grande, in the gulf of Fonseca, may be considered as a north-westerly continuation of the series.

Between these three lines of elevations the traveller can pass on a level road from the Atlantic to the Pacific; and, in the direction to the latter, this may be done by two principal routes,—one on the south-western side of the Maribios, from Leon to Realejo; the other on the north-eastern side of that chain, from the northern corner of the lake of Managua through the plain of the Rio de Palma and the Estero Real to the gulf of Fonseca.

On the 31st of January I left Leon on my return to Granada. From Managua I took the regular road to *Nindiri* and Masaya. The first of these two places is a large Indian village, representing one of the most charming scenes I have ever seen. Its little thatched huts are built with great regularity in rectangular streets, with plantain gardens behind them. Most of them are situated in the shade of orange, mango, and other fruit-trees, and half concealed by groups of the most exquisite ornamental flowers, while the tallest cocoa-palms gently waft their crowns above them. Brown girls with smiling faces stood in the doorways, greeting the passing traveller in a friendly tone with their "goodooawee, Americano!"—good-bye, American!

In the neighbourhood of Nindiri the road crosses an old stream of lava ejected from the crater of the volcano of Masaya. From the summit of the mountain it has descended into the plain, where it was arrested by the horizontality of the surface, and the progress of cooling. It is an awful sight, looking as if a broad stream of melted iron, raised in wild commotion like the sea in a storm, had suddenly concreted. It is narrow above and widening below, bordered all around with the trees of the forest, the contrast producing an effect not less striking than that of the trees growing on the side of a glacier. The points and edges of this mass of lava are so formidable, that the idea of making an excursion on it is given up with great damage to the shoes after the first experiment of a few steps. Some strange hollow cylinders or tubes, somewhat similar in appearance to huge hollow trunks of trees burnt to charcoal, but formed of the lava, have arrested the attention of travellers, some of whom have conjectured that these masses were really produced by the lava surrounding trees. I have spoken of similar formations occurring on the sides of the volcano of Telica, and it is my opinion that they have been caused by portions of half-cooled lava rolled along on the surface of the stream, as in the case of Nindiri, or on the ground as in the case of Telica, while a development of gas was going on in their interior; a process by which cylindrical balloons, opened afterwards in one way or the other, may have been formed, though by this explanation I do not pretend to deny the possibility of these tubes being casts formed round the trunks of trees, only the fact that hollow masses of lava exist in many other forms at the same localities has made me doubt it.[1]

I spent a night at Masaya, a considerable town with a very active Indian population in its suburbs. More luxuriant plantain gardens, and finer fruit trees cannot be seen. All the fences are living hedges of piñuela or wild pineapple. On the market place, early in the morning, many interesting and highly creditable articles of Indian skill

---

[1] An eruption of the Volcano of Masaya has taken place since the time when I was in Nicaragua.

and industry are offered for sale; fine hammocks, mats made of reeds with tasteful designs in different colours worked into them, and some of them large enough to cover the whole floor of a room in one piece,—*jicaras* and *guacales* (cups and basins made of calabashes) ornamented with reliefs,—earthenware, saddlery, and various other objects. For their skill, taste, and application, the Indians of Masaya are in high reputation throughout Nicaragua.

CHAPTER VII.

A Visit to the Island of Ometepe and the Isthmus of Rivas — Indian Antipathies — Violent Attack of Fever — Muyogalpa — Cutaneous Diseases — The Two Peaks — Meteorological Phenomena — Return to the Main Land — Gothic Blood — Rivas — Slope to the Pacific — Brito — A Jicaral — La Concordia — A Californian Vessel in search of an Imaginary Town — San Juan del Sur — Nagascolo — The Transit Road — Slow Combustion of Wood — Wasps and their Sense of Hearing — Virgin Bay — Rio de las Lajas — Political Characters: Laureano Pineda and Fruto Chamorro.

In the latter part of February I visited the Island of Ometepe and the Isthmus of Rivas, or Nicaragua Proper.

The population of the island is almost exclusively Indian, and, as already stated, of the Aztec race. Few white men have ever lived amongst them, and the Indian blood seems to have remained unmixed in this locality. With the purity of the race and the greater isolation of the inhabitants, a more obstinate antipathy against Europeans and their descendants than is to be found with the other Indians of Nicaragua, has descended to the present age, and only a very short time has elapsed since the secret practice of idolatry was proved to exist on the island. A German, named Woeniger, had settled there and established a cotton plantation. One day, returning after a short absence, he found his family murdered and his house burned down. I met the man on the Isthmus of Rivas, where he was employed by the Canal Company as superintendent of the transit road. In this capacity he had several hundred Indians under his directions, whom he treated in such a haughty and repulsive manner that I was not at all astonished to hear, some years later, that they had murdered him also. After Woeniger, and for a while together with him, another German, named Campe, lived on the island. I saw him often at Granada, where he had retired with his family. He spoke favourably of the character of the Indians of Ometepe, though he said that it was always advisable to be cautious with them. As for himself, although he possessed a property on the island, and had acquired considerable influence with the population, he did not like to live there.

I found a passage in one of the canoes in which the islanders bring their oranges, water-melons, cocoa-nuts and other fruits to Granada. Campe had promised, through one of his friends amongst them, to make an agreement for me, and on the 12th of February he came to inform me that the owner of one of these canoes had agreed to take me over for six reales. In half an hour I was ready. To carry some baggage and the arms I always wore on my rambles in Nicaragua down to the landing-place, I went there on horseback. But when I found the Indian stretched on the sand of the beach near his canoe, he asked six dollars instead of six reales for my passage. This was eight times the amount agreed upon. My remonstrances, however, were of no avail, and when I became angry the man turned on his heel without taking any further notice of my presence. In the mean time Campe arrived, to whom I applied, requesting him to settle the difficulty; but though he tried to bring the Indian to reason, it was to no effect. "That man"—the Indian told him, speaking of me—"is riding about on his horse, armed with gun and pistols, and with an appearance as if he held command here. Such people we don't like on our island, and I shall not take him over for any sum he may be willing to pay."

Alongside the canoe of this obstinate fellow lay the most pitiable nutshell in which a man could dream of navigating a rough water, such as the lake of Nicaragua, during the season of the trade-wind—a hollow tree, just large enough to carry two or three persons with a few dozens of water-melons, cocoa-nuts, or other fruits. It was occupied by an old man and a young boy. When I asked the former whether he was willing to take me to the island he made all kinds of objections, but ultimately consented, and, not to give him time to repent, I took immediate possession of his craft.

It was late in the afternoon when we left the playa of Granada, and our course, as far as the point of the *isletas*, being straight in the face of the wind, the old Indian and his grandson had to work hard at the oars to reach that locality before night. Here we spent some hours, till the moon had risen and the wind calmed a little. From that point onwards our course was a south-easterly one, so that the use of a sail became possible. The lake was very rough, and when, a little before noon on the next day, we arrived at the island, I had been in a continual bath for five or six hours, and felt so cold from the wind to which I had been exposed all the time, that I ordered the Indian to put me on shore at the first human habitation. When I paid him the dollar agreed upon for my passage, and wanted to add some reales as a token of my satisfaction, he refused to accept the additional sum. I then presented it to the boy, upon which the old man clasped me in his arms with gratitude.

I was well received by the inhabitants of a hut which, concealed between trees and shrubs, was situated a few hundred steps from the water. Here I dried my clothes, while some chocolate, cultivated on the spot, was prepared for me, and after a dinner of wild pigeons, which I shot from the next tree, I felt quite comfortable. Soon, however, an extraordinary sleepiness came over me, and when I awoke towards the evening I was shivering from an attack of fever, which became very violent during the night. The hut had only one room, occupied by several women, one of whom had the fever likewise; and no accommodations remaining for me within, I had to pass the night on a wooden bench in the open air, and for several hours remained in a delirious state. In the morning I took six grains of quinine, after which I had no return of the attack, but my strength was broken to such a degree that I felt compelled to abandon my original intention of ascending the summit of the peak of Ometepe.

The wind had been exceedingly high during the night, and large branches of trees were broken down by it around the house. The sky at the same time was cloudless, and the moon and stars shone in all their brilliancy. This strange contrast is a main feature in the climate of Nicaragua during the dry season. I took a walk on the beach in the morning. It was strewed with three different species of bivalve shells ejected by the waves during the night. At one place the lake was so full of fish that a boy in a single throw of his net caught enough for the dinner of the whole family. The fishes belonged to the two species called *Mojarra* and *Guapote*, which are always to be bought in the market of Granada. I sent these two and four other species of fishes from the lake of Nicaragua to my friend Professor Agassiz, and they all proved to be hitherto undescribed, representing six new species and two new genera.

The island has two villages and a number of scattered habitations like that which afforded me, I cannot say a shelter, but at least the good-will and services of its inmates and the comforts of the wooden bench before its door; advantages not at all to be despised under the circumstances. Cacao and the different fruits of the country are the chief productions of the island, the greater part of which, however, is a wilderness of forests interrupted by savanas and tracts of park-like country. It abounds in all sorts of game,—as deer, different kinds of fowl of the family of the *curassows* common throughout Nicaragua, monkeys, panthers, &c.

I went to the village of *Muyogalpa*. The name, in the Aztec language, means *Mosquito Town*, from *moyotl*, mosquito, and *calpa*, a group of houses. The road led through the bush and over patches of savanas, where some half-starved horses and cows were straggling about to find nourishment between the parched grass. During the wet season when the savanas are covered with a fresh vegetation, these animals are better provided. Some of the trees and bushes were covered with beautiful flowers. The habitations of the village are built either of canes or of mud, thatched with straw or palm leaves. Some of them stand in a group on the shore of the lake, where the situation of the village is marked by some very tall cocoa-palms. The rest of the huts are scattered in the bush.

In the family of one of the principal men of the village, I saw a boy of four years, with large horny excrescences on various parts of the body. They were of a conical form, and looked very much as if the top of a cow's horn had been sawed off and planted on the skin. As one of these deformities was placed on his forehead, he looked exactly as if the real horn of an animal was growing there. He had another growing on the chin, a third, of smaller dimensions but very pointed, on the under lip, and several others were seen on his lower extremities. With the exception of these monstrous formations, the skin of the boy was very clean and smooth. He was, however, squint-eyed in an unusual degree, and his sister, a little girl one or two years older, had the same deformity, but no cutaneous excrescences. The parents of these children, undoubtedly of pure Indian race, were of fine and healthy appearance. Other persons in the village, however, had the marks of cutaneous diseases.

Cutaneous excrescences, like those just described, I saw at Granada. A young woman had them on the joints of her fingers. She applied to Dr. B. to have the horns cut off, and I was present when he tried to perform the operation. Near the point the substance was without sensation, but as the doctor attempted to cut deeper and blood-vessels appeared, the patient declared that she could not bear the pain, and the attempt was abandoned.

As far as I had an opportunity of examining the rocks of the island, they are formed of basaltic lava, like that of the isletas, which, as I have remarked, must have been produced by an eruption of the Mombacho. In the same manner the lava of Ometepe, together with the whole material of the island, must have been the production of the two craters by which the two cones of the island have been formed. In the beginning two separate islands must have existed here, till they were connected by the increasing mass and extent of the ejected matter, or were soldered together by a stream of lava. There is little land fit for cultivation. In most places the shores are steep and rocky, with no flats between them and the mountain sides. The soil capable of cultivation is formed by volcanic tuff, like that around Granada. Where this formation borders on the lake, steep embankments and deep ravines are produced, some of the latter very similar to the fissures existing near that city, and which have been described in a former chapter.

One of the two peaks of the island bears the name of *Ometepe*, which, in this application, may be called absurd, as a term meaning "*two mountains*" cannot be justly applied to designate *one* of them. The other is called the peak of *Madera*. According to Baron Bülow, the former has an altitude of 5100, the latter of 4190 feet. The former can be ascended without difficulty. Its lower region is covered with forests, the higher with savanas, and in general its sides appear to be of a nature very closely resembling those of the Telica. The peak of Madera is thickly wooded from the water's edge to the summit. There may be considerable difficulties in penetrating through the forest, which, as I imagine, conceals some objects of Indian antiquity.

During the dry season, while for months a spotless sky is spread over Nicaragua, a thick cloud covers the top of the peak of Ometepe, and, if examined on the spot, may be observed to be in a constant process of originating on the north-eastern side of the summit, to roll over it in a direction to the south-west, where it is in an equally constant process of dissolving. The north-eastern trade wind, striking against the side of the mountain, is forced to cross the apex, and passing thus from a warmer into a colder region of the atmosphere, is obliged to part with a portion of the water it held in dissolution. Thus the cloud is produced on the windward side of the summit. On the lee side, the reverse takes place. The wind descends from the colder to the warmer region, where the cloud is dissolved, not, however, before a part of its water has collected in heavy rain-drops which I have observed to fall, even at the northern foot of the mountain, from a thin and almost transparent veil surrounding the cone. I have already mentioned this kind of local precipitation in reference to the summit of the Mombacho. During the five days of my sojourn, I never saw the summit uncovered for a single moment. Another observation I made during this time was that of the regular gusts of wind which poured down the side of the mountain every evening. As to the peak of Madera, I cannot tell whether it exhibits the same phenomena in an equally regular manner. From a distance, however, I have seen it capped with a similar cloud, and this is occasionally the case with the summit of mount Mombacho.

I found considerable difficulty in engaging a canoe to bring me to San Jorge, an Indian village on the neighbouring main, which may be called the port of Rivas. At that time of the year it was very easy to go there, and the transit could be made in little more than an hour; but this rendered it the more difficult to return, and canoes from the island have often to wait many days at San Jorge before a temporary subsidence of the trade-wind will allow them to effect a home-passage.

I brought a letter to a man of distinction amongst the inhabitants of the village. His features, though intelligent in expression, bespoke the Indian with a mixture of negro blood in his lineage. His wife, on the contrary, was a tall ladylike woman of very fine appearance and noble demeanour, and altogether so superior to everything around her that she seemed to be a stranger mingled with the vulgar denizens of the place. The truth was that she belonged to a family of pure Spanish, and perhaps I might say of Gothic, descent. The last remnants of this element, if any such be left even now, will soon be lost in the progressing mixture of races in Central America.

The road from San Jorge to Rivas leads through the

very garden of Nicaragua. Plantations of cacao, fields of maize, orchards loaded with every description of fruit, form a wall of the most luxuriant vegetation on either side, so that the view is entirely restricted to the closest objects, with the exception only of the two cones of Ometepe rising majestically into the air. The whole region is of unsurpassed fertility, and it is impossible to calculate what it might produce if cultivated with care and intelligence. Cacao, however, is the principal production of this section of Nicaragua. The view from the hills to the west of the town is rich beyond description. From their foot, the plain, entirely covered with verdure, slopes gently down to the lake.

Rivas itself was more than half in ruins, and a more dreary sight than these crumbling walls could scarcely be looked upon, bearing as they did the double marks of destruction by earthquake and by a most sanguinary civil war. Rivas had suffered the horrors of both within a short interval of time. At the period of my visit the hopes and expectations excited by the canal project had produced a spirit of activity and enterprise which, had the scheme been carried on, would soon have replaced these ruins by new buildings. Everywhere I saw hands employed in tearing down old walls, in manufacturing sun-dried bricks, in cutting timber, and in other occupations connected with the building of houses. The impulse given to the whole country by the prospects of a brighter future, of course, was more strongly felt at Rivas, a town situated almost upon the line which, it was generally supposed, the inter-oceanic canal would follow. It is generally known how these expectations have been deceived. The disappointment was followed by renewed civil wars and by the ravages of the cholera, so that, if the condition of Rivas has changed since the time of my visit, it can only have been for the worse.

From what seemed to have transpired as the result of a preliminary survey, it was stated by persons in connexion with the engineers then at work on the isthmus of Rivas, that the canal would follow the line of deepest depression between the mouth of the *Rio de las Lajas*, on the lake of Nicaragua, and a place called *Brito*, on the coast of the Pacific. As I wished to form a general idea of the nature of that section of the country, I took a horse and guide and set out in the direction of the designated locality.

I do not pretend to give an opinion in reference to the great object contemplated in the survey which was in progress of execution at that time. An official report of this survey has since been printed, and to this authentic document I must refer the reader for reliable information on the matter. According to my impression, the principal difficulty here, as on any other of the different lines that have been proposed within the territory of Nicaragua, must consist in the insufficiency of the quantity of water which may be required for feeding a canal deep and wide enough for all the vessels which would avail themselves of the advantage of this passage between the two oceans. For even if a cut was made through the isthmus between the lake of Nicaragua and the Pacific Ocean deep enough to supply the canal from the lake, the question still remains to be decided, whether the additional drainage thus produced would not lower the surface of the lake at a rate which would render the plan impracticable. This consideration I know does not contain an absolute impossibility, in as far as the quantity of water leaving the lake by the San Juan river might, under certain circumstances, be regulated in such a manner as to reduce the drainage in both directions to the amount it has now in one. But in reference to any line that might be recommended between the lake of Managua and the Pacific Ocean, the above consideration, if I am not greatly mistaken, actually embraces an impossibility. From the statements in the fifth chapter, it results that the lake of Managua at the present time has no outlet whatever, or at least none during the dry season. Under these conditions that lake, in the most favourable case, has a stationary level; and as a double drainage would be necessary to connect it with the lower lake on one side, and with the Pacific Ocean on the other, there can be no doubt that a rapid decrease of level would be the result of its being included in the canal line.

The country between Rivas and Brito is hilly, and in general must be very healthy. The whole tract from hence to the north-west, including the country around Jinotépet, and farther on, is in this, as in many other respects, highly fitted for the settlement of immigrants, if ever the stream of European emigration should be directed to Nicaragua. Here, while inhabiting a fertile, a healthy, and a most lovely country, they would have the inestimable advantage of a situation on the Pacific and on the Atlantic coast of the continent at once, a distance of a few miles being all that would separate the settler from the lake on one side, and from the ocean on the other.

Leaving Rivas, the road, passing between plantations and gardens in the most charming situations, gradually ascends a range of hills; when the summit is reached, the country forms a kind of table-land, with savanas, interrupted by bushes and clusters of trees. The coyol, or wine-palm, is growing scattered here and there over these prairies. Farther on towards the Pacific the road enters a forest, the trees of which become taller and of a more vigorous growth as the traveller approaches the ocean. In this forest I came to a rivulet of the clearest water, running over a bed of sand and pebbles, and full of little fishes and delicate univalve shells; and here I hit upon the signals of the surveying engineers of the canal company. Emerging from the forest I came to a place called *La Salina*, being a salt-marsh surrounded by a growth of shrubs of a very peculiar character. Some Indians were here to fetch a mule's load of salt, which at the dry portions thinly covered the ground. Where the bottom was not dry it formed a deep mud of a stiff clayey consistence, and appeared to be impassable.

Where the ocean opened to the view, the coast swept in a long, smooth bend from north-west to south-east. As far as I could see, there was nothing but a beach of one or two hundred paces between the water and the trees of the forest. Nothing could be smoother and cleaner than the white sand of this beach, but here and there a black rugged cliff stood out from it, where, as the long swell of the Pacific, in regular intervals, rolled over the beach, each wave was dashed into a cloud of spray. In the south-eastern direction the *Punta de Santa Helena*, one of the western headlands of the mountains of Costarica, closed the view.

It had been my intention to proceed along the coast in that direction as far as the little bay of *Concordia*, or San Juan del Sur, which at that time was an uninhabited district, like that called Brito, where I now found myself. My guide, however, assured me that I could neither pass along the coast, as some cliffs, he said, interrupted the line of beach, nor through the forest, where there was no road in the direction I intended to travel. Thus I was obliged to return to Rivas, and thence start anew for San Juan del Sur.

From Rivas to the latter place the traveller has to follow a road which, after having reached the shore of the Pacific, leads along it into the State of Costarica. With the exception of a few cattle-farms situated in the woods, the country in this direction may be called a wilderness, exhibiting nature, however, in great variety. Here I saw for the first time what is called a *Jicaral*, or tract of land overgrown by *jícara trees*. It is quite a characteristic feature in the country, and must be described in a few words. The tree is the *Crescentia Cujete*, or calabash-tree, well known by the use which is made of the hard shell of its fruit in manufacturing vessels for domestic purposes. The drinking cups, constructed from a smaller species of an oval form, are called *jícaras*, while the bowls or basins prepared from a large variety of a compressed subglobular shape, sometimes of as much as one foot in diameter, are named *Juacales*. For the purpose of manufacturing these vessels, the tree is cultivated. Here, however, I am speaking of the wild tree, which bears fruits of the size of a large orange. The tree is small, with a great number of long, thin, worm-shaped branches, covered all along with small and very poor leaves of their own, but bearing an additional vegetation of parasitic *Bromeliaceæ*, in tufts of stiff leaves striped red and green, in parrot-like colours, so that a superficial observer may believe these tufts to be the flowers of the tree. To form an idea of a *Jicaral*, a number of these trees must be imagined scattered over a horizontal portion of the country, the soil of which consists of a black stiff clay, and which is so situated as to become overflowed in the rainy season, when the entire district is transformed into a marsh. During the dry season the soil becomes nearly as hard as stone, and cracked in all directions, so that it is sometimes exceedingly rough, and with its dark colour appears almost like a field of lava. Between the trees some tufts of a coarse kind of grass, and bushes of the aroma mimosa, with the sweet-scented yellow catkins, are scattered. The ground under the trees is strewed with the fruits, which are eagerly sought and eaten by the cattle, the succulent pulp allaying at the same time their hunger and thirst. But the skeletons of cows, horses, and mules lying about form an essential feature of a more extended *Jicaral*, as a considerable number of these animals die in these localities from want of food and water during the dry season. On a large scale a region of Jicarales extends all along the foot of the table-land of Chontales, Matagalpa, and New Segovia.

Another peculiar feature of the country between Rivas and San Juan del Sur consists in some small localities with permanent moisture, covered with thickets, of ever-green trees with glossy leaves like those of most tropical species of *Ficus*, to which they may belong. A considerable quantity of milk exudes from the broken branches or leaves. Around these dark green groups of trees the country was covered with dry grass and scattered shrubs which, at that time of the year, stood loaded with yellow, white, pink, and lilac-coloured flowers, the whole producing the effect of an immense park.

Farther west, where the hills began to be higher, reaching, as far as an estimate may be reliable, an elevation at least of one thousand feet above the sea, the road entered the forest, which, in this region, follows the coast of the Pacific. I came to a brook rushing in cascades through a ravine, where I saw many of the trees called *Ufle* or *Ugle*, one of the several species from which india-rubber is collected. The rocks over which the brook passes, and those in its vicinity, are recent deposits of carbonate of lime from its water, in parallel layers, and of a structure resembling that of stalactites. Tertiary rocks of limestone and sandstone, some of them in a metamorphic state, similar to the rocks of the hills west of Jinotépet, seem to constitute the coast range in this direction also, but the country is so thickly covered with vegetation that the mere passing traveller has little opportunity of making a series of observations calculated to convey a positive idea of the geological character of the region. On my way from San Juan del Sur to Virgin Bay I saw fragments of limestone heaped up near a lime-kiln, but I could not discover any fossils included in them. They were from a neighbouring quarry, but the necessity of reaching a certain locality before night did not allow me to visit it.

On the bank of a little river my guide, by throwing a stone, killed a most beautiful specimen of a vulture of the species called the *rey de zapilotes*, or king of vultures. I regretted that I had not the means of taking it with me and preserving it. This bird, I suppose, is the *Cozgacoate* of Oviedo. The Aztec name, according to Mr. Buschmann, is *Cozcaquauhtli*, from *quauhtli*, eagle, and *cozcoatl*, a jewel, a compound which the learned linguist translates by "the eagle with the collar."[1] I was astonished to see the dexterity of my guide in throwing a stone. But I have been assured by persons of reliable authority that some of the herdsmen of Nicaragua are able to kill a deer in that manner.

The little bay of *Concordia*, where one year later the

[1] Professor Lichtenstein, according to Mr. Buschmann's statement, was uncertain whether the *Cozgacoate* of Oviedo was Vultur sarcoramphus, gryphus, or icterus. I should say that the bird which my guide killed was either the Sarcoramphus Papa, or a species very similar to it.

town of *San Juan del Sur*—or St. John on the South Sea—had sprung up, was, at the time of my visit, without a human habitation. It was however decided that the steamers from San Francisco should run in here. This, then, was the western terminus of the road which, under the name of the *Nicaragua transit road*, was at that time in progress of being opened through the woods, and has since become famous in the system of American communication as well as in the history of American speculations and politics, and in that of Central American revolutions and civil wars. At the time of my visit, the line of the road had only begun to be marked by a cut through the woods, and when I arrived on the shore of the bay, three or four men were engaged in erecting a hut of branches which might have been called the first house of the town of San Juan del Sur, and which, for the night I spent at this interesting place, afforded me the necessary shelter. Besides this shed, no traces of human activity were seen in the bay. The country all around was covered with a forest of lofty trees reaching down to high-water mark. Between a low growth of mangroves a little river empties itself into the bay. The beach, at its mouth, was covered with thousands of small shells of snails, which, as I came near, all ran away with amusing celerity, each of them being inhabited by a diminutive crab that had taken possession of it.

In the roadstead before the bay was a vessel at anchor, from which, while I was riding along the beach, a boat was sent on shore. From this two gentlemen landed, one of whom addressed me in the English language, asking where the town of *San Juan del Sur* was situated. "We are in its main street here," I answered, "and there," I added, pointing to the shed, "you see the principal hotel."

From the explanations following this introductory conversation it appeared that the gentleman who accosted me was a Mr. Hall, of San Francisco, owner of the brigantine in the road, and which had left the golden gate for the purpose of buying provisions at San Juan del Sur. The reader may imagine Mr. Hall's disappointment when he heard that he had made a voyage of several thousand miles to an imaginary city, for the purpose of laying in stores at a place where there were not provisions enough to sustain the life of six persons for a single day, and where even my horse was in a starving condition, obstinately refusing to eat the leaves of any of the trees or shrubs that grew in the neighbourhood. Mr. Hall learned the true state of things with the calm mood of a man who had seen the origin of Sacramento and Stockton, and merely remarked that at San Francisco the plan of the town of San Juan del Sur, with the names of the streets and the situation of the public buildings, had been circulated, and that building lots had been offered for sale.

My night's rest under the shed was disturbed by hundreds of minute ticks which entered my clothes and began to burrow themselves in my skin. These insects have been described by all travellers as one of the greatest annoyances in Central America, but they are quite as bad in Texas, Louisiana and other southern states of the Union; and even a single walk through the grass, in some public places of New Orleans may expose you to the attacks of this kind of vermin. But at last I was lulled to sleep by the loud noise of the wind, which, though the stars shone bright and the air was soft and warm, bent the old trees of the forest, and by the roaring surf of the South Sea, sending its spray up to where I was stretched on the ground. When I rose in the morning the beach was covered with the dead bodies of a large species of eels thrown out by the waves together with other sea animals. This kind of fish, which has a skin spotted like that of a panther, is said to be poisonous, and it is even asserted that it communicates death to other animals approaching it in the water.

The bay is of an almost circular form, with a narrow entrance between perpendicular rocks. Close by, on the other side of the hill by which it is locked in to the northward, is the bay of *Nagascolo*, somewhat smaller, but of a similar form. The narrow neck of land between the upper part of the two bays has but a slight elevation, and if ever a town of importance should spring up here, it might easily extend across this locality from the bay of Concordia to that of Nagascolo.

Five years had elapsed when, in October, 1855, returning from California, I visited this place again. The rush of travellers, and the haste in passing on to the other side of the isthmus, did not leave me time to examine the town of *San Juan del Sur*, which, since my first visit, had risen here, nor to ask for information as to the number of its houses and inhabitants. But my impression is that there could not be more than twenty houses. These were built of wood, and the materials had been sent, ready for erection, from the United States. They were pleasantly situated, scattered amongst the trees that had been spared from the primitive forest, and the little place looked quite snug and comfortable.

What may have become of this rising town since the transit has been interrupted in consequence of the proceedings of Walker, the filibuster, I am unable to tell. When I passed, in 1855, the place was the head-quarters of this adventurer, and I saw him sitting in his tent outside the town. It was on the 3rd of October, not long before he succeeded in taking possession of the city of Granada and making himself, for a short time, master of Nicaragua. But of this remarkable episode in the history of Central America I shall take an opportunity of speaking more in a subsequent chapter.

In 1855 the transit road between San Juan del Sur and Virgin Bay was in a tolerably good condition, and the passengers of the steamer Cortes, in whose company I passed over the Isthmus, found it dry enough even then, in the rainy season, to walk over a great portion, for the purpose of obtaining some exercise between the two sea-voyages. This walk was a real pleasure trip, which we all enjoyed; the beauty of the scenery in passing the hills, and the purity of the air, making the whole party feel delighted with the country.

But I must not forget that I have to return to February, 1851. At that time no transit road existed, and the line it was to follow was scarcely marked in its extent by a cut through the woods. In reference to the two termini, on the lake and on the Pacific, considerable pains were taken to keep the public in ignorance. But having once hit upon the line, I followed it as much as I could on my return to the shore of the lake, which I reached at the place where the little town of Virgin Bay was founded shortly after. The distance between this place and San Juan del Sur is twelve miles. Riding through the forest I saw several trunks of trees lying on the ground in a state of slow combustion. The fire, having begun at one of their ends, was glowing, without flame, like that of a cigar, and its progress was so gradual, that, as long as I stood by, I could not observe the slightest advancement. From the ashes on the ground, however, I could see that a considerable portion of the trunks had already been consumed, and my guide assured me that more than a month ago he had seen these trunks on fire. According to this rate of progress, a quarter of a year must have been necessary to accomplish the total combustion of one of these trunks. Whether the statement of my guide was exact, of course, I am unable to tell.

I passed the night at the Hacienda de la Sebadilla, situated near the road at about equal distances from the lake and the ocean. In the evening I met an Englishman of my acquaintance, who superintended a body of Indians at work on the road, and invited me to pass the night with him at the hacienda where he had his quarters, promising to accompany me to Rivas the next morning.

We started very early and followed the cut through the bush. On the trees near the road I saw numerous large wasps' nests of an irregular oval form. My guide told me that it was not good to speak loud in the vicinity of these nests, as the wasps become easily irritated by a noise and would attack me. I gave little credit to his statement. But soon after, when I had remained behind for a few hundred paces, and the extraordinary dimensions of one of these nests, which could not have less than four or five feet in diameter, induced me to call my companion to look at it, the insects suddenly rushed forth and surrounded me. I put spurs to my horse and fled with all the speed of which it was capable. My companion, whom I passed, followed in the same manner, while the infuriated insects were all the time upon us, many of them getting into our hair and darting their stings wherever they could find access to our skin. I trembled for the consequences, as the stings were burning like fire, but the pain was of short duration, the swelling very slight and soon passed away, and the consequences were less severe than I have known to follow from the bite of as many mosquitos. On another occasion the report of a gun produced the same effect in exciting the wrath of a swarm of wasps. I shot a bird, when a companion of mine who stood near raised such a cry that in the first moment I thought I had shot him. His terror, however, was caused by the sudden attack of a swarm of wasps rushing from their nest immediately after the shot had been fired.

At that time no habitation existed at the place called *Bahia de la Virgen*, or *Virgin Bay*. The name was simply applied to a little indenture of the shore of the lake. The beach, here, is a bed of black lava. In 1855 the little town built since the period of my first visit consisted of a number of wooden houses, all of them being hotels, forming a single street which runs straight down to the landing place of the lake steamers. The largest building was that of the Transit Company, containing the offices, store-rooms, and residence of their agent. From the shallowness of the water the steamers cannot come close to the shore, and as the lake has generally a very heavy surf here, the embarking as well as disembarking of some hundred passengers was connected with considerable inconveniences. At the landing place speculating girls with brown faces and black eyes had established their stalls for the sale of chocolate, coffee, lemonade, liquors, oranges, pine-apples, and other fruits of the country. The town, at that time, was the dearest and most inhospitable place I have ever heard of. For as much room on the bare floor in one of the hotels as I wanted to lie upon for the night, without any other accommodation, I had to pay three dollars. Outside of the house was a wooden bench of which a man had taken possession, when one of the waiters of the house came up to him with the information that if he wanted to sit there he must pay for it.

Between Virgin Bay and the village of San Jorge, the *Rio de las Lajas*—the little river mentioned above—empties into the lake. During the dry season its mouth is closed by a dry sand-bar. But above the bar the water is deep even at that time of the year, and the river is said to extend for a considerable distance upwards in this manner, passing through a dense forest. During the rainy season it conveys much water to the lake. According to general information, as I have stated above, this was to be the eastern terminus of the projected Ship-canal between the lake and the Pacific. The land on one side of the river-mouth was the property of an old farmer whom I found fully convinced that a few years hence all the vessels of the world would pass his house on their way between the Atlantic and Pacific, and he was already making preparations to furnish them with dry beans, sweet potatoes, and other vegetables. I asked him whether he would not sell some of his land? "There is no man who has got money enough to buy my land"—he answered with a smile. But he was willing to let a portion of it for a few years at the rate of ten dollars the cavalleria—an extent of between one and two hundred acres. His economical notions appeared to be altogether deranged by the contrast of his great expectations with the modesty of his customary habits.

At any rate the mouth of the Rio de las Lajas is one of the most favoured localities on the shores of the lake of Nicaragua. Soil and climate are excellent, and most tropical productions might be cultivated here with advantage. The situation is as desirable as can be imagined—

and as to the natural charms of the site for a family residence, they cannot be surpassed in any part of the world.

From this place I returned to Rivas, whence I sent to Granada for my horse. While waiting for it, I made the acquaintance of two men who have acted prominent parts in the recent history of Nicaragua. One of them was the licentiate *Laureano Pineda*, at that time a lawyer at Rivas, but shortly after elected *Director Supremo* of the Republic, though he filled the presidential chair for a few weeks only. Mr. Pineda had the appearance and manners of a gentleman equally dignified and popular. It has been said that when he was elected, and he departed to the capital, he remarked that he knew he was going to his death, but that he was resolved to do his duty as a citizen. He was well aware of the exasperated feelings of the different political parties. These his election was intended to allay, but only contributed to bring to an outbreak. Scarcely had he been inaugurated when both parties accused each other mutually of meditating violence, and these accusations were followed by the fact. One night the whole government of Leon was quietly arrested. The gentlemen composing it were taken from their houses, placed on horses, and carried out of the country. The banishment of Mr. Pineda was not of long duration. From the State of San Salvador, where he had taken refuge, an English vessel brought him to San Juan del Sur, whence he came back to Rivas. The state of politics, however, had completely changed in the mean time, and he was not placed in office again.

A public character of much superior interest was *Fruto Chamorro*, at that time Prefect of the department of Rivas. I had a conversation with him with regard to a projected settlement of Germans at San Juan del Sur, an idea to which he was decidedly opposed. Nicaragua, he told me in a polite but most determined manner, did not like to see foreigners settle on its territory; and when I replied by representing the contrary views of General Muñoz, he remarked that the influence of General Muñoz would soon terminate.[1] A few months later Fruto Chamorro, at the head of a military force of some hundred men, marched on Leon, where the party to which Muñoz belonged had established an opposition government. The latter fell into the hands of his adversary, and narrowly escaping the fate of being shot, was banished from the country. Of both men I shall have to speak more hereafter.

It was the 4th of March when I returned to Granada. The road leads through some very fine sections of country, particularly those near the southern foot of the Mombacho. The southern side of this mountain presents a much more interesting aspect than the northern. The southern wall of the crater being broken down, the inner side of the northern wall can be seen from that quarter.

I passed the night at *Nandaime*, a large village, situated in the plain, at the south-western base of the Mombacho. This plain is kept moist and green throughout the year by the local exudations caused by the mountain as stated on a former occasion. It has several permanent springs, and the inhabitants are much engaged in the cultivation of rice, for which commodity Nandaime is the chief place of production in Nicaragua.

---

[1] After my return to Granada I wrote to the General on this subject, mentioning the ideas of his political adversary. In his answer, dated Leon the 20th of March, the General says:—"Mi influencia estará siempre en favor de la colonizacion, y mucho mas del pueblo Aleman, que por muchos titulos y grande interes es acreedor á nuestras deferencias." The opposite views of these two men were the views of their parties.

CHAPTER VIII.

An Excursion to the Province of Chontales and to Upper Mosquitia — Estero Panaloya — The Jicarales — Masapa — Savanas on Fire — Parallel Chains — Juigalpa — Opals in Nicaragua — Old Indian Fortifications — The Gold Region — The Aquilucho — Minerals — Acoyapa — Snakes in Nicaragua — A beautiful Species of Spoonbill — The Supa, or Pijivaye — The Nancite — The Edge of the Table-land — Hydrographical Remarks — Change of Scenery — View from the Summit — Climate of the Table-land — The Woolwa Indians and the Ancient Chontalli — Village of Lovago and its Population — Aztec Colonies — Manners of the Woolwas — Hacienda de San José — Nicaraguan Curassows — A White Harpy.

On the 21st of May a party of four, of which I formed one, started from Granada on a trip to the province or district of *Chontales.* This name is given to the country extending from the north-eastern shores of the lake to the table-land of Upper Mosquitia.

The ride in the cool air of the morning along the smooth sand beach of the lake was refreshing and delightful. I know nothing in natural scenery to be compared with the beauty of a fine morning in Nicaragua. We had to follow the beach for a distance of twenty miles in a northerly direction. Our horses, moving at a quick travelling pace, kept close to the water's edge, where the sand was moist, and consequently forming a firm bottom. Their hoofs were bathed from time to time by a wave, and a better and more pleasant road could not be imagined. Flocks of plovers, avocettes, snipes, sandpipers, and other birds of the waterside, ran before the feet of our horses. To our left was the bush, where parrots were chattering on the boughs of every tree. To our right the view passed over

VIEW TAKEN FROM THE EDGE OF THE TABLE-LAND OF UPPER MOSQUITIA.

Book I., Chap. 8

the lake and was bounded in the distance by the mountains of Juigalpa, towards which our journey tended. The sky above this bright landscape was of unmingled purity, the impression being heightened by here and there a *Tijereta*, or *Frigate*, soaring without any perceptible motion of its wings, high above the surface of the water. This bird, of which there are two kinds here, corresponding to two different species of *Tachypetes* or *Fregata*, is an essential feature of Nicaraguan lake scenery. The Spanish name is derived from *tijera*—a pair of scissors—designating the two long feathers in the tail of the bird.

At a little village, called *Los Cocos*, the road leaves the shore and enters a forest of tall trees, amongst which are many palms with fan-shaped leaves, and trees with their roots dividing at a considerable elevation above the ground. Passing through this forest we arrived at the *Estero Panaloya*, a long, deep, and narrow branch of the lake, which, as long as the Rio de Tipitapa was running, formed the mouth of that river. The name *Panaloyan*, according to Mr. Buschmann, means a ferry, from the Aztec verb *pano* —"to ferry over." The Spanish name of the locality is *Paso Real*—the King's ferry.

Our passage across the Estero was connected with some difficulties arising from one of our horses being unable to swim and threatening to sink the ferry boat. We succeeded, however, in safely reaching the other side, where we continued our journey without delay. The road led through tracts of forest and extensive *Jicarales*, where I was astonished to see some globular cacti with small red fruits growing on a soil which, for at least three quarters of the year, is a morass; though at that time the ground was dry, with deep cracks running through it in all directions, and hard as a rock. This was a section of the Jicaral region mentioned in the last chapter as extending along the foot of the table-land of Chontales, Matagalpa, and New Segovia. During the rains, the communication with those higher regions of the country is almost entirely interrupted by this belt of marshes, and even during the dry season the soil of some portions becomes hard only at the surface, while other localities, where permanent springs exist, remain marshy throughout the year. We passed some of these places, which were frequented by numerous musk-ducks almost as large as geese.

Towards the evening we arrived at the buildings of the hacienda of Masapa, where we intended to pass the night. They are situated on a broad and flat dome-shaped elevation, between the higher mountains which commence in that neighbourhood. The rocks in this district have a trachytic and phonolitic character, either in a more homogeneous or in a porphyritic state. A ridge of mountains begins here at the shore of the lake, continuing in a south-easterly direction, and terminating south of Acayopa. The situation of the hacienda is very fine, but the soil suffers from want of moisture during the dry season, though a never-failing little river is at a short distance. Absolutely nothing was to be found here to feed our horses, and we had to send them several miles off, to a patch of grass where they remained during the night. The hacienda, like all haciendas of Chontales, is a mere cattle farm, without any agricultural improvements. Before the commencement of the rains the dry grass is set on fire, and with the approaching darkness we saw the savanas of the neighbouring heights burning in several places. As the grass is generally of a thin growth on these rocky mountain sides, the fire can do little harm; though, during that night, we were told it consumed a valuable stock of Brazil-wood, cut and piled up for exportation on a hill in the vicinity. Continuing our journey on the following morning, we had to pass through the fire of a burning savana. The line of progressing combustion ran across a valley through which the road passed. But from the scantiness of the grass in consequence of the rocky nature of the soil, the flames were not dangerous, and our horses crossed them without resistance. We felt, however, a very sensible increase of the temperature in the valley, in which we found the air close, and the smoke extremely annoying. Of the shrubs and trees which stood scattered in the valley, the leaves only had suffered from the fire, and no trunks or branches were seen actually burning or recently ignited. This is very different in some of the savanas of the United States. In western Texas I saw the trunks of oak-trees burning many days after the fire had passed over the prairie.

Our road continued through a wide longitudinal valley between two main ridges of mountains parallel to each other; but the space thus included, instead of exhibiting one general bottom, is filled up with minor elevations in the form of flat domes, broad transversal yokes, and lower hills, by which it is divided into different hydrographic sections. The highest mountains were all the time to our left. Before reaching the town of Juigalpa, and while the road led along the side of a mountain, some hills with regular slopes and terraces like those of a modern fortress were seen on the opposite side of the valley. The whole conveyed the impression of an artificial formation, and I was sorry that neither time nor circumstances permitted a minute examination. The sky was threatening with the first thunderstorm of the rainy season, which begins sooner in the mountains of this region than in the low country around the lakes. The hour was late in the day, and we were still at a considerable distance from Juigalpa. Since that time, however, I have seen the map of Nicaragua, published by Don Fermin Ferrer,[1] in which "*ruins*" are indicated between Acoyapa and San Migueleto; and, from this fact as well as from the descriptions of certain old Indian fortifications in Guatemala, given by the Abbé Brasseur de Bourbourg, I have little doubt that what I saw from a distance on the road west of Juigalpa, were the remains of some old Indian stronghold.

Before we could reach *Juigalpa* a torrent of rain poured down upon us, making the mountain path so slippery that we had considerable trouble in descending into the valley. The town is situated at the foot of one of the highest mountains in the chain, which is seen from a great distance in the lower country as well as on the table-land, though I should not estimate its altitude at more than five thousand feet. It is steep and rocky, and the greater part covered with forest. The country around this mountain, which I may call the *Cerro de Juigalpa*, has the reputation of being rich in gold, and a company of inhabitants of Juigalpa and Granada had begun to work a mine at the sources of the *Rio Mico*, and had accumulated a large quantity of a yellow substance of which they were uncertain whether it was gold or not. The samples shown to me by a North American, who introduced himself as the director of the mine, were iron pyrites included in calcareous spar, which, according to the general geological character of this section of country, should be supposed to form a vein in the por-

[1] Geographical Map of the Republic of Nicaragua, by Fermin Ferrer, 1855 —without an indication of the place of publication, which, however, may be justly supposed to be New York. The map, with the exception of a few specialties, is without peculiar value.

phyry. With the pyrites gold seems to be really associated here in a considerable proportion, as the Indians bring sometimes grains of gold in quills for sale to Juigalpa. The director of the mine, however, was unable to distinguish between the gold and the pyrites, and, of course, cannot be supposed to have understood any method of extracting the precious metal. The rocks of this region are all trachytic and phonolitic porphyries, with frequent inclusions of opal and of various minerals of the Zeolite family. A little hill in the immediate vicinity of the town is composed of a beautiful light-green porphyry.

Opals have lost much of their interest and value since they can be produced by art. But, nevertheless, it may be worth while to state that it is not in Honduras alone that they are found in Central America. In Nicaragua, they occur at Chontales and Matagalpa, and the *Cerro del Diamante*, near the little town of Teustépet, as well as the *Cerro de Martinez*, east of Acoyapa, have been indicated to me as the principal localities for these precious stones.

From Juigalpa to Acoyapa the road continues between the same two parallel chains, as in the tract from Masapa to Juigalpa. On this part of our way I found a feather from the wing of a bird of extraordinary size, the quill being thicker than that of a swan. I was told that it was the feather of a large bird of prey called the *Aquilucho*, living in the highest mountains of this region, and so powerful that it carries away young sheep and the largest monkeys to its nest. A reliable authority at Acoyapa, whom I questioned on the subject, corroborated these statements, adding that the *Aquilucho* is even in the habit of killing calves. The bird must be either a *condor*, or—what appears more likely—a large *harpyia*.

As we approached nearer to Acoyapa, the transversal

yokes of the mountains became higher. Near the Hacienda de Pompoá, situated half-way between the latter place and Juigalpa, the porphyry included masses of white foliated *Heulandite* and radiated *Mesotype;* the latter with well-formed terminal faces of the crystals. This mineral is of common occurrence between the hacienda and Acoyapa, and all the white pebbles in the little river near that town are of Mesotype. In the neighbourhood of Acoyapa, the ridge which had continued between our road and the lake all the way from Masapa suddenly terminates, and the valley opens towards the latter. But a broad bar of low basaltic or doleritic hills is placed before the opening, separating the bottom-land of the valley from the shores of the lake, and leaving an outlet only for the little river on which the town is situated.

Acoyapa is the chief town of Chontales. Together with the farms of the surrounding country, it has a population of about 2600 inhabitants. The principal wealth of the province is in its pastures and in the cattle, horses and mules raised on them. Mules, hides, and cheese are the articles of export. The valleys of this region are hotter and less healthy than the shores of the lake, while the table-land beyond the principal chain of mountains north-east of Acoyapa is healthier than both regions. The town is situated on a little hill, at the foot of which, under the shade of large trees, the river flows. During the dry season there is scarcely water, and when I saw it it was little more than a number of water-holes in a bed of sand and pebbles. When the rains prevail, however, it seems to accumulate a considerable quantity of water, as may be judged from the large boulders heaped up in some portions of its bed. This is the condition of all the smaller rivers of this region.

With regard to the name of this stream, I am in an uncertainty of which I cannot tell whether it is my own fault or not. As I understood the people of Acoyapa, they called their river *Rio Mico,* the Monkey River. But it must be remarked that a river of the same name is on the other side of the principal chain, running in an opposite direction and being a tributary of the Bluefield. Fermin Ferrer, in his maps of Nicaragua above mentioned, and Mr. Squier in the map to his "Notes on Central America," call the river of Acoyapa *Rio Poderoso.* According to Mr. Buschmann, the name *Acoyapa* signifies "a place where the water expands;" from the Aztec words *atl,* water, and *coyahua,* to spread. I cannot see, however, how this corresponds with the nature of the locality, unless it be referred to an extensive jicaral in the valley below the town.

We were received in the house of the first Alcalde, who we found to be a very intelligent and obliging person, to whom I am indebted for much information respecting the independent Indians of the neighbouring district of Mosquitia. On one of the nights we passed in his house, illumined by the light of the moon, a companion of mine called me to see a large snake passing between the wooden bars of the window into our room. The reader must be aware that in the whole State of Nicaragua, and I suppose throughout Central America in general, glass windows are unknown. A rat then was seen running up the wall, to hide itself under the thatch of the house, which, as there was no ceiling between, we had immediately over us. The snake followed it with a spring, and soon the screaming of the rat told us that it was caught by its enemy. This snake was of a species called *ratonera,* or rat-snake, and being totally harmless and even useful, is tolerated in the houses. As to poisonous reptiles I have never seen any in Nicaragua, with the exception of a beautiful specimen of the coral-snake, which had been killed and was brought to me at Granada, and I could not learn one single case of a person having died from the bite of a serpent in the interior of the country. This was not the case at San Juan del Norte, where the son of one of the principal merchants had been killed in that manner and other similar instances were recorded. But still this cannot be compared with the danger from venomous reptiles in Texas, New Mexico, and other southern and western parts of the Union. In some tracts along the Rio Grande a rattlesnake may be seen every few hundred paces, and at San Antonio in Texas no summer passes without some persons of the lower classes, mostly Mexicans, dying from the bite of the mocassin. In Nicaragua too a species of rattlesnake—*cascabela*—is found, but it cannot be very abundant, as I never encountered it in my travels. Two kinds of snakes are said to be particularly dangerous in the coast region near San Juan del Norte and in the woods of the San Juan river,—one of them called the *culebra tobova*, the other the *vibora de sangre*, and to these the fatal cases which I heard mentioned at San Juan were ascribed.

A little basin of water, at the foot of the steep hill on which the town is situated, was a place of rendezvous for various kinds of large aquatic birds, which at certain hours I saw there assembled in flocks. Amongst them were two kinds of white herons; a very large white bird with black wings, head and neck entirely naked, and the whole very much like the *Jabiru* or Mycteria Americana. There was also a rose-coloured spoonbill with a rhombic shape of its bill, the whole bird of the most delicate beauty, with different kinds of bitterns, and others. The white herons are called *garza*, the large white bird with the black wings and the naked head and neck has the two names of *garzon* or *guaïron*, and the spoonbill is known by the name of *garza morena*. I shot specimens of all these different kinds, without being able to preserve them for scientific purposes.

While my companions remained at Acoyapa, I made an excursion to the table-land on the other side of the dividing ridge. From what I have already observed in describing the road from Masapa to Acoyapa, I need not say that the dividing ridge is to the *north-east* of Acoya; but as all the former maps have laid down this town on the table-land of Mosquitia, instead of placing it between the dividing ridge and the lake, it may be useful to state this fact expressly. The Alcalde provided me with a guide, and I started from Acoyapa in the direction to the sources of the Rio Mico; that is to say, the Rio Mico which is a tributary of the Bluefield river.

The road led in a north-north-easterly direction, first across an open plain, then over hills covered with shrubs and trees, at last through a valley, along the dry bed of a torrent lined with high trees and thickets of bamboo and of a diminutive palm-tree called *Supa* in the language of the Woolwa Indians, and *Pijivaye*[1] in the dialect of Nicaragua. The stem of the little tree is rarely higher than six feet and thicker than a finger. It bears a cluster of nuts of the size of a walnut, which are eaten, and, when roasted, have a taste very much like the chestnut. The bed of the torrent is filled with blocks and boulders of various sizes, all of porphyritic rocks with a predominating

[1] The above word is spelled according to the rules of Spanish pronunciation.

trachytic or phonolitic basis. The sides of the hills and mountains are rocky, but covered with grass and bushes. Amongst the latter a shrub or little tree called *Nancite* is characteristic, and prevails to such a degree that it determines the aspect of vegetation in the greater part of Chontales. The shrub is found in the lower country likewise, and I have seen it often in the environs of Granada. It has a stunted growth, like some dwarf-oaks; bears clusters of red berries of a sub-acid taste, which are preserved and eaten like cranberries; and the bark is said to be a superior material for tanning. If the latter statement is correct, this bark might become of commercial importance, as any quantity of it may be obtained from these regions.

From the valley the path ascended a steep mountain side, where a family lived in a hut, keeping some goats and chickens; but I could see no trace of cultivation in the neighbourhood, and I was really unable to conceive how these people managed to sustain life. Farther on, the path led along the brim of a precipice, from which I looked down upon a valley covered with a forest of high trees. The roaring of a number of howling-monkeys, sounding almost like that of lions, was heard from below.

When I had reached the summit of the ascent, I saw myself on the edge of the table-land, and a beautiful park-like country, with green prairies, clusters of trees and little groves lay expanded before me. Here numerous springs give rise to brooks and rivulets which, by their confluence, form the *Rio Mico*. This river, together with the *Rio Siquias*, into which it empties, and the *Rio Arama*, which likewise empties into the latter, from the same side and a little lower down, make up the *Boswas* or *Boswash*. This name, in the language of the Woolwas, means "the three rivers," from *bos*, three, and *was*, water, or river. The

Boswas flows to Bluefield; but whether it is the Bluefield river itself, or only one of its tributaries, I was unable to learn. Looking over the nearer portion of the table-land, my eyes were arrested by a flat wooded ridge slightly elevated above the average level, following the course of the river just mentioned. These woods, I was told, continue along it down to the sea-shore; from which statement, however, it would be erroneous to conclude that the whole country in this direction is covered with forests. The greater part of Mosquitia, on the contrary, consists of savanas, the woods following the course of the rivers and the direction of the elevations only. Where the soil is sandy, the woods are formed by scattered pine-trees with groups of palmettos. Of this kind of vegetation, however, there was no trace in the region I visited on that occasion. Trees and shrubs were mostly different from those in the lower country of Nicaragua. One of the trees scattered here and there over the savana was covered with large rose-coloured flowers. If I am not mistaken, it was the *Bignonia leucoxylon,* a tree which grows in the low country along the Belize river, in British Honduras, and is known there by the name of "mayflower." The air of the table-land was cool and refreshing, with a gentle breeze from the north-east. Here and there in the distance a house or hut was seen, while herds of cows and horses were grazing in the plain in all directions.

The change of scenery, on reaching the summit of the ascent, had been so complete and so sudden that it seemed as if a hundred miles had intervened between looking forward and backward. In the latter direction, which was that to the south-south-west, the view followed the valley through which I had ascended. Mountains of considerable elevation are on both sides, the highest being the Cerro de Juigalpa, which stands to the right, and is marked by its abrupt steepness. Where the valley opened into the plain of Acoyapa, the view passed over the lower country, beyond which the lake expanded itself at the foot of an extensive region of mountains and hills. Just before the opening of the valley, the two peaks of Ometepe rose from the water. Beyond this island the hills of the Isthmus of Rivas were seen, and on the farthest horizon, faintly traced, the volcanoes of Costarica were discernible. The Mombacho, a little more to the right, marked the site of Granada.[1]

A house stood at the very edge of the plateau, so as to command the view down the valley, as described.

Continuing my journey over the table-land, I was struck by observing the number of springs in this region. Within a circuit of not many miles in diameter a river is formed on which the canoes of the Indians can pass down to Bluefields. Most of these springs are surrounded by trees and thickets of bamboo, and of the little supa palm mentioned above. At one of these localities, while passing under a tree, I disturbed the peace of a family of monkeys. With loud and angry chatterings they fled, and soon were hidden between the branches. But in this hasty flight a young one had been left behind on a branch just above the path, and so near that I could reach it with the muzzle of my gun. I stopped my horse to look at the little creature, which seemed to be so much frightened that it did not dare to move when its mother came back to save it. It was interesting to watch the struggle between fear and maternal love in the old monkey, alternately approaching, now

[1] The view accompanying this page was taken at one or two hundred feet below the summit.

retiring, hiding herself in the thicket, and then appearing again. Several times she stretched her arm towards her offspring, but as her eyes met mine, she again lost courage. At last the better feeling prevailed; with a sudden desperate jump she reached the little thing, clasped it in her arm, and in an instant was out of sight.

It was yet early in the afternoon when I reached the habitation of the outermost Nicaraguan settler in this direction, who gave me a friendly reception, and, when I left the next morning, refused to take payment, accepting only some powder and shot, of which I made him a present. The first of these two articles is rare and valuable in this district, the latter not to be had at all. The Chontaleños, or inhabitants of Chontales, are accustomed to hunt with bow and arrows, like the Indians. The small habitation in which I was received by Don Tomas S. was exceedingly clean, and nicely built of bamboo-reeds, to the exclusion of almost any other material. Even the furniture—consisting of a table, some benches and bedsteads—was composed of the same. Don Tomas, when I arrived, was occupied in preparing cheese, which is done on a large scale here, and he offered me a guacal full of fresh cream of as delicate a taste as I have ever enjoyed in Switzerland. The Nicaraguan cheese, however, is dry and of an inferior quality. But a large quantity is made and consumed in the country, and the inhabitants consider it a great delicacy. What is the cause of its inferior quality I cannot tell; it cannot be in the nature of the milk, which is good everywhere in Nicaragua. As far as my eyes could reach from the habitation of Don Tomas, the savana was covered with herds. The scene would have reminded me of Switzerland, if the country had not been so different in its natural features from the region of the Alps.

The savanas of this table-land are green throughout the year, there being no such distinction as that of a dry and a wet season, or of summer and winter. The temperature is always mild, and a due proportion of sunshine and rain prevails at all periods. Gigantic trees are scattered here and there over these prairies, affording shades to which the herds repair during the noontide heat. The trees and shrubs are principally exogenous, a few *goyol-trees* being the only kind of palm, which, with the exception of the little *supa*, I saw on the table-land.

In this district the outermost settlers from Nicaragua dwell in immediate contact with the independent Indians of the Mosquito territory. As some families of them lived in the neighbourhood of Don Tomas I went to see them, and my friendly host accompanied me. After we had proceeded three miles, passing the Rio Mico—which, at the place of the passage, was a little river running over pebbles of porphyry—we came to an impenetrable thicket of shrubs and reeds, where we halted, alighted from our horses, and entered an almost imperceptible path leading into the jungle. In a zigzag, like the entrance to a fortress, this path suddenly brought us to a large open shed, under which eight or ten Indians—men, women, and children—were assembled. Apparently they were surprised and felt uneasy at our arrival. Their good neighbour, Don Tomas, took pains to dissipate the suspicion I seemed to inspire, and I too did my best to insinuate myself into their friendly feelings; but I was unable to overcome the mistrust of the old women of the family even by making them a present of cigars, some small silver coins, and other trifles. On our way back Don Tomas gave me an explanation of their behaviour. These Indians believed me to be an Englishman from Bluefields, who, under the authority of the King of Mosquitia, had come to exact some services from them. On several occasions such exactions had been made, and parties had been sent up from Bluefields to press a number of men into the service of the king, or rather of his British tutors, for the purpose of cutting wood or doing other work on the river. The tribe of Indians to whom I paid a visit had lived somewhat lower down, but had retired to these upper regions for the purpose of remaining unmolested by the government of the *Rey-King*—the title which, by a composition of the Spanish and English words for the character of royalty, they gave to the Zambo sovereign of Mosquitia. Don Tomas told me that they suspected "the son of the Rey-King" would come with soldiers to carry them down to the coast by force, and compel them to work there.

When we arrived, all the individuals under the shed were completely naked, but the women hastened to put on an apron; the men, though more leisurely, did the same, and after a while the whole family, according to Indian notions, were in a becoming state for appearing before a foreign visitor. I observed that the more aged amongst them were suffering, or had been suffering, from cutaneous affections. Their skin, which, in a healthy state, was of a dark brown colour, showed large spots of a lighter shade, where it peeled off, and the marks of boils and sores were visible on different parts of their bodies. All of them were deformed by the disproportioned extension of the abdomen. The expression of their faces was not disagreeable, though their features were more of the broad Mongolic than of the sharper type of the Aztec and Chorotegan races in the lower country. If my memory serves me well, their physiognomy bore a considerable degree of resemblance to that of the Indians of the southern part of the State of California between the Colorado desert and Los Angeles.

A fire was burning under the roof on which some fish and a number of plantains were roasting. The fishes were of the species which, at Granada, is called guapote. I saw, besides, some little stores of mandioca-roots, sugar-cane, pine-apples, supa-nuts, and a fine guanávana. The latter, which is a well-known fruit of exquisite flavour and taste, is extremely rare at Granada, and, as it is not very likely that the foresight of these Indians should extend to planting of fruit-trees, must be supposed to grow wild in this region. The mandioca, however, the sugar-cane, and the pine-apples, are cultivated near their habitations. I saw them fishing on the river, which they did with bow and arrows, passing slowly and quietly along in a small canoe. The arrows, for that purpose, have a peculiar construction, being composed of two pieces, one of reed of the length of a common arrow forming the shaft; the other of very hard wood, to which an iron point is fixed. The wooden piece is inserted into the reed in such a manner as to separate from it in consequence of the movements of the fish which has been hit; when the former remains in the body of the fish, the latter, attached to it by a thread, swims on the water. The whole arrow is about six feet long. The iron points are of English manufacture, imported from Bluefields. Fish seemed to be a principal nourishment of these people. But the country is rich in game of all sorts. Manatees are in the river, tapirs in the thickets on its banks, deer, rabbits, cavias, pheasants, curassows, partridges, &c., everywhere in the bush and on the savana.

From an old man, who seemed to be the head of the family and tolerably well understood the Spanish language,

I succeeded in collecting a number of words and grammatical forms of the language of the tribe. On returning to New York I communicated this vocabulary to my friend Mr. Squier, who published it in his valuable work on Nicaragua, where it is to be found vol. ii. pp. 324, 325. In his preface Mr. Squier states that, according to subsequent investigations, my vocabulary is of the *Woolwa* language. Having no doubt as to the correctness of this statement, I have adopted it as a fact that the tribe to which the family I saw belonged were *Woolwas*, though they did not mention that word when I asked them for their name as a nation. In answer to my questions on this point, they said their appellation was *Rey-King*, by which, no doubt, it was their intention to show their loyalty to the sovereign of Bluefields. The whole tribe, I was told, could muster four hundred adult males under a chief of their own, who was well spoken of by Don Tomas. The fact, however, of the vocabulary which I collected being of the Woolwa dialect, does not diminish the interest attached to it as a specimen of what is probably the old *Chondal* language of Oviedo and other early writers. This probability I am going to show.

By the Nicaraguans these Indians are called *Caribes*; but no importance is to be attached to this denomination. The Caribs of the Mosquito territory and of British Honduras, as is well known, are of West Indian origin, having been transplanted, in 1796, from the island of St. Vincent to Ruatan, and afterwards to Honduras, whence they have spread over the whole extent of coast from Cape Gracias á Dios to Belize. Now, my investigations have elucidated the fact that the Indian population of a village, called *Lóvago*, are of the same race with the Woolwas, and as that village, like another called *Lovigisca*, both situated a few miles distant from Acoyapa, has existed, and its inhabitants have been Christians long before the time of the transmigration of the Caribs, it is beyond any doubt that the application of the name of the latter to the tribe of the Woolwas is erroneous. As to the Indians of Lóvago, one of my travelling companions, Dr. Bernhard, who was called to visit a sick person in that village, brought me the information that all the words of my Woolwa vocabulary, with the exception of one only, were understood at Lóvago, though the Indian dialect of the village was nearly extinct. From this fact we may conclude that the whole Indian population of Chontales, in the whole or in part, were of the same race with the Woolwas. Mr. Squier has discovered certain traces of affinity between the language of the Woolwas and that of other tribes farther to the north and north-west, to whom he has applied the general appellation of the *Lenca* race. Thus the name *Boswas*, or "the three rivers," derived from the Woolwa language, corresponds to the names *Amacwas* and *Was-presinia*, which are those of two tributaries of the Patuca.[1]

From all these particulars it is probable that the old Chontales Indians, who, according to Oviedo, spoke one of the five Indian dialects of Nicaragua, were the same race as the *Lencas* of Mr. Squier—a race spread all over Mosquitia and part of the State of Honduras.

One fact seems to oppose this opinion. The people of Lóvago, in their conversation with my travelling companion, stated that their ancestors, as well as those of the inhabitants of the little town of *Camoapan*, about sixty miles to the north-west, had come from the neighbourhood of Masaya. It is not very probable that this statement

[1] Squier, 'The States of Central America.' London, 1858, p. 247.

should refer to the time before the arrival of the Spaniards. But even if this should be the case, it never could have any other meaning than that some colonies of the more civilized nations of Nicaragua had settled amongst the ruder tribes of Chontales, and that those of Lóvago had sprung from a mixture of both; for even now the latter speak of the Woolwas as of their own people in its original condition, and with the manners and customs still preserved which had once been their own.

The question may be put whether those colonies were of the Aztec or of the Chorotegan element in the Nicaraguan population. That they came from the vicinity of Masaya says nothing, as both races were and still are neighbours in that section of the country. The fact that many of the local names of Chontales are derived from the Aztec language seems to decide the question, though that fact may appear by far too general to bear directly upon it. Aztec local names are scattered almost over the whole of Central America, in regions where no other vestiges of any historical influence of the race can be shown. These names must be considered as the monuments either of an old and far-ascending Aztec rule, or of the migrations of certain fragments of the Aztec race such as afterwards settled on the isthmus of Rivas and on the islands of the lake, or they mark the site of old mercantile colonies of the Aztecs, such as we know from the early historians this energetic nation was in the habit of establishing amongst the tribes of the adjoining regions. Thus, in Chontales, Matagalpa, and Nuevo Segovia, where the Aztecs are not known to have ever been established as a nation, we find geographical names such as Panaloyan, Acoyapa, Camoapan, Comalapa, Tecolostote, Matagalpa, Juygalpa, Totogalpa, Teustépet, and many others, all Aztec words, most of which have been translated by Mr. Buschmann in his essay on Aztec local names.

Even the name of *Chontales*, or *Chondales*—an appellation which repeatedly occurs in Mexican and Central American history and ethnology—is of the Aztec origin, and there is little doubt that in the old Indian times of Nicaragua it was used to designate the Woolwas and others of the ruder tribes which still inhabit the country to the north-east of the lake, and most probably all belong to the Lenca race. *Chontalli*, according to Mr. Buschmann, in the Aztec language, means a foreigner, and consequently an uncivilized man, like the Greek *βάρβαρος* and the Sanskrit *mlêtscha.* The country of Chontales, therefore, means the country of the savages. The same name is given to a mountainous district in the State of San Salvador, where Aztecs likewise lived in the vicinity of other tribes less advanced in civilization. Tribes, called Chontales, are mentioned by the Mexican historians as existing near Tlascala, in Oaxaca and Tabasco. When the Tlascaltecs made their submission to Cortés, they stated that the fault of the hostilities committed lay with the wild tribes of the mountains, the Otomis and Chontales. Thus the word has a very general signification; but if, in Nicaragua, it was used in reference to a distinct nation and language, there is not the slightest reason to suppose that this nation and language should not have been identical with the Woolwas of the present time, and the same of which Dr. Bernhard found the descendants in the village of Lóvago, though here they may have been mixed with a colony of Aztecs.

From the inhabitants of the village just named, Dr. Bernhard received some information concerning the old manners of the race, in giving which they invariably identified themselves with the Indians of the table-land. At Lóvago, they said, little remained of the customs of old; but with the people of the interior—"*por dentro*"—the ancient manners had been left unchanged. These latter are living in a state of polygamy; but a man has never more than three wives, who in most cases occupy separate dwellings, and usually have a great number of children. When a young man intends to marry he kills a deer, which, with a quantity of firewood, he places before the door of the girl. If she accepts this present the marriage takes place. When the husband dies the wife cuts her hair and burns the hut, and the same is done *vice versâ*. The dead are buried with all their property, and for a certain time some gruel of maize is daily placed on the grave. At certain times of the year they celebrate festivals or perform ceremonies at which no stranger nor any of their women and children are admitted. On these occasions they pretend "to dance with their god"—*bailan con su Dios de ellos*, as the alcalde of Acoyapa expressed it. This they do, singing at the same time with a loud voice. At these festivals certain feats of gymnastics are performed, each of them jumping over the next; the jumping man, at the same time, deals the other a blow over the shoulders, and if the latter does not show signs of being affected by the pain, he is acknowledged as an "hombre valiente"—one of the braves. Similar customs have been observed amongst various tribes belonging to races and countries widely different and distant from each other: they are of little interest. I would, however, not omit these particulars, as they are well calculated to convey an idea of the mental development of this people.

The next day I returned to Acoyapa, and on the 28th we left that place on our way back to Granada. As it was our intention to return by water, we took the road to the landing-place of *San Ubaldo,* which may be called the port of Acoyapa.

On this trip we passed some days on the hacienda of *San José*, the owner of which, Don Luciano de la Cuadra, received us with perfect hospitality. We had to wait here for a passage to Granada until the 3rd of June, there being but little intercourse across the lake in this direction. The time was spent in walks and rambles in the vicinity of the house, partly from a desire to satisfy our curiosity, partly from the more serious inducement to improve the fare of our dinner table. The hacienda of Don Luciano, according to the true Chontales style, was a mere cattle-farm, without the slightest agricultural improvement. Not even bananas or plantains were cultivated, and a few goyol-palms, together with two or three orange-trees, represented all the productions of the vegetable kingdom on this extensive and splendid estate. Bread is not known in Nicaraguan country places, and even at Granada it was only eaten by a few foreigners, all the other inhabitants contenting themselves with tortillas. Our host had several thousand cows on the savanas around his habitation, but he had neither milk nor butter. He ordered a cow to be killed the day after our arrival; but as meat will scarcely remain fresh for a day in that climate, especially during the rainy season, which had now set in, the eatable parts of the animal were cut into slices to be dried in the air during the intervals between the different showers that fell throughout the day. The vultures carried away half of it before our eyes, and what remained, and was brought to us for dinner the next two or three days, was of a *haut-goût* rather too strong for our taste. We tried to supply our table by shooting doves and quails, of which there were numbers everywhere; but both were of a diminutive size; and the former in particular were such beautiful little creatures that we soon discontinued our sport. There are three kinds of very small pigeons common in Nicaragua. One of them, called the *Cola-larga*, or long-tail, is of an ashy colour, and the size of a small thrush or common blackbird; the two others, called *Tortola* and *Carmelita*, are smaller still; and the latter, which is scarcely as large as a common lark, has some round spots of a splendid blue on the wings. There was no want of larger game in the vicinity, especially of the different kinds of curassows—large birds of the size of a small turkey, and, according to my opinion, amongst the most delicate wild-fowl which exists. One of the species, common in Nicaragua, is called *Pavon*, or *Pajuil*, and seems to be the *Crax Alector*. Another is of a very fine plumage, reddish-brown with white spots, somewhat similar to the banded curassow, or *Crax fasciolata*. A third, which is the most common of the three, is of a greyish black, and is called *Pava*. This is often stated to be the female of the pavon, but the opinion is erroneous, the pava not even appearing to belong to the same genus as the pavon, and having more the character of a *Penelope* or *Salpiza*. I shot several of these birds during our stay at the hacienda of San José; but the cook always ate the breast and left us the bones; and as we were the guests of the house we could not complain of this impudence, which seems to be the general fashion in Central America.

On one of my walks at San José I shot a small kind of eagle, or rather *Harpy*, carrying one of the large green parrots called *Lora* in its claws. It was a bird of prey of the proudest appearance, of the most ferocious valour, and of an incredible tenacity of life. With the exception of the long feathers of the wings and tail, which were of a dark-bluish grey, the whole bird was of the purest white. Its legs were covered with feathers to the toes, which were armed with the most formidable claws, very long, of semicircular form, and sharp as needles. Its head was large and broad like that of an owl, with long feathers in the neck, which being erected gave the bird a most savage aspect. Its eyes were very large, with yellow iris; and the indomitable courage in their expression only died away with the extinction of life. I had to crush almost every bone of the chest of this animal before it was dead.

On the 3rd of June we were informed that a bongo had arrived at San Ubaldo, and was going to sail for Granada in the evening. In this we took a passage, and arrived at home the next morning. Our horses had been sent back by land.

CHAPTER IX.

State of Political Affairs in Nicaragua — The different Parties — Interference of Foreign Interests — The Canal Project and the Accessory Transit Company — Outbreak of the Civil War of 1851 — The Author hastens to Leon — Insecurity of the Road — The Aristocracy of Science and Virtue — Arrival at Leon — The Leonese Government protests against the Contract with the Transit Company — General Muñoz, his Character, his Party Position, and his Death — Character, Political Career, and Death of Fruto Chamorro — The Author returns to Granada, and thence to the United States.

DURING the rambles which have been the subject of the foregoing chapters, the political horizon of Nicaragua had darkened more and more, and in the first days of August one of those revolutions broke out by which several of the Spanish-American republics have gradually ruined themselves. These civil wars and dissensions reflect a sad picture, and it may appear an unprofitable task to direct the reader's attention to such occurrences. Their interest, however, might be easily underrated; and the author is of opinion that he should not pass over a page of American history but imperfectly known and understood by those who have not been present on the spot, and still less a page containing particulars of certain far-reaching practical consequences.

When, on the separation of the Central Amerian provinces from Spain, the Royalists associated themselves in a revolutionary movement which they were unable to resist, they did so in the secret hope of establishing a Central American monarchy. Their political opponents, on the other side, aimed at a republican confederacy, after the model of the North American Union. The latter succeeded. The Royalists, unwilling to submit, asked the assistance of the ephemeral Mexican Emperor Iturbide; and when, in consequence of this application, a Mexican army entered Guatemala, the fugitive Republican Congress decreed the annexation of Central America to the United States. The shortness of Iturbide's career relieved the country from the necessity of choosing between the two annexations, either to the then existing empire of Mexico or to the North American Union. But that decree of annexation to the United States decided the character of the interference of foreign powers in the domestic affairs of Central America; and all the subsequent phases of political dissension and civil war in that unfortunate country, down to William Walker, who was called in by the remnants of the same party which, in 1822, decreed the annexation to the United States, take their origin from that desperate position of parties in the first year of independence. From that date it was decided that thenceforth Central America should be a prey to foreign influences—that the royalists or aristocrats, called "serviles," had to look to England; the republicans or democrats, called "liberales," to the United States, for sympathy and support in their struggle for power, and the realization of their political system. From that time also throughout Central America, the former might be called the English, the latter the American party; and as the latter were those who established, supported, defended, and, after its having been overturned, strove to restore the federal constitution and government, British influence in Central America, as a matter of course, directed itself against all federal tendencies.

From causes which do not enter into the subject of this rapid glance over the history of Central American federalism, these anti-federal influences have been strongest in Guatemala and Costarica; while in the three remaining States, the federal party continued to strive against them and to aim at the reconstruction of the Union dissolved in 1837. Various attempts to realize that purpose had been made by Nicaragua, Salvador, and Honduras, and conventions of delegates, instructed to frame a new constitution, had been held at Chinandega in Nicaragua in 1842, at Sonsonate in Salvador in 1846, and at Nacaome in Honduras in 1847, without leading to any result; when, in 1849, the influence of the United States was brought to bear upon the question. The government of Washington instructed its diplomatic agent in Central America to assist those republics in their endeavours to re-establish the federation; and encouraged by him, the State of Nicaragua took the lead in a new attempt. As in former cases, Guatemala and Costarica excluded themselves from the common cause of Central American nationality. But the representatives of the three middle States assembled at Leon and drew up a federal constitution which was signed on the 8th of November, unanimously ratified by the legislative assemblies of the same three States and published in the *Correo del Istmo* of the 16th of December, 1849. In accordance with this constitution, the representatives of the three States assembled in the month of December of the following year, and José Barrundia, who had been the President of the Central American Republic of 1821, was elected President of the new confederation. General elections were ordered to take place of representatives to the first regular national congress, to assemble in December, 1851, and participation in which was left open to Guatemala and Costarica.

To frustrate the success of these labours, has been one

of the principal motives by which certain foreign influences were actuated in promoting the revolutionary outbreak of 1851 in Nicaragua. To frustrate the endeavours of the Accessory Transit Company—that metamorphosis of the Atlantic and Pacific Ship Canal Company of New York—was another motive of almost equal weight with the same foreign influences. Both motives, by the peculiar turn which things had taken in Nicaragua, came into conflict with each other; the federalists of Leon being precisely that of the two Nicaraguan parties which was opposed to the new contract demanded by the Accessory Transit Company. But before I enter on a few explanatory remarks with reference to this view of the matter, I have to add some facts of interest by which the history of that last attempt to form a Central American nationality is brought down to the moment when I left Nicaragua—the more so as these facts seem to have remained unnoticed in some political transactions of a more general significance. To Mr. Guerrero, one of the members of the then existing federal government, I am indebted for the original documents of which the following statements are an abstract.

The federal, or, as it was called, the national government, with Mr. Barrundia at its head, was installed on the 9th of January, 1851, and the fact communicated to the political agents of all foreign powers represented in any of the Central American States. By the new federal compact the three States of the confederation had given up the right of entertaining separate intercourse with foreign powers, all diplomatic relation having been ceded to the national government. The three States of the confederation, accordingly, broke off their diplomatic intercourse. By the State of Nicaragua, in particular, this was done by a decree of its legislative assembly dated the 31st of May, and by a circular note to the foreign powers with whom it had been in political relations, dated June 4th. And in a communication, dated June 10th, the national government was informed by Nicaragua that this State had fulfilled its federal duties in that respect, and Mr. Marcoleta, who, till then, had been accredited as Chargé d'Affaires of the republic of Nicaragua to the government of Washington, was recommended to the same position under the authority of the national government of Central America.

It is a remarkable fact that on this occasion England and the United States took the same view of the question, both concurring in not taking any notice of these communications, nor of the existence of the new Central American confederation in general, though it had been formed under the influence of the latter of the two powers. The government of President Taylor had given place to that of President Fillmore, and with the change of administration a change of system in reference to Central American affairs had also occurred at Washington. When, in July, the diplomatic agent, who was to follow Mr. Squier in Central America, was sent out by the government of the United States, he insisted upon being received by the government of Nicaragua and obstinately refused to enter into any communications with the national government. The British Consul General did the same. To the official communication of the establishment and inauguration of that government he gave no answer, and in a confidential letter to one of the ministers, he used the most undiplomatic language which, as far as I know, is on record in the history of modern international transactions.[1]

[1] A copy of the letter of Mr. Frederick Chatfield to Mr. Pablo Buitrago, then one of the members of the national government, was communicated to me by Mr. Guerrero, another member of that government, in the presence and with the consent of his colleague. It is dated: Legacion de S. M. B., Gua-

In this hopeless state of federal affairs, the revolution of which I am going to speak in connexion with my last movements in Nicaragua, broke out at Leon.

As in the other States of Central America the parties in Nicaragua, though subordinate to the more general distinctions of which I have just traced the origin, had developed themselves according to certain local conditions. Here the aristocratic party, anti-federal as in all the States, had been called, by a popular name, the Timbucos, while the democrats had received the designation of Calandracas—the latter name derived, if I am not mistaken, from *Calandra*, the lark, meaning to express that the party was that of the poor who live like the birds of the fields. The former party had their head-quarters in the city of Granada, the latter in that of Leon, and thus the political division was of a sectional character. The Timbucos, therefore, in the records of Nicaraguan events, have been often called the Granadinos, their antagonists the Leonese; and as the most distinguished leader of the latter at the time of which I am going to speak more in particular, was Fruto Chamorro, they assumed at that special period the name of the Chamorristas. The names Timbucos, Granadinos, and Chamorristas, therefore, are different appellations of the same party, which is the Nicaraguan fraction of what might most appropriately be called the conservative party of Central America. In 1849, while the liberals held the reins of government, the conservatives of Granada and Rivas made an attempt to wrest them from their hands by inciting an insurrection of the Indians. A man named Samoza,

temala, 13 de Junio, 1851. As it is not the intention of the author to enter more deeply into the matter here, he contents himself with remarking that he published that interesting document, in its original Spanish, in a note to p. 449 of the first volume of the German edition of the present work, 'Aus Amerika. Von Julius Fröbel. Leipzig, 1857-1858.'

who had been at the head of a band of highway robbers, but had some chivalrous traits in his character, was their instrument in attempting to effect this purpose. But when Samoza, who rapidly made himself master of the whole district of Nicaragua Proper, and occupied Rivas with his Indians, showed that he was about to imitate Carrera after the Timbucos of Nicaragua had imitated the "Serviles" of Guatemala, a general consternation pervaded the party who had stirred up the insurrection; and they were the first to call on the government for protection against an impending general calamity. General Muñoz, at the head of a military force, hastened from Leon to Rivas, where, after a hot fight in the streets and houses, he routed the insurgents, who had sacked the city, and Samoza was taken prisoner and executed.

This happened shortly before my arrival in Nicaragua, and the result had produced a general disposition to forget old animosities and establish the prosperity of the country on the basis of mutual justice and toleration. This was the spirit which presided over the election of the new Director Supremo, Mr. Pineda. It was, however, impossible, under existing circumstances, that the parties should keep the peace for any length of time.

Amongst the prominent men of the democratic party, the most formidable to the Conservatives was General Muñoz, commander-in-chief of the troops of the Republic. They hated him because the military force of the country was in his hands, which, however, he had not made use of in any unlawful manner—because he was in favour of innovations and reforms that were disliked by them, or threatened to curtail their interests — because he was a strong supporter of all federal tendencies, and from various other reasons. But the General, at the same time, had been opposed to British influence, and though he was on good private terms with the more influential Englishmen living at Léon, he had reasons to consider them as his enemies. Now the interests of a society of speculators as powerful as the Atlantic and Pacific Ship-Canal Company came in conflict with his views on a question of national economy, and thus losing the support of the American influence he seemed unable to resist the combined attacks of his adversaries.

The interference of the Canal Company marks a new period in the history of Central American troubles and dissensions. Be it that the results of the survey had been less favourable than had been expected, or that the want of sympathy which the enterprise had found with the capitalists of London had produced the effect; at any rate the Canal Company had formed the conviction that it would be an advantageous transaction to get rid of the obligation of opening a navigable communication between the two oceans across Central America, without losing the available part of the immense monopolies and privileges awarded for the realization of the great work. With the view to obtain this result an accessory contract was proposed to Nicaragua by the Company, who were to constitute themselves in the capacity of holders of this second contract under the name of the Accessory Transit Company. The obligations of the latter were to be, to open a carriage-road across the Isthmus of Rivas; and to supply the necessary means for the transit across Nicaragua, on this road, as well as on the river and lake. For fulfilling this obligation, together with some financial engagements, the Company were to have the monopoly of steam-navigation and various other valuable advantages.

Muñoz and the whole democratic party, actuated by

patriotic as well as sectional views, were opposed to the granting of the transit contract, while their political adversaries at Granada and Rivas, situated so as to derive immediate advantages from the transit through the southern section of the country, were inclined to yield to the arguments of the friends and agents of the Company. Thus certain American interests, sufficiently strong to act upon the government of the United States, became associated with a Nicaraguan party which had always been considered as peculiarly inclined to enter into English views. And while thus American interests in Nicaragua were in conflict with themselves the same was the case with British interests in the country. These, of course, were decidedly opposed to the transit scheme. If the canal, as it now appeared, was not to be constructed, and if the transit project could be frustrated, there would be some hope to drive the Yankees out of the field in Nicaragua, and "to free so desirable a spot in the commercial world from the competition of so adventurous a race as the North Americans."[1] To produce this effect was the object of all who were in the British interest in Nicaragua; and thus it happened that these same agencies found reasons to support the Leonese party, with General Muñoz, in their opposition to the transit contract.

President Pineda, though belonging to the party of Granada and Rivas, was of the opinion of his political antagonists in this particular question. The intrigues of the New York speculators accordingly turned against him, and by a combination of various interests brought into

[1] See No. 9, p. 40, of the 'Documentos relativos á la legacion de los estados de Nicaragua y Honduras cerca el gabinete Británico, sobre el territorio de Mosquitos y puerto de San Juan del Norte. Los publica el Señor Don Francisco Castellon, Ministro Plenipotenciario y Enviado Extraordinario de dichos estados. Granada, 1851.' There is an English edition likewise.

simultaneous action, he and his government were driven from office. A revolution broke out at Leon in the night between the 3rd and 4th of August, and a provisional government, with the senator Justo Abaunza at its head, was established. At Managua the legislature of the State was assembled at that time. When the news of what had happened at Leon reached them, that body, following the advice of the agent of the American Company, elected a provisional government of their own with José del Montenegro at its head, and removed to Granada. At the latter place a few hundred troops were assembled, and the command was given to Fruto Chamorro, while at Leon Muñoz was preparing to march on Granada. Nicaragua had thus two governments and two armies ready to fight each other. The agent of the Canal Company knew how to avail himself of these troubles, and on the 19th of August the contract of the Accessory Transit Company was ratified by the Legislative Assembly sitting at Granada. The day after having put his signature to the instrument, the provisional director, Montenegro, died. The confusion at Granada became general. As the foreigners living in that city almost unanimously sympathised with the Leonese party, they were summoned by the authorities in power at Granada to deliver their arms, to enter the ranks of the troops to be employed against the Leonese, or to leave the country. At a meeting of almost all the foreigners then at Granada, it was determined to refuse compliance with all these three requests, to organize for mutual protection, and to resist by force, if necessity should occur, all attempts to infringe upon their neutral position in the civil war which was impending. In the mean time public excitement and anxiety increased. On one side it was stated that the Leonese under Muñoz were approaching; on the other it was asserted that General Guardiola—the tiger of Honduras, as he had been called—was coming in aid of Granada, though his Indian cut-throats were feared more, even as friends, than the Leonese as enemies. Barricades were erected in the streets. One of my German friends who, when emigrating to Nicaragua, had taken with him a flag with the old German colours, striped black, red and gold—an ideal banner of German nationality—hoisted it over the gate of his house. Who would believe it, that the colours of the German empire, past or future, could have inspired some ladies of Granada with absolute confidence, and that soon the rooms of my friend were filled with cases and boxes containing the more valuable portion of the moveable property of the good señoras!

Such was the state of things at Granada, when, to hold a conversation with General Muñoz, I started on a hasty trip to Leon. A young German accompanied me. It was in the evening of the 21st of August, and just in the very moment when we mounted our horses a drummer was beating through the streets, and an order issued that no one should leave the city without a special permission and passport from the "Comandante." We set spurs to our horses and never drew rein till we had reached Masaya.

To protect Granada against a sudden attack of the Leonese, the Granadinos under Chamorro had taken possession of Managua. The "army" consisted of 200 men, at the utmost; but the road was covered with soldiers and recruits hastening to join him. We had taken our breakfast at Managua the next morning, and were ready to proceed, when a man in a dressing-gown and nightcap, followed by an officer in uniform, appeared, and subjected us to an interrogatory in reference to our journey. We were allowed to pass. "Who was the man in undress?" I asked the waiter. "*El general del ejército!*" answered the boy, with importance. It was Don Fruto Chamorro himself, who, since I had had a dispute with him at Rivas, had become general of the Granadinos, and soon afterwards became President of Nicaragua. Undoubtedly he recognized me, and knew that what I answered to his questions was untrue. But he behaved with perfect politeness.

The country between Managua and Leon, at that time, was in a very unsettled state, and the roads were infested by deserters and stragglers from both parties. While passing through the forest between Managua and Mateares I had advanced ahead of my companion for a quarter of a mile, and was just trying to lead my horse over a narrow and slippery path between the trees on one side and a deep mud-hole on the other, when two men, each of them with a pistol in one hand and one of the long and heavy knives called *machete* in the other, stepped forward from the thicket. To turn my horse was impossible. I drew and cocked a pistol, and thus, without a word being spoken on either side, I passed on. When I had cleared the mud-hole, I turned to wait for my companion, after which the two fellows disappeared in the bush. General Muñoz, to whom I narrated the fact, asked me why I had not shot them down. "What business had the ruffians to stand at the road-side in the forest with arms in hand?" he said, when I objected that they had made no attack upon me. It was one of the merits of the general that under his influence the country had enjoyed a degree of security unknown before as well as after his time.

The next day, while resting a few hours at Pueblo Nuevo, one of those violent thunderstorms broke out which are not uncommon in this western part of the country during the rainy season. The eastern and western sides of Nicaragua, and, I believe, of Central America in general, are very different in this respect. The whole western coast of the Continent, from Nicaragua to the Peninsula of California, is frequently visited by thunderstorms of a frightful violence. Mazatlan, for instance, is ill-reputed for this feature of its climate; while at San Francisco, on the contrary, thunderstorms are of rare occurrence, and not very heavy. In our case, we had reason to congratulate ourselves on having reached a shelter before it broke out. The flashes of lightning were most frightful, and the claps of thunder altogether appalling. The rain poured down so densely that it seemed doubtful whether a man could breathe in such an atmosphere. The house we had entered was inhabited by a widow and her two daughters. As soon as we had alighted, the curate of the village, curious to see the foreign travellers, hastened to pay a visit to the ladies; and now, while heavy strokes of lightning fell in every direction on the trees of the forest, the trembling women looked to the priest for consolation, and the young divine availed himself of the opportunity of showing his superior information. "When I was a boy," he said, "I too was afraid of thunder and lightning. But since that time I have studied philosophy "—a terrible clap—"*Ave Maria santisima!*—and our professor has taught us that the heavenly bodies are too high up to fall down upon us." Another clap—"*Jesu Cristo, mi mejor pararayo!*" The next stroke drove the trembling padre into a dark room, where the women had taken refuge, and as long as the storm lasted we heard their loud and pious "*ora pro nobis;*" but scarcely had it passed away, and the thunder was heard from a certain distance, when the philosophical curate, followed by the widow and her daughters, issued forth from their place of concealment, and calling a little boy who passed by: "Juan!" he said, in a tone of mental superiority, "go quickly to my mother and tell her she need not be frightened, there is no danger at all."

While waiting till the waters had subsided on the roads, we had the advantage of a prolonged conversation with this enlightened member of the Nicaraguan clergy. He had a small English volume in his pocket, and tried his utmost to prove that he could read it. He asked me for an explanation of the different meanings of the word "*sir.*" "I understand," he said, after I had answered his questions, "In England they have an aristocracy, but in Nicaragua no aristocracy exists besides that of science and virtue—*en Nicaragua no hay otra nobleza que de la ciencia y de la virtù.*"

At Leon I appeared as the bearer of important intelligence. They knew nothing there of what had happened at Granada. I could tell them that the transit contract had been ratified, that Montenegro was dead, and that Chamorro had taken possession of Managua. The first of these news made a strong impression upon the Englishmen residing at Leon, with whom General Muñoz was now the man for the situation of the moment.

With the general himself the paramount interest was entirely of a military character. When I told him that Chamorro was concentrating his forces at Managua, he triumphantly remarked: "here I shall have an opportunity of demonstrating some superior military tactics—*aqui puedo yo hacer unas operaciones muy militares;*" and he proceeded to explain how he could send troops by sea from Realejo to San Juan del Sur, whence they could pass to

Rivas and take that city, as well as Granada, by surprise; or how he could despatch them in canoes over the lake of Managua, land them at Tipitapa, and again take Granada by surprise; and other stratagems of equal depth in military science. Poor general! he had neither a vessel for the sea-passage of his troops, nor canoes for the lake, nor troops to spare, nor money to pay them; though certain foreigners at Leon had loudly proclaimed that they would supply the necessary funds.

Late in the evening before my departure from Leon, which took place on the 27th, the General came to see me in the hotel, handing me a package of documents and dispatches which I was requested by the provisional government to take with me to the United States. Some of them were intended to be delivered to the government of Washington; others to be published in the principal journals of the Union. The most important of the papers was a formal protest of the provisional government of Leon, against the contract which that of Granada had entered into with the Accessory Transit Company of New York. In this protest the Leonese government took the unobjectionable ground that, if during a civil war a foreigner enters into an agreement with one of the parties, he makes his rights and claims dependent upon the fate of the party on which he thinks proper to rely; the Leonese government declaring in advance, that they would not recognize the contract entered into by their political antagonists, if ever the undivided and legal authority over the State should fall into their hands.

It was the last time that I saw the General, who had become my warm friend. I intended, after a short visit to the United States, to return to Nicaragua. But soon after I had reached New York, the news arrived that Leon had been taken by the Granadinos. Muñoz had become the prisoner of Chamorro, and would have been shot, but for the interference of his English friends, who succeeded in commuting his sentence of death into banishment from the State. Of all the "*operaciones muy militares*" none had been executed. After the capture of Leon, Chamorro was regularly elected Supreme Director of the State by the concurrence of both sections of the country. He was magnanimous enough to recal his adversary from exile, and intrust him anew with the command of the troops of the State; and Muñoz was sufficiently ungrateful again to take side with the Leonese party when they revolted against the government of Chamorro in 1854. In this respect Chamorro proved himself the better man and the nobler character. The Leonese, on that occasion, placed Francisco Castellon at the head of their oppositional government, and with him Muñoz once more became one of the chiefs of that party. Chamorro attacked Leon a second time, but was driven back to Granada, followed by the Leonese, who besieged that city, but were obliged to retreat in turn. In this impossibility of deciding the fate of the country, Castellon and his friends, amongst whom was Muñoz, called in the aid of William Walker. When the latter, on his first attack upon Rivas, was deserted by the native troops placed under his command, Muñoz was said to have acted as a traitor to his North American auxiliaries, though the question may be raised, which of the two—the North Americans or the Nicaraguans—first thought of using the others as an instrument for their own purposes? In the mean time the Leonese government was attacked by a force from Honduras. Muñoz marched against and completely routed these invaders, but he found his death in the engagement.

Though he had many defects in his character, the general *José Trinidad Muñoz* was the most enlightened man of his time in Nicaragua. He knew that his country, and Central America in general, could only be redeemed by the aid of foreign elements of population from Europe and North America. He had all the ambition which might be expected in a Spanish American general, and according to his system a military government was the most adapted to the condition of society in Nicaragua. But if he had been in possession of absolute power he would have used it to advance the interests of the country. To dispose of the public lands in favour of immigration, to promote the naturalization of foreigners, to introduce complete religious toleration, to establish a system of public education, to secularize the so-called "capellanias"—and in any way to concur in the re-establishment of the Central American federation—were amongst the political measures he had in view.

At Managua, on my way back to Granada, his antagonist, again in the nightcap, inspected and interrogated me a second time. At this interview I had to risk more than on the former occasion, but General Chamorro acted again in a very gentlemanlike manner, and everything passed on without difficulty.

Fruto Chamorro died in 1854, exhausted by the hardships and cares of a continued civil war, in which he was the leader of one of the two parties, representing at the same time the legal executive authority of the republic. In the tragedy of the decay of Hispano-American life in Central America he has acted a part to which sympathy cannot be refused. I believe that he was a true friend of his country, and with the honesty and firmness of his character he could have effected much good if his notions had been less circumscribed. But by the course of events, his natural stubbornness and the narrowness of his views incessantly increased, and his political ideas became more and more reactionary. Under his leadership the disinclination towards foreigners, which he had shown privately before, and which caused the legislature of the State to reject a proposition of law facilitating the settlement of foreigners in the country, became avowedly an essential part of the political creed of the conservative party of Nicaragua. One extreme called the other into life. The democratic party, seeing and understanding the degree of prosperity, progress, wealth and power derived by the United States from foreign emigration, and fully conceiving that, with all its natural wealth and advantages of situation, Central America has no other hope of escape from ruin than the acquisition of assistance in skill, intelligence, activity, enterprise and capital from the same source, demanded foreign assistance at any cost; and thus, while the revolution had again broken out at Leon in 1854, the party, under the leadership of Francisco Castellon, took the desperate resolution of calling in the military assistance of a band of North-American adventurers under William Walker. The sequel is known to the world.

On the 28th of August I returned to Granada, where barricades obstructed every street. I did not, however, remain to witness the farther development of affairs. I left Granada on the 2nd of September, on my way back to New York. At San Juan del Norte, which had considerably increased during the time I had spent in the interior, I made the acquaintance of Captain Samuel Shepherd, known by his claims to the proprietorship of I forget how many thousand square miles of land in the kingdom of Mosquitia. Captain Shepherd, who died a few years ago, appeared to me a remarkable character,—one of those men who leave an impression in the memory of all who have encountered them. He was above seventy when I saw him, but though he was almost blind, and had lately broken several ribs by a fall, he still retained the traces of a powerful constitution and great energy. He told me that he had lived on the Mosquito coast from his youth without ever having been seriously ill. The country in general, he stated to be perfectly healthy. When, upon his questions, I told the old gentleman that I had visited the Rio Mico, he threw up his arms and hands, "That country is all mine," exclaimed he, as if inspired by a vision of the beauty and riches of his property.

I left San Juan del Norte on the 12th of September, and on the 21st arrived at New York, after an absence of exactly one year.

CHAPTER X.

A Visit to Honduras — Belize — An Excursion on the River — Sites and Scenery — Information in reference to the Remnants of the Belgian Colony of St. Thomas — The Boom — Ruins in British Honduras — Manati Lagoon — Negro Settlement — Types of the Black Race under favourable Circumstances — Manati Cave — Subterraneous Rivers — Geological Remarks.

Before proceeding to the general remarks on Central America which are to fill the closing chapter of this Book, I have to give a short account of a visit paid to the British settlement of Belize and the coast of the State of Honduras during the early part of 1857.

I made this little trip accompanied by my family and by a friend who had come with us from New Orleans, and my movements were restricted within the boundaries of what we could accomplish under such circumstances. Nevertheless, and though in some cases we intended little more than the satisfaction of curiosity, I may not be quite hopeless of contributing to the reader's information and entertainment by my descriptions.

It was the 8th of February when we left the mouth of the Mississippi. The sea was very rough, and our brig, called the *Creole*, rather an elderly lady, and much afflicted with dropsy, supplied accommodation of a very dubious character; but the northerly gale by which the waves were raised drove us in little more than five days into the harbour of Belize. The communication between the latter place and New Orleans is carried on by a few schooners and brigs, of which, generally, one sails every fortnight. They are all of a very inferior class of vessels.

The goods which they carry to the British settlement are principally provisions, such as flour, salt meat, hams, liquors, &c., chiefly for the mahogany cuttings. On their return to New Orleans they usually call at Ruatan, where they take in plantains, bananas, and cocoa-nuts, as a home freight.

I abstain from a description of the little town of Belize, as I may fairly suppose it to be sufficiently known in England. This, however, is not to be expected of the natural character of the country, the charms of its scenery being but very indifferently appreciated by the inhabitants.

During the first days of March we made an excursion of two days paddling up the river. Downward the current brought us back in one day. The course is very crooked, so that the farthest point of our excursion could have been reached on horseback in six or seven hours—the land-road, which runs on the northern side of the river, cutting off the bends. We travelled in one of the long canoes called pitpans, rowed by six Caribs. It was provided with an awning, under which we were well protected against the sun. I was indebted for these accommodations to the kind attentions of Mr. Travis, of the firm of James Hyde and Co.

The Belize river empties itself by two channels which separate at a place called Haulover, where the old piratical settlement of Wallace, and afterwards the seat of government of what is now called British Honduras, was originally situated, and remained so until it was removed to the outlet of the southern channel. Here the present town is built along the sea-shore, on both sides connected by a wooden bridge. This southern branch of the river-mouth may be six or seven miles long, forming a narrow passage through a thicket of mangroves. The northern channel, which carries out by far the greater portion of water, is wide, and in that direction the sea is seen from Haulover at a short distance. From hence upwards, to a place called the Boom, where the river is artificially narrowed and shut in by an iron chain for the purpose of arresting the mahogany flooded down from the upper cuttings, the stream has a respectable appearance, and might be navigated by steam-boats.

Leaving Belize, we took the southern channel, and thus had a fine opportunity of seeing the characteristic scenery produced by mangrove thickets lining the banks of a river within the limits of tide-water. Thousands of interwoven branches of an inverted vegetation, as it were, lifting the main trunks of the trees above the flood and representing what might be called the legs of the forest, form a labyrinth of arches and grottoes under which a canoe may pass, and where a whole fleet of such small craft might hide itself from view at a hundred yards distance. It is evident that, in addition to the coral reefs of the coast, these thickets must have greatly contributed to the security of the first adventurous settlers who had established themselves here in spite of Spanish persecution and vengeance. By the variety of so grotesque a foreground, the general monotony of our passage through this region was agreeably relieved. Our Caribs paddled away in the best humour, showing their dexterity in the handling of their little oars by now and then giving a double stroke to the water in the time required for a single one, or by letting them wheel round upon their hand so as to be again in the right position when required by the regular movement of the little crew, while in a low voice they sang their songs of strange melody in unintelligible language.

A little above the Haulover the mangroves disappear. The banks rise above the level of the water and begin to be fit for cultivation; though in time of inundations, during the rainy season, the whole country is occasionally overflowed. Now and then we pass a little hut, half hidden between some giant plantain-leaves, and overshadowed by a few cocoa-nut trees. After three or four hours' rowing we reached the plantation of Mr. R., a German, who owns a considerable tract of land here. Most agreeably we were surprised by the neatness of the small dwelling in which we were received with all the hospitality we could have expected from good countrymen. Mr. and Mrs. R., both from the borders of the Rhine, had been amongst the first settlers of the ill-fated Belgian colony of St. Thomas, on the coast of Guatemala, where they spent many years before retiring to their present residence. The situation of their house is delightful. The river, here a noble stream, passes before the door, the opposite bank offering an admirable view of Dr. Y.'s country seat, one of the oldest cultivations and residences on the Belize river. A long avenue of cocoa-nut trees, planted at regular distances, extends along the bank, from which an ever green meadow, bordered by forest-trees, spreads towards the interior.

Mr. and Mrs. R. have a very favourable opinion of the climate of the country in which they are now residing, and whoever sees them will not doubt their assurances of its salubrity, though they confess they have not escaped some attacks of intermittent fever. They bear, however, an almost equally favourable impression of the climate of St. Thomas, in defiance of the terrible reputation which that place has acquired by the mortality of the colonists. There are several other persons at Belize who have belonged to that colony, and I took considerable interest in collecting and comparing their statements with reference

M 2

to the unlucky fate of the settlement. But all agree that the climate had very little to do with it. The country is described by them as rich and beautiful, the climate as good; but of the company who speculated in bringing the settlers out, and principally of the directors of the settlement itself, they spoke in terms of strong reprobation. By a foolish system of arrangement and an iniquitous exertion of arbitrary power, the colonists, placed in an absolute wilderness, where the existence of a well-prepared location with dwelling-houses, built in advance for each of them, had been promised by the company, were deprived of their individual liberty, and subjected to forced labour for the benefit of what was called "the community." And while thus reduced to a state little better than that of slaves they were allowed to perish from want of wholesome food, almost all the provisions sent out by the company being unfit for the sustenance of human life. Under these circumstances the greater number of the colonists either died or removed to some other locality. Some, however, principally Germans, remained, and are said to be now well contented and in tolerably good circumstances. In consequence of the non-fulfilment of their contract by the company, the colony of St. Thomas has reverted to the sovereignty of Guatemala, and the remaining settlers are doing far better under the rule of Carrera than they did before under the direction of European speculators. Some of them cultivate yams and other vegetables on a larger scale than is customary in this neighbourhood, and from time to time bring them to market on their own boats to Belize. The realization of the Honduras railway project would place them in a very advantageous situation, as even Omoa is obliged to procure many necessary articles of life from the Caribs.

This is all I had an opportunity of learning of the history and present state of St. Thomas—a place which has become so conspicuous in the development of unfavourable opinions as regards colonization in tropical regions. *Relata refero.*

As we continued to ascend the river the scenery became still more beautiful. Lined by thickets of an elegant but diminutive species of palm-tree, which might be kept among the ornamental plants of a drawing-room, showing on a miniature scale all the relative proportions of the most characteristic representatives of *palmaceae*—fringed, still higher up, by the gigantic light-green wafts of the *bamboo*, that drop gently over the water's surface, like the downy plumes of delicate marabouts—the banks rise some twenty or thirty feet above the average height of the river. Fine savanas extend on either side, interrupted, in a park-like manner, by patches of forest or clusters of trees. Here the majestic shafts of the cabbage-palm, representing a natural prototype of the Grecian column, and smooth as its marble, stand in plastic beauty; while the *Corozo*, or *Cahoon-nut tree*, may be considered as the most perfect representative of the picturesque in tropical vegetation. With its trunk clad in the richest attire of parasitic *aroideae*, *orchideae*, or *bromeliaceae*, its feathery leaves bent into elegant curves by the weight of their own luxuriance or the burden of ornamental climbers:—this species of palm might be compared to a beautiful Indian maiden, such as may have adorned the court of the Aztec princes or of the Yncas of Peru.

At no place, as far as I had an opportunity of seeing the country, do these palm-trees unite in composing a more delightful scene than in the neighbourhood of what is called the *Boom.* Here they stand, scattered along the smooth surface of a beautiful prairie, over which numerous herds of cattle are roaming. Both land and cattle are the property of Mr. B., a wealthy individual, if the mere possession of valuable materials, without the inclination of turning them to a useful purpose, constitutes wealth. But while we passed a night under the hospitable roof of Mr. B., we had an opportunity of seeing the owner of many square leagues of land and of thousands of cattle deprived even of that degree of comfort which in the United States may be found in the log-cabin of the squatter; and this in the neighbourhood of a town like Belize, where cattle for the consumption of the inhabitants is imported almost weekly by sea from Omoa. A Yankee, in the position of Mr. B., would have monopolized the cattle-market of Belize. His lands he would have parcelled out in half a thousand farms. He would have laid out on his property on the river a town; and farms, as well as town-lots, he would have sold to some thousands of emigrants, whom he would have known how to induce to settle there; and after having realized millions by this process, he would either have built a palace as his family seat at the Boom, or have retired to some of the fashionable cities in the United States or in Europe.

The *Boom*, under more favourable circumstances, will not fail to become the site of a considerable town, and a delightful site it will be. We left early in the morning, and about three o'clock in the afternoon arrived at *Baker's*, where we remained for the rest of the day, spending a part of the time in a walk to the neighbouring "*pine ridge.*"

As from the borders of the river the traveller passes to this new region, the whole aspect of nature becomes changed —the luxuriance of tropical vegetation disappears. Surrounded, by scattered pine-trees and groups of palmettos, we found ourselves on a sandy soil, covered with a scanty growth of grass of very inferior quality. The country is far superior in aspect to the pine-regions of the Carolinas; but nevertheless the visitor might imagine himself to have been suddenly removed to some district in the "Palmetto State."

I had no opportunity of examining or inquiring into the agricultural qualifications of the pine regions which comprise so great a portion of eastern Central America. Some parts are said to have very fine pastures, and numerous ponds or little lakes form natural reservoirs of good drinking water, never failing even in the dry season. The soil, however, appears to be poor, though it may be quite fit for the cultivation of some particular kinds of vegetable produce; but one thing is certain, the pine regions of this country supply an inexhaustible source of turpentine. The quantity of resinous matter contained in the wood is so great, that when a torch is wanted here a piece is split from the side of the first trunk met with, and it will burn as freely as any torch artificially manufactured.

In the higher regions of the interior, the pine districts, I was told, present a better aspect. In the State of Honduras they are the richest grazing districts, nourishing millions of cattle, which an intelligent Swiss gentleman just from the interior of that State, whom I met at Omoa, told me are fully equal to the best breed in Switzerland.

A few miles from Baker's is a sugar plantation, owned by a resident of Belize, and called New Boston. I was greatly mortified when, after my return to Belize, I learned from a young Frenchman that on this plantation are Indian ruins of the same character as those of Yucatan, and that idols and other antiquities have often been found there.

The following day we returned. Had we extended our trip higher up the river, some hours would have brought us to the lower rapids—the first of a series of falls which interrupt the navigation. Canoes can ascend higher, but must be dragged overland at these rapids.

As far as I examined the Belize river, I received a very favourable impression of it, and the country higher up, I was told, is still in a state of general improvement. Nothing but the political history of the British settlement can explain the manner in which the natural advantages of this fine region have been neglected.

A few days later we made an excursion to the *Manati Lagoon*, the inlet to which is situated on the coast about twenty miles south from Belize. Mr. Dieseldorff, a German merchant established here, obliged us by offering his fine little sloop, drawing 3½ feet of water, which would just allow entrance into the lagoon. She was manned with two herculean negroes—experienced sailors as well as woodsmen — such as may be found in the mahogany works of this region. Provisions were laid in for a few days, and on the morning of the 10th we passed over the bar of the Belize river and took our course along the coast to the southward. We kept close enough to the land to see the huts of the village of Sherboon, at the mouth of the river of that name. Inside the bar I was told a second village exists, composed of the habitations of mahogany-cutters, to whom the banks of this river afford an active occupation. The cuttings of the house of Young, Toledo, and Co. are as high up in the interior as the head waters of its southern branch. By-and-bye, as we proceeded, the hills and mountains of the southern part of the British territory rose higher, until, as we came close to the shore, they were again concealed by the trees of the forest which extends along the beach. After a navigation of four or five hours, we anchored before the inlet to what appeared to be a narrow river, lined with mangroves, but which was, in fact, the connecting channel between the sea and the lagoon, through which the salt water runs in and out with the tides. The tide being low at the time, the water over the bar was too shallow to allow us to pass; but, after having spent some hours very pleasantly on the beach, we at last drifted in with the influx of high tide.

The channel is several miles long, narrow and winding. From time to time the high mangroves on either side intercepted the faint breeze of the evening; then our two boatmen took to the oars, and their powerful arms kept the sloop in motion. Our progress, however, was necessarily very slow, and the sun had set when we arrived at the end of the channel, where a scene of striking effect was suddenly unrolled before our view. Through an opening between the two walls of mangroves a double stream of light, in the brightest hues of gold and vermilion, burst upon our eyes. Emanating from the western horizon, above a chain of steep and densely-wooded hills, its rays were reflected from the surface of a wide and forest-bound basin of water which lay expanded at their foot. A mysterious region of darkness between two oceans of light, these hills, wrapt already in the shades of night, stood like a barrier between an upper and a lower sky.

Here we entered the Manati Lagoon. Its water, in the neighbourhood of the outlet, is very shallow. Our sloop touched the ground several times, when our two sailors would jump into the water to get her afloat again. We anchored near a long and narrow strip of land, running out for many miles into the lagoon, from its southern extremity to the northward. Here, between groups of cocoa-nut trees, and unknown to the rest of the world, are the habitations of a small population of negroes and mulattoes, who, according to the languages they speak, must have gathered together from different quarters of the globe—some speaking French, some Spanish, some English in preference, and others a language composed, no doubt, of an idiom of African origin, mixed up with elements of the various European dialects used in the West Indies. Of this settlement of black squatters scarcely anything was known at Belize, where even the best-informed told us that we should be obliged to bivouac in the wilderness, wherever we might land around the lagoon—a statement to which our boatmen would only respond with a smile, or a mysterious "let us take care of that and you will see." Indeed here they had their own houses, though they had left them uninhabited for a considerable time while they were working in some of the mahogany cuttings of the interior, or in the port of Belize. All the neighbours around were their friends or relations, with whom they passed the night, leaving us on board our sloop as we refused their invitation to go on shore with them that evening. Next morning they returned and landed us close to some cane-huts, surrounded by palm-trees on a strip of land not more than one hundred yards broad. Black and brown women and children gathered around us. Of the male portion of the little settlement, only a few appeared to be present. No trace of cultivated land was to be seen, and indeed the soil, though overgrown with trees, shrubs, grass and herbs, seemed to be very poor—a mere accumulation of sand. Fresh water is nowhere to be found on this long and narrow dike: it is brought in canoes from some places on the opposite shores. But the refreshing liquid of the cocoa-nut is so plentifully at hand and so generally in use as to make water almost superfluous for drinking purposes.

Though well recommended by our boatmen, as I supposed we were, the population of this secluded place appeared to be ill disposed towards us, or at least not to like our visit. But this, if it really was so, must be confessed to be very natural. Who can doubt that, wherever on American soil an independent black population exists, sufficient causes for disliking white people must be retained in their memory? and who can dispute that they will be disturbed in their peace and in the enjoyment of their freedom as soon as white men begin to settle around them? At present their life is that of almost absolute independence and of undisturbed tranquillity—not of idleness, but neither of toil. The lagoon contains an inexhaustible quantity and great variety of the most excellent fish, and its shores are swarming with game—principally the small species of wild hog called the *pecari*. But to provide for more than mere existence, the men, leaving their families under the safeguard of the natural seclusion of this hidden spot, migrate for some portion of the year, returning with the earnings of a highly creditable activity in the mahogany cuttings.

An exception to the cold manner in which we were received by the rest of this community occurred in the instance of a young mulatto woman of very prepossessing and even interesting appearance, who, politely approaching Mrs. F., invited us to her habitation, where she fulfilled the duties of hospitality with a remarkable degree of delicacy and good manners, doing the honours of the place in a style which made us call her the Queen of Manati, or the Black Preciosa of British Honduras. There was nothing of the awkward and ungraceful movements about her that generally distinguish the negro race. Quite the contrary; whatever she did was expressive of a natural good taste, not often to be found in civilized society. Her very appearance was striking. She was dressed in a tunic of white muslin; a blue handkerchief was tied round her head in the turban-like fashion of the West Indies; and a string of white beads fell around her bronze-coloured neck. Her features, though not denying her near connexion with the negro race, were very fine, and left a most favourable impression. Life and intellect flashed from her eyes, while her teeth were as white and well set as those of the most perfect coloured beauty can possibly be imagined. No wonder that one of our young travelling companions, born on the cold banks of the Elbe, fell in love with this attractive daughter of a fiery clime, who, however, received his addresses with a sublime mixture of dignity and good-humoured satire.

While speaking favourably of the free negroes of this territory, I cannot omit mentioning the excellent qualities of our two boatmen. If our Preciosa was a happy representation of the natural graces that can be expected in a black woman, Mr. Barnard, one of the two negroes, was a type of manliness in the best sense of the word. Uncommonly tall, and of herculean frame, but perfectly well proportioned; used to all the hardships of a sailor and woodsman, and still easy in his movements: he was as good-natured as he was naturally intelligent, and as polite as he was dignified in his entire deportment. He tried to comply with our wishes as soon as he knew them, and to the comforts of my family he paid an attention which left almost nothing to me to take care of. When, with a few strokes of his machete, he opened a cocoa-nut which he held between his fingers, or when he split it in two while it rested freely upon the palm of his left hand, and then offered it to one of our company, a more easy, and at the same time striking, display of physical power and natural politeness could not possibly be conceived.

The reader will allow me to assure him that these portrait sketches of a black woman and a black man are conscientiously taken from nature. I must add, however, that in general free negroes born in the tropical regions of America are a race more favourably developed than negroes, free or slaves, under the less genial climate and institutions of the United States.

By several islands, peninsulas, and tongues of land, the lagoon of Manati is divided into several branches and subordinate basins; and by a narrow channel, such as that by which we had entered, it is connected with another, and still larger, lagoon, situated to the northward. The shores of this latter are entirely uninhabited. From the west, a stream, called the Manati River, enters into the first lagoon. By several falls or rapids, it descends from the mountainous regions situated in that direction. Some ten or fifteen miles before reaching the lagoon, it passes through the interior of a mountain in a natural tunnel, navigable for small canoes; the Manati River thus repeating a remarkable feature characteristic of the physical geography of Yucatan and Honduras.[1] This tunnel is known by the name of the *Great Manati Cave*, and it had been our intention to visit the locality; but to proceed up the river was declared a very toilsome and difficult task at this time of the year, when we should be obliged to drag our canoe over the sand more than a dozen times. There is, however, another cave, called the *Cave of Ben Lomond*, in this neighbourhood. It is situated in a rocky hill, at the north-western corner of the lagoon. A Scotch gentleman at Belize, the owner of that tract of

---

[1] Lake *Yojoa*, in the State of Honduras, has, according to the statements of Mr. Emory Edwards, published by Mr. Squier, a considerable number of subterraneous outlets.

land, where he once intended to establish a sugar plantation, christened it with that name. The same gentleman established another sugar plantation on the south-western side of the lagoon, and called it *Cumberland Hall;* but here, as well as at Ben Lomond, the project, when half realized, was given up, and a vast amount of money sacrificed. I visited the latter place also, and saw a very fine dwelling-house overgrown by the rank vegetation of several years; and costly machinery cast away in an absolute wilderness.

As we were once about seeing caves, we resolved to see that of Ben Lomond, and for that locality we accordingly steered.

After a navigation of some hours we anchored in the shallow water of a bay, before a fine park-like savana, with pine-trees and palmettos, extending about a mile inland to the foot of a ridge of steep and thickly-wooded hills. One of them contained the cave we proposed to visit; by an accident I was prevented from seeing its interior, and therefore can give no description of it. Some gentlemen belonging to our party were more fortunate, and, according to their relation, the cave contains all the wonders of subterranean scenery, such as stalactitic formations of fantastic shapes, large halls and narrow passages, shafts and tunnels leading up and down. For myself, while standing before the entrance, I discovered that the two boatmen, whom I believed to have continued on the beach, had followed us; my family, who had remained there while I went to reconnoitre the approach to the cave, thus being left entirely alone and unprotected in an absolute wilderness. Without losing a moment, I hastened to join them. In the mean time heavy clouds had collected and a thunderstorm was approaching. We had not time enough to take refuge on board our sloop before it burst over us in all its violence. The quantity of water pouring down was frightful. Drenched to the skin in a minute, we reached the sloop with some difficulty, where we tried to make the best of our situation, while our friends were in danger of being cut off from us. After the rain had continued for about an hour it began to overflow the plain at the foot of the hill, and in returning to the beach they had to wade up to their waists through the water.

The scenery at the entrance of the cave is wild and romantic to the utmost. From the darkest shades of a tropical thicket, with a dense undergrowth of young palms, a perpendicular wall of silver-gray rock rises to the height of one hundred feet or more. Thick ropes of gigantic vines stretch over its surface from top to bottom, some of them straight, others wound in a spiral line. At the foot of this wall is the entrance to a large vault with stalactites hanging from its roof and the background lost in darkness.

The soil of the savana was naturally swampy, and after this inundation several days would have been necessary to render it again passable. Without waiting, therefore, until another visit to the cave should become practicable, we returned to Belize.

The country around Manati Lagoon is of a very attractive character. The soil is not rich, but this, in a tropical region with more than sufficient rain, is a recommendation rather than a drawback. With respect to the salubrity of the climate, I could obtain no information; our own experience, however, short as it was, speaks in favour of it. The steep hills of this region are composed of a metamorphic limestone, which, where I had an opportunity of a closer inspection, took the form of a crystalline, variegated marble, which seemed to have excellent qualities for architectural purposes. As to the geology of the territory in general, there seems to be some analogy with that of Western Texas. According to the descriptions which were given to me during my conversations with a gentleman who had visited the interior, the higher mountains at the sources of the Belize River and Sherboon are composed of a centre of plutonic rocks, flanked by strata of black slates, and layers of sandstone with gypsum are resting upon the latter. These strata, which form the pine ridges of the territory, may belong to the new red sandstone, while the limestone ridges, with the caves and tunnels, may be of the jurassic formation.

CASTLE OF OMOA.

Book I., Chap. 11.

CHAPTER XI.

Visit to Honduras, continued — Omoa — Pleasant Navigation of the Gulf of Honduras — Carib Villages of the British Territory — The Zapodilla Keys — Cerro de Guyamel — Omoa — The Malinche, or Guacamayo — Wild Scenery in the Neighbourhood — Climatic Influences of Northerly Winds — Oak Trees by the side of Cocoa Palms — Northern Birds of Passage — Excursion to the Northern Terminus of the Honduras inter-Oceanic Railway — Carib Village of Tulian — Severity of Caribean Criminal Justice — Port Cortez and Alvarado Lagoon — Prospects of this Locality — The Honduras inter-Oceanic Railway.

ON the 28th of March we left Belize for *Omoa*, one of the two seaports which, at the present time, the State of Honduras possesses on its Atlantic side. Four or five small schooners keep up the communication between that place and Belize; their crews, as well as their masters, are either negroes or Caribs, from whom nothing beyond the merest elements of the art of navigation can be expected. Nevertheless, these vessels find their way. The passage, however, it must be confessed, needs no great skill; the greater part of the distance, which is generally made in one day and a half or two days, leads through a portion of the Bay of Honduras, well protected against the heavy swells of the ocean by an almost continuous line of reefs and keys. It is a quiet sea, on which even the nut-shell canoe of the negro woman or Carib boy may pass safely along. In one of these coasting-vessels we took our passage.

The little trip is a very pleasant one: the climate is delightful, the water smooth, the aspect of the coast on one side and of the keys on the other highly interesting. As we proceeded, the mountains in the southern portion of the British territory rose conspicuously in sight: first, the hills in the vicinity of Manati Lagoon; then, farther on, the serrated outlines of the Coxcomb Mountains, which, in boldness of form, bear some similarity to the summit of Mount Pilatus in Switzerland. Two Carib villages, called North and South Stanncreek, are situated on this section of the coast. Towards the east we had a continued line of low coral islands, with mangroves and cocoa-nut trees; here and there the sail of some Carib fishing-boat appeared between them. It is by this industrious race that the market of Belize is chiefly provided with fish. The islands are without water, but, if they were to be inhabited, it would be easy to provide for the want by cisterns, as is done at Belize, where no other drinking-water exists except that collected from the rains. The islands, moreover, produce such a number of cocoa-nuts that fresh water could almost be dispensed with. The end of the chain in the direction towards Omoa is formed by the *Zapodilla Keys*, where the course of vessels crosses over to the opposite side of the Gulf. They are a group of delightful little islands, whither the inhabitants of Omoa resort on pleasure-trips to inhale the pure sea-breeze and enjoy a few days of sport. The surrounding sea abounds in many kinds of fish.

On the morning of the 30th, at daybreak, the coast of the State of Honduras extended before our view. A chain of very high mountains, called the *Cerro de Guyamel*, rises to the west of Omoa, and contributes to the scenery a grand and very interesting character. By one of the calms which are of daily occurrence here, we were kept immoveable in sight of Omoa for several hours. The daily sea-breeze at last drove us in, and at eleven o'clock we cast anchor in front of the old castle, which stands as a monument of Spanish greatness as well as of its decay, and as a *memento mori* to the race on which the inheritance of the latter alone seems to have devolved. A large shed under the wall is the custom-house of the port. In its shade a dozen of idlers of both sexes, stretched on the ground, or swinging in their hammocks to the sleepy notes of an accordion, were recovering from the toils of their vocation. During a conversation with the director of the customs—or "*Ministro de la Aduana*," as his title runs—I was indiscreet enough to ask how many soldiers were in the castle; when that high dignitary fixed a piercing eye upon me, and "Sir!"—he answered with a strong accent —"the whole coast is sufficiently guarded by the military force of this republic!" My innocent curiosity had excited his suspicion, and he tried to discourage me in case I should be connected with some filibustering scheme to take possession of the fortress by a *coup de main*. The garrison, I learned the next day, consisted of twenty men, but, if it was not strong in numbers, it was at least potent in drumming. After we had been some weeks at Omoa, and suspicions had subsided, I not only received permission to see the interior of the castle, but the *comandante* himself came to accompany us with all the politeness of a Hispano-American cavallero.

But to return to the moment of our arrival—we were waiting for the boat to bring us on shore, when a man with the fair complexion of a northerner, in company with a black beauty, came on board, and while Miss Lucinda embraced our captain, Mr. F. addressed us with the cordial and good-natured air of a German mechanic. "You are Germans, I hear," he said. "Have you come to see Honduras? Omoa is a fine place, I assure you, and a very gay one too. We have a ball every Saturday, where a considerable quantity of champagne is consumed. I, of course, have never to pay for it: there are some very liberal gentlemen here, who are in the habit of treating the rest. Every Sunday we have our recreations likewise. This is the day for our democratic assemblies, and Monday and Tuesday are the days for the nigger balls. No want of fine girls here!" And in this strain our countryman continued, freely communicating his store of knowledge respecting the ladies of Omoa, by which he expected to excite our warm interest. He told us he was a jeweller by profession, who made himself useful at this place by repairing the gold chains of the girls, a job which he confessed he never did well enough to let the chains last for more than a single evening. Never did I meet a man more contented with his position, and certainly, if the "*travail attrayant*" of the Fourierists is more than a Utopian dream, the happy jeweller of Omoa enjoyed, and I hope still enjoys, its reality.

The situation of Omoa, though endowed with all the charms of tropical scenery, with the most luxuriant vegetation, is neither healthy nor favourable to commercial interests; and as soon as a communication is opened from Puerto Cortéz into the interior it will lose what little importance it has now as a port of entry. With the merchants the rest of the population will remove to the latter place, where all the conditions unite for a town of greater extent. In expectation of such a change, some of the inhabitants, even at the time of our visit, had discontinued to keep their houses in repair.

The town is situated a quarter of a mile from the beach, a savana extending across the intervening space. To the eastward of the latter is an eminence, from which a view over the gulf and the coast to the westward, with its high mountains, is to be obtained. The splendid *Poinciana pulcherrima*, in a yellow and scarlet variety, forms a thicket of shrubbery on this elevation. This beautiful plant, called *Malinche* in Nicaragua, bears the name of *Guacamayo* in Honduras. Both names have a historical, and, it may be said, a poetical interest; the former being the name of the Indian mistress of Hernando Cortéz, while the latter is originally that given to the large red parrot, called Ara and Lapa in other parts of South and Central America—a bird which, with the Maya Indians of Yucatan, seems to have been sacred, and dedicated to the sun.[1] On the highest point of the eminence a flagstaff is raised, and a guard kept to signalize vessels coming in sight. In former times this guard was stationed on the summit of one of the higher hills in the rear, but the men were so often devoured by the jaguars that the post had to be abandoned. These ferocious beasts are by no means rare in the vicinity of Omoa even now; and one of them, not many years ago, ventured into the very streets of the town.

Immediately behind the place steep hills, covered with primitive forest, begin, and form a wilderness almost impenetrable. A little river flows down from between the mountains. One day, in company with a friend, I tried to follow its course for five or six miles. For half the distance we suffered no other inconvenience than that of being compelled to pass several times through the water from one side to the other. Higher up, however, the density of vegetation on the banks would not allow us to proceed

[1] At Itzamal there "was a temple dedicated to Kinich Kakmó, an idol fashioned like the sun, with the beak of a bird: he was surrounded by rays of fire, and descended to burn the offered sacrifice at mid-day, as the *vacamuya*—a bright-feathered parrot—descends in its flight." Fancourt, History of Yucatan, pp. 124, 125.

otherwise than by the bed of the river itself. The latter is a transparent stream rushing down in cascades, over rocks of *gneiss*, *mica-slate*, and *amphibolic schists*, overshadowed by gigantic trees. Its embankments are covered with a variety of ferns, and with a mossy carpet of creeping *lycopodiaceæ*. With our guns to carry, and with the wish to keep them dry, it was no easy matter to pass along in the midst of the river, now wading through a widened portion of it, then leaping from one slippery rock to the other, where the water foamed around, rushing through the narrow passages between blocks and boulders. We at last found it too difficult to proceed farther. We then left the river and tried to ascend one of the hills on its side, which we succeeded in doing. But with scarcely any possibility of looking beyond the next trees, whilst the forest extended over steep ridges and through narrow gorges in almost every direction, we had to retrace our steps, and reached home completely exhausted with fatigue.

What struck me on my little excursions in the vicinity of Omoa, was the small number of tropical birds, while different kinds of aquatic birds of a more northern climate were numerous. Mr. Julius Levy, at Belize, a young gentleman who takes a very lively and intelligent interest in the natural history of these regions, told me that during the winter the greater number of birds to be seen on the coast of British Honduras belong to the fauna of the United States, while the characteristic birds of the tropical region, such as parrots, toucans and others, have disappeared. This also seems to be the case on the coast of the State of Honduras; but I did not make a similar observation in Nicaragua. The influence of the northers of the Mexican gulf does not seem to reach as far as the latter country; while they sweep over Yucatan and are very sensibly felt at Omoa, communicating to the regions within the limits of their farthest extent certain features of an *extra-tropical* character of nature. Thus, in reference to the flora of British Honduras, I have seen *oak trees* growing by the side of *cocoa-nut trees* on the shore of Manati-Lagoon.[1] At Omoa, while tropical birds have only to pass over the coast range of mountains to be out of reach of the cold winds, every gale from the north throws numbers of snipes, ducks, teals, &c., on this coast.

During our stay at Omoa I visited the northern terminus of the projected Honduras Inter-oceanic Railway. The locality, inhabited at that time by a few Caribs, and by a lonely family of settlers of whom I shall say more, had been hitherto known by the name of *Puerto Caballos;* which, with the authorization of the government of Honduras, has now been changed by the projectors of the railway into that of *Port Cortéz;* while a beautiful lagoon, separated from the sea by a strip of land of a few hundred yards in width, formerly called the *Laguna de Puerto Caballos*, has been christened *Alvarado Lagoon*, thus associating in a very appropriate manner the memory of the two great "conquistadores." I made the excursion in company with the American Consul and several other friends. The distance is such as to allow going and returning the same day, either by land on horseback, or by water. We chose the latter, leaving Omoa early in the morning in a canoe with two Carib boatmen, and taking our course along the coast in an east-northeasterly direction.

The aspect of the land remains essentially the same towards that quarter. Everywhere the forest reaches down to the sea-shore, either with a narrow sand-beach before it, or with the coast breaking off in the shape of a perpendi-

---

[1] At the locality called "Cumberland Hall" by Mr. MacDonald.

cular wall of some red material, either clay or sandstone, which I could not approach near enough to distinguish. Steep ridges of wooded hills follow the coast, sending down some small streams, like that of Omoa: the *Tulian, Cieneguita* and *Marques*. The mouth of the latter is connected with the Laguna de Alvarado. Where these little rivers reach the sea, and at the connecting channel between the latter one and the laguna, small communities of Caribs have built their villages. We landed at *Tulian*, where we took our breakfast in the habitation of the chief, or "*general*," as he is styled. Before his door some heavy chains attracted my attention, and, on inquiry, I was informed that these chains—together with an apparatus consisting of two blocks of wood prepared to fit to each other so as to leave certain circular openings between them—were intended for securing malefactors. The criminal law of the Caribs seems to be exceedingly harsh, and in other respects also this remarkable and highly respectable race is distinguished by an uncommon discipline and severity of manners. In their engagements as mahogany cutters, or for any other work to be executed, they are always to be depended on; the responsibility for each member of a company of labourers resting with their own captain with whom the contract is made. But, on the other hand, they expect the strictest fulfilment of obligations on the side of their employers, and when the term for which they have been engaged—and which in the mahogany cuttings is generally eight months—is over, they stop working, and it is almost impossible to induce them to continue even for a single day. A gentleman, who has had much experience with this race, assured me that they were in the habit of punishing the intercourse of their women with men of other races in the most cruel manner, by whipping the unfortunate female slowly to death. Whatever may be thought of such a cruelty, the fact is a striking exhibition of the national energy of a tribe which—when transplanted at the latter end of the passed century to Honduras from the island of St. Vincent—consisted of little more than five thousand persons, and is now settled along the whole extent of coast from Cape Gracias à Dios to Belize, being able to furnish between four and five thousand prime hands to the mahogany works. While the men are absent in this and other occupations, the women cultivate the fields. Mandioca is the principal product of their agricultural industry, and the Casade, or bread made of mandioca flour, is known by the name of Carib bread at Omoa and Belize, where they bring it for sale. Omoa is dependent upon them for this, as well as for many other articles of food. Almost every morning their canoes arrive loaded with all kinds of fish and molluscs, iguanas, mandiocca, yams, plantains, and cocoa-nuts; while the Hispano-American inhabitants of the town are far too lazy to provide for their own wants.

At Tulian the habitations of this people, situated in a grove of cocoa-nut trees, were built of a wooden framework, which is filled up with clay, the whole thatched with palm leaves. Their fields were situated at a little distance, and I had no time to visit them. They had formerly been more extensive; but the cows of Omoa, roaming about for many miles, as is the custom in that country, had found these plantations, and by their devastations had caused a part of the inhabitants of the village to remove to the Laguna de Alvarado, to which place I was told the rest were preparing to follow them. As soon as a town shall spring into existence at the northern terminus of the Honduras Inter-oceanic Railway the presence of this Carib settlement must become eminently useful.

Port Cortéz and Alvarado Lagoon, taken together, constitute a most admirable situation for a maritime city. Nature has prepared here all the essential conditions for the existence even of a large commercial city, destined to become the centre of business for the whole eastern side of Central America; and there is little doubt that, as soon as the railway is constructed, a considerable population will assemble at once at this spot. There is an almost unlimited space along the sea-shore as well as round the lagoon. The plain, which spreads towards the interior, is capable of an extensive and most productive cultivation. The climate is delightful, the heat being greatly tempered by the sea-breeze. The rise and fall of tide is scarcely perceptible on this coast, a fact which is calculated to contribute in an essential manner to the healthiness of the situation. There is no want of fresh water for the use of a large city, a fact which constitutes another essential condition of salubrity. Good building materials of every kind are to be found in any quantity in the immediate neighbourhood. But all these advantages, however important, are secondary to the excellence of the harbour, which is the only first-class seaport on the Atlantic coast of Central America. According to authorities perfectly competent in the matter, it offers all the necessary protection and accommodation. It is shut in on all sides except the west, but even in that direction the sea is broken by a reef which acts as a natural breakwater, without embarassing the entrance. But the general formation and run of the coasts surrounding the Gulf of Honduras seem to keep off the high winds from that quarter. Near its northern shore it has a depth of from four to eight fathoms, even within a hundred yards of the land.

On the strip of sand which separates the lagoon from the port, and which at the narrowest place scarcely reaches one hundred paces in width, with an elevation of about two feet above the water, we found a European, named Fischer, settled with his family. Here he had built his house, surrounded by cocoa-nut trees planted by himself, and which already bore a rich harvest of fruit. With the exception of his own efforts towards the cultivation of the place, he lived in an absolute wilderness, with no human beings but a few Caribs in the neighbourhood. His life, however, had not even the comforts of a Carib family. For his own and his family's sustenance he was dependent on the game of the forest, the fish of the lagoon, and the cocoa-nuts of his plantation. When I asked him how he could have resolved to live here, and with a family, he answered that he felt proud to be the first settler at a place where he was sure a large and wealthy city was destined to originate, supplanting with its palaces the trees of the wilderness; and that, if he was to die before the accomplishment of this expectation, he would do so with the satisfaction of knowing that civilization would be triumphant over his grave! I have heard with much pleasure that Mr. Fischer had lived to see the engineers of the Honduras Inter-oceanic Railway survey the locality where he had built his house; and I trust the company, who are acting the part of destiny there, will recompense the strong faith of this enthusiastic believer by something more consolatory than simply letting him enjoy the spectacle of his cocoa-nut trees falling by the axe of civilization.

As to these trees, I must state that on one of them I counted more than four hundred cocoa-nuts, and that nowhere have I found the liquid of the nuts of a more exquisite taste.

As Mr. Fischer had a canoe on the lagoon, we crossed it in several directions. It has a length of two miles and a half, and a width of about one mile and a half, with an oval form. Its water is salted, with an almost uniform depth of from eighteen to twenty-four feet, and the whole could be easily converted into a perfectly protected natural dock for vessels drawing from sixteen to twenty feet of water. On its northern shore twenty-four feet have been found, within thirty yards of the beach. While crossing this little basin, our attention was drawn to the incredible number of *medusæ* in the water. They were so numerous that it was difficult to wet the hand without risking the burning effect of their contact, to which they owe the name of sea-nettles. At the same time other portions of the lagoon were absolutely alive with large shoals of fish.

The scenery of the neighbouring country is very attractive, particularly by the contrast of the sea-shore with the high mountains that rise on the coast in the direction towards Omoa. During our visit we were greatly annoyed by mosquitoes and sand-flies, which I have scarcely ever seen more troublesome than on the beach of Port Cortéz. This annoyance, however, will disappear as soon as the locality becomes cleared of trees and shrubs.

Amongst the different projects for a highway across the Isthmus of Central America, that of a railroad through the State of Honduras, from Port Cortéz to the Bay of Fonseca, is the most promising. The advantages of the excellent harbour on the Atlantic side have just been mentioned. Those offered by the Bay of Fonseca, on the Pacific side, are still greater and of an extraordinary character, as it may justly be doubted if there be another point on the entire Pacific coast of America that has the natural inducements which are here afforded for a great commercial establishment. A line of railway between these two first-class seaports has been surveyed and found to contain no extraordinary difficulty of any kind. This survey has not only been executed by the engineers of the company which is in possession of the grant from the government of Honduras, but Colonel E. Stanton, of the Royal Engineers, who was sent out by the British ministry to verify the labours and statements of the company's surveying corps, has corroborated these results and declared the enterprise practicable throughout and in every respect. The length of the railway, according to these surveys, will be about 200 miles from sea to sea, and the time occupied between New York and San Francisco, by this route, will not exceed fourteen days, while the passage between these two places, *viâ* Panamá, has averaged upwards of twenty-four days; and, in one way or the other, all the various routes, existing or projected, for the purpose of connecting the eastern and the western world across the Central American Isthmus, must remain far behind the advantages offered by the Honduras Inter-oceanic Railway. The Ship Canal through Nicaragua, it is true, *if it were feasible*, would be a work of a higher order altogether than any railway through Central America, whatever line the latter might follow. But, though we are now told that the time for the realization of that great project has ultimately come, we must be allowed to remain in doubt with regard to the question whether any of the existing generation will live to see ocean vessels pass through Nicaragua. It may be that the possibility, in an abstract sense, is only an affair of time and money; but if it really be so, I venture to say that all the time and money left at the disposal of the present generation from other schemes of a more urgent character will prove insufficient. The feasibility of a ship canal between Lake Nicaragua and the Pacific, though even this may be surrounded by difficulties arising from the necessity of feeding the canal from the lake, is but a subordinate consideration in the matter. An incomparably greater amount of labour and cost will be caused by the necessity of a thorough canalization of the San Juan river, and of extensive constructions for the purpose of establishing an efficient harbour on the Atlantic as well as on the Pacific terminus of the line. But even if all these difficulties were at once overcome, the existence of the canal, no doubt, would affect the commerce of the world in an extraordinary manner, but it would by no means diminish the utility of a railway between Port Cortéz and the Bay of Fonseca: quite on the contrary, it would enhance it. Then a degree of civilization and prosperity, of which we can now only form a faint idea, would be developed all around the shores of the Pacific, and every means of quick travelling and of quick transport of the more important articles of traffic would correspondingly rise in value—a consideration under which the canal through Nicaragua could never pretend to compete with the Honduras railway. All this must be obvious to whoever takes the trouble of thoroughly considering the question. As to the difficulties of the Nicaragua canal enterprise, we ought to entertain too high an opinion of the intelligence and technical experience of those French gentlemen who have recently undertaken to perform the work, than to suppose that they do not see and completely understand the nature and difficulties of the enterprise. This, however, is not the matter in argument. The real purpose contemplated in *beginning* the canal may have nothing to do with the question whether it is *intended* to be *finished.*

Amongst the other routes and projects, that of a railroad across the Isthmus of Tehuantepec is the only one which seems to compete with that through Honduras; but its advantages are entirely neutralized by the absence of harbour accommodation on both sides. This route, moreover, may suit the interests of New Orleans; but it neither corresponds to those of New York nor of England.

The steaming distances from Liverpool to San Francisco, touching at Jamaica, are: by way of Panamá 7980 miles; Nicaragua 7720 miles; Tehuantepec 7740 miles; Honduras 7320 miles. The distance between New York and San Francisco, by Panamá, is 5224 miles; by Nicaragua 4700 miles; by Tehuantepec 4200 miles; by Honduras 4121 miles—a saving by way of Honduras, as compared with Panamá, of 1103 miles. All the advantages of the Honduras route, taken together, will produce a saving in time, as compared with that by Panamá, of from eight to ten days between the Atlantic ports of the United States, as well as between Europe and California, Oregon, Vancouver, China, Japan, and the whole North Pacific.

The general state of commercial and political affairs alone has delayed the realization of an enterprise of such a character, and at the head of which are men of the highest standing in the financial world, who are resolved to launch it at the right time, and are sparing no effort to secure its success.

CHAPTER XII.

General Remarks on Central America — Geographical Position and Political Importance — Natural Advantages and future Prospects — How the Interests of England and those of the United States, in reference to the Central American Question, could be harmonized — European Immigration — Prejudices against the Climate refuted — Native Labourers fully available, and how to be treated.

By its geographical position in connection with the recent development and future prospects of commerce and civilization in the countries of the Pacific Ocean, Central America claims an unusual degree of attention. California and Oregon, British Columbia, Australia, Japan and China: each of these names carries heavy weight in the scale of the political importance of Central America. No full justice, however, would be done to that interesting region, if it was to be considered only according to the importance attached to its different transit routes. If the isthmus which connects Africa and Asia, separating the Arabian Gulf from the Mediterranean, offers nothing to the civilization of the present age but the fact that it separates what should be connected and connects what might just as well be separated, the case of Central America is quite different. Here is an extensive country endowed with all the charms and wealth of nature, uniting the advantages of an archipelago with those of being the most favoured portion of a continent; a country open to the commerce of the world in every direction; a country with a diversity of soil and climate and a variety of sites suitable to every constitution, taste, and occupation—and all this within the reach of the two great Oceans of the world; a country rich in many of the most precious and valuable productions of the mineral kingdom, nourishing millions of the most useful domestic animals, and capable of producing the most valuable commodities of the vegetable kingdom of every zone—from the potato, barley, and oats of Ireland and Scotland, up to the sugar, coffee, and chocolate; the cotton and indigo, the banana; the cocoanut and spices of the Eastern Archipelago; a country inhabited by a people unable to govern themselves, it is true, either in politics or in industrial pursuits, but a people of excellent and very useful qualities, if well directed by superior intellect, and eminently fitted, by the gradations of caste arising from the mixture of three great races, to correspond to the wants of a topographical character so diversified. And this country is thrown by providence in the midst of the main stream in which the expanding civilization of our age has begun to move. All these combined advantages are without a parallel, and I have no hesitation in avowing that, according to my conviction, Central America, everything taken into consideration, is the most favoured spot on the surface of the globe; and is destined to act an important and glorious part in the history of the future.

The North Americans, who in such matters are gifted with the instinct of the pioneer—an instinct by which they discover the most eligible site for a new town, in what direction it will extend, and in what street the building lots will be most valuable:—the North Americans have understood the splendid character of Central American prospects; while, if anything is beyond the conception of common sense, it is the system followed by England in this magnificent country. If England, instead of having contributed systematically to the utter ruin of those helpless republics, had followed the opposite course lending assistance to their liberal party—a party which has always been in favour of foreign immigration, religious tolerance, and other means of improvement and progress—a confederation of Central American States would now exist, strong enough by the influx of population, intellect and capital from abroad, to preclude any idea of an annexation to the United States, or of the re-introduction of slavery. All the civil wars down to the invasion of William Walker, would have been avoided, and prosperous communities would now be in a condition to buy ten times the amount of British goods which the bankrupt inhabitants of ruined cities and neglected plantations can ever afford to purchase. Mosquitia and Yucatan might have formed two acceding States of the confederation, and I cannot see why British Honduras should not have contributed to raise the number to eight. England would not have lost; she would have gained in every respect by such a development of Central American politics: a development which has been, and still is, in the hands of the British Government. By following such a course, England would have avoided many disagreeable transactions and useless difficulties with the United States, while the result would have heightened British influence in American affairs in a manner too noble and too legitimate not to be approved in the United States by all the adversaries of slavery, of filibusterism, of imprudent territorial extension, and of political iniquity. Such a result would have harmonized the true interests of England with those of the United States, with those of Central America itself, and with those of civilization in general.

Even now it is not too late. Whatever complications

in reference to Central America may still exist, or may yet originate, the aim of England should always be the establishment and prosperity of an independent Central American confederacy, strengthened by the immigration of hands, intellect, skill, capital, and enterprise, as they cannot fail to be attracted by improvements such as the Honduras Inter-oceanic Railway; by the facilities thus offered in every sphere of intercourse with the rest of the world; by the opportunity of profitable investments; and by the inviting nature of the country, its beautiful scenery, its fertility and climate.

Immigration, above all other sources, is destined to become the great means of Central American regeneration; and in this respect it is of importance that the prevailing prejudices in reference to tropical climates in general, and especially as to the climate of Central America, should be refuted.

There is no doubt that there are some unhealthy localities on the coasts of Central America; Chagres, Aspinwall, Panama, and Ysabal may be named amongst them. But New Orleans, Mobile, and Charleston, with the whole coast of Texas, are at least equally pernicious to life; and, though slavery exists at all these places, certain occupations are carried on there by white men, and principally by Irish and German immigrants, fully as fatiguing and exposing as the greater part of the labour performed by the negro slave. Thousands of emigrants from the north of Europe arrive annually at New Orleans and on the coast of Texas, and there is not the slightest reason why they could not, with an equal degree of safety, reach the worst places on the coast of Central America. These worst places, however, can be avoided; none of those named above being situated where an emigrant coming to settle in the country would find any inducement to establish himself. Greytown, Bluefields, Truxillo, Port Cortéz, and Belize would be the ports where he should land. All these places are healthy. Emigrants, moreover, would have no occasion to stay on the coast, but might at once proceed into the interior, where they would find a climate altogether superior to any within the confines of the United States.

The prejudices against tropical climates in general, intentionally propagated by the jealousy of the colonial system of former times, have been revived and sustained in more recent periods by a strange concurrence of opposite interests. It has been asserted by the defenders of negro slavery—and those who have learned how to appreciate the lazy life of a wealthy European in a tropical country will declare the statement to be absolutely correct—that white men are unable to work in a hot climate. On the other hand, some of the organs of public opinion in the United States opposed to the extension of slavery and the annexation of territory where slavery could be introduced, not only concur in decrying the climate of tropical latitudes, but even surpass their antagonists in their denunciations. Their intention may be honest, but it is never judicious to support a good cause by false pretences.

The following facts, not generally known in Europe, will contribute to throw light on the question of "white labour" in regions where the climate is generally supposed to exclude its exercise to any available extent.

At New Orleans the market is provided with vegetables mostly cultivated by Germans. They are the owners of the greater number of gardens that surround the city,—at Lafayette, Algiers, the Half-way House, and Carrolton,—

in which these vegetables are grown;—and they neither keep slaves nor do they employ hired negroes. If they are able to engage hired hands, those hands are Germans like themselves.

In Western Texas, where, in certain districts, Germans form the greater number of the population, German farmers, on their own property and in good circumstances, cultivate the cotton by their personal labour. But there, under a sun as hot as it ever is in Honduras, at a short distance from a coast where the yellow fever rages, I have met with gentlemen who had been officers, professors, men of science, lawyers, or of similar positions in Germany,—some of whom had even been wealthy proprietors and used to all the comforts and charms of refined European life,—standing behind the plough; and I have never heard them complain of this or any other agricultural occupation in the hot climate being injurious to health.

In travelling through Georgia and Alabama, I became acquainted with a wealthy planter of Louisiana. Our conversation turned upon the question of slave and free labour, and their relative merits, when that gentleman remarked, "Alabama has great resources in mineral wealth, but the State wants entirely a different population to turn them to profit. I have been a slaveholder all my lifetime; but I have my eyes open." "Do you think, then," I asked him, "that the climate of the Carolinas, of Georgia, Alabama, and Louisiana, would allow negro labour to be generally supplanted by the free labour of white men?" "Certainly, I think so," was his answer. "There are very unhealthy places in those States, but they are fatal to negroes also. I have employed Germans in occupations in which they had to expose themselves to the hottest sun during the whole day, and I found that they endured it just as well as my negroes did. The pretended inability of white men to work in a hot climate is all nonsense."

I have heard similar opinions from other gentlemen, derived from the same experience. It might be objected that in these cases the experience was made in countries where the heat of the summer months is very excessive indeed, but which are not exactly marked by the tropical features. This is true. But the pine and oak regions of Honduras and Guatemala have even less of what is generally called a tropical character, and are by far more healthy in many other respects.

If the white race should be unable to perform exactly the same amount of labour in a hot as in a temperate climate, it must not be forgotten that there is no necessity for their doing so. In those countries where agricultural labour is restricted by the character of the climate, agricultural labour, in the same and perhaps in a much higher ratio, is more productive.

Speaking, however, of European immigration to Central America, the intention cannot be to recommend that region to European agriculturists entirely without capital. But there is scarcely any necessity for making this remark, as mere labouring hands seeking employment will scarcely find the means of getting there. Mere hands are not wanted in Central America, the unemployed portion of the population being numerous and willing enough, sufficiently active, and endowed with many qualities which, if well directed, will make them highly available. What they want is to be freed from military conscription, from revolution, and civil war—to be set to work in a sensible way—to be directed with firmness, without the haughty and overbearing manner of which Englishmen and Anglo-Americans are so often guilty towards their inferiors—and to be treated with kindness and honesty. The last condition is most essential. Native employers rarely pay their labourers in cash, and almost universally deal with them in a fraudulent manner. A European settler in Honduras, or any other part of Central America, who knows how to act with good sense, firmness, conciliation, and strict integrity towards the natives, will never be in want of hands to carry on his work. The population, of course, has become lazy and disorderly by the long unsettled state of public affairs and by the general ruin of agriculture, mines, and commerce. It will be the gratifying lot of the promoters of enterprises such as the Honduras Railway, and of those who may hereafter settle in that region or in any other district of Central America, to redeem so beautiful a country from the baneful effects of a most deplorable period.

Book II.

JOURNEY FROM NEW YORK

BY MISSOURI

TO THE NORTH OF MEXICO;

STAY AT CHIHUAHUA,

AND

RETURN THROUGH TEXAS.

CHAPTER I.

Objects of the Journey — Trade with Chihuahua — From New York to the Frontier of Missouri — Railway Journey and Scenery between New York and Lake Erie — Cincinnati — On the Ohio, the Mississippi, and the Missouri — Western Philosophers — Dangers by Steamers — Weyne City—Independence.

IN the spring of 1852 I made the acquaintance of Mr. Samuel Kaufmann, of the firm of Messrs. Mayer and Co., trading with Chihuahua, who invited me to accompany one of the transports of the Firm from Missouri to Chihuahua. The back wilds of the North American Continent, still traversed by Indians, are even at the present day so unsafe and inhospitable for travelling that it is impossible to cross them except in parties; and a person who has not the means to equip an expedition himself is obliged to join some other caravan. I here met with an opportunity of this kind, with pleasant companions, and readily joined the party. Our caravan, which was to start from Independence, on the Missouri, consisted of eighteen or twenty waggons, each drawn by ten mules, with the requisite number for relays, and the complement of drivers, muleteers, &c. The whole party was under the conduct of a second partner of the Firm, Mr. H. Mayer.

The State of Chihuahua, which is the farthest one in Mexico from any sea-port, has for a long time received the chief part of the merchandize connected with its trade by route through the interior of the United States—the so-called Santa-Fé road. On a first glance at the distances upon the map, this appears scarcely conceivable; but the fact is explained when the attending circumstances are known. The extraordinary facility of the transport by railways, canals, and steamers on the rivers in the United States from New York to the Missouri—the natural facilities of the roads through the prairies west of that river—the cheapness of journeying in this country, where the feed of the draught-cattle costs little or nothing—the bold spirit of enterprize, and the skilful management of the transport in the United States—lastly, the origin of this intercourse from the pedlar-trade on the frontiers and the traffic with the Indians—have for some time given to this route, although about six times the length of the distance of Chihuahua from the nearest Mexican port, a preference to the transport on beasts of burden over the difficult passes of the mountains of Mexico, with the indolence and timidity of the Mexicans. Of late years, however, these commercial relations have undergone a change. The North Americans have begun to prefer the much shorter journey by Texas to the Missouri route, as the rapid advance of the colonization of Western Texas enables the traders to provide themselves here with draught-cattle and provisions for the journey to Northern Mexico; and the Mexican Government under Santa Ana, by raising the import dues, and enforcing them strictly on the United States frontier, while facilitating the importations through the sea-ports of the country, enabled the merchandize brought to Chihuahua from the south by the interior to be sold cheaper than that carried to El Paso across the frontiers, either from the Missouri or Texas. At the time, however, to which my narrative refers, this change had not yet been effected; and the caravan with which I travelled still preferred the longest of all possible routes. The merchandize sent by railway and steamboat to the Missouri, was loaded on waggons at Weyne City (near Independence), and was thus conveyed to New Mexico, and down the Rio Grande to El Paso, where it passed the frontier, and thence to the town of Chihuahua. El Paso was at that time the only place of entry on the Chihuahua frontier. The Presidio del Norte, further south on the Rio Grande, has since been added as a second, and the road through Texas has thus acquired a decided preference.

These commercial expeditions through the interior of the Continent are attended by considerable danger to life as well as property, and great personal courage and perseverance are required to bear the fatigue and privations attending them. It is the more surprising to find German Jews taking a prominent part in this commerce, and exhibiting a fearless courage rarely attributed to the Jewish nation.

In company with Mr. H. Mayer I started from New York on the morning of the 16th of June; the steam-ferry conveyed us over the North River to Jersey City, where we took the train for Dunkerke on Lake Erie. The railway is constructed in the bold and careless manner peculiar to the North Americans. We were swept along on rails laid down upon the edge of steep mountain declivities, or round projecting rocks, through the wooded and mountainous country. The air was close, and the rocking and shaking motion of the carriage, together with the dust and heat, extremely fatiguing. The country, however, offered a refreshing aspect; for some distance the railway runs at a considerable height along a mountain ridge, with views alternating right and left into the wooded valleys. From the Delaware to Lake Erie the country increases in beauty: the railway runs through green valleys, richly watered by rivulets, between beautifully wooded hills. The pine forests prevailing on the Delaware give way to a different class of trees, and only a hemlock-fir or white pine, here and there, stands amidst oaks, maples, locusts, and other trees of foliage. On the meadows and clearings stand new houses, singly or in groups, indicating the first lines of streets in towns still to be built. Everywhere the natural wealth of the country and the active industry of man were to be seen. We travelled over the last portion of this road in the night, and embarked at Dunkerke on Lake Erie for Cleveland.

The night on the lake was tranquil and pleasantly cool. In the morning we coasted the shore, which is flat, covered with wood, but cleared in many places. Here and there stands a single house. Most of the farms of this country are situated somewhat inland, and are not visible from the water. Early in the morning we reached Cleveland.

The site of this town on the high bank of Lake Erie is uncommonly fine; but we were not allowed to stop there. On landing from the steamboat, we immediately entered the railway carriages; in a few minutes we were out of sight of the town, and proceeded without stop through the forests of Ohio.

In this section the traveller has an opportunity of seeing the whole beauty of North American forest scenery. The grouping of the masses, and the varieties of form and colouring, are endless, and often present the most beautiful effects, in which the tall and slender elms, with their thick and yet light foliage, are prominent features.

An accident deprived me of even a passing view of a great part of the State of Ohio. Between La Grange and Wellington, shortly before our arrival, a collision of two trains had happened. The wreck presented a picture of the fearful effects of velocity,—an immense heap of *débris* of smashed carriages. Whether any lives were lost I could not ascertain, and the passengers in our train talked of nothing but the disagreeable delay caused by the accident;—this seemed to be their only care. It was impossible to wait for a clearance of the track; we had therefore to get out and walk to Wellington, at no great distance, and there await a train from Cincinnati, to exchange its passengers with our train, and take us to that place. Meanwhile a great storm came on. The rain poured down in streams, and compelled the passengers, three to four hundred in number, to remain crowded together until eight o'clock in the evening in a small room, —the only one in which we could obtain shelter. The rest of the route was travelled in the night, and during incessant torrents of rain we reached Cincinnati at daybreak.

We were obliged to remain four days in this city. Various matters of business connected with our journey had to be transacted, and Mr. M. intended to be married here. In the United States this ceremony, with all its preparations, can be performed in half an hour, and to devote a whole day to it would be a waste of time. But the lady was to accompany her husband on the long and arduous journey to Chihuahua, and might therefore claim a few days. The stoppage gave me an opportunity to see the city and its environs. The hill at the foot of which Cincinnati is built commands a splendid view over the city, over the valley of the Ohio, and the surrounding hills. It reminds me somewhat of the valley of the Neckar; but the country around Cincinnati is on a much larger scale, and the more luxuriant trees of this region give it a more southern character. The tall elms on the other side of the Ohio give to the town of Covington quite an aristocratic appearance. On this side Cincinnati branches inland, into all the little valleys or defiles between the hills which enclose the chief valley; while at the same time the city rises on the side of them, and—with some detached houses in the finest situations—even reaches the top of the elevation. The hills on this side are more considerable than those on the Kentucky side; and, while the latter are wooded, groups of trees are scattered over the former on a kind of lawn, or around the country-houses, commanding the most beautiful points of view. These hills seem formed for the growth of the vine, and the vineyards here and there complete a certain European aspect, which appears to me to distinguish Cincinnati from other American towns.

In the afternoon of the 23rd we left Cincinnati. The rainy weather obliged us to remain in the cabin of the steamboat, in which we had taken a passage to Louisville. In the evening I went on deck for a moment. The boat, like all the western steamers, was one of those large and elegant, but unsolid edifices, in which the motion of the machine and of the water is felt throughout the whole structure. The planks of the deck bent under my footsteps, and the whole woodwork of the vessel shared the motion and trembling of the river waves. It seemed as if it must have gone to pieces every instant.

Early the next morning we reached Louisville, and on the following day embarked for St. Louis. It was the 25th of June, and it may not be uninteresting to mention that in the morning we breakfasted in the saloon with a fire. The sun's rays were hot, but the air was chilly in the shade.

Our voyage lay the whole day between wooded hills,

horizontal limestone strata cropping out here and there. Alternately right and left lay a beautiful plain on the concave side of the river bends. We occasionally passed some commencement of a village, consisting of a few houses, or a single house, with a small plot of cultivated land. The shores were generally wooded. Oaks and elms, with occasionally pines, appeared to be the predominant trees. The next morning we had before us flat shores, with groves of poplars, succeeded on the left side, below the mouth of the Wabash, by hills, which continued as far as Paduca, toward the mouth of the Tennesee. On the Ohio I observed no other animals than a large dark-grey heron, some carrion vultures, and numerous small white gulls. In the evening, after sunset, we reached Cairo, and ran into the Mississippi.

I was interested by a conversation I overheard between two of my travelling companions, a Kentucky farmer, and a methodist preacher from Indiana. It began with the subject of steamboats, and passed on to that of flying-machines; which led the farmer—a shrewd little old man, with a bald pate and white curls behind his ears—to speak of the flight of angels and spirits. The preacher said he had heard of the invention of a machine which was propelled "by electricity, like the flight of the eagle."

"What is your idea, sir, of the spirits of men after death?" asked the little farmer. "Do you think they will be able to move with extraordinary velocity from one place to another?"

"Unquestionably," answered the preacher.

"Well," continued the farmer, "but as to the angels there's a difficulty I can't get over, and I am curious, sir, to know your opinion on the subject. You will allow that even a spirit cannot be in two places at the same time. Now, when God sends the angels upon earth for the service of man, and gives them a commission, they will have to convey information and receive fresh instructions; and the question is, how quickly they are able to do this: for if they are to help man, and have first to fly away and fetch instructions, this might take too much time, and the help come too late."

The minister sought to remove these scruples by observing that spirits can receive instructions in any place, since they are everywhere "in that spiritual atmosphere which unites them with the Lord." The farmer, however, seemed to take a peculiar pleasure in his casuistry, and to be little satisfied with this reasoning.

The conversation here took a turn, and passed to the rapping spirits and the Misses Fox of Rochester, when a third gentleman joined the party. All three were entirely opposed to the theory. The farmer said he would believe the ladies if they did not take money; but, as it was, he considered the rapping of their spirits a mere money speculation. "And the chief speculation is still to come," added the minister, who had evidently some experience in such matters. "A book will be written, containing a collection of the revelations of spirits; the book will be declared a sacred one, and much money will be obtained by its sale." He appeared to have a prejudice against unorthodox spirits, but at the same time made this scientific observation,—that whenever a sound was made, like the spirit-rapping, it could only be in accordance with natural laws. "The matter," observed the farmer, "is the cause of much unhappiness;" adding, that "in the lunatic asylum of the State of Kentucky there were fifteen ladies who had gone insane from these spiritual tricks. A young lady received a letter pretending to be written by a spirit, in which she was called on to write to her deceased parents: if they had been received among the blessed they would reply immediately. The girl did as she was directed, and, receiving no answer, concluded that her parents were amongst the condemned. This conviction affected her so much that she lost her reason." "I cannot say whether the spirits really exist or not," observed the third gentleman; "but, even if they do, I see no practical utility in it." In this all agreed, and so the conversation dropped.

The next day we passed some beautiful parts of the Valley of the Mississippi. The hills (or bluffs, as they are called) occasionally approached close to the river, and their steep, often rocky, acclivities imparted a peculiar character to this otherwise monotonous landscape of wood and water.

At night we reached St. Louis, where we stopped two days for business connected with the objects of our journey. I had only a few hours free, to pay a visit to some friends resident in this town and to make some new and valuable acquaintances. Of the town and its environs I saw too little to add anything to what is already known of St. Louis.

On the 30th we embarked for Weyne City, a small place, consisting of a few houses, which may be called the harbour of Independence. We left St. Louis at noon, and in the afternoon reached the mouth of the Missouri, whose thick and yellow water contrasts strongly with the clear stream of the Upper Mississippi. This difference is perceptible even far below St. Louis, after the confluence, on the two sides of the united stream—nay, in fact, as far down as the mouth of the Ohio, until the whole Mississippi gradually becomes one and the same clayey stream. On entering the Missouri our steamer had to struggle against a strong current. At the confluence of these two rivers their outer shores are high and form flat hills.

Towards evening, the western shore of the Missouri was formed by a fine wooded highland, at the foot of which extends a long low bank of horizontal limestone strata. Oaks, locust-trees, lime-trees, elms, sycamores, with every description of underwood, shade this rocky bank, and numerous springs gush forth at its base. Here and there stands some miserable log-house, inhabited by Frenchmen of the old Missouri population, whose cultivated land probably lies at the back of the hills, no trace of cultivation being visible near the river.

A thunderstorm obliged us to lay to for the night. As we proceeded next morning, the shores of the river rose on each side, high and wooded; in some clearing was occasionally seen a house, surrounded by a patch of meadow. The bottom-land near the river is overgrown with poplars, sycamores, and willows. The river washes away the shores here and there on each side, carrying the old trees into the water. At these spots, on the opposite side, sandbanks are formed—a new shore—which is soon so thickly covered by a young growth of poplars, plane-trees, and willows, that at a distance it has more the appearance of a luxuriant cornfield than of a young forest. The forests on the banks of the river thus being composed of portions of a different age, give an agreeable variation to the landscape.

Jefferson City, the capital of Missouri, which we passed at noon on July 2nd, is a small place, consisting mostly of scattered houses, built on a high bank cleared of trees and furrowed by ravines. The Capitol, a large stone building, with a semicircular portico and a tower with a cupola in the centre, stands on a green hill, just above the river, surmounting a rocky bank. In the night we passed Boonville, in the morning Glasgow, and later in the day Brunswick. Of all the places I have seen on this river, Miami is the most beautifully situated, on a steep grassy hill, crowned with oaks, and rising somewhat abruptly from the river. Before reaching Lexington, the next day, I saw, upon a sandbank in the river, a long line of wild geese, which kept up a comical race with our steamer. It was indeed laughable to see the efforts the stupid animals made to prevent our passing them, whilst our boat was moving slowly against the strong current. Lexington is situated partly upon a height, partly at its foot, on the bank of the river, every house having immediately in the rear its own coal-pit. The entire hill, on the side of which a coal stratum crops out, is perforated in this manner. On the shore were lying the remains of a steamboat, which had been blown up here a few months before. In the middle of the hill-side stood some elm-trees, upon one of which the body of the captain had been flung. Several hundred persons lost their lives by this accident. Were it the custom here—as it is in Mexico, in places where murders have been committed—to erect memorials at places where these accidents by steam have occurred, such *mementos mori* would never be out of sight, either on the steamboats or in the railway carriages of the United States.

The Missouri here makes a great bend—a rapid and impetuous river, difficult to navigate. Its current, on the side of the convex shore, is impeded by large sandbanks; and on the side of the concave bank it is so choked by sunken trees (snags) that it is difficult to steer a boat between these obstructions. A few miles from the mouth of the Fishing river, below Sibley, formerly Fort Osage, we actually ran upon one of these snags, in which one wheel of our boat was caught. The steamer cracked and fell on her side, the water rushed over the lower deck and extinguished the fire. Boxes, casks, and a quantity of furniture which formed part of the freight, fell from the lower, middle, and upper decks into the water, and floated down the river, together with our firewood. The boat had meanwhile got extricated, but she was now carried down the river sideways, and ran the risk of drifting upon other snags and being broken in two. However, we succeeded in reaching the shore, and lay to. At the moment the boat fell on one side supper had just been served: the tables were upset; plates and dishes, jugs, cups and saucers, and all the good things prepared for us, lay scattered on the floor, and we had to wait until eleven o'clock before a fresh supper could be prepared. The coolness of the Americans—even of the female sex—on such occurrences is exemplary, and compensates in a great measure for their carelessness. The visible danger in which on this occasion we were placed did not at all interrupt the cheerful conversation of the ladies, who were gathered on the stern of the vessel. After six hours' labour the boat was free to continue her voyage by moonlight, but we had still to work our way for four or five miles through a dangerous passage, beset with innumerable snags, before getting into safe navigable water, which we reached at one o'clock in the morning.

The next morning, under a clear sky, such a fresh west wind met us that the steamer, which had great difficulty in making head against the stream, was almost stopped in her course. At noon, however, we reached Weyne City, where we disembarked.

The air had been agreeably cool on the river; on shore

the heat was oppressive, for which this place is noted. In the evening a carriage arrived from Independence, which conveyed us to this first station of our journey. The distance is about four miles inland. The ascent from the river to the higher country is by a steep hill and very bad, but a tolerable road leads from hence to the town. Upon this road I now saw before me a journey of about *fifteen hundred* English miles.

CHAPTER II.

Stay at Independence — Frontier Places of Missouri — Caravans of Traders and Emigrants — Means of Conveyance — Northern and Southern Methodists — Negro Belief — Censorship and Indulgence — A Religious Curiosity — Historical and Political Views — A Political Murder — Preparations for Departure — Beyond the Limits of Civilization.

Independence is a small town, with the character of a frontier place engaged in an extensive carrying trade. At a distance of ten to twelve miles from it, on the road to Santa Fé, were the last farms, on the edge of the great Prairie, and at a few days' journey further the road to Oregon separates from that to New Mexico and Chihuahua. The town is surrounded by wheelwrights' shops, large premises filled with new waggons, painted red, green, or blue, and the whole trade of the place consists in supplying the wants of trading and emigrant caravans, which start from this and from a few other stations on the Missouri for New Mexico, Utah, California, and Oregon. At certain times of the year the intercourse with these distant countries imparts great animation to this small town. During the last spring the number of emigrants to California collected here had been very large, and the place is said to have resembled a fair, although those people generally live encamped outside the town. The season for these trains was now too far advanced, it being no longer possible to pass the Salt Lake before the winter. Some emigrants, however, who intended to winter among the Mormons, had still time for their journey, and the communication with Santa Fé and Mexico is not entirely stopped even in winter, although a journey across the prairies at that season is always dangerous and fatiguing. Formerly Independence had the exclusive benefit of this communication "over the plains," as this far western region is designated; but at the time of my visit Westport, lying twelve miles higher up the Missouri, disputed the monopoly. Still higher up succeed Fort Leavenworth, Weston, St. Joseph, and Council Bluffs—all starting-points for emigrants to California, Utah, and Oregon. Beside these, the Mormons have Kanesville, opposite St. Joseph, whence their caravans usually depart for the New Jerusalem on the Salt Lake. I cannot say what changes may have taken place since. From the extensive region west of Missouri, which, at that time, was still belonging to the Indians, the two territories of Kansas and Nebrasca have since been formed, and many a new town has since risen into existence in the last few years. The whole first part of my journey passed through what is now called Kansas, a region become famous in the history of the struggles between the enemies and advocates of slavery.

Then we here were in one of those towns which, situated on the limits of a desert, may be compared to a harbour; and perhaps, in spite of the new settlements of Kansas, Independence may have maintained this character. The camel has been called the ship of the desert; but until the camels introduced of late into Texas by the Government of the United States shall have increased sufficiently to play a similar part in the New World, the trader's waggon must be called the ship of the prairie: and indeed the waggon drawn by mules stands in the same relation to that drawn by oxen as the steamboat to the sailing-vessel. Formerly oxen were here used in preference as draught-cattle for the journeys across the prairies; but mules have gradually superseded them. Teams of mules are quicker than yokes of oxen, and the mule is also better able to endure heat and want of water. Mules, however, cost three times as much as oxen, and in the Indian territory they are a property far more in danger. Oxen are seldom stolen by the Indians; whereas the stealing of mules is regarded by them as a great and honourable exploit. The large demand for draught-cattle of both kinds for the numerous caravans travelling west, has naturally given a considerable stimulus to cattle-breeding in the State of Missouri. The mules reared here are noted for their beauty, size, and strength, and although inferior to the small Mexican mules in briskness and endurance, they readily find purchasers even in Mexico, where they are sought for chiefly for carriage teams: the trading caravans, therefore, passing between the Missouri frontier and Northern Mexico generally bring back only part of their mules. From California, Oregon, and Utah, draught-cattle very rarely return to the east: a part of them die on the road—a much larger proportion of oxen than mules—which is partly owing to the former having much less power of endurance, and partly to their not being treated with the same care, being a less valuable property. In this manner the caravans across the prairies cause a very considerable traffic in animals, independent of the exportation of cattle to California and Oregon.

I remained at Independence from July 5 to August 17, our caravan being detained for the arrival of merchandize from New York and by the purchase of the necessary mules. During my stay here I witnessed the stupid and brutal treatment to which draught-cattle are sometimes exposed. It is perhaps natural: waggoners are in no country noted for their refinement, and least of all can we expect to find this in a system of transport, in which the labour of the teamster almost equals that of his beasts. The worst instances of such cruelty I imagined I had witnessed in Nicaragua with the ox-carts; but what I saw in this town far exceeded the goading practised with lances by the Nicaraguan *carreteros*, although the animals are often covered with blood. In front of a house in which I was staying, an ox, one of a team of eight pairs, fell down from exhaustion, after toiling up the four miles of bad road from the Missouri, and, in spite of beating, kicking, and other drivers' resources, the poor creature was quite unable to recover its legs, strangled as it was by the yoke. The men twisted its tail and pulled it until it almost gave way. Vain ingenuity! Then, in order to rouse him, they trod on the nostrils of the half-strangled beast, which was lying with its muzzle on the ground, panting heavily, and alternately snorting and inhaling the dust. All was in vain, and severer means were now resorted to: a small quantity of gunpowder was placed under the animal's nostrils and fired. The effect was magical; but it showed itself in the other beast under the same yoke, which made the most extraordinary bounds, stamped with its fore-legs on the body of its fellow-ox, twisting the head of the latter with the yoke, and threatening to break its neck. Not until after exhausting all these efforts and torments was the poor creature released from the yoke, and a pailful of cold water poured over it. The animal with difficulty now raised itself on its tottering legs, and as soon as it succeeded it made a fierce rush on the nearest of its tormentors, who, I am sorry to say, escaped. The ox was now removed, and died the next day.

Independence, with its environs, then contained four thousand inhabitants and seven churches. There were both northern and southern Methodists resident here—the former appealing to the authority of the Bible against, and the latter in favour of, slavery. The northern Methodists admit amongst them none who keep slaves; but the slaves themselves, of course, belong to the southern Methodists. "It is the will of God that the blacks are to be slaves," said a negro, who was preaching during my stay here; "we must bear our fate; but in a future world we shall be white men and free." A German whom I met here told me that the blacks believe the damned among the negroes to become monkeys; but if in this shape they behave well, they are advanced to the state of a negro again, and bliss is eventually possible to them, consisting in their turning white, becoming winged, and so on. Whether such ideas are fostered by the Christian clergy I do not know, but I am almost inclined to this opinion; nor am I able to say what position in Missouri a sect may at the present time hold who exclude from their church every slaveholder: the struggles in and about Kansas must, however, render this position somewhat critical.* At Independence I heard much said about the strict discipline observed by the Methodists with regard to morality and manners. A young lady was expelled from their church for having danced on a Sunday, and a young man had received a warning for having attended a circus. But it is a remarkable fact, as I have been assured, that the church grants a *furlough* for sinning—that is to say, she permits a temporary separation from the community, which permission is taken advantage of by those who wish to seek the amusements of the world. This is evidently analogous to an indulgence granted by the Roman Catholic Church, and it is an interesting proof, in an historical point of view, that endeavours to establish principles with excessive severity render a compromise with their opposite inevitable.

Now that I am on the subject of religion, I will here mention a singular book which fell into my hands at Independence, and which I perused for want of another. It contains the confessions, religious opinions, and justifications of Mr. Warder Cresson, of Philadelphia, who was first a Quaker, then a Shaker, then a Millerite, and lastly made a pilgrimage to Jerusalem and there became a Jew. On his return his family took steps to get him declared insane and have him sent to an asylum: Mr. Cresson, however, instituted a desperate lawsuit, which he won. The characteristic part in this man's state of mind is the combination of the wildest fanaticism with the most prosaic realism. He insists on interpreting every sentence in the Old Testament according to the letter: the passage "Blessed are they who walk on the ways of Jerusalem" is, in his view, a command to him to leave his family and all his interests in Philadelphia, and to repair to Jerusalem by the shortest route. He advises every one to do the same, and, for the convenience of all who are willing to follow his advice, he gives the following information at the end of his book: "From Philadelphia to Jerusalem 21 days and a quarter: first class, 190 dollars 75 cents.; second class, 135 dollars 50 cents."[1] In the year 1854, according to Mr. Cresson's interpretation, the kingdom of God was to commence, when every one judged worthy was to receive his portion of the inheritance at Jerusalem; and the fear of receiving less than others appears to have been

[1] 'The key of David. David is the true Messiah, &c. &c. Also Reasons for becoming a Jew; with a Revision of the late Law-suit for Lunacy on that account. By Warder Cresson.' Philadelphia, 5612.

a principal motive for his journey thither—a trait which depicts clearly the realistic character of the course of ideas that urged this strange man to embrace Judaism.

At Independence I made the acquaintance of a man who in his way is no less singular than Mr. Warder Cresson. Mr. ——, who though known in the State of Missouri for his eccentricity, nevertheless holds a respected position, has, for a North-American, the most extravagant views of political life and interests. He regards the "American" as the "most ancient and primitive civilization of mankind," and laments that this is not acknowledged by the world at large. This culture, he admits, has become degenerate in America itself; but in China it is still found in a pure state. Hence salvation must come to America from China, and this consists in the introduction of the "Chinese constitution," viz. the "patriarchal democracy of the Celestial Empire." The political life of the United States is, "through European influences," in a state of complete demoralization, and the Chinese constitution alone contains the elements of regeneration. For this reason a railroad to the Pacific is of such vast importance, since by its means the Chinese trade will be conducted straight across the North-American continent. This trade must bring in its train Chinese civilization. All that is usually alleged against China is mere calumny, spread purposely, just like those calumnies which are circulated in Europe about the United States. Mr. —— belongs to the class of American malcontents, in whose character is mixed an immeasurable portion of national conceit with a general discontent at the state of things in the United States. This class of people is not rare, and belong to the better elements of the Know-nothing order.

These characters, with their forced American nationality, represent the reverse of our former long-haired Teutonists. "We Germans," said the latter, "are the first people in the world: at present, it is true, matters stand badly with us; but our ancestors, they were a people!" The former say, "We Americans are the first people in the world: at present, it is true, matters stand very badly with us; but our descendants, they will be a people!" But as the sons of Arminius, proud of their past, understood that a past has no value if it has no future, and therefore prepared themselves for this future by their athletic exercises; so the sons of Uncle Sam, proud of their future, seem to opine that a future, without a past, is of no value, and therefore they attempt to found an American culture upon Indianism. "We want the prestige of antiquity," said Mr. ——, to me; "but we have it! See the Indian mounds in our West!" It was upon this tendency of the American mind, which is not exclusively peculiar to the United States, but is also met with in the Spanish-American countries, that the cunning founder of the Mormon sect originally calculated, in making the American Indians play so prominent a part in the sacred history he invented. It is an endeavour, mentally and historically, as has been done politically, to emancipate themselves from Europe; and they imagine they can attain this object by denying their physical and mental origin. In the same manner the Mexicans, at the time of their separation from Spain, called themselves the sons of Montezuma—*hijos de Montezuma.* The history of how many a people may in the earliest times of mankind have been falsified in this manner!

Our waggons were loaded at Weyne City in the first week of August, and drawn by hired teams of oxen on to the open prairie, where, in charge of Mexican lads, our mules had been out at grass. On the 17th of August, in company with Mr. Mayer and his wife, I followed the caravan, which, when we overtook it, had already passed the frontier of the State of Missouri, and entered the large tract which at that time still belonged to the Indians west of the United States, but is now opened to the colonization of the whites, under the name of the Kansas territory.

CHAPTER III.

The Caravan, its Arrangements — Waggons, Freight and Requirements for the Journey — The Commander and his Men — Anglo-Americans and Mexicans — Man and Animal — Characteristic of the Mule — Aristocrats, Mes-alliances, Parvenus, and Rabble in the Animal Kingdom — The First Breaking-in and Harnessing Wild Mules — The Corral — Order of Journey and Prarie Roads — The Camp and its Comforts — Night Watches, and Usages of Caravan Life — Astronomical and Musical Amusements — Dangerous Charms of the Wilderness.

Before inviting the reader to accompany me on the long journey from Missouri to Chihuahua, I must endeavour to give him a general idea of the arrangement and locomotion of a caravan on its journey through the western wildernesses of the North American continent.

The waggons generally carry from five to six thousand pounds weight, and are yoked with five pairs, if drawn, like ours, by mules. A single driver guides them, now seated on the saddled mule, now walking by the side. In difficult places the drivers assist one another, and sometimes the teams have to be doubled: that is to say, the three or four fore pairs of the one waggon are attached in a line to the other, in order to get the waggons over some height or through some deep morass. On these occasions sometimes eight or ten men are engaged about a single waggon. As the caravan must keep together, it can only proceed, under such circumstances, a few English miles in a day. I shall hereafter have occasion to speak of an effort that occupied a fortnight to get twenty-six waggons over the short distance of twelve English miles. In other parts, on the contrary, the roads across the prairies are so good that seventy to eighty miles can be travelled in four and twenty hours, if want of water (as is often the case in these parts) renders it necessary to travel so quickly. Of this likewise I shall have occasion to mention a few instances.

The waggons are very strongly built, and their durability is almost inconceivable. They suffer mostly from the dryness of the air on reaching the higher regions of the West, and for this reason the wheels must be watered whenever an opportunity offers. Without some unfortunate accident, however, a good teamster can take his waggon across the continent without incurring any breakage. Nevertheless, a caravan carries with it the most important articles of harness and parts of the waggon in extra quantities, so that a broken axle, a worn-out collar, or a broken chain, &c., can be instantly replaced.

A store of shoes for the mules, which are not always shod, and seldom completely, must likewise be taken; and wheelwrights' tools, shovels and hoes, windlasses, levers, crowbars, axes, and hatchets for cutting wood, are also indispensable articles.

The provender consists of flour, bacon, dried beans, coffee, and sugar. Spirits are never given on these journeys, unless the master or conductor of the caravan is induced by great toil or especial privations to unlock his holy of holies, and to give his men a portion to refresh them. Brandy is only taken as medicine; but coffee, on the contrary, is an indispensable article, and is drunk twice a day in large quantities. The refreshing and strengthening effect of this drink, under great toils, in heat as well as cold, in rain and dry, is extraordinary. The dried beans form one chief article of food—the indispensable *frijoles* of the Mexicans and all the other Spanish Americans; but all depends on the kind of beans and the mode of preparing them. They are boiled in water till soft; a part of the water is then evaporated, and a pan, with some fat in it, is placed on the fire; the beans are poured into it, salt is added, they are left to stew for a moment, and the most savoury and nourishing food a hungry traveller can desire is prepared. It is well known that this dish is never wanting at the most luxurious Mexican table, where it invariably concludes the meal before the dessert is served; but to do full justice to it pure soft water is required. The broth, as is well known, contains the most nutritious part, and, indeed, I have often taken it out of the kettle and drank it, when returning from my night-watch to the camp-fire, hungry, frozen, and exhausted, and have found it as good and as strengthening as a cup of broth. Bread is daily baked in the camp, and is generally eaten hot.

For the chief table of our caravan, to which I had the advantage to belong, we had a quantity of choice delicacies with us, — preserved meats and fine vegetables, cauliflowers, asparagus, oysters and lobsters, sardines in oil, delicate hams, pickles and preserved fruits, tea and chocolate, claret and champagne. For these luxuries we were indebted to the presence of a lady in our caravan; but the gentlemen of such a party of travellers are generally provided with some of these articles. Sardines are especial favourites, and their consumption in the prairies is so large that the track of tin boxes strewn along the route is alone a sufficient clue to mark the road from Independence to Santa Fé.

The caravan has to be amply provided with arms and ammunition. Every driver and muleteer is called upon to furnish himself with a gun in good order, a rifle or musket, —which he must always have at hand,—and many carry pistols also. I had myself a brace of six-barrelled revolvers, of the army bore, with a double-barrelled gun, so that I had always fourteen shots at command. Mr. Mayer and our waggon-master were armed in the same manner.

The caravan is likewise furnished with a store of clothes, shoes, hats, knives, tobacco, and other articles of daily want; the proprietor or conductor generally undertaking the task of providing all the articles which the party require for their equipment. An account for these is opened with each driver and servant, to be repaid out of their future wages. The prices are fixed very high, and with reason, as losses are unavoidable; and as during the journey a great quantity of these articles is consumed, there remains to a man, at the end of it, out of his wages (twelve to twenty dollars a month), seldom more than the means of making himself merry a few days, like the sailor on shore; after which he is obliged to seek fresh service, either returning by the same road or proceeding on by another. Thus we find on the prairie-roads, and at the stations on their limits, a moving population of drivers and muleteers, which we can only compare to sailors at sea and in port; and everywhere in travelling in these parts—at Independence or Westport on the Missouri, at Santa Fé or El Paso on the Rio Grande, at Chihuahua in Northern Mexico, at San Antonio in Texas, at Los Angeles in California, or in the Mormon city on the great Salt Lake—the traveller will, from time to time, meet again the same fellows, lounging about like idle sailors on the landing-place of a harbour.

The commander of a caravan is the waggon-master: the Mexicans entitle him the *mayor-domo.* The proprietor, unless he himself takes the command, is to the waggon-master (if present on the journey) in the position of a supercargo to the captain of a ship. This was the case in our caravan; and Mr. Mayer, although dissatisfied with his waggon-master, avoided any decided interference with the command. The waggon-master, on the contrary, often tried to throw the responsibility of a decision on the proprietor. The former was an Anglo-American by birth; I have never seen a more idle and effeminate man. Though he had made the journey several times, he would, towards the latter part, when we suffered much from the cold nights, creep forth in the morning from under his eight or ten blankets, whilst I had slept under a single pair: he had to be called at least three times ere he could be roused up to take the night-watch. There is, nevertheless, a common prejudice that only an Anglo-American is fitted for a waggon-master. The truth is, that if the crew consist of Anglo-Americans, scarcely a waggon-master of any other nation will know how to deal with them. If, on the contrary, they are Mexicans, a German who understands the language and his business as a driver will be able to take this office perfectly well. In a mixed body of Anglo-Americans and Mexicans discord will continually occur, and the latter seldom escape without maltreatment from the former, in whom the idea that a man of a darker complexion is thereby excluded from equal rights with them is with difficulty eradicated. "Shoot him!" "Hang him!" "Whip him!" are exclamations heard from the lips of his Anglo-American companions, when any small fault is committed by a Mexican; and "I never killed a white man," is usually considered by the latter as completely clearing their character from any unfavourable suspicion. Amongst Anglo-Americans, however, who have lived in Mexico any length of time, this prejudice of race is often found effaced, and a more humane feeling has taken its place; to this the intercourse with Mexican women is usually the first step. Thus the corrupt morals of the frontier towns of Mexico have their humanizing influence, and we observe how the civilization of the human race frequently follows strange channels.

The Anglo-Americans have unquestionably the superiority in driving the waggons, whereas the Mexicans are the only useful muleteers—*muleros.* The business of the latter consists in bringing up the mules for the relay; in catching the draught-cattle with the *laso* when required and handing them over to the driver, in keeping the herd together when unyoked, &c. Irish people, sometimes even Scotch and English, pass for Anglo-Americans; and even the Germans, when with Mexicans, pass for *Americanos,* although they are generally on more intimate terms with the Mexicans. As drivers, the Germans are not cool enough; they become irritated and morose under fatigues and privations, and often vent this on the cattle. The Mexican exhibits in danger the mere passive courage of the fatalist, although examples of distinguished heroism are not wanting among them. Toils and privations they bear with an almost incredible equanimity and even cheerfulness. Often have I observed our Mexicans, stretched in the mud under the waggons, hungry and wet, passing the time in songs and joking. They are cruel to the draught and saddle animals, because they expect from them what is impossible; but they understand their temper thoroughly, especially that of the mules, and know how to attain by cunning and coaxing what an Anglo-American fruitlessly attempts to effect by force. Whilst the latter vainly strives in every way to put the bit into the mouth of some obstinate mule, the Mexican looks on with compassion and contempt. "Estos hombres son bárbaros, no saben nada!"—these men are barbarians, they understand nothing!—said one of these men to me on such an occasion. For instance, a little spirited mule, which afterwards became the favourite of the whole party and went by the pet name of "*la Niña*," resisted all the attempts of a big, stout Kentuckian to tame it; when Pedro, unable longer to bear it, exclaimed, "Let me try!" and taking from his hand the end of the cord, which was tied in a noose round the animal's neck, he first let the mule, trembling with excitement, have a few minutes' rest; then he approached it slowly and gently, patted its back, tickled its neck and behind its ears, and soothed it with words of endearment: "*O Niña! O mulita! Mulita bonita!*"—O my child! O my little mule! My pretty little mule!—said he, in a soft tone. Meanwhile he drew the bridle over its head, and, unobserved, put the bit into its mouth, the creature offering no resistance. I remember another mule, to which his Mexican muleteer gave the classical name of Lais. Lais was in the same favour with Leandro as Niña was with friend Pedro. Once, however, I saw him in an indescribable rage with the animal. Trembling with fury, he raised the butt-end of his whip against it: "*O, si fueras Mejicana!*"—Oh, were you but a Mexican!—he muttered, letting his arm fall again. The Mexican did not dare to lay hands on the Anglo-Saxon beast. The Mexican drivers and muleteers are not only superior to the Anglo-American in patience, frugality, and good-humour under fatigue and privation, but also in manner. They do not swear; for the occasional repetition of an improper word in the Spanish language cannot be compared to the innumerable curses of the Anglo-American driver.

From drivers and muleteers we may pass to mules,

which are in many respects far more interesting than the former, and whose natural disposition is an attractive subject to the observer of nature. One of the most striking characteristics of the mule is his aversion to the ass, and the pride he takes in his relationship to the horse; which instincts are met, with obtrusiveness in the ass, and by indifference in the horse. If an ass at any time—urged by the vanity peculiar to its race as related to the mule—happens to fall in with a drove of mules, he will, in all probability, be kicked and lamed by his proud relatives. A horse, on the contrary, takes a distinguished position in a drove of mules. The latter crowd round him, and follow his movements, exhibiting a violent jealousy, each striving to stand nearest to their high-bred relative; this instinct is employed to keep together the droves of mules, on a journey or at pasture, by putting a mare to the drove, with a bell round her neck, and called the "Bell-mare,"—by the Mexicans, "*la yegua madre*" (Mother-mare). This animal is led day and night by a cord; and the whole drove is thus kept under control, and will not leave their queen. It is therefore very difficult to separate the drove. The man who leads the mare is instructed, in case of an attack from the Indians, to leap instantly upon the back of this animal, and take refuge in the waggon-encampment, whither the drove is sure to follow him. Even if the Indians succeed in separating any from the drove, they find it difficult to carry them off. The animals incessantly attempt to turn back, and the travellers are thus enabled to overtake the robbers and recover the stolen animals. The Indians, in consequence, use every means to get possession of the mare; and, if they succeed in this, the whole drove is lost to their owners. If several horses are in a drove of mules, the danger is that the latter becomes dispersed; and this is the reason that, in these journeys, saddle-horses are not allowed to go loose, but are led by a cord.

A large drove of mules, however, generally contains one or another democratic individual, which has attained to the consciousness of its natural animal dignity and native rights, and therefore asserts a kind of independence. We had, for instance, in our drove, a white mule which regularly separated from the others at the time of harnessing. When the mules were driven from the pasture into the waggon-encampment, where they are caught by the *laso*, the white mule accompanied the rest up to the entrance; but here it made a sudden leap aside, ran off to the distance of half-a-mile, and from this point watched the camp with fixed attention, until the caravan was in motion. It then returned quietly, and joined the relay. Sometimes, to show who was master, two Mexicans were sent out to catch the fugitive; and the animal was then, of course, harnessed for the day. The loss of time, however, and the fatigue of the saddle-horses, prevented a repetition of these measures. The animal had its own way, and, whilst its brethren were hard worked, it made simply a journey of pleasure from the Missouri to Chihuahua.

An educated Mexican told me a counterpart to this. In a certain convent, six mules were kept, each of which was employed daily by turns: one of these animals knew its own day in the week so well that, on that morning, it regularly endeavoured to keep the yard-door closed, by planting itself against it, and thus preventing the servant's coming to fetch it to work.

It is impossible to describe the scene of the first harnessing of some hundred mules, until then quite wild, and which have never had a bit in their mouths, nor a saddle on their backs. The waggons are drawn up, so as to form three-fourths of a circle, whilst the space left open is the entrance to the court-yard of this encampment. In the intervals between them the waggons are connected by a cord tied from wheel to wheel. The mules are driven into the court, when the entrance is also closed by a cord drawn across it. Two men, armed with whips, are placed at this entrance, in order to drive back any of the mules which may attempt to leap over the cord or creep under it. The Mexicans call this waggon-encampment, which serves both for catching the animals and as a place of protection against the Indians, a "*corral*,"—a word which signifies any yard or enclosed place, where cattle are kept. The Anglo-Americans have changed the word into "carrel."

The reader may picture to himself two to three hundred wild mules crowded together in this space, with ten to fifteen men among them, each endeavouring to fling the *laso* over the heads of the animals, one after another, to force the bit into their mouths, and to lead each to its place before the waggon to which it has to be harnessed. In a caravan of twenty to thirty waggons, this first attempt occupies the greater part of a day, leaving no time to get the waggons in motion. The mules well know the *laso*, and strive to escape it in every way possible: they crowd closely together, first on one side then on another of the *corral*, their heads turned to the centre, and hidden as much as possible; others thrust their heads under the waggons or between the wheels, to prevent the *laso* reaching their necks; while, again, others are even more cunning: they stand stock-still, as if they were actually holding their necks patiently for the noose; but the expression of their eye, fixedly watching at the same time the man with the *laso*, betrays their cunning. The man now whirls the cord, in serpentine coils, round and round over his head; the noose flies hissing, with the precision of an arrow, to its object; whilst the animal stands as if rooted to the spot, but making a small side-motion of its head, and the *laso* misses.

All these stratagems, however, are useless. Whilst the drove rush from side to side of the *corral*, one mule after another feels the *laso* twisted round its neck. Then it tears away madly into the midst of its companions, dragging the man who holds the cord from one side of the *corral* to the other. A second and a third now come to his aid. The hard breathing of the half-strangled animal is heard amidst all the uproar and confusion of the scene. At length the men succeed in drawing the end of the cord between the spokes of a wheel, and the animal is gradually brought nearer and nearer to this point. As soon as it is close to the wheel, the cord is drawn round its body, and again pulled through the spokes, so that the whole body is now brought into a noose. Thereupon the men endeavour to force the bit between its teeth, and, just as they seem to have accomplished this, the animal in despair makes a last effort; it throws itself on the ground, frees its legs from the cord by rolling over, jumps up, and, with the noose still tightly drawn round its neck, disappears in the thickest of the drove. The chase now begins anew, until the animal has a second noose around its neck: half-strangled, it is now flung on the ground and mastered by forcible means, until the bit is in its mouth, and the cord, with a second noose, fixed round its nostril. Upon this, it is let out of the *corral*; and now begins the attempt to put it to, and harness it to the waggon. The creature again makes the most violent struggles; and, considering that in this manner ten animals are put to every carriage, and that this operation goes on at the same time in different points in the *corral*, and before twenty or thirty waggons, the reader may form an idea of the confusion of the whole scene. When trying to put them to, the animals entangle themselves in the harness, fling themselves on the ground, trample upon and kick one another, sometimes break loose, and run off with part of the harness, the Mexicans in pursuit, mounted on the swiftest horses in the caravan. The mule, with the draught-chains clattering at its heels, gallops madly on, until the noose is again round its neck, when it is brought in and harnessed anew.

When at length all the waggons are in readiness, the *corral* is opened; the supernumerary animals are let out, with the bell-mare, and the caravan is now ready-to start. The mules are now, for the first time, put to draught; for the first time they feel the bridle and the lash of the driver, who takes his place on the saddled mule.

Fresh confusion! *Here*, it is impossible to get the team to move, — *there*, another team tries to run away with its waggon. Here, one pair of mules make a desperate effort to advance, whilst a second pair holds back,—there, the leaders turn sharp round, drag the next pair after it, and threaten to snap the axle-tree. Here, an animal falls,—there, a chain breaks. Amidst the cracking of whips, and shouting and swearing of the drivers, at last one team gets into a regular pace, when suddenly they strike off from the beaten road, dragging the waggon into a morass, or wedging it fast between trees. The broken harness has to be mended, the waggon has to be dragged out of the morass, and the tree standing in the way has to be felled; before all this is accomplished another waggon is in a similar plight! Thus the day passes, in the utmost excitement and fatigue both to man and beast, until in the evening a new *corral* is formed, with great trouble, perhaps scarcely a thousand yards distant from the former. The animals are unyoked, and driven to grass and water; and the men, after lighting their fires, set about satisfying their hunger and thirst.

The next morning matters are somewhat improved; in many the obstinate nature of the animals is subdued, and the men have begun to learn their disposition. The yoking and harnessing is accomplished in three to four hours, and the caravan succeeds in proceeding a few miles. Under the most favourable circumstances, however, the yoking a caravan of twenty to thirty waggons takes at least an hour and a half.

The waggons have their fixed order in the camp as well as on the road. No one is allowed to pass another, and those in advance are ordered to wait for those behind. The danger of an attack from the Indians obliges the caravan to keep together as much as possible, and for this reason, it sometimes travels in double column; a great part of the Santa Fé road has, in consequence, double tracks. I must here observe that the roads over the prairies are for the most part well marked out, and it would be quite erroneous to imagine these journeys made over trackless wilds. Now and then, it is true, a daring caravan-conductor attempts a new route, with a view to cut off an angle to reach some watering-place, or to avoid a hill, and in these cases he has of course to make his own path. The wheel-tracks of a waggon-caravan are distinguishable for several years in the prairie: a different vegetation springs up on them—herbaceous plants, for instance, supersede the grasses, and not unfrequently the course which waggons have many years ago followed may be traced by a line of tall sunflowers, extending for miles over the grassy plain.

The caravan usually travels from early in the morning until eleven o'clock; it then stops to rest, to cook, to eat, to water the mules, and let them graze. In the afternoon a second journey is performed: the night encampment is formed if possible before dark, and the drove is taken to water and turned out to grass for the night. In selecting a place for encampment, attention must be paid to the different kinds of grass, which are of very unequal value as fodder for the cattle; likewise to the vicinity, abundance, quality, and accessibility of the water; to the facility of arrival and departure, and security against the Indians. The waggon-master rides on before, to reconnoitre the country for this purpose—a task often accompanied with danger. The order of march is, however, frequently reversed, the journey being made by night and the party resting by day.

As soon as the teams are unharnessed, the first watch has to mount guard, whilst the others light their camp-fires, prepare their meal, eat, smoke, chat, and repose, until their turn comes to relieve guard. For this purpose the men are divided into corps, each with its leader, and they relieve one another every two hours. Under the protection of this well-armed guard, the animals are kept out at grass during the night. Shortly before daybreak, however, the herd is driven into the *corral,* as pillaging bands of Indians prefer this time for their attacks: the camp is then aroused, and harnessing begins.

It need hardly be mentioned that the only couch for sleeping is the ground, upon which is spread a blanket or the skin of some animal: the saddle serves for a pillow, and a few blankets give the necessary warmth to the body. The traveller lays his gun—his faithful bed-fellow—under his blanket. When the ground is dry and not too uneven, and there is neither rain nor snow, the traveller soon finds such a bed comfortable enough: when it rains, shelter may be found under the waggons, unless you chance to drop into a puddle or a brook. The waggons are provided with a double covering of sailcloth, drawn over wooden hoops, and long enough to be pulled down to the point of the axletree: this forms a roof, under which, placed upon the axletree, the leathern harness can be kept dry; and this is the place where the driver usually sleeps.

I must observe that, as far as I was personally concerned, we were provided with a tent, which, together with a companion, I used during the first nights; but as the trouble of putting it up and taking it down usually fell to my lot, and the tent mostly afforded shelter when it was least wanted, whereas in bad weather it was generally blown down by the wind, I gave up the use of this very questionable comfort. Our caravan had also two travelling-carriages in its train, which could be closed up and the seats converted into a couch. Half of one of these carriages was at my disposal. Thus I had the comfort of being able to drive and ride alternately; but for my night-couch I generally preferred to lie on the ground in the open air, as it was disagreeable to be unable to see at any time what was passing around. I slept on a buffalo-skin, covered with a few blankets; but I never took off my clothes at night during the whole journey, and my shoes only three or four times in the one hundred and five nights we spent on the road to Chihuahua.

The night-watches are the severest part of these journeys, especially after forced marches, which a want of water sometimes compelled us to make. Even the constant fear of being surprised and scalped by an Indian has at times not prevented my falling asleep whilst standing at my post. During the whole journey, however, I only two or three times neglected my duty on guard. On the high plateaus of New Mexico, five to seven thousand feet above the level of the sea, the intense cold in October and November also greatly increased the discomforts of these nocturnal military herdsman's duties, from which no one who travels in these caravans is exempt, unless, like Mr. Mayer, he is accompanied by his wife. But as in the United States a part of the privileges which ladies enjoy extend to their husbands or cavaliers, the courtesy of the drivers has introduced the considerate practice, on the prairie-roads, of exempting a husband travelling with his wife from sharing these night-watches. Mr. Mayer was, in consequence, in a most enviable position; and as often as a comparison of his lot with mine forced itself upon me when on guard, Leporello's "Keine Ruh' bei Tag und Nacht" (no rest day or night), resounded in my ear, and I involuntarily fell to humming the air. Moreover the snail's pace of Time during these night-watches called up all kinds of musical recollections, from my early childhood till the time of my departure from Europe. My voice soon awakened the echo of the prairie-wolves, and their howling and whining lasted till morning.

My musical amusements were properly against rule, and in the most dangerous parts I was obliged to forego them: instead, therefore, I chose astronomy as a pastime, and was soon enabled, by the help of the stars, to calculate the expiration of my time on guard within ten minutes, and to succeed in retracing my road in the dark to the camp, across the prairie or through a Mexican *chaparral*, from the herd grazing at a mile distant.

On the whole, the rude and hard life on such a journey through the wilderness has great charms, which may gain a fascinating power over the mind; and at the moment I am writing this I indeed scarcely know whether they do not surpass those of civilized life. At all events I have spent, during these travels, some of the most cheerful hours of my life in a state of mind free from all weight. The experienced traveller, however, should warn his civilized fellow-man against these charms of life in the wilderness. He to whom fate has shown the questionable favour of having enjoyed both will maintain a divided interest as long as he lives.

CHAPTER IV.

Departure from Independence — Outskirts of the Prairie — Commencement of the Caravan Journey — Indian Signal Station — Wolves and Indians — Uncomfortable Night-Quarters — Journey by Moonlight — Solitude of the Prairie — Breeds of Dogs, and Races of Men — Geological Remarks — The Prairie — Council Grove — Yerba-loco — Small Prairie Rivers — Landscape Scenery — Buffalo-Herds, and Hunting — Marmots and their Villages — Their Companionship with Owls and Rattlesnakes — Californian Ground-Squirrel — Meteorological Observations.

I have already said that I left Independence on the 17th of August, in company with Mr. and Mrs. M., in order to follow the caravan. In a few hours we had left behind woods and cultivated lands, with the last traces of human habitation, and found ourselves on the edge of the wide steppes which stretch hence westwards over the greater part of the North American continent, reaching even in some places, with a few interruptions, the shore of the Pacific.

To give a correct idea of this border-country it must be observed, that from the valley of the Missouri upwards the prairie lies on an elevation, whilst the woods which clothe the slopes of the valley break off where the elevation begins to form an undivided plain, and, following some small precipitous valleys and ravines, extend here and there into the steppes. From the margin of the prairie there is a view on all sides down into the lower woodlands.

The farms of this border-land produce an agreeable impression. Fields covered with heavy sheaves of wheat and maize showed the fertility of the soil. The meadows, watered by brooks, were covered with rich grass, and the scarlet blossoms of the Asklepias, the white Œnothera, and golden sunflowers invested the foreground with the most brilliant colours.

We encamped for the night, and reached the caravan early the next morning, continuing our journey with it. A brilliant sky rested over the wide-spreading plain before us, which was still broken here and there, park-like, by groups of trees and strips of wood. Upon an elevation near the road stood three pyramids of stones, roughly piled one upon another, the highest twelve or fifteen feet high. I could learn nothing of their origin. Later on I saw, in various places in the prairie, similar but rougher heaps of stones. Sometimes green boughs stuck between the stones, which led me to infer that these were signals of communication agreed upon by the Indians. For the greater part of the day I rode in advance of the caravan. The first prairie-fowls showed themselves, and the pursuit of these, with the examination of some plants quite new to me, filled all the time until we reached our night-quarters. This point went by the name of the "Lone Elm Tree." An elm had stood here; but some travellers, to whom a cup of warm coffee gave greater pleasure than the sight of a tree in the steppes, had cut it down not long before we passed: the barbarous act was already perpetrated, and we might, therefore, use the pieces of wood lying about for our camp-fire.

Our way led us through the strip of land between the Kansas and Osage rivers, rising gradually, with beautiful views, on to the neighbouring country. Towards the south the ground sloped gradually down into valleys, and was, on the whole, more flat; but towards the north, the descents into the valleys were steep and precipitous. Far away in both directions were to be seen rivulets, bordered with trees, winding along through the meadows.

At the Rock Creek we met a party of Indians, armed with lance and tomahawk; and the next morning we found them seated on one side of our camp, and a troop of wolves on the other, awaiting our departure to seize any food or other articles we might leave behind.

One night a terrible storm burst over our heads. I was lying with two companions under the tent, when the wind blew it down upon us. We immediately raised it again; but in a few minutes it was once more overthrown. The rain poured in torrents, and we had no shelter, no resource but to remain lying quietly. The wet canvas lay cold on my face, and soon a stream of water was running down my neck. I crept under the counterpane, and at last fell asleep.

A few days afterwards we encamped on the Fish Creek—an appropriate name. Here we caught with our rods a number of small perch, and as these fish sparkled on my line brilliant humming-birds chirped around me.

We continued our journey by moonlight. The long row of waggons, with their white tilts, and shadows all of the same shape and size, moving along the road at equal distances, offered a curious sight. No sound was heard but the tinkling of the bell borne by a horse in the rear of the caravan, which was now and then drowned in the song of lament from one of our Mexicans. Later on I often heard this same song in night journeys in Mexico. It must be of Indian origin. Perhaps the Aztec prisoners of war, before being sacrificed to the great Huitzilopochtli, may have sung such a funeral song; an opera-composer might very well adopt the *motive:* it begins with a loud continued scream of anguish, modulating into a few minor intervals, expressive rather of physical than mental pain.

On first hearing it I fancied it, at a distance, the howling of wolves.

In our day's journey to Council Grove I missed the keys of my luggage, and rode back *twelve* or *fifteen* miles to our encampment, where the first object I saw was my bunch of keys lying on the grass. I rejoined our caravan before it encamped for the night. During this ride I was reminded, by the stillness and solitude of the prairie, of similar impressions of loneliness made on me by the high places of the Alps. Whilst riding along the plain I observed some Indians riding towards me. On a sudden they vanished as if they had sunk into the earth. Being, however, well armed I continued my ride, only taking the precaution to turn a little out of the road at the spot where these figures had disappeared. Whilst doing so, the men, with their horses, re-appeared near to me. There was probably some dip in the ground, concealed by the grass, the even growth of which renders it difficult to perceive any inequality in the plain. I observed there were two men and one woman, accompanied by a dog, which flew at me fiercely, and was not called off till I levelled my gun at it.

The Indian's dog has, like his master, natural hostility to the white man,—an instinctive enmity which is fully returned by the dog of the latter. A large dog belonging to our caravan could not be held back whenever he saw an Indian, but instantly flew at his throat. He had the same hostility towards dark-coloured Mexicans of the lower class, whilst toward the whites he was perfectly tame. Horses and mules take fright, and shy at the sight of Indians, until they become quite used to them; and even a friendly visit from the Indians occasions an uproar and alarm throughout the caravan.

As far as the vicinity of Pleasant Valley our road had

lain over a tract of carboniferous limestone; but, on an elevation in this part, a limestone stratum appears of quite a different geological character. The chief colour is white, softly shaded like marble, or marked with black dendritic lines. It is dense, hard, and impregnated with silica, which is often secreted in masses of flint. This limestone forms at Council Grove a terrace, ascending which the road runs, still rising, in a westerly direction. On the other side of Diamond Spring, near Lost Spring, commence the marl and conglomerate strata of the new red sandstone.

I observed no organic remains in the limestone of Pleasant Valley and Council Grove; but, in journeying across it, I came to the opinion that one step had brought me from the carboniferous limestone to the cretaceous formation. At the foot of the terrace formed by these strata, just as at the lower edge of the cretaceous strata in Texas, clear springs gush forth, the excellent water of which is very distinguishable from the peaty water of the strata of coal-limestone and the saline or alkaline water of the new red sandstone. Marcou, in his geological map of the United States, lays down the new red sandstone as commencing near Pleasant Valley, with insulated masses of the cretaceous formation lying about on the former. If this is the leading feature of this part of the country, the Santa-Fé road appears to pass over such a chalk island, which exactly covers the limit between the new red sandstone and the carboniferous limestone. We travelled through part of this country by night, and I could not, therefore, follow an uninterrupted line of observation.

On the Little Arkansas rises an elevation in the prairie, the sharp edge of which is formed of layers of light-grey sandstone. This termination of a plateau to the north-west extends along the Arkansas river as the northern boundary of its valley, and the road runs along at the foot of this plateau until it crosses the river above Fort Atkinson. The characteristic features of this plateau are the small rocks on Walnut Creek, at Pawnee Rock and Pawnee Fork, and on the so-called Caches; and the geological phenomena of these are repeated on the north side of the Cimarron, on the so-called Lower and Middle Springs. The conglomerate which appears here (clearly a higher stratum of the new red sandstone than that which furnishes the masses of quicksand on the Arkansas and Cimarron) is loosely held together by a white, powdery, or rather flour-like cement, and contains boulders of quartz, jasper, cornelian, flint, granite, syenite, trap, red, brown, black and green lava, scoriæ, and brown pitchstone. Wherever the cement occurs in layers without boulders, a number of indistinct formations of organic origin are visible in the white mealy mass, which deserve to be examined under the microscope. The more distinct forms have the appearance of delicate roots and twigs, and in the fractures numerous small holes, like little tubes, are seen in many places. Here and there this net-work of organic remains is very hard, being penetrated by hydrated oxide of iron. A harder stratum forms the surface of these rocks, protects them against decomposition, and is the cause of the formation of this plateau. At Walnut Creek, Pawnee Rock and Pawnee Fork, this roof presents peculiar dark-brown masses, looking like half-fused sandstone, and as if they had formerly composed the surface of contact between the sandstone and a layer of lava which had flowed over it. Wislicenus asserts that these formations are of volcanic origin; and on the Rabbit's Ears and the Round Mound, volcanic mountains on the sources of the Nutria or northern branch of the Canadian river, are found ejected masses of half-fused sandstone, just similar to those above-mentioned. In other places, on the contrary, the harder layers that cover the sandstone and conglomerate appeared to be merely sandy and ferruginous incrustations of limestone, with a cellular appearance. On the Pawnee Fork a dense limestone has provided, and probably still provides, the materials for such incrustations by solution and filtration. Upon the surface of contact are found brown sandy stalactites and sandy limestone crystals, similar to the so-called crystallized sandstone of Fontainebleau.

A rough, sandy, dolomitic limestone, which overlies the softer sandstone and conglomerate on the Cimarron, separates these layers of the new red sandstone formation from the upper and more recent masses of sandstone, which at first appear in piled-up blocks. Their substance is remarkable for the quantity of quartz and mica it includes; for the occasional entire absence of any perceptible cement; for the complete amalgamation of its grains of quartz into a solid quartz rock; for its great hardness and bright colours of all shades, from the purest white to a brilliant brick or brown red, or from light yellow to brown. Numerous knots of brown ironstone, partially detached by the wearing effects of the weather, stand out on the surface in concentric films, and form one of the characteristic features of the formation. The stratification of this higher and more recent sandstone is distinctly visible on the so-called Upper Springs, upon the south side of the Cimarron, and on the Cold Spring and Cedar Spring. Undermost are seen the layers of conglomerate and sandstone which form the quicksands of the Arkansas and the Cimarron; over them the rough limestone, as a roof, and above this the more recent and hard sandstone which I have just described.

The strata of the latter, if I am not mistaken, are not parallel with those underlying it.

I have no doubt that this upper sandstone belongs to the Jura formation pointed out by Marcou as occurring here. On the Ocaté, a cleft running out into the valley of the Upper Canadian, this sandstone contains vegetable remains, consisting of indistinct twigs and dicotyledonous leaves. At the same time numerous little round elevations of a white colour are seen upon the planes of separation in the red or yellowish chief mass, which give the rock a spotted appearance and an oolithic character.

Upon these strata of sandstone, which contain the beds of Rabbit's Ears Creek, Rock Creek, Whetstone Creek, and other creeks, and over which the trap-lavas of the Rabbit's Ears and the Round Mound have poured, there lie in the vicinity of Waggon Mound, on the plateau across which the road leads to Las Vegas, still higher strata of a limestone, now lighter, now darker, and of a very hard dark grey sandy marl-slate containing innumerable and here and there separate masses of calcareous spar. The trap-lavas of Waggon Mound have broken through and spread over these upper layers.

At Las Vegas, on the north-east side of the valley, the limestone of the Jura formation terminates in nearly horizontal stratification, and on the opposite side of the valley a steep ridge of sandstone runs from N.N.W. to S.S.E.; its strata, inclined E.N.E., passing under that limestone. Probably it is the new red sandstone uplifted from the west which reappears here. Through a narrow cleft which intersects this ridge to its base—so narrow that a loaded waggon can hardly pass between the rocks—the road to Santa-Fé leads on level ground into a labyrinth of irregular valleys and ravines, without water, where horizontal strata of sandstone with superincumbent limestone reappear. The Cañon Blanco and Cañon del Toro are defiles in this sandstone which Marcou assigns to the Jura formation. Upon a table-shaped mountain of sandstone, near Anton Chico, a small place on the Upper Pecos, are again found the vegetable remains of the Ocaté, with other parts of plants appearing like reeds. South of Cañon Blanco the country again forms an undivided and horizontal plateau, which to the west, on the Rio Grande, is bordered by a succession of plutonic-metamorphysic, perhaps also volcanic and partly sedimentary groups of mountains of steep alpine forms, between which defiles descend to the Rio Grande Valley. Upon this plateau, at the Ojo de Berendo or Antilope Spring, occurs white limestone resting upon sandstone. This plateau clearly bears a detached portion of the Jura formation of the Llano Estacado. But this formation appears in a great measure to have been washed away, and the new red sandstone laid bare. The same thing occurs near the little Salt Lake, towards which the streams of Manzanas, Cuarrá, &c., flow from the above-mentioned groups of mountains. Over this sandstone the road runs through the pass of Cuarrá and Avó into the valley of the Salado, a salt brook which flows through the new red sandstone, and then cuts its way through a ravine of a deeper-lying limestone, and through this arrives at the valley of the Rio Grande. Our way did not lead us through this ravine, but over a steep mountain of limestone overlying the sandstone, and in this way reached the valley of the river above La Joyita. Thus there appear here upon the east side of the Rio Grande, in a narrow space, three or four different formations which, according to Marcou, fill up the whole period from the carboniferous limestone to the chalk, with plutonic, metamorphic, and volcanic masses interposed.

I have made this digression from the thread of my narrative in order to give briefly such superficial geological remarks as our mode of travelling from Missouri to the Rio Grande permitted. Our frequent night journeys prevented a more complete and connected series of observations. I must now recall my reader's attention to the eastern portion of the prairie, where I have other phenomena and travelling incidents to relate.

Irrespective of any geological consideration in reference to the appearance of the cretaceous formation in Pleasant Valley, it is certain that this, together with the greater elevation of the ground, is accompanied by a remarkable change in the whole natural features of the prairie. Both air and soil are more dry upon the higher ground and new character of the strata. The dew, which had fallen plentifully on the lower step of the plateau, is seen here sparingly. The traveller is sensible of the change of climate, in his improved healthy feeling and increased activity. The vegetation is in general shorter and not so rank.

Council Grove, where we arrived August 27th, will unquestionably become one day an important place. The situation is beautiful, and possesses many advantages. At the time we visited it, this place consisted of about ten houses, inhabited by white men and Indian women. A little higher up the brook stood, detached, the Mission-house, a somewhat large stone building, surrounded by hedged-in fields. This Mission, which was established by the Methodists among the Caw-Indians, has been, I believe, disturbed by the newer lawless state of the territory of late years. About a mile distant down the stream was a camp, composed of twelve to fifteen leather tents, belonging to the Caws. The country around is rich in natural beauty on a small scale. The rivulets, bordered by trees and bushes, wind along through beautiful flowery valleys, between hills covered with grass. These form the sources of the Neosho, which flows into the Arkansas.

Near Diamond Spring, where on one of the heights was an Indian burial-place, an ox was caught by one of our people and slaughtered in the evening. It had evidently strayed from some caravan that had preceded us. We tried to shorten our stay at Lost Spring, where we watered our animals. A certain poisonous plant growing here, called by the Mexicans *Yerba-loco* (mad-herb), is much feared: the specimen shown to me appeared to be an Astragalus. Here, again, as I have already mentioned, a different kind of rock begins, and with the increasing loose sand on Cotton Wood Creek the poplars commence. Hitherto the creeks had been bordered by a variety of bushes and trees, of which oaks had formed a predominant feature. The ground here is one vast level plain, and the deep bed of the river just mentioned looks like a straight line of tree-tops rising a little above its edge. The grass here was short, and even at this season already withered. Myriads of locusts were hopping around, whilst mosquitos of an unusual size plagued both man and beast.

At noon, on September 1st, we stopped on the Little Arkansas to rest. The bed of this river is, like all others hereabouts, deeply hollowed in the prairie,—not in rock, but in alluvial clay.

I have remarked how easily hollows in the ground may escape observation. The grassy plain nowhere presents any determined lines, no geometric perspective;—and, as the nature of the atmosphere either excludes the perception of distances by different degrees of distinctness in which objects may be seen, or confuses it by the unequal temperature of the strata of air, it is impossible to avoid optical delusions. I mistook a rabbit near me for a stag in the distance, and some ravens walking along the road for men; one of the foremost waggons passing through the bed of a river seemed to sink into the earth. Along the valley of the Little Arkansas grow elms and poplars; which, seen from the plain, look as if their tops grew out of the ground.

As soon as you descend to the bed of a river, a peculiar little world opens to your view in the barren prairie: the trees grow up from out of the depth, on the sides of which are sunflowers the height of two to three men, and vines entwine luxuriantly amidst the underwood.

Whilst ascending the elevation on the west, commencing here with sandstone layers, I had an interesting view of the sandhills on the Arkansas river, to which we were very near. The range of these hills appears like strips of land variegated white and green—an effect produced by single bushes scattered upon the white sand. Close to these hills an interesting formation of the ground was seen under a remarkable evening light. Small conical hills, overgrown, like the surrounding country, with grass, rose like gigantic mole-hills from the gently undulating plain, casting dark shadows, with the appearance of black spots and stripes. The grass around was of a brilliant green for the time of year—a sign that the neighbourhood of these peculiar elevations, which were perhaps originally merely drift sandhills, must be rich in moisture: the capillary attraction, as I repeatedly observed afterwards, often draws a great quantity of moisture to the surface of the loose sand, especially in hollows amongst sandhills.

In this neighbourhood we first saw some single buffaloes, their numbers increasing as we proceeded. Two days before, I had seen at sunrise, standing out against the rosy hue of the eastern horizon, a large black figure, which fixed my attention until I discovered it to be a stray buffalo, which, for some cause or other, had separated from the herds grazing farther west. We, however, saw no more of these animals until we reached these herds. One evening, as our waggons were driving along in a golden glow, we were suddenly surrounded by small bands of buffaloes, which formed the commencement of a large herd. One of the animals was immediately pursued, and the hunter soon returned to the camp, announcing it to be killed, and asking some of our people to ride back with him and fetch the carcass. Night, however, had meanwhile come on, and the animal could not be found; nevertheless, our desire for buffalo tongue and marrow-bones did not go long unsatisfied, and a few days later several of our people even fell sick from feasting immoderately on the flesh. In the morning, on looking around, the plain was covered with innumerable buffaloes. The herd was immense, but divided into separate bodies. From September 1st to the 8th we journeyed through them incessantly. They spread chiefly along the north bank of the Arkansas, but in some places we saw them also covering the opposite shore. Occasionally crowds of them approached so close to our caravan as to threaten to occasion a disorder, and while the oxen of a train of waggons following our caravan were led to drink, it was difficult to prevent their mixing with the buffaloes. During the night the bellowing of these animals was heard all around our camp, accompanied by the howling of innumerable wolves which always follow buffalo herds, killing the calves, the sick, and old. I do not know whether the buffalo-wolf is a distinct species; those we saw were white and very large. On the 6th, whilst moving along between Pawnee Fork and Coon Creek, the buffalo herds formed a close line at least eight miles long upon the northern heights. Doubtless this herd, which surrounded us for a week whilst travelling, consisted of millions of animals, and formed one body, journeying along in company. I must, with my own eyes, have seen hundreds of thousands. Further on, after passing through this herd, we found the grass of the prairie cropped closely off, to the great inconvenience of our draught animals. The buffaloes had journeyed along, grazing as they went, and for hundreds of miles farther south the carcases of these beasts lay scattered about on the plain in such abundance that not a spot was free from the traces of their bones.

During our journey through this buffalo-herd we were of course never in want of fresh meat. In half an hour, or less, an animal could always be procured; and even after having left that part of the prairie where the buffaloes were grazing, our store of fresh meat held out for another week, as in these high and dry regions, especially at that season, fresh meat keeps good for a long time and is at last dried up by the air without being corrupted. Before our buffalo-meat was exhausted we fell in with herds of antelopes. Further west, immense flocks of ducks covered every pool in the prairie; and on the Rio Grande we found, in addition, geese, cranes, hares, quails, and other small game, so that our table was always well supplied. During the greatest abundance the flesh of calves and young cows was alone deemed good enough, and of many slain animals we ate only the tongues and marrowbones. The liver also of young animals is delicious, and the marrow from the leg-bones is one of the greatest delicacies. If the reader desires a characteristic picture of good living in the prairie, let him imagine a troop of travellers seated round a fire of buffalo-dung, upon which a buffalo marrowbone is being roasted. When it is believed to be sufficiently done, the bone is split open with a hatchet and the marrow taken out in a solid lump. In contrast to these delicacies of the wilderness must be placed the flesh of an old bull, which is almost uneatable, and obstinately resists all attempts of cookery to convert it into anything more digestible than a hank of cord. The scene of a tribe of Indians hunting a herd of buffaloes is exciting and wild enough; many travellers have described this, but I had never an opportunity of witnessing one. Buffalo-hunting was pursued on a small scale by our party—I might say, "*en detail.*" If meat was wanted, a man rode forth into the midst of the herd, with a six-barrelled revolver. The great mass of buffaloes is divided into herds, and these again into bands, each under the guidance of a single bull. The connection of this immense mass is never quite broken up, though the single bands rove about always following their leader independently in a straight line. The hunter selects one of the animals from a troop, and pursues it. Now this part of the herd is set in commotion. All the different troops near immediately begin running in all directions over the plain, always following their leader in a straight line, and leaving their beaten tracks only when compelled to do so; the latter cross each other continually, quite like ordinary footpaths. The issue of the chase depends on the horse and the skill of the rider. The horse is kept on the left side of the buffalo, and the huntsman may approach the animal so closely before firing as almost to touch its shoulder with his pistol.

None but a very unskilful huntsman ever expends his six charges without bringing down the animal. I have never seen resistance on the part of the buffalo, nor any combined defence of an attacked troop. I also observed that the whole herd never took other notice of an enemy in the midst of them than that the nearest bands moved aside. The numerous burrows of the prairie marmot render this chace dangerous, and only a horse accustomed to the ground, especially to buffalo hunting, is recommended to a novice. As I had no such horse, I was prevented taking an active part in the sport. A young man belonging to our caravan, who one day wished to try his luck, rode over a buffalo-calf, and was thrown from his horse, but without incurring any serious injury.

Amongst our muleteers was a Mexican, who had been for about eight years a slave among the Comanches, and went by the name of "Comanche" in the caravan. This man was very skilful in flinging the laso, and caught with it not only several buffalo-calves, but one day a full-grown cow, when, unaided, he threw down the animal and bound its legs. When he announced this feat at the camp I rode back with him to see where the cow lay. After the lad had thrown the laso round the creature's neck, whilst it stood still resisting its efforts, he rode, continuing to hold the cord tightly, several times round it, and in this manner gradually wound the cord around its legs tighter and tighter, till at last he overthrew the animal with a jerk. He then jumped quickly off his horse, and tied the four legs together with the end of the cord. We killed the animal by a single shot, and "Comanche" immediately began to cut as much flesh from the carcass as we thought needed in the camp, without stopping to skin or clean the beast. As the lad was performing his task with incredible agility, cutting off at every incision several pounds of flesh, he presented a most barbaric appearance: man looked like a wild beast in the spectacle before me. The chief part of the carcass was left to the wolves and vultures, which, as soon as we had left, immediately took possession of their booty.

The place where the buffalo-cow was caught and killed was a large burrow of the sociable prairie marmots, which have very incorrectly been called the prairie dogs. On a level spot of ground where all the vegetation is destroyed, and whose clayey surface is as hard as a barn-floor, rise innumerable heaps of earth, each with an opening at the top similar to the crater of a volcano: this is the entrance to the dwelling of a marmot-family. A certain number of such families dig their holes near together, and form what is called a prairie-dog village. In many places these villages occur in such numbers (sometimes with a small space between them, at others nearly touching each other) that they spread over hundreds of square miles. The little creatures allow but scanty vegetation to spring up near them, which often exposes the draught cattle of passing caravans to a dangerous want of fodder. This I met with afterwards further south, upon the road from San Antonio to El Paso, where in many places the grass is scanty enough without this additional cause.

The prairie-marmot has often been described by travellers. The idea that these gnawing animals share their dwellings with owls and rattlesnakes had always appeared to me fabulous, until I saw the fact with my own eyes. Not only is it true, but it invariably is the case, without exception. On approaching a marmot-village, the real possessors and builders of the dwellings are everywhere seen popping their heads with curiosity but cautiously out of their holes, or sitting on the heaps of earth near the opening, and those who are away from their burrows immediately run home. Suddenly a whistling call is heard around, and the animals have all at once disappeared: at the same time little owlets, grey-brown, sprinkled with yellowish-white, with soft noiseless plumage, are seen fluttering about from one hole to another. Many fly in to their four-footed companions, while others alight at the entrance and sit with a demure look as if keeping watch over the dwellings. The little bird, whose body is not larger than a turtle-dove's (its full plumage makes it look much larger), can see perfectly well in broad daylight. It was not till afterwards that I convinced myself of the presence of the third fellow-tenant, nor do I know for a fact whether the rattlesnake is as regular an inhabitant of these marmot-holes as the little owl. I have frequently seen rattlesnakes basking in the sun before the entrances, and coming out of or going into the holes. The manner in which the snake rewards the hospitality shown to it interested me particularly: it takes upon itself the task of freeing its kind host from a too numerous progeny—a fact of which I was convinced by actually finding a young marmot in the stomach of a rattlesnake, inhabiting a marmot-burrow. Whether it does the same with the owlets, or whether these turn their especial attention to the young rattlesnakes, I cannot say.

It is a remarkable fact that the ground-squirrel, which in a part of the State of California lays waste fields and meadows, also shares its subterranean dwellings with owls and rattlesnakes. There I have much oftener remarked the presence of rattlesnakes than among marmots. The owlet is either the same or a nearly-related species of that which lives with the marmots.

During the last three days of August a hot south wind was blowing. In the night of the 1st of September signs of a change in the wind were perceptible: it lightened in the north under a cloudless sky. Towards morning there were broken clouds, and by noon the north wind set in: from that time we had several very cold nights. No dew had fallen during the south wind; but as soon as the north wind set in, the grass was quite wet in the morning, and my feet became dreadfully benumbed with cold during my night-watch: the howling of the wolves also increased. Later on we were repeatedly exposed anew to a hot south wind, which caused illness among our people. I shall have occasion to notice the sudden change from this American sirocco to an icy north wind.

CHAPTER V.

Continuation — The Arkansas — Wolves — A Stampede — Comanches and Kiowas — Visit of Chiefs — Indian Mourning, and Military Decorations — Fort Atkinson — Further Intercourse with the Kiowas — Pillaging Expeditions to Mexico, and Mexican Prisoners — Use of the Spanish Language among the Prairie-Indians — Gradual Destruction of the Character of the Race — Indian Tribes converted into Bands of Robbers — Eastern limit of the Apaches — Indian Rock-tomb — Indian Ideas of a Future Life — Slave Trade among the Indians — Crossing the River — Indian Visits to the Camp — A Step from the Sublime to the Ridiculous.

THE 3rd of September brought us to the bank of the Arkansas, at the spot where it reaches the extreme point of its northern bend. In the evening we encamped a few hundred yards from the river on a green sward of buffalo-grass. The shores of the river are composed of clay, as on the Missouri, the Ohio, and the Mississippi: the surface of the water was at that time from four to six feet below the level of the prairie. The shores are undermined by the water and gradually fall away, whilst on the opposite shore of the river sandbanks are formed. The water is clayey, and the bed is composed of dangerous quicksands, upon which no one can safely stand still long when bathing. At this season the river was fordable at any place. At the foot of the vertical embankments poplars and willows grow here and there. But the prairie extends everywhere to the edge of the embankments, in the sides of which were several wolves'-dens very near to us, from out of which we heard a continual howling and whining of the young cubs. At night the noise and howling of the old and young wolves produced a music quite indescribable:

wolves and buffaloes were continually crossing the river in our neighbourhood. As long as the plain is covered with buffaloes, the wolves are in no want of food, and some generally accompany the herd in their wanderings. We and our animals had nothing to fear from them; but our stock of meat had to be nightly defended by our dog. Enticed by the meat, the wolves, as well as the smaller species, called by the Mexicans the Coyote,[1] approached so near us, that, if the shooting without necessity at night had not been against the rules of travelling, I could every moonlight night have shot one of these animals of prey without rising from my couch. I was told that in Nicaragua the coyotes, when in great numbers, have actually ventured to attack men; but in the prairies I never heard of such an occurrence. Although our mules were in no actual danger from the wolves and coyotes, they were continually disturbed by these nocturnal invaders stealing around us, whose visits may easily be attended by serious consequences.

One night, when encamped on the Arkansas, I was on guard at about a thousand paces from our camp. Near me was a white mule, which always used to graze with its head turned away from the others, and invariably outside the drove of mules, as if it were their sentinel. As I happened to be looking at the animal it suddenly left off grazing, and looked into the darkness in a watchful and wary manner. On a sudden it snorted loudly and made a tremendous bound backwards: the whole drove, consisting of two hundred animals, was simultaneously seized with a like panic, and rushed off at full speed. All this happened so instantaneously, that before I had recovered from my

[1] An Aztec name—*coyotl*.

surprise the sound of their wild flight over the plain was heard receding further and further into the far distance, and I found myself alone in the dark solitude of the prairie. The fires in the camp were extinguished, so that for the moment I knew not whither to turn nor what course to pursue. I soon, however, heard steps close to me, and stumbled upon one of my comrades on guard, then upon a second and a third, until I had rejoined the whole body of sentinels, with the exception of a Mexican lad, whose duty it was to lead the bell-mare. In a short time he also was discovered. He had nearly paid the forfeit of his life for a neglect of duty: in order to be able to sleep whilst on guard, he had tied the cord of the bell-mare round his leg, so that when the drove of mules suddenly ran away, he was dragged along with them for some distance. Fortunately the cord got loose and the lad was left lying on the prairie, the only damage done being tattered clothes and some bruises. Meanwhile the camp was astir; the noise made by the mules running away had been heard by our men—some threw themselves on the saddle-horses, which were always tied up to the waggons, and the pursuit of the run-away animals was commenced: fortunately they had stopped at no great distance, and their flight was easily tracked, from the nature of the soil on the banks of the river. In the course of half an hour they were all safely lodged again in the *corral*.

What Greek herdsmen used to term "panic terrors" is called by the American waggoners a "stampede," and next to a surprise by the Indians, and a fire in the prairie, this is one of the greatest dangers incurred on a caravan journey through a North-American wilderness. Besides the fear, in such an occurrence, of a man's being run over and trampled to death by the whole drove of animals (comparatively a trifling misfortune), should there be Indians in the neighbourhood the whole drove may be lost; and for this reason predatory Indians seek to occasion a "stampede." The loss of the animals generally includes that of the waggons and property and the ruin of the proprietors, not unfrequently attended by the death of some of the party.

The next day, in passing Jackson's Grove, a few poplars and willows growing on the bank of the Arkansas, we perceived on both sides of the river numerous bands of Indians riding toward us. We were here only a day's journey distant from Fort Atkinson, and had hardly cause to fear any attack from the Indians, whose appearance, moreover, was pacific. We found that these people were Comanches, on their journey east to hunt buffaloes. They inquired eagerly after the direction where the buffaloes were to be found, and about their enemies, the Pawnees, of whom they seemed to be in great dread, and on whose hunting-ground they did not venture to enter.

During the summer there had been in the neighbourhood of the Fort an assembly of Indian tribes, numbering altogether several thousand men, for the purpose of receiving the presents of the Government, which are due to them according to treaty. The Government agent for these tribes had not made his appearance as soon as he was expected, and the Indians had threatened to attack the next caravans if the presents did not arrive soon. The young warriors had been clamouring for the immediate commencement of hostilities, and the interference of the older and more sensible chief alone prevented an outbreak. Under these circumstances it was fortunate for us that a short time before our passing this way the presents had arrived, and had given the greatest satisfaction to the

Indians; having, according to the expressions of the chiefs who visited us, exceeded their expectations. The distribution of these gifts is a wise stroke of policy in the Indian department of the government of Washington, as the savages by these means become gradually dependent on the wants of civilized life.

In the afternoon we descried on the opposite side of the river a large Indian encampment of tents, nearly opposite to which we pitched our *corral*; and soon a great number of men and women came riding through the river to visit us.

On this occasion several of the principal chiefs of the northern Comanches honoured us with their presence, all provided with written certificates of their names and character; given them partly by the government agents and partly by some officer of the United States army, who holds the command in these parts. These documents, which they eagerly showed us, are intended as vouchers to travellers for the character of the native chiefs, and present, in fact, a ludicrous reverse of the passport system in the Old World, being at the same time the only passports met with in the United States. The wording of these certificates reads ludicrously enough; take, for instance, the following:—"The possessor of this paper is the *Red Sleeve*, a celebrated chief of the Apaches, who is on friendly terms with the whites. Travellers will do well to show him kindness and respect, but they must at the same time be on their guard." Under this is written the *visa* of travelling traders: "The *Red Sleeve* has visited our camp, and conducted himself, with his followers, respectably." Further on: "Do not trust this fellow—he is a rascally Indian." When such a voucher is presented to you, with that taciturn gravity of which an Indian only is capable, you are obliged to control your features like an Indian, not to betray the humour of the thing,—an indiscretion which might have disagreeable consequences.

On this occasion of the visit of the Comanches to our camp, beside a number of inferior people, the chiefs To-ho-pe-te-ca-ne, or the "*White Tent*," and Way-ya-ba-tosh-a, or the "*White Eagle*," came to pay their respects. These names, and their translation, are copied from the vouchers which these grand personages presented to us. After these came an older man, distinguished as much by his noble mien as his simple dress. The latter consisted merely of a blue woollen blanket wrapped round his body. His hair was cropped short, after the fashion of the whites, and no ornament of any kind was visible. He was accompanied by a Mexican prisoner, who acted as interpreter, and told us that this was the great chief Okh-ákh-tzo-mo, who had come to visit us; and the reason he appeared in this simple dress and with cropped hair was that he was mourning the death of his son, whom the Pawnees had killed, and for whom he had not yet been able to take blood-revenge. The two younger men had appeared in our presence in the full attire of Comanche warriors, clothed in leather, with richly-ornamented mocassins, their faces daubed with red paint, and their heads ornamented with eagle's feathers; their thick and long plaited hair hanging down their backs, loaded with silver plates, growing smaller downward,—in the neck of the size of a saucer, at the end of the plait as large as half a dollar. These silver plates are made in Mexico expressly for the Comanches, and are an important article in the trade with these savages, which is carried on at the Presidio del Norte, at San Carlos, and at the Presidio del Rio Grande. At last an old man came into our camp who wore, over his Indian nether garments made of leather, the blue blanket-coat of a North American from the West. A pair of gilt epaulettes were attached to the coat—one on his breast, the other dangling at his back between his shoulders—by which the old Comanche prince (for such was the rank of our guest) was distinguished. His Indian highness, however, was not too proud, like the other notabilities of his tribe, to present to us a certificate of his character, in the handwriting of the commandant of a neighbouring fort, which stated that its possessor had formerly been one of the most dangerous and cruel enemies of the whites; but that he had latterly altered his disposition, and, from his influence with the Comanche tribes, was entitled to be treated with respect, but at the same time with great precaution. This man shook hands with marked formality with those whom he thought to be the chief among us, and gave us assurances of his friendship. We smoked with him, and treated him with coffee, as we had done with the others. His features were strongly marked,—his brow furrowed with deep wrinkles, his nose large and arched, and over a coffee-coloured face his straight hair hung in numerous plaits, through which glistened the characteristic vacant Indian eye. He had his wife with him, a fat, elderly woman, whose face retained the traces of some beauty, and the type of the better class of Mexican families. This person had probably been stolen in her childhood; she did not dismount, but sat astride upon her horse, like all Indian women, taking no part in our conversation with the old Indian chief. Some young females of the lower class of Indians, however—one a very pretty girl—kept up an animated chat with our drivers, and evidently tried to turn their coquetry to profit.

Amongst the crowd we saw many stolen Mexican boys

and girls, who seemed on the whole to be not badly treated. A light-haired, blue-eyed boy, with a fair complexion, and an open brow, must have come from a German settlement in Western Texas. When addressed in German, however, he did not answer. Another boy told us, in Spanish, that some years since he had been carried off with his sister from Mexico, and that his occupation during his detention consisted in herding his master's horses.

In the evening, before dark, Okh-ákh-tzo-mo exhibited his authority by ordering our Indian visitors to leave the camp and return home. To some, who did not obey immediately, he applied his horsewhip. Our camp was soon deserted, and we could at length enjoy our long-desired repose.

These Comanches belong to the tribe which the Mexicans call *Cibuleros*, that is, Buffalo-hunters (from *Cibulo*, the buffalo); they live almost exclusively on buffalo-meat. They are on good terms with the Kiowas, who had a large encampment above the fort, and some of whom accompanied them on this visit. The language of the two tribes appears to differ entirely, but several of those present could speak both languages.

On September 10th we reached Fort Atkinson. It is a group of adobe buildings, with canvas roofs,—something between a house and a tent. The word "fort," in America, does not always convey the notion of fortifications: the term, here, merely signifies a permanent camp of eighty foot-soldiers; but to all these posts is attached a well-stored magazine where clothing, saddlery, ironmongery, tinware, and provisions may be obtained, from the indispensable flour and bacon up to preserved oysters and champagne. The travelling caravans lay in stores at these stations for their journey. We were, however, so well provided with the chief delicacies, that we had, in these places, to sell—not to buy.

In the Fort I saw an old Kiowa, the ugliest Indian I ever beheld. I can compare the expression of this fellow only to that of an hyæna. But he had a beauty of his own: his mouth was drawn up on one side; one of his eyes was half closed by the drooping eyelid, the other unusually wide open. He had a young Mexican woman with him, whose whole face was daubed with red paint. She begged us to purchase her,—her husband asking only two mules in exchange. He had, probably to enhance her value, expended so much red paint upon her face. It is characteristic of Indian bestiality, that the hind part of the horse which the old brute rode was painted round the root of the tail as carefully as the face of his wife.

We halted a few miles above the Fort, and numbers of the Kiowas visited our camp. One of them was introduced by his Mexican interpreter, as a great "Captain," and he showed considerable pretensions to rank. On our leaving him a short time unnoticed, being otherwise occupied, his interpreter asked, "Why don't your captains speak with him?" We then saluted him with all formality, and he sat down. "Why don't the other white men come and speak with him?" said the interpreter, pointing to our American drivers. "Because they are no captains, but my slaves," replied Mr. Mayer, with admirable presence of mind; and this answer, flattering as it was to the Kiowa chief, had the happiest effect. The man became very conversable,—even cordial. With delight he told us how often he had accompanied predatory expeditions into Mexico—a "*Campaña*," as he expressed it—and how much these enterprizes had brought him. He mentioned several Mexican localities which he had helped to plunder.

"There," said he, "*Caballos, mulas, muchachos, muchachas, —mucho!—bueno!*"—(Horses, mules, boys, girls,—much! —good!) "Here, on the Arkansas, *Nada!*"—nothing. He had three boys with him, two of them his own children, the third stolen from Mexico. The last, however, was treated by him quite as his own children. We gave him some biscuit, which he distributed equally among the three boys.

These people spoke Spanish with tolerable facility, and the interpreter of the Chief appeared to hold merely an office of etiquette. I heard groups of women and children conversing in Spanish.

It is evident that, by naturalizing Mexican prisoners, the Indian race must become gradually effaced. Anglo-American desperadoes of the worst kind, robbers and murderers by profession, join these pillaging hordes, and gain great influence over them; and if this system continues unchecked,—whilst the race changes, but their occupation and mode of life remain the same,—the Indian tribes will gradually be transformed into robber hordes. It is a well-known fact that foreigners of European and semi-European extraction, when naturalized among the Indians of the wilderness, are the worst and most dangerous robbers.

It is very erroneous to imagine that the Indians have a natural and instinctive hatred of the white race. A white man, otherwise qualified, who has a taste to be naturalized among the Indians, is always received by them with welcome, and may attain to high honours in the tribe. But what the Indian hates is civilization, as much in his own race as among the whites. He makes no distinction of race in this respect, as is evident from the fact that there exists no less hostility between the settled and civilized Indians of Mexico and the savage tribes of the wilderness, than between the latter and the civilized whites. Even the Pimas, who dwell on the Gila, and form a valiant vanguard of old Mexican civilization against the Apaches and other plundering tribes of the north and east, speak of the latter in the same terms as civilized people speak of barbarians. "They are savages who do not pursue agriculture." The antagonism, consequently, is not one of race, but of mode of life,—the same which existed between the civilized States of the old Anahuac and the surrounding savages. I shall hereafter revert to this subject when speaking of the Apaches.

These Kiowas were likewise on their way eastward, on an expedition to hunt buffaloes; they eagerly enquired all particulars relative to the hunting-grounds in the east. They had quite as strong an enmity to the Pawnees as the Comanches, but seemed to be less afraid of them. They expressed the same hostility to the Mexican Apaches, whom they mentioned only with abuse.

We met, a few days afterwards, on the other side of the river, a great chieftain of the eastern tribe of the Apaches, in another troop of Kiowas, with whom he seemed to be concerting a pillaging foray. Single tribes of the Apaches, I heard, live as far east as this district—a fact apparently not generally known.

Neither the Comanches nor the Kiowas who visited us accepted brandy; but they drank coffee and tea immoderately, very much sweetened. They eat sugar in large quantities. Our guests were very suspicious; and we were obliged to partake in their presence of everything we offered them, before they touched it. The old Comanche, with his gilt epaulettes, even smoked our tobacco with hesitation, and asked whether there might not be something in it to send him to sleep. Such fears are not unfounded; it is a fact that the whites have attempted to poison whole tribes of Indians, and I have myself often heard the question discussed how this could be effected in the best manner. A story of the designed introduction of the small-pox amongst a remote Indian tribe is current in the west, and I have heard it related with every particular.

Fort Atkinson must be an interesting station for a botanist. The slight variations in height in the soil exhibit a great variety in the character of the vegetation within a very small space. Yellow sunflowers, of various kinds, red Cinnias, blue Delphiniums and Salvias, white-leaved Euphorbias, and innumerable other flowers and herbs show a varied mixture of bright colours in the tall grass. Raised only a little above this flowery meadow, on the banks of the above-described conglomerate, and between detached masses of quartz, jasper, lava, &c., is another world of plants, on a dwarflike scale,—pigmy Asters, with small violet flowers; elegant little mallows, with crimson and vermillion blossoms; low, grey, woolly Artemisias, of an alpine character, with a strong aromatic scent, similar to the *A. muttelina* of the Alps; dwarflike Asclepias; small white Syngenesistæ, with only four marginal blossoms, which look like *Cruciferæ*,—every kind of such plants in miniature, occasionally mixed with a leather-like *Opuntia*, cover the short scanty turf.

In places a gulley has been washed away into the banks of conglomerate, in which gourds creep over the ground, while here and there grows an Archemone, or some other prickly plant, of which I do not know the name, in the crevices and furrows of the marl.

Whilst encamped above the Fort I followed these conglomerate banks in pursuit of a wolf, but without being able to get within shot; he at last disappeared in a cavern among the rocks. As I was examining the entrance of this hole I observed a second opening filled up with loose stones. In removing these I found in the interior, wrapt in a piece of mouldering cloth, a quantity of human bones —part of a skeleton. The skull was in good preservation, and the jaws retained a set of fine white teeth, which, however, easily dropped out. Near these remains I found a leather bag, full of red paint, the tanned hide of a stag, a leather strap, which had evidently been a bridle, and a lump of buffalo-dung. These bones had, no doubt, belonged to the corpse of some Indian, and were here not in their original place of interment. The former grave may have been disturbed, and the friends or members of the tribe have probably collected these remains, and placed them here. The bones were much older than the cloth in which they were wrapt, and evidently the latter had never contained any of the flesh of the body. It consisted of a piece of the canvas which the caravans use for waggon-coverings. The offerings lying near the bones showed the notions which the friends of the deceased entertained of a future life. The dead man, they imagined, will require in another world a leather garment, red paint, to daub himself with, a bridle for his horse, and buffalo-dung to make a fire. The absence of all weapons was remarkable.

On our journey the next day, a Kiowa, riding over the plain, came up to us, his wife and son remaining at a distance, until, seeing there was nothing to fear, he fetched them also. The man and woman had a clever and good-natured physiognomy: they both looked with great interest and evident pleasure on Mrs. M., who, with her husband, rode before me; they then came up to me, inspected my carriage with much curiosity, and asked whether I too had not a wife. On my replying in the negative they offered to fetch me a girl out of their camp; at the same time depicting in a lively manner by signs and words her charms and beauty. At last the man placed the forefinger of one hand on that of the other, adding an expressive "*Bueno!*" (good). "This woman," he said, pointing to his companion, "is a mere common woman"—*mujer car . . . . a*; "the other, young, good—*otra, chiquita, buena!*" So saying he held his fingers pointed before his breast. I replied that we were travelling further without delay, and that I could not wait for the girl; to which he answered that his wife would fetch her, and in two days they would overtake us. On my positively declining the offer they both laughed, and rode off. Probably their intention was to sell me the girl, perhaps a Mexican, whom they had made prisoner. I might doubtless have had her for a few cups of well-sweetened coffee, as companion in our next camp; for these procurers brought us the next evening a woman, richly bedaubed with red paint, who first tried her fortune in vain among the gentlemen of our party, and whom I afterwards saw amongst a group of our drivers by a camp-fire.

From numerous enquiries I made respecting the customs of the Indians, I believe that most of the tribes keep prostitutes on purpose; either prisoners or women whom some peculiar circumstance has reduced to this degraded state. It is these women who are offered to strangers.

On the 12th of September we crossed the Arkansas, the passage being successfully effected in three hours by our whole caravan. The bottom of the river is a quicksand, which is visible in parts above the surface of the water, apparently dry. If a waggon passes quickly over it the wheels rumble as if crossing a rocky path; but if it stops for an instant the ground grows fluid, the wheels sink in, and shortly stand fixed, as if walled in; the skill of the driver, therefore, consists in keeping the waggon in motion at all hazards. Sixteen mules were attached to each of our waggons, and at least four drivers walked by the side of each team to urge on the animals.

We encamped on a low meadow on the other side of the river. The Indians, who during our passage had assembled in great numbers on the shore, accompanied us to our camp, waited until our dinner was prepared, and then offered unceremoniously to share our meal.

Amongst our visitors was a man who introduced himself as a chieftain of rank among the Kiowas. He wore the usual leather dress, with a blue blanket over it, and round his head a red handkerchief twisted in the fashion of a turban, which gave him quite an Asiatic appearance. The thought struck me of offering him a pair of old black trousers and an old silk waistcoat. Another one added a shabby felt hat, and this present was received with a delight which banished from the old man's face that impassive expression which Indian etiquette dictates. He unceremoniously pulled off his dress—by no means valueless—and donned these cast-off clothes. When the old hat had supplanted his red turban, a small looking-glass was added to the present. In this the man gazed at himself for a long time with speechless astonishment, until at last he broke out into the first gentle and then increasingly loud exclamations of "*Bueno!*" In his rapture he wanted to give me in return his whole equipment—leather garment, blanket, bow, quiver, and arrows, a bag embroidered with pearls, the red handkerchief—in short, all he had about him. When I gave him to understand that I did not accept any payment, but had freely made him this present, he extended his arms as if to embrace some huge object, and declared that I was a "Capitan *tan* grande!" (Such a big captain!)

He now ordered all his people present to leave our camp; he himself had had enough, and thought the others might likewise be satisfied. He flung himself on his horse and, without taking leave, rode off, continually looking in the mirror and feeling himself with his hands.

CHAPTER VI.

Continuation — Country between the Arkansas and the Cimarron — Plants and Zones of Vegetation in Miniature — Water for Drinking and Washing — Wild-ducks — A Fugitive Murderer visits our Camp — Deserters from the Western Forts — Nature of the Soil — The Tarantula — Effects of Refraction — Valley of the Cimarron — The River — Electric Phenomena — Thunderstorm — Herds of Antelopes — The Bed of the Cimarron suddenly filled with Water — Passage of the River — Aspect of the Country — Juniper-bushes — Distant Mountains — Curiosity of the Antelopes — The Rabbit's Ears—Fissure in the Lava — The Round Mound — Spurs of the Raton Mountains — Cienagas and Water-fowl — The Canadian — The Cañon of the Ocaté — Waggon Mounds — Salt Lake — Forests — La Mora — Settlements, and Agriculture—A Projected Town — A Day of Rest for Cattle and Men — Watershed between the Mississippi and the Rio Grande.

OUR road now continued in a W.S.W. direction, rising gradually from the river over loose sand, which rendered the journey very fatiguing. The country around presented a desolate aspect, with here and there only a tuft of grass rising from the sand, a cactus, or a sunflower. We gradually approached a layer of firmer ground, a sandy clay, forming a level plateau, and growing a short turf of buffalo-grass. Now and then the latter is broken by a barren spot, or by a group of large-leaved Asclepiæ, white Euphorbiæ, grey Artemisæ, white-blossomed Asters, or by one of the innumerable yellow-flowering plants of the family of *Compositæ*. Most of these plants occur in groups of the same species, according to the peculiarity of the soil on which they grow. There are circular depressions in the ground, which are at times filled with water, the bottom being coated with stiff clay. These depressions are very flat, the water in the middle being rarely two feet deep. All round their edge the ground rises a few feet, until it reaches the surrounding level, and this embankment is surrounded with annular zones of vegetation, in which are seen in successive rows most of the plants that grow on the plain in groups. This phenomenon, therefore, is no doubt attributable to the same causes that regulate the formation of the zones, and arises from the circumstance that the smallest variations of height in the soil cause differently mixed strata and other conditions of moisture to appear on the surface. These are phenomena showing some of the laws which regulate the geographical distribution of plants on the smallest scale, and the shallow basins of water, many being only a few paces in diameter, may be called lakes *en miniature*.

Water is found in this desert—for such indeed the tract between the Arkansas and the Cimarron must be called—in a second form: in irregular holes in the sand, called by the waggoners "sand-pans." The reader may easily conceive that in both these natural reservoirs the fluid is neither very clear nor pure; and I must remark, that in this journey, as well as on my subsequent travels through the interior of the continent, I speak of pure water as of exceptional occurrence. When I use the term *water* it generally designates a brackish mud, and for a long time I have drank water which was not clean enough to wash my face in. On these muddy pools in the desert between the Arkansas and the Cimarron, I saw on this journey the first wild ducks. They increased in numbers as we proceeded westward.

We travelled throughout the night, and the following morning encamped close to a pool of water. The wind blew cold from the north, and one of our drivers was suffering so much from rheumatism as to be quite disabled from service. I advised him to take a bath in the pool, and after this to have himself rubbed hard. The remedy was completely successful. The wind suddenly shifted from the north, and a very close south wind succeeded, the change causing dizziness and vomiting in several of our people. I found throughout the whole journey that a southerly wind invariably produced a disagreeable and often injurious effect on the body. Even north of the Arkansas, during such a warm wind, one of our drivers, a tall and strong-built blue-eyed Kentuckian, fell senseless and in convulsions on the ground as I was walking by his side and speaking with him. I bled him, by which he recovered.

Whilst encamped by this pool we saw a single horseman come up to us across the plain; he dismounted and claimed hospitality. During his stay he confided to us the fact that he had shot a man in New Mexico, and had, in consequence, been obliged to fly. It requires desperate resolution to travel from New Mexico to Missouri alone; this man, however, had a horse and a gun. We repeatedly met, at different points of our journey, deserters from the forts of New Mexico, who had travelled on foot for many hundred miles over the wilderness alone and unarmed. Some of them had subsisted for weeks together on locusts, lizards and frogs, before we supplied them with provisions.

The further we advanced the more sterile the plateau became and the harder the soil, which, as far as the eye reached, presented a perfectly level plain. Proceeding over a tract of loose sand, we came to Sand Creek, the bed of which was dry, and on the further side the soil was again hard and level. The stratum of hard clay always lies above the loose sand.

Here I saw, for the first time, one of those large hairy spiders called *tarantula* by the Mexicans, but differing from the European tarantula. They are found in the deserts and steppes from the Arkansas to California, as well as throughout a great part of Mexico; and this insect, the very sight of which creates a disagreeable feeling, is with reason more feared than the rattlesnake. Its bite is perhaps less immediately dangerous, but its consequences are far more difficult of cure than those of the bite of the rattlesnake. During my travels in North America persons of my party were, on two occasions, bitten by rattlesnakes; in both cases they drank brandy in large quantities as an antidote, and the danger passed without any subsequent inconvenience. One of our drivers, on the contrary, told me that his brother had lost an eye from the bite of a tarantula near the temple, and had subsequently become idiotic.

On the third day of our journey through the desert, towards evening, the refraction raised into the air, above the horizon, the picture of the heights on the other side of the Cimarron. This effect of the unequally-heated strata of air often produces strange phenomena on these plains. Objects which appear on the horizon are lengthened out to a gigantic size, and a buffalo-herd on the Arkansas looked like a group of trees.

Soon after, we had in reality a view of the valley of the Cimarron. With the green pasture, but without either tree or shrub, enclosed on both sides by banks of sandstone and conglomerate, this slight depression presented a true oasis in the desert, between the greyish-brown barren heights of the plateau on either side. But the oasis itself is here only a milder form of desert nature. The river—if I may call it so—formed at the point where we reached it a small stagnant and brackish brook, running amongst reeds and rushes. On its bank, however, we found some springs of sweet water, the so-named "Lower Springs," near which we halted.

In the evening the lightning played all around, and heavy clouds promised rain; but only a few drops fell. As I was standing on guard, between nine and eleven o'clock, I saw a waving light over the heights on the north side of the valley: its motion resembled that of the fluctuating reflections of the Fata Morgana, under a gentle agitation of the air. Two bright points suddenly appeared, like rising stars, but soon vanished again. This light I observed for above half an hour. During the whole time the sky was clouded, and there is no doubt that this luminous phenomenon was seated within the stratum of air immediately above the ground.

On the north side of the river the road runs along it — one while through the valley, at another ascending to the plateau over banks of sand and conglomerate. Small semi-spherical cacti grew at the top upon the hard clay soil, while here and there small patches of grass, of different species, covered the ground. In the distance we saw hills of drift-sand, the forms of which recalled those of the snow on Alpine summits heaped up by the wind. When at the bottom we again came upon the river: nothing was to be seen of it but a few saltwater-pools between drift-sand and scattered reeds. In some places there was hardly any river's bed perceptible: the drift-sand had filled it up, and salt-grass or reeds had overgrown it. It looked as if no water had flowed here for years, and this may perhaps have been the case. The sand was covered with salts, which, to judge from the taste, consisted of a mixture of common salt and sulphate of magnesia.

On the 17th of September we neared the "Middle Springs" at nightfall, as a storm was approaching, and at ten o'clock we reached the spot for our encampment just as it began. It was a wild scene—the drivers bringing up the waggons to form the *corral*—the unyoking and collecting the animals in the pitch darkness, and amid thunder and lightning.

Scarcely was this business finished when the most fearful hurricane came sweeping from the north that I have ever witnessed in the North-American steppes. The violence of the wind, which shook even the heaviest waggons, baffled attempts to seek protection from clothing, and a doubled woollen coat of the thickest cloth, together with two blankets, in which I wrapped myself, were penetrated by the cold wind as if it was thin muslin. The mules trembled and crowded together, seeking shelter behind anything; and whilst I was standing on guard one or other of these animals was constantly pressing against me, on the lee side, as a kind of shelter against the wind. At the same time the wind swept along mingled rain and snow, and the darkness was so great that we were knocking against carriages and animals without being able to see them. After two hours I left my post on guard, stiff with cold and wet through, and in this state I was obliged to pass the night, finding shelter only in our travelling-carriage. From my own experience as well as the example of others I have convinced myself that there exist in civilized life the most ridiculous prejudices as to what man can bear without injury to his health.

The climate of the country around the Cimarron is in bad repute: it was here that, a few years ago, more than a hundred mules perished in one night from cold, belonging to Mr. Speier, a well-known trader to Santa-Fé and Chihuahua. Their scattered bones are still to be seen.

The middle springs are clear sources on the north side

of the river, in a little rocky valley, enclosed by banks of sandstone and conglomerate. Further up the character of the principal valley improves: the soil, although sandy, becomes firmer, and is more overgrown with grass. At a distance, toward the west, are seen the first mountains—high table-lands, completely level at the top—and toward the south several side-valleys branch off from the chief one.

On the 20th the caravan was delayed by a team becoming restive and breaking the axletree of a waggon, just as at nightfall we were about to pass the dry bed of the Cimarron to encamp on the other side. We remained on the north side. The next morning, at daybreak, the bed of the river was filled with a deep and rapid stream, which rendered its passage impossible: here we halted two days, to await the subsidence of the water. After it had fallen a little we found, on the third day, a spot where a passage was practicable, and reached the other bank safely. Probably, during the last hurricane from the north, there had been a heavy fall of snow in the Raton mountains, and the sudden melting of the snows during the south wind had afterwards caused the sudden filling of the bed of the river; for this took place in the most beautiful weather and with a cloudless sky.

In this part of the country our sportsmen shot the first antelopes. I had already seen two of these animals at a distance when we first reached the Arkansas. They are indeed rarely seen so far east: here they were more frequently seen, and in herds of twenty to thirty.

From the banks of the Cimarron, which we left on the 23rd of September, the general level of the country rises much more steeply than hitherto. We had travelled from Independence to Council Grove, at a mean elevation of about 1100 feet above the level of the sea. This elevation in our route west had increased to 1500 feet: we had crossed the Arkansas at about 2700, and the Cimarron at 3800 feet. The continuation of our journey now led us rapidly to a table-land of 5000 to 6000, and nearly 7000 feet. These latter heights, it must be observed, were of the general level of the country, although at the foot of the mountains of New Mexico.

On the first day's journey on the south side of the Cimarron we reached the neighbourhood of the so-called "Upper Springs." Here, where the sandstone of the Jura-formation commences with towering masses of rock, the country increases in interest. I ascended to the rocky summit over the first rising ground, on the right of the road. On the highest point I found clear water in the little hollows of the rocks. In different places were breastworks, built of stones—probably Indian places of ambush. I had a wide view over the country: overhead was a cloudless sky; distant unknown sounds reached my ear; high in the air passed a flock of cranes in a wedge-like double line—an appearance we saw more frequently as we advanced westwards.

The Upper Springs are a spot, not without the peculiar charms of the wilderness. Between naked sandstone rocks, on which is merely a scanty growth of yucca bushes, lies a small valley of meadow-land, with a group of poplars on a brook which further down is dried up again. Through the opening of the valley the view extends down to the level of the prairie, which reaches to the distant eastern horizon, and has the appearance of the ocean. Here we halted to take our noon-day dinner. On starting again we had towards evening one of the most interesting landscape scenes at the side of our road. Over the valley of the upper Cimarron, shut in by terraces of rock, the view stretched to the opposite plateau, the declivities of which were everywhere overbrowed by rocks. In the north-west it is divided into several distinct plateaus, tables, square chests, and blocks, the surfaces of which form one horizontal line. Above these rise, at a greater distance, single domes,—evidently volcanic cones, similar to those which, a few days' journey further south-west, we passed on our road. The whole scene, with its red-brown, black-brown, yellow-brown, violet and blue tints, produced the most peculiar impression.

At the Cedar Spring, where the first bushes of the juniper-cedar, with scented wood, begin, appeared in the distance west-north-west the tops of the Raton mountains; and in the direction of west-south-west the domes of Rabbit's Ears and Round Mound. We came to a small hollow, where, on the dry bed of a brook, a few scantily-growing vines intertwined between young willows and poplars.

I had gone in advance of the caravan, and was examining some small plants on the ground on the other side of the height, when I heard a noise behind me, and looking round I saw—at a distance of five or six paces—two antelopes, which eyed me attentively; but before I could snatch up my gun which lay by my side, and prepare for a shot, these nimble creatures were off, flying over the ground like a shadow. It is well known that the antelope is equally curious and timid: the first of these qualities is taken advantage of by sportsmen; they wave a red cloth tied to the end of the barrel, and frequently succeed thus in enticing one of these animals within shot-range.

The Rabbit's Ears, two trap domes, rising from the same basis, we left lying beyond a deep fissure, which, for many miles, passes through the entire thickness of the trap lava down to the underlying sandstone. Without perceiving this cleft, over the edges of which only the top of a few juniper-trees were seen, I rode straight toward the foot of the two domes—a general uprising of the prairie—until I saw at my feet the deep chasm in the rock, which cuts off all communication with the other side. This fissure proves that the rise of the ground, which forms the basis of the two cones, has been caused by upheaval. The cones may have arisen in part (as is evidently the case with Round Mound) from the heaping up of thrown-out masses, and at the same time streams of lava have overflowed the country around the point of eruption.

We drove along the cleft for some distance, until it wore away and allowed us to cross to the other side. Here the ground was again higher, and we proceeded toward Round Mount—another trap dome—which I ascended, whilst the caravan encamped at its foot. The mountain stands on a bladder-like rising of the ground (similar to the base of Rabbit's Ears), whose upraising has caused another similar fissure. I could only see this latter from the top of the mount, at a distance. The base is all around strewn with red and brown scoria and small ejected pieces of lava and half-melted sandstone: it rises to a height of about eight hundred feet above the plain, consisting of strata of lava overlaying one another. The rocks of the summit were clothed with a thick covering of yellow lichens: on its sides I found a pretty little Liliacea, and the first specimen of the *Opuntia arborescens*, a plant which in the north of Mexico is one of the natural features of the country. A small alpine-looking Artemisia, with grey felt-like leaves and of an exceedingly aromatic scent, formed great part of the vegetation on this cone: the grass of the prairie grew up the sides and to the top of the mountain. Here I was rewarded by a grand view. To the north-west rose the flat but regular cone of Fisher's Peak—an old volcano, with small truncated cones in the plain at its foot, whilst behind them the snow-capped summits of the Rocky Mountains appeared. The eastern chain of this great range of mountains reaches its southern extremity in these parts, and the road to Santa Fé runs around it. A line of black stripes extended parallel to the horizon, through the plain at the foot of the small hills. I suspected these stripes to be the brows of the abrupt edges of flat masses of lava, which lie at a small elevation above the level of the plain.

The continuation of the road, after crossing several small valleys, leads round the rocky extremities of the Raton Mountains and its spurs—rows of naked cones on the plateau, with rampart-like contreforts. These spurs radiate from a centre, and in the space between these radii the prairie rises in angular sections. Fragments of sandstone and trap, the former often with marks of the influence of heat, lay strewn on the road. We passed in the dark the "Point of Rocks," the extreme spur of this mountain-group. The specimens which I picked up on the road in the dark proved the next morning to be a dioritic trap.

At this place the road passes over a flat elevation of the plateau, not less than 6500 feet above the level of the sea. Thence, as far as the Canadian or False Red River, it again sinks for about 900 feet. On the summit we found small shallow lakes—*cienagas*—surrounded by a green border of reeds: they were covered with flocks of geese, ducks, and water-hens.

On the 30th we passed the Canadian River, which flows rapidly over a bed of sandstone. It issues from the high mountains, the valleys of which were opening towards us. Some Anglo-Americans are said to have settled there, attracted by the advantageous nature of the country. Below us the river falls into a hollow—*cañada* —into which, also, the fissure of the Ocaté opens.

We travelled round this deep and narrow cleft (Cañon del Ocaté) at its head. The view down into this chasm, locked in by perpendicular sandstone walls, is exceedingly wild. The edge is bordered by pine trees, and pines stretch forth their heads from out the depth of the abyss. In the middle of a barren and level plain is this precipice, which leads down into a deep wilderness hidden from sight,—one of the most fearful scenes I have ever witnessed.

The "Waggon Mounds," which the road passes further on, are pointed summits of trap. The rock is the same as that of the Rabbit's Ears and Round Mount; but it presents here, as in numerous rocky points, fissures and precipitous declivities of the surrounding country, an almost columnar formation — and thus approaches the character of a real basalt. The traveller first climbs over limestone, over which the trap has poured. In the lowest stratum, in contact with the limestone, it has a schisteous character: towards the top it becomes massy, and irregularly burst and cleft. Red and brown scoriæ lie here and there on the surface of the declivity.

Before reaching the foot of the mountain, a semicircle of the plateau, closed in by the steep declivity of the higher *mesa* [1] or terrace covered with the trap lava, is seen to the right of the road. This amphitheatre contains a salt lake, in the shape of a crescent, its convex side following the course of the rocky acclivity. The efflorescence of this lake, which covers the soil with a white deposit, appears chiefly to consist of soda.

---

[1] *Mesas*, i. e. tables: the mountain plateaus and terraces that are so frequent in Mexico are so called in Spanish.

South of the principal summit extends a line of trap-rocks with pointed and columnar tops, rendering still more gloomy the wild character of the adjacent country, which is intersected by the rocky hollows of the Canadian River which are covered with pine forest.

Passing over a high vaulted limestone plateau, intersected by the sandstone valleys of Wolf Creek and Duck Creek, we descended into the valley of the Mora, a small river, on which, higher up, at the foot of the mountain-range, lies the small New Mexican town of the same name. Immediately below, in the valley, are the first New Mexican settlements—the house of Mr. Waters—and further below Barclay's Fort, a fortified private dwelling, occupied by that gentleman and his New Mexican servants.

On the road from the Waggon Mounds to this spot are seen, to the right, the first heights covered with forest (pines); whilst to the left the view extends into the wooded lateral hollows of the Canadian. Here and there the road itself touches the forest—the first met with from the Missouri frontier to this place. The road, in this region, runs over a terrace, above which the mountains rise in the west, whilst in the east the above-mentioned defiles intersect it, and thus form the transition to the lower country.

The Anglo-Americans call the little river whose valley we here reached, as well as the little town, "Moro,"—probably from the word "moor." But the name is Mora, a word which signifies a mulberry, or the mulberry-tree.[1] Near the house of Mr. Waters, which, being the first dwelling of civilized man after a wilderness of many hundred miles, deserves mention, two small rivers meet, one of which

[1] In the same manner the tops of the mountain-chain that rises behind this little town should be called the *Mora* Peaks, and *not* the *Moro* Peaks.

is *the* Mora—properly so called; the other a tributary of it. From this circumstance the place is called the "Junta," or the Confluence. The country around this spot and up the two small rivers forms a splendid plain surrounded by mountains, and covered partly with natural pasture and partly with fields of maize. It belongs to a company, who propose to found here a town, for which the locality is especially adapted. Insecurity from the marauding Indians is perhaps the only obstacle opposed to the success of such an enterprize. About a mile above the Junta stands Barclay's Fort, on the Mora, a quadrangle of buildings surrounded by a wall, and provided with two cannon. I have before mentioned that this is simply a private dwelling. Such names as Barclay's Fort, Bent's Fort, Layton's Fort, often give erroneous notions to European geographers: these spots are merely fortified private establishments.

From the Junta downward the little river Mora, after leaving the plain, enters a wooded valley partly enclosed by rocks, which lower down deepens and narrows into a hollow, conducting the clear water of the Mora to the Canadian River.

We rested here a whole day for the sake of our mules, and bought for them some maize for fodder, which they greatly needed after their hard toil and the poor food of the withered winter grass. Nevertheless, we had not hitherto lost a single animal of our drove. Our people too gave themselves up to enjoyment, after their fashion; some got intoxicated, and began quarrelling; others disappeared from the camp, and did not return till the next morning,—when I heard that this frontier locality, but just reclaimed from a perfect desert, was inhabited by a number of Mexican girls, who make a trade of selling their favours to passing travellers. Small cottages, situated here and there in some corner, are the dwellings of these girls. I was told that even larger establishments, devoted to this traffic, are connected with certain settlements in this part of the country. Thus here, on the western edge of the great North American desert, are found the counterpart of African caravan-stations.

On the other hand, it was pleasing to see here the beginnings of a sound culture, and to witness the courage with which this has been attempted. The new works of irrigation, for which the river has been used (throughout New Mexico the basis of all agriculture), and the maize-fields and plantations of other vegetables, produced an agreeable impression. No one who has not experienced this can, perhaps, quite understand the charm that attaches to any spot where human effort is perceptible after a long residence in a perfect wilderness.

The buildings of this infant settlement are erected of *adobes*, with flat roofs, in the Mexican fashion, which carries one—although in a territory of the United States—quite into another world. Indeed, the whole of New Mexico has, and will retain, a character quite foreign to the spirit of the United States.

On the 5th of October we arrived at Las Vegas, a miserable place in a valley running north and south, at the foot of the sandstone mountain mentioned in the preceding chapter. The valley lies at an elevation of 6000 to 7000 feet above the sea. Wheat and maize are grown here. The inhabitants of Las Vegas are a miserable population of New Mexicans; amongst them have settled some Anglo-American retail dealers, innkeepers, and speculators, who inhabit the less miserable dwellings. The buildings are all constructed of adobes, mostly consisting of a single room, and furnished with a small hole for a window. Upon the mud walls unhewn rafters are laid, which are covered with clay, forming a flat-roof. If the little window-aperture is closed with a plate of gypsum, this is a domestic luxury of very rare occurrence. It is difficult to picture to oneself the wretched appearance of such a New Mexican frontier town. When, in addition to all this, an isolation from the world greater than that upon any of the larger islands in the Pacific, and the constant insecurity of life and property from wild Indians is considered, the reader may imagine the life of a man who has been accustomed to civilization. Nevertheless, its position on the Santa Fé road offers great advantages, which some foreigners settled here have turned to advantage. A German resident has grown rich here, leaving at his death a considerable fortune, which gave rise to a lawsuit respecting the inheritance.

After travelling about fifteen miles further, passing through the above-mentioned rocky pass of the sandstone range, we arrived at its western side, and there encamped for the night in a valley, without water, between sandstone mountains, and overgrown with pines and juniper trees.

CHAPTER VII.

Continuation — Journey along the Edge of the Plateau on the Eastern Side of the Rio Grande — The Upper Pecos Valleys — Character of the Country — Breeding of Sheep — Caravan Law — Mexicans in Service of Anglo-American Masters — Anton Chico — Cañon Blanco — Cold Nights — Singular Hospitality and Corresponding Reward — Plateau of Manzanas — Landscape Scenery — Ruins and Mountain-Pass of Cuarrá — Larks, Magpies, and Daisies in New Mexico — Descent into the Valley — Steep Alluvial Terraces — Vegetation — Volcanic Hills in the Valley — View from the Summit — Tree Vegetation near the River — Water-fowl — La Joyita.

THE country on the Upper Pecos, which we had entered through the defile of Las Vegas, is a succession of wide and narrow clefts and valleys, between table-shaped sandstone mountains which they encompass, and larger mountain plateaus, which these valleys intersect, from the strata of the Jurassic formation down to that of the new red sandstone. A thin forest of pines and juniper trees, with an underwood of dwarf oaks, spreads over hill and valley, here and there interrupted by pasture-land, whilst there is occasionally seen on the sandy or stony soil, amongst trees and bushes, a low *Yucca*, a small *Opuntia arborescens*, a white-flowering Aster, a delicate crimson Phlox, or some other plant flowering in that season.

A considerable breeding of sheep is carried on in this part of New Mexico, as well as in other sections of the territory; and we met, in these deserts, large flocks of sheep, under the care of shepherds, armed with bow and arrow. They are driven for the night into sheep-folds, to protect them against the wolves; but whenever the Indians have an appetite for roast mutton, flocks and shepherds are pretty much at their mercy. We paid a dollar a-piece for some sheep purchased for our caravan. The breed is a small one. I do not venture to judge of the value of the wool, but the meat has an excellent flavour.

There had been a storm and rain during one of the nights we spent in this part of the country, and at daybreak the guard mentioned that a valuable horse had disappeared from the *corral*, and that at the same time one of our Mexican muleteers was missing who, probably, had decamped with the animal. The recent rain enabled us to track and follow him. Arrangements were made for the pursuit of the deserter, who, as we discovered on a closer examination, had also broken open the boxes of some of his companions, and taken part of their contents. The nearest human dwellings were distant about a day's journey, with the little village of Anton Chico not far off: but the thief, in order to secure himself and his booty, had taken the road to Las Vegas; and here we recovered our horse the next day, although nearly destroyed by an incessant gallop of forty to fifty miles. We could not catch the thief: he had sold the animal, which was worth several hundred dollars, for five dollars and a blanket.

Whilst we were busied with the pursuit of the thief the attention of the party was drawn to a Mexican lad, one of our muleteers,—the same who, at the nocturnal "stampede" on the Arkansas, had been dragged along. We thought it probable that the theft might have been committed whilst he was on guard at the *corral;* and, according to the mode of dealing practised toward Mexicans by the Anglo-Americans, this suspicion was sufficient to justify inquisitorial violence. My heart revolted at the sight of the boy tied to a waggon-wheel: it was out of my power to interfere, and when a stout American driver advanced with a heavy mule-whip, I stepped aside to avoid witnessing any further proceedings. I, however, heard the lad called upon to confess, and his repeated assertion of his innocence. Then the lash descended—"For the love of God, sir, do not beat me!"—"Speak! confess!" —A second time the whip descended.—"For the sake of your mother's life, sir, do not strike me!"—"Speak! confess!"—A third stroke followed.—"For the sake of the beautiful eyes of your wife! Stop! I will confess." The lad now confessed that the thief had threatened him with death should he betray him; that hereupon he had let the horse pass out, and the thief ride off while he was on guard, without raising an alarm; but that he knew nothing more, and was no further implicated in the theft.

Such occurrences frequently happen in the North American trading-caravans, in whose service Mexicans are engaged; and these people are, indeed, under the Anglo-Americans in a position quite unprotected by law. The conductors of the caravans subject them to penal discipline, which is allowed neither by the laws of the United States nor by those of the Mexican Republic; for in Mexico, the law gives the master no right to the corporal chastisement of his peons. The Mexican victim of Anglo-American violence there has, commonly, no legal protection: the most distant attempt to deal with an Anglo-American, who has hired himself out as a labourer, as is so frequently done with Mexicans on the journey and in the frontier places, would doubtless result in the instant death of any one who should venture the attempt; and not until the Mexicans, in their intercourse with Anglo-American masters, venture their lives in resisting attempts against their honour and liberty, in the same decided manner, will they be secure from such treatment. He who can assert his rights will always be treated by the Anglo-Americans with consideration; but woe to the weak who are unable to defend themselves! The general consent of public opinion in the United States, adjudges the rights of man to him only who has the power to assert them. Whatever laudable qualities the Anglo-American may possess, he wants one of the essential graces of man —generosity of the strong toward the weak;—no observant person can regard the gallantry shown to ladies in the United States in this light, inasmuch as, if for no other reason, the female sex has here assumed the position of the stronger part, on account of the smaller number in which it exists at the beginning in every colony.

Anton Chico is a small place of wretched appearance resembling Las Vegas; but which has a still more death-like aspect from its distance from the high-road. The stony heights of the surrounding country, dotted here and there with single juniper-bushes, impart to it a desolate and gloomy character; and the dilapidated mud-walls, against which, wrapt in his old shabby *serape,* a man is occasionally seen leaning, to thaw his stiffened limbs in the sun, with groups of women and children seated on the ground, all present a concentrated picture of North Mexican misery.

Half a mile below this spot, our caravan crossed the Pecos, a small muddy river, on the other side of which the road ascends from the sandstone soil of the valley to a flat limestone hill, upon which we found a little rain-water in the hollows of the rocks. Pines, juniper-trees, and dwarf-oaks, covered the country in a park-like appearance. Stretching toward W.N.W., a dry rocky valley, called the Cañon Blanco, or White Defile, passes from the Pecos Valley through the plateau of white sandstone of the Jura formation, which separates the Pecos from the Rio Grande. The road from Anton Chico to Albuquerque, by Galisteo, leads through it; and we took this road with the intention of turning, after a time, on to the plateau in a southerly direction. The valley forms an open forest of pines and juniper-trees, between sandstone rocks. We were obliged to encamp here for the night, unable to find water for our animals; even the quantity reserved for ourselves only sufficed to cook our coffee.

From Anton Chico a man had followed us on foot, who now approached our camp-fires and begged permission to pass the night under our protection, being afraid of lighting a fire for himself alone in the wilderness. The night was very cold, and this fellow had scarcely sufficient clothing to cover himself. Objections were raised in our camp against admitting this stranger: he might be associated with some band of robbers, and engaged in plundering our caravan, or, at all events, he might run off in the night with one of our animals. In order, therefore, to afford protection to this man, and guard at the same time our own safety, we required that he should let himself be tied to a waggon-wheel for the night: to this he assented. Our Mexicans brought a cord, and, with all kinds of good-humoured bantering, they tied their countryman fast. The prisoner was of course allowed all sufficient comforts for his night's rest. They prepared him a warm bed close to the wheel, brought him tortillas, frijoles, and coffee, wrapped him in a blanket, and then left him till the morning, when he was released.

Whatever the man may have thought of this hospitality, he did not show himself again the following day, and our generosity was not appealed to a second time. We halted the next night on a prairie, with juniper-trees growing here and there. As I was standing in the moonlight guarding the herd and leaning on my gun, a shot suddenly fell in the camp, and I heard the cry of "Thief! thief!" A pursuit was at once made in the surrounding underwood, and several shots were fired; but neither the report of the guns nor the pursuit was successful. A pair of boots had been stolen from the bedside of one of our drivers, which in the morning were found not far off in the grass. All were of opinion that the thief had been no other than our guest of the preceding night. I cannot decide whether gratitude for the hospitality shown him had urged him, or whether he followed us, as our people said, from Chico to this place—seventy to eighty miles through the wilderness—with the design of stealing the boots.

The Cañon Blanco contracts westward to a narrower defile, called the Cañon del Toro, through which the road runs to Galisteo and Albuquerque. Here we turned southward on to a plateau of easy ascent: at the top all tree vegetation suddenly vanished. From a level prairie the view extended down upon the wooded valleys of the Pecos and into a deep country encompassed with red sandstone rocks, and belonging to the Rio Grande, whilst at a distance, behind the neighbourhood of Santa Fé, rose the snow-capped peaks of the mountains of Mora and Taos.

We rested for the night near a small lake, with pretty good water. The air was so cold, that in the morning my blanket was covered with hoar-frost and my beard was frozen.

The plateau between the Pecos and the Rio Grande, which we now traversed, is bordered on the west, along the Rio Grande, by a line of isolated mountain groups of interesting Alpine forms, between which defiles lead down into the valley. They are the Placer Mountains, Sandilla Mountains, Manzana Mountains, and other groups whose names I did not learn. These groups are surrounded at their base with woods of juniper-trees. At distances the rocks rise out of the plain, like steep cliffs out of the sea. On the other side rugged declivities descend into deeper valleys, which I shall describe further on.

Our journey across this plateau, which I may call the Plateau of Manzanas, took a southerly direction slightly deviating to the west. For some distance we proceeded along the above-mentioned groups of mountains, until we at last turned down into the valley of the Rio Grande, through the Pass of Cuarrá. From the Cañon Blanco we had pursued an untrodden route across the prairie, with scarcely any waggon-track until we came to a road which, leaving Chilili, Manzanas, and other small places at the foot of the mountains on the right, leads from Galisteo to Cuarrá, and, under the Spanish rule, probably led further south to the mysterious Gran Quivira. Those places appeared situated in a pleasant and sheltered position, between the wooded spurs of the mountains, and on clear brooks, which, however, soon disappear in the prairie. The latter is highest in the north, on the Cañon Blanco; it declines to the south, and the road then passes from the Jura formation to the new red sandstone. Loose sand appears, covered here and there with saline efflorescence, and grey Chenopodiaceæ, together with succulent kali plants, succeed in patches.

The road led past a deep round hole in the sandy clay, which was filled with a muddy brackish and stinking water. Further on we came to the Ojo de Verendo—the "Spring of the Antelopes"—a source of clear and wholesome water, rising at the foot of a limestone bank that covers the sand: it collects into a little basin at the side. This stratum of limestone extends from the base of the Manzana

Mountain to this spot, where it terminates.* A little further south we found a similar spring, with a basin just like the former: here we rested, and I bagged a dish of snipes for our table; but in vain endeavoured to secure a large ibis-like bird which kept alighting here and there on the edge of this little lake. This bird was white, with black wings and a long curved beak: it had the flight and cry of the curlew.

To the east of our road we saw, stretching in the distance, a sandy acclivity, which, heightened by refraction, presented striking pictures of high rocky walls. A salt lake lies in this direction, probably at the foot of this ascent, into which, at certain times, flow the waters of the brooks of Chilili, Manzanas, and Cuarrá. Toward evening, when the effects of the refraction had disappeared, the effects of sunset gave a magic charm even to this desert. Under the crimson sky towards the east, the heights of the above-mentioned acclivity were grouped in picturesque forms, and hues of red, lilac, and blue cast over them; nearer the foreground, brown, green and yellow stripes intermingled in the plain; whilst in the immediate neighbourhood, the prairie, with dark yucca-bushes scattered here and there, presented the appearance of a carpet with a graceful pattern.

We rode through the Manzanas river, over glittering masses of micaceous slate; and, judging by the detached blocks and the width of its bed, now almost dry, it must at times have a large mass of water. The road soon after led into an ascending valley between sandstone mountains, which, projecting eastwards, rise above the level plain. The mountains appeared to form a jagged part of the summit of the plateau itself. A few large-leaved poplars were growing by the side of a clear brook, descending into the valley with a steep fall. Then succeeded fields of maize, in which the people were busied with the harvest; and suddenly there stood before me some old and high walls of brown sandstone, in the middle of a valley, between high poplars and pines, with a wooded mountain in the background. These were the ruins of Cuarrá, which have without doubt a Christian origin, although, like many others in New Mexico, they have been attributed to the Indians. They consist of the walls of a church, built of sandstone without mortar. The builders were doubtless Indians, but the architect, some missionary, must have had a Byzantine type in his mind when designing the building. The ruin has but little historic interest. Very probably the church, together with the other buildings of a flourishing mission, the walls of which still exist, was destroyed in the great rising of the Indians, when the Spaniards, after their first settlement in New Mexico, were driven out of the country, and had to conquer it a second time. At no great distance from Cuarrá are the ruins of Avó; said to be still larger than those of Cuarrá, and doubtless connected with the same history.

The site of Cuarrá is remarkable: we seem transplanted into a mountainous corner of Germany, with the ruins of some old robber-castle; until, on closer examination, we are reminded of being in the land of the Cactus and of the Indians, and that the building was no castle, but a church.

Cuarrá has the rank of an Indian *pueblo*, but the number of the inhabitants is limited to a few families, who have used the old ruins as their dwelling. The *pueblo* erected on the ruins, after the destruction of the mission, has evidently never had many inhabitants, otherwise there must have been remains of a second period. The present tenants cultivate a few fields of maize and gourds, and keep a few domestic animals. I had great difficulty in procuring half a dozen eggs.

From this point the road runs through a wooded valley, between high mountains of sandstone which in the distance are surmounted by still loftier heights of limestone, while a base of deeper limestone is underlying them. At the entrance of this valley the landscape is completely changed. In parts, we passed through a forest of lofty pines; in others, through a scattered wood of pines and juniper-trees. The latter has often a very picturesque growth. Like other species of the *Juniperus* and certain *Taxodiæ*, the juniper of this region shows a remarkable variety of character in its form and growth, according to age and *habitat*. The cypress remains, however, the fundamental type of its physiogonomy. But the reader must not think of the stiff-twisted forms of the *Juniperus Virginiana*, which disfigure so many a landscape in the United States. Red sandstone rocks rise above this wood, in part presenting the appearance of walls with battlements and loopholes. In riding for a whole day uninterruptedly, down a steep road, we were able to form an idea of the great height of this plateau, at its highest point little under 7000 feet.[1] Upon a kind of side terrace of the declivity, where the sandstone rests upon the limestone, we came to the sources of a saltish and alkaline brook, running for some distance through the grass, from one hole to another, until it falls westwards into a deep and narrow cleft, and through the latter finds its way down into the valley of the Rio Grande. The limestone rocks of this gorge show in several places the entrances to caverns. The brook itself is called "*Salado*"

[1] There no doubt exist measurements of the altitude of Manzanas and Cuarrá, as some officers of the United States have made surveys of this part of the country. They are, however, unknown to me. The Rio Grande, in this section, is 4800 feet above the level of the sea.

(the Saltish), designating the quality of its waters. Whilst roaming about near our camp, I was surprised by the chattering of a magpie in a tree: the bird was marked just like the European magpie, but was rather smaller. It is interesting how a trifle of this kind may affect the traveller, and transport him back to his distant home. I also met with a lark, whose notes somewhat reminded me of the European skylark. A bird's note gives indications of its genus and family, whichremain the same in remote countries, so that the bird can be recognised by a careful observer at a distance.[1] The same must be said of the flight of birds, but in a less remarkable degree. I was here also surprised by the appearance of a little flower, which properly belongs to the lark and magpie,—a pretty *Pellis*, quite like the *Pellis perennis*,—the German daisy. The white little flowers had the same red colour beneath, and were also tipped with crimson. Here too I saw for the first time a beautiful woodpecker, probably *Picus badioides*, which I afterwards often met with in the valley of the Rio Grande.

Two roads lead hence into the valley of the Rio Grande, one leaving the defile of the Salado on the left, the other on the right. The defile itself seems to be impassable for man and beast. We chose the latter road, which led us straight towards a limestone mountain, in a pass of which we halted for the night, and through which we descended into the valley the following day, on a rough and rocky road, not without danger to our waggons. The limestone of this small group belongs probably to the cretaceous formation which, according to Marcou's observations, occupies here a narrow strip on the Rio Grande.

---

[1] A celebrated naturalist and ethnologist remarked to me justly, that this fact gave a warning not to draw from the affinity of languages too general conclusions for the unity of the human race.

On the evening of October 16th we reached the western foot of the mountain. We had reached the Mora on the 3rd, and had thus travelled for thirteen days along, as it were, the edge of the plateau, which in the east borders the valley of the Rio Grande, having at the same time touched the e treme eastern settlements of New Mexico.

We had however not yet reached the actual soil of the lower valley, but only one of those inclined plains of débris which descend, in all the wider parts of the valley of the Rio Grande, from the foot of the mountains, or the adjacent steppes, close to the river, and which here break off, with a steep edge, jagged by small hollows and fissures. The soil of these steep lateral terraces, consists of large alluvial strata of sand, clay, and detached masses of rock. This region is quite destitute of water, excepting what falls at rare intervals, and only during three months of the year; it bears a vegetation, composed of some species of grass, mostly in isolated spots, shrub-like *Artemisiæ* and *Chenopodiaceæ*, *Algarobbiæ*, *Larrea* bushes, the long green but mostly leafless thorns of the *Fouquiera*, and other thorn-bushes with or without leaves, various *Opuntiæ* and *Echinocactæ*, as well as several species of *Jucca* both dwarf and tall. This region is incapable of cultivation, which is limited in the valley to the bottom lands along the river, as far as they can be watered. The lateral terraces occupy the greater part of the valley, so that the cultivation is restricted to a narrow strip, and even this is interrupted in the narrows of the valley. The bottom along the river is therefore the only part of the valley of the Rio Grande where trees are found. A kind of poplar, low and broad, is seen in groups and in small woods, and some willows grow on the edge of the river. The valley, otherwise, from one mountain-top to another is treeless, and like a large basin in the desert.

Of this general character I formed a clear idea in ascending a small isolated mountain, of volcanic origin, rising out of the alluvial masses of the eastern side-terrace. The lower masses of the rock consist of a dense, grey, trachytic lava; the upper, of a lava of darker colour and more basaltic or doleritic nature, becoming more and more porous and spongy towards the summit, till, on the top, it appears in black lumps thrown one over another, perforated, eaten into, jagged, crooked, and forced up, like a scoria not completely vitrified. The rock contains, from top to bottom, numerous concretions of a milk-coloured chalcedony, sometimes hyalitic, small pieces of which lay strewn about everywhere. The view from the summit of this isolated mountain is grand, and most peculiar. Wherever the eye stretches to the edge of the wide prairie valley it sees in the distance some detached mountain-group, its bare and rugged sides descending to the valley, and from whose base the slanting plain of débris, clothed in a naked and monotonous grey-brown, descends in long lines to the river, which is indicated only by some distant poplars.

I saw upon this summit the first shrub of the *Larrea Mexicana*, which, further south, forms such an important feature in the vegetation of the steppes, from the plateaus of Texas down to the lower Gila, and which in the valley of the Rio Grande likewise begins to predominate, only farther south. It is remarkable, in approaching the extensive province of certain plants, to see them first appear upon the summits of isolated mountains, and especially when, as here, the district of this vegetation lies further south. This remark applies also to the *Opuntia arborescens*, of which I found the first small tree on the top of Round Mount.

We reached the river near some houses, called, I believe, Nutrias, and first saw here again for a long time a large stream. Our thirsty animals were watered, and all the men who could get the time hastened down to bathe. The quicksand-banks of the river were covered with thousands of wild geese, ducks, and cranes, but they did not come within shot. The next day we passed a beautifully situated place called "La Joya," and halted near "La Joyita," a little lower down, where we encamped for the night.

SIERRA DE LOS ÓRGANOS.

Book II., Chap. 8.

CHAPTER VIII.

Valley of the Rio Grande — Irrigation Canals — Encampment near La Joyita — Visit of the Apaches — Indian Hieroglyphics — Augitic Lava over the alluvial Masses of the Valley — The River breaks through a Bar of Lava — Water-fowl, and ill Success in hunting — Hills of Drift Sand — Excesses of our Waggoners — A view of Socorro — Valley of Valverde — Basalt — Bushes of the Mezquite — Rattlesnakes — Tarantulas — Quails — The Paisano — San Cristóval — Desert of the Dead — Geological Remarks, and Landscape Scenery — A Vegetable Monster — Doñana — Sierra de los Órganos — Fruit — Fletcher's Rancho — A *Memento Mori* — Deserters from Fort Fillmore — Grounds of Discontent — Narrows of the Rio Grande near El Paso — Franklin and Macgoffinville.

THE numerous and extensive canals for irrigation—*acequias* —give to the valley of the Rio Grande a peculiar character in reference to its cultivation, and produce a pleasing impression on the traveller coming from the Steppe. This valley is by nature a long and narrow strip of oasis, in a desert extending on both sides for thousands of square miles; or rather, it is a chain of basin-like oases, separated by rocky passes and barren defiles. The river annually overflows the valley more or less, but, from the great deficiency of rain and the want of springs and brooks to water the land, the moisture left behind by the inundation would not suffice. It is true that from out of the high and rocky mountains, with which the edge of the plateau is bordered on both sides of the valley in isolated groups, defiles and ravines extend down, whose rugged appearance and detached rocks show that at times they form the beds of mountain torrents; but these beds are perfectly dry, except when, as is rarely the case, violent torrents of rain fall in the mountains: these temporary streams run instantly into the river, and, instead of fertilizing the adjacent valley, only spread devastation over it. As soon as the time of high-water is past, the river falls much below the level of the valley, and the banks appear like perpendicular declivities of sand or clay. In this point, as well as in the muddy colour of its waters, the Rio Grande resembles the Missouri, Arkansas, Ohio, Lower Mississippi, Californian Colorado, and many other rivers of North America. On the Rio Grande, likewise, the banks—undermined by the stream—fall in from time to time; the poplars and willows bordering them fall into the river: whilst on the opposite side new banks are formed, and covered with young wood. Here and there the stream forces for itself a new channel, and the old one remains a stagnant water among the poplar groves of the valley. Owing to the steep banks, the river is often inaccessible for many miles; so that a caravan may suffer from want of water for its animals, in the immediate vicinity of the river. If the beasts suffer greatly from thirst, there is a danger of their discovering some access to the water, getting down into the river, and being unable to get out again. If possible, therefore, the caravan encamps near some irrigation canal, as we did at Joyita.

Much as the valley of the Rio Grande has suffered from the continual irruptions of the wild Indians, especially the Apaches, it is not uncommon to see two or three irrigation canals, each capable of driving a mill, running through the valley for miles, at different levels, in order to convey the water to fields further distant from the river and lying higher. This system of agriculture is foreign to the inhabitants of the United States, and opposed to their spirit of personal independence; as a system of irrigation on a larger scale presupposes express legislative interference, and a restriction of the free disposal of his land by each individual. In Texas, where the Mexicans have followed the same system of agriculture—in the vicinity of San Antonio for instance—are seen the ancient *acequias* of the times of the Spaniards, gone to ruin and decay. The farmers who have immigrated from the United States—from feelings of blind contempt for the Mexicans, and the accidental occurrence of a series of comparatively rainy years—have allowed these canals to fall to ruin; they have, however, had to suffer severely for this neglect, in the subsequent years of drought. In New Mexico nature is too capricious, and immigration too inconsiderable, to cause any fear of the entire abandonment of the well-founded old system, which is in all probability of Indian origin.

In our camp at Joyita I first saw face to face some Indians of the dreaded Apache nation. Whilst taking our noonday meal, two Indians came riding up, who dismounted, shook hands with us, and invited themselves with great naïveté to partake of our repast. Th were clothed in leather, and armed with good guns, which they laid aside. They told us they belonged to the tribe of the Mescaleros,[1] and one of them pretended to be a chieftain,—an assertion however which the fellow's bad manners proved to be false. In general, the Indian chieftains observe a dignified demeanour, and marked etiquette. The physiognomy of these two men, who after a short time were joined by a woman, nearly approached the common Chinese type, chiefly in the broad flat nose; but there are also seen among this people very various physiognomies, and I afterwards saw several sharply cut profiles of noble proportions.

[1] *Mescal* is a kind of agave, of which the roots are eaten. The Californian Indians have treated me with a sweet agave-root, which, I believe, comes from the so-called wild species of mescal. Mescal is also the name of a kind of brandy prepared from the agave. The Apache tribe takes its name from the plant. The root is an essential article of food amongst many Indian races.

As they have children by great numbers of stolen Mexican women, and as boy prisoners are continually adopted by the tribe, it grows more and more difficult to distinguish the original form of the face and colour of the skin.

I wished to avail myself of this opportunity to collect a few words of the Apache language, but I had great difficulty in attaining my object, even to a very limited extent. My questions at first displeased them, and I received no answers: I then bethought me of a ruse, which was successful. I declared that I knew the Apache language, and uttered the Comanche words which I had on a former occasion noted down. The hatred of the Apaches for the Comanches aroused such indignation among our guests, that, to prove the superiority of their language to that of the Comanches, they told me a number of words.

I learned from these people that not all the Apache tribes speak the same language: for instance, that of the Coppermine Apaches and Gila Apaches differs widely from theirs, and is not understood by them.

In the evening our guests took their leave. That night I slept at the edge of our camp, which was on a level plain near the village; and near me lay our cook. On a sudden we were aroused by the sound of horses' hoofs, and the fierce barking of our dog. Scarcely five paces distant we saw two mounted Indians. In an instant my gun was levelled at one, and the cook, snatching up one of my pistols, aimed at the other, whilst the dog seized one of the horses by the throat. "No tira, compadre!" (don't fire, comrade!) exclaimed one of the men. "Don't you know your friends, the Apaches, who are come again to drink coffee with you?" An explanation followed, in which we made them understand that we could not receive their visit at night, and that they must go away; but that they would be very welcome to join our early breakfast. They reluctantly yielded, but not without lively protestations; and when some way off, one shouted to me, "Hark-ye, comrade! the Apaches are good—the Apaches are your friends—but yonder dwell rogues!" meaning the people of the neighbouring village, the name of which, La Joyita, signifies "the little jewel." The next morning we waited in vain for our guests at breakfast, and afterwards saw them riding with eight or ten others over a neighbouring hill. The object of their nocturnal visit had doubtless been to test our vigilance; and as our complete guard was about half a mile off, with the drove of mules, disagreeable occurrences might have happened at the camp.

Below La Joyita the valley narrows, and the river forces its way through a cleft intersecting an elevated plain which crosses the former. On its western side rise high and steep mountains, with columnar formations, probably consisting of masses of porphyry. There is a hot spring somewhere among these mountains. The flat barrier which crosses the valley consists of an augitic lava, through which the Rio Grande has made its way; the remaining portions are seen on either bank of the river. The road passes over these lava hills, on the east side of the valley, and is very heavy from the quicksands which here and there cover the rocks. Whilst the caravan was toiling along this road, I followed the cutting which the river had made, and climbed about the rocks on the hill-side. In one place, where the unfrequented footpath led from the valley to the hill-top, I observed blocks of stone with figures cut on them. In the course of my narrative I shall have to speak of many similar sculptures, and shall therefore reserve for the present some general remarks on this subject.

Near this spot the stratum of augitic lava appears in a highly interesting manner above the alluvial masses. The superposition resembles that of the Californian table-mountain, famed for its auriferous alluvial substratum.

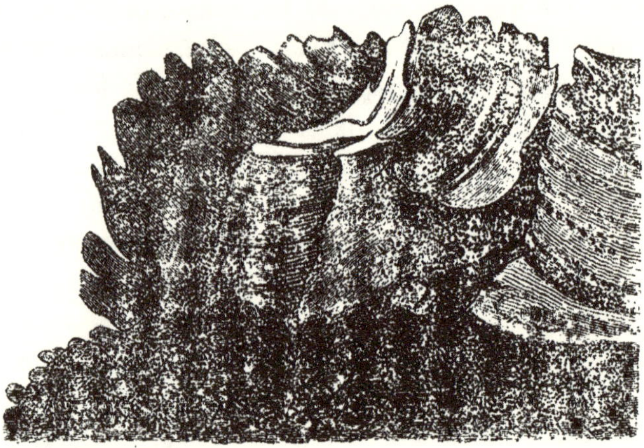

Further on, the Rio Grande winds through beautiful meadows, dotted here and there with groups of poplars; while the banks of the river are covered with the same trees. At the commencement of this opening of the valley I came to an old branch of the river, covered with thousands of various kinds of geese and ducks, whilst large flocks of cranes lined the shores. With the aid of some bushes, I crept along till I came within gun-shot. On my discharging both barrels into the midst of these flocks of birds, a cloud of water-fowl rose on the wing; the flapping of wings and the screams filled the air. In the water geese and ducks were fluttering about, which I had wounded but not killed, and, on my approaching them, they had still strength left to escape. I waded into the water up to the waist, with a pistol in my hand, but only succeeded in capturing a single duck, which I secured by a pistol-shot.

In this excursion from our caravan, I came to high and extensive quicksand hills covering the augitic rock. Their shape was exactly that of the snowdrifts met with on the summits of the Alps; and, indeed, these formations in the landscape reminded me vividly of the Alpine scenery. I had wandered miles away from my companions, when I recollected the peril of my position. I loaded my gun with buck-shot, and set out to find the nearest way to rejoin the caravan.

Our next night-encampment was below Sabino. Some of our people begged to be allowed to return to the village, and join in a dance. On this occasion a North American so excited the jealousy of a native peasant, that he was surrounded, and a general attack was made upon him. At this he drew a small pistol from his pocket, and, like Don Juan, fired into the crowd of people in the room; fortunately, however, the affair turned out quite as harmless as in the opera—no one was hurt, and the culprit was unheeded. I have before observed that the Mexicans living on the borders suffer much from the insolence and violence of the North Americans. The next night one of our North American drivers found one of our Mexican muleteers asleep at his post, and, to arouse him, he gave him a blow which laid open his head with a wound about two inches long; it nearly killed him, and the driver openly boasted that this had been his intention.

The road down the valley lay sometimes along the bottom, and sometimes over the hills forming the lowest lateral terrace. In a geological point of view, the latter are in part merely the separated portions of the alluvial masses adjacent to the mountains, or they consist of flats and bars of basaltic or augitic streams of lava, which have filled a part of the valley, as at Joyita. Such a bar, forming, near Fort Conrad and Valverde, a semicircular and perpendicular precipice toward the bottom of the valley, consists of a basaltic rock, partly dense and partly porous, with numerous grains of Olivin, and a white chalky filling or coating of many of the cavities—a substance which I have not been able to subject to further examination. Upon the surface of the masses of lava spread over the alluvial soil of the valley, more recent alluvial deposits of pebbles, gravel, and sand have been deposited.

The bottom land at the foot of this hill has a vigorous vegetation of tall grasses and various shrubs, between scattered poplars. The soil is highly fit for cultivation. One of the most beautiful sections in this neighbourhood is the Valverde bottom, where a small town of the same name formerly stood. Were it not, like the rest of the valley, exposed to the attacks of the Indians, this would be one of the most eligible spots for a settlement that I have seen in the course of my American wanderings. At the time of our passing, only one North American resided there, with a few Mexican servants. The land did not belong to him, but he had taken possession of it.

One of the many interesting scenes of landscape which the valley of the Rio Grande presents to the traveller, is the view from the hills below Parida, on to the opposite side of the valley, with the town of Socorro lying at the foot of high mountains. The road on the hill runs close to the edge of a steep precipice, at the foot of which the Rio Grande—its bed half filled up with grey sandbanks—winds between poplars and willows, through extensive meadows. On the limit of the latter, indicated in the distance by the sharp line of an irrigation canal, lies the town, with its flat roofs; and behind it rises the mountain—bare of trees from the base to the summit—in terraces, one above another, and supported by columnar rocks. As in all the mountains which enclose the Rio Grande, detached bushes of Mezquite, Larrea, and various kinds of Artemisiæ, with an occasional Yucca or Cactus, compose the characteristic vegetation of the foreground of this landscape. Where sandy alluvial masses form the soil, the mezquite[1] is quite the predominant plant. I do not know whether all the mezquite bushes or trees, from Texas to California, are included by botanists in the single species *Algarobbia glandulosa.* If so, this mimosa-like plant is a perfect vegetable Proteus. In new Mexico it is a shrub, with branches and twigs spreading out upon the ground, and springing directly from the roots: in Texas, the plant is represented by a small tree: on the Gila and Colorado, it is a tree of considerable size, regular growth, and grouped into small woods and groves. In comparing these varieties, their appearance is so different that an unscientific man may well imagine that he has presented to him various species of the same genus. The Mexicans distinguish two kinds: the pods of one are edible, those of the other are not considered so. I shall have occasion to mention this shrub or tree hereafter, and will then complete what I have to say respecting it. On the middle section of the Rio Grande, the mezquite bush generally grows upon little hillocks of loose sand, which are drifted around them by the wind. The plant here evidently prefers such a soil; for where the ground is firm and strong, the *Larrea Mexicana* takes its place. The mezquite bushes and their sand-hills are a favourite resort of rattlesnakes and tarantulas. In some

[1] The North Americans, who mutilate every Spanish and Mexican name, have converted *Mezquite* into *Musquito;* and from Texas to California, in books and newspapers, are seen the words "Musquito-tree," "Musquito-shrub," "Musquito-grass," and so on. The word has no connection with musquito or gnat, but is an Aztec word:—*Mezquitl.* The grass takes its name from the shrub, as in Texas it grows in the same districts.

parts of New Mexico, rattlesnakes are met with at every few hundred paces, and in our journey I have sometimes killed five or six in a few hours, lying in our very path. The danger here is, however, small, and far less than in the grass of the prairie. In New Mexico the ground between the single bushes is generally barren, so that in the daytime it is not easy to tread upon a snake unawares. In going out to hunt the beautiful Californian quails, with the curved tuft of feathers on their heads, it is necessary to be more cautious, when the sportsman is often obliged to force his way into the thorny mezquite bush. The flesh of this elegant little bird is excellent; it is continually met with on the Gila and Colorado. The earth-cuckoo (*Geococcyx viaticus*) is also peculiar to this and similar localities. I often saw it running about, and later I shot several in other parts of the country. They run so swiftly that, on ground overgrown with underwood, it is very difficult to get them. The Mexicans call this bird *Paisano* (peasant), a corruption of *Faesano* (pheasant). It much resembles a pheasant, especially in its long tail and great speed in running, but is much smaller. In Texas and California it is known by the name of "Correcamino" (road-runner). I have been repeatedly told that it lives chiefly on rattlesnakes.

Leaving the Valverde bottom behind us, and Fort Conrad, which is situated in this vicinity, to our side, we reached a spot known by the name of San Cristóval. This place was probably once inhabited. It is a small section of the valley, enclosed on the east and south by the acclivity of a basaltic plateau. The river runs in a westerly direction through a series of narrows between this plateau and the mountains rising above it; and pursues its course, for about a hundred miles, through a rocky defile, which is quite impassable for waggons, and scarcely capable of cultivation. The road, therefore, ascends, in a southerly direction, over the basaltic terrace, and continues along a plateau covered with prairie, between distant mountain-chains, east and west, for about ninety miles. This eastern lateral terrace of the Rio Grande, which on a mean average is about seven or eight hundred feet higher than the bed of the river (which falls in this part of its course nearly four hundred feet), is known by the name of "*The Dead Man's Journey*" (Jornada del Muerto). It has, however, a worse reputation than it deserves, for these ninety miles are seldom entirely wanting in water; and even were this the case, there is nothing very formidable in it for a traveller journeying with baggage-waggons from Texas to California. With mules, the entire distance may be travelled without water; there is excellent grass the whole way, and the road for the most part very good.

This certainly was not the case at the outset. The ascent was covered with deep sand, from which rose basaltic cliffs, and in parts the road passed over a rough ground of rocks. We at length reached the plain on the terrace: about half our waggons had arrived on the summit, when a storm came on, and we were drenched to the skin. In this plight we had to work until late at night, doubling our teams, to bring up the remainder of our waggons. There was no fodder for the mules above, and we were obliged to drive them down again into the valley, where they were placed under guard for the night. The next day our journey was neither arduous nor disagreeable. The grass on the plain was already somewhat withered, from the advanced season; but by the roadside were many beautiful autumnal flowers; and we saw here, for the first time, a tree-like species of Yucca, which, together with the grey rocks of the mountains, gave the scene an entirely new and striking character. Stags, hares, rabbits, and flocks of cranes, enlivened this wilderness, over which we pursued our way undisturbed for thirty miles, until we reached the lagoon, where we encamped for the night.

This, as well as a smaller lagoon, a few miles further south, contains water for about three months in the year, collected during the rains. Both have neither an inlet nor an outlet. Immense flocks of ducks covered their surface, whilst hundreds of gigantic grey cranes were stalking about in the long grass on the shores. These birds were very shy, and would not let us come within shot. In the night I heard the rushing sound of flocks of cranes, geese, and ducks, over our heads; they flew in a westerly direction across the desert, toward the Rio Grande.

We halted the next day, for our noontide rest, at the second lagoon. All around rose barren, steep, and grotesque mountains, in single groups or isolated chains, on the borders of the prairie. The terrace stretches between them to the north, south and west, down to the Rio Grande, while to the east a communication with the table-lands on the Pecos exists over the mountain-passes between the Sierra de los Jumanes, the Sierra del Caballo, and other mountain chains. The rain in the afternoon prevented our reaching the so-called Aleman, a place we had fixed upon for our night encampment, from the water found there. The night cleared up, and the next morning the ground was covered with hoar-frost.

Pursuing our journey, we came to a range of hills, stretching directly across the plain. The soil was composed of red clay, with pebbles and fragments of limestone, ferruginous sandstone, flint, hornstone, carniola, jasper, quartz, and silicified wood. The *Larrea Mexicana* forms the prevailing vegetation. Other tracts are covered with various kinds of shrubs, especially of the wormwood family (*Artemisiæ*), and a grey-leaved *Chenopodiacea*. Scattered between these shrubs grow tree-like Yuccas. As the traveller proceeds south their stems grow taller; the plant assumes the appearance of a small palm-tree, and accordingly is called "*Palmilla*" by the Mexicans. The disproportionate thickness of the stem is produced by the withered leaves clinging around it. Toward evening we reached a small group of low trachytic hills. The trachyte is bordered by limestone, which in appearance resembles that on the Ojo de Verendo. The trachyte exhibits some degree of stratification, and in some parts encloses fragments of hornblende, flint, with other kinds of rock, and thus forms a breccia. This spot is known to the American traders as the "Point of Rocks." The Mexicans call it "Perilla."

The mountains bounding the terrace of the Jornada to the west, consist of isolated groups. Those to the east, form a long unbroken chain divided in sections, becoming towards the south more lofty, precipitous, and indented. The next morning a snowy peak of the Sierra Blanca (White Mountains) was visible behind a depression of the nearer chain. On the south side of the terrace, where the road descends towards the Rio Grande, a circular group of dark rocky hills stands forth like an island in the plain, apparently the remains of an old volcano. Behind these, to the left, rose the sharp peaks of the Sierra de los Organos, the southern extremity of the above-named chain. The setting sun shed a marvellous beauty upon these mountains, the small group standing out in a dusky brown, with black shadows, while the prominent peaks of the more distant Sierra de los Organos were bathed in tender hues of lilac and violet, with deep blue shadows, so that they resembled a mass of solid lepidolite.

We encamped for the night where the terrace begins to slope in a southerly direction. When we rose, at 3 A.M., the plain was white with hoar frost. On our way we set fire to the dry leaves of some yuccas, which burned with a high crackling flame, enclosing the whole stem, and affording us considerable warmth as we passed. By the time the sun had risen we had reached the valley. Our early march in the dark prevented my examining the afore-named isolated group of rocks, which, in a geological point of view, must be very interesting. If I was not deceived by the distance, volcanic, plutonic, metamorphic, and sedimentary rocks are compressed into a small space here, and easily to be examined; the whole representing quite a small geological laboratory.

By the river the scenery was equally interesting. A lofty, precipitous, rocky mountain, towered on the other side of the valley. Poplars grew on the plain, and the sandy hill by which we had descended was covered with tall yuccas and many varieties of shrubs; while behind this, to the east, the distant peaks of the loftier mountains arose, looking surprisingly near. Here for the first time I saw the gigantic Echinocactus Wislizeni, a perfect vegetable monster. Let the reader imagine a barrel-shaped, deeply-ribbed, green mass, from three to four feet high, and from two to three feet thick, covered with bunches of thorns long and strong enough to inflict a deadly wound; the centre ones of each bunch being curved, so as to form perfect hooks. The rock of the precipice along which the road passes is sandstone, exhibiting the influence of volcanic agencies. The mountain on the opposite side of the valley appears to be of the same formation. The fragments of the alluvial hills are of trapp, basalt, porphyry, trachyte, and almost every variety of quartz and chalcedony.

We encamped for the night about a mile above Doñana, a small village beautifully situated. The peaks of the Sierra de los Organos, although nearly half a day's journey distant, rose apparently so close behind the flat roofs of the houses, that they seemed to form a rocky wall immediately adjoining the village.

This chain, which contains a productive silver mine, forms one of the most striking and interesting features of the scenery along the Rio Grande. It consists of a mass of lofty rocks whose vertical position has given it the name of the Organ Mountains. The central portion of the chain is, however, alone entitled to this name, as north and south of it the masses become broader and more compact.

Fruit trees and the vine are much cultivated in this valley. At Doñana, and afterwards at Las Cruzes, we bought excellent grapes, good apples, and tolerable pears. Wine, raisins, dried peaches and pears, form a considerable source of trade, and are exported from the valley of the Rio Grande to Chihuahua. The dried pears of El Paso are the best in the world.

A large fortified house, named from its owner, Fletcher's Rancho, stands solitary on the road between Doñana and Las Cruzes. An extensive estate belongs to it, but the owner pays more attention to trade than to agriculture, and the house is in fact a large store. The locality of this magazine was, in all probability, chosen with reference to the smuggling trade with Mesilla. This large and prosperous village lies on the other side of the Rio Grande, and at that period had not been sold by Mexico to the United States, an event which took place a few years later. But goods may be stored here in a lonely house with greater safety than an estate can be cultivated, for the Apaches prefer exercising their marauding propensities upon flocks and shepherds to attacking a house. Here I received a very practical warning as to the need for caution upon the high road, through the most populous parts of New Mexico. I had remained at Fletcher's Rancho about half an hour after our caravan had started, and was riding after it, when I met two North Americans with whom I exchanged a few words. Some days afterwards, at El Paso, I learned that they had been murdered by some Indians, at no great distance from the spot where I had spoken to them.

Fort Fillmore, which is merely a military station, had at this time a garrison of 200 infantry and 200 dragoons. We encamped two miles lower down the valley, where its breadth is very great, and where the river divides, enclosing an island of many square miles in extent, between its branches. A German soldier from the fort came to us here. He complained of bad treatment, but his jovial, well-fed appearance, and excellent clothing, formed a ludicrous contrast to his words. He carried a fine hunting-gun, and intended to improve his dinner by shooting a hare or a wild turkey; such game abounding in the valley. But his immediate purpose was to desert; and I actually met him some time later on Mexican territory, whither he and several of his companions at Fillmore, all with good arms and excellent horses, had made their way. At Chihuahua the higher Mexican officers had beautiful American horses, which had all crossed the frontier in this manner, and been bought for a mere trifle. I questioned this man as to the causes of his discontent, and learned that they arose from some arbitrary diminution of the extra pay allowed for field and building work,—a kind of labour occasionally required of the garrison of a fort.

This extra pay should be 18 cents daily, and the portion curtailed went into the pockets of the commandant, the quartermaster, and other officers, who not only lived in luxury, but were able to save money. So said the soldier. But, if this be really true, we must doubly admire Uncle Sam's liberality, which is so great, that, after all such embezzlement, the soldier has still more than he can use. At all these forts the traveller can purchase superfluous rations and cloaks; the latter often so little worn, that many a German burgher would be but too thankful to possess one. It is scarcely possible in Europe to form an idea of the luxurious equipment and maintenance of the army in the United States; and, if this consideration were the principal one under a military point of view, the system would be admirable indeed. This liberality, however, is of the same character as the wasteful expenditure of Congress in printing their public documents, from which no great literary fame can result. The United States government acts, in these respects, like a rich parvenu of insufficient education, who, by lavish expenditure, strives, though unsuccessfully, to gain the position of a gentleman. The cause of the frequent desertions from the frontier forts is simply this:—the officers turn with haughty pride from the common soldiers, and thus the beneficial influences over the men, which they could so easily exercise, are lost. In these frontier forts,—placed, as they mostly are, in unpeopled localities,—an enlightened intercourse between officer and man is of the utmost importance. Most of these desertions are caused by intolerable *ennui*.

The valley below Fort Fillmore is uninhabited for a considerable distance. We bivouacked at a spot where the road runs close to the river. This place, which is called Los Alamitos, or The Poplar Trees, is one of the most beautiful along the Rio Grande. We were in a grove of scattered old poplar trees, between which we could see the rugged forms of the Sierra de la Soledad rising above the valley. Our mules grazed here by the light of the moon, and, as usual, were well watched. But in spite of our care, one of them, in the morning, was found to have an arrow wound in his leg; proving that an Indian must have crept very near us.

In order to expedite arrangements at the custom-house on the Mexican frontier at El Paso, Mr. Mayer decided on riding on before our caravan, and I accompanied him. The distance was about twenty-five or thirty miles. There was nothing remarkable in the valley till we came to the spot where the river breaks through the narrow pass above El Paso; but at this point the country becomes very interesting. The mountain chain on the east throws out a spur here, which is separated from the chief mass of the Soledad and the Organos by a deep saddle; and this spur continues on the other side of the river in a northerly direction, though forming here only an isolated group. Between these higher mountains, the valley is filled with rocky and stony hills, through which the river has formed for itself a narrow bed. Sandstone rocks mark the entrance of this valley; while lower down the substance of the hills may be called a granito-porphyry. Connected with these are metamorphic strata, which appear to have been originally sandstone, in which shells are easily distinguished.[1] At the base of the rapid stands a mill belonging to Mr. Hart, a North American officer engaged in the Mexican war, who, having married a Mexican lady of one of the first

[1] Mr. Bartlett, in his 'Personal Narrative,' speaks of limestone. I have seen none. As my two journeys took place under circumstances which precluded any delay for a scientific purpose, he may be right.

families of the State of Chihuahua, erected this—in such a country—remarkably fine building, and provided it with good machinery. It needed considerable courage to choose such a home. The road over the adjacent hills is bad and unsafe. The drivers, even of the poorest bullock-carts, carry guns with their whips. The situation of the mill is wild and strange, marked by the most striking peculiarities of North Mexican nature. The mountains on each side the valley are rocky ridges,—bare, grey, and curiously formed. Alluvial terraces extend from their base into the valley, and, uniting with the rocks near the river, form a bar across the valley. The river rushes here with a strong current through the fallen rocks. A few old poplars, the only trees in the whole region, grow on its banks. But notwithstanding this absence of anything like masses of verdure, we find among these rocks and fragments a most varied, interesting, and beautiful flora. Among an almost infinite variety of low shrubs (as I have already described in the upper portion of the valley) rise clusters of the long green shoots of the Fouquiera. A tall yucca, with its broad sword-shaped leaves and naked stem, throws up its palm-shaped crown; while here and there is seen the monstrous mass of a giant echinocactus. The creeping opuntia spreads over the stony ground, and small echinocacti peep up between rank mammillarias. Then a small agave, in bunches not larger than a lettuce, and called by the Mexicans Lechuguilla, or Wild Salad, covers the ground like grass. All these, stiff, bristling, and thorny, harmonize curiously with the stony soil and bare rugged mountains. But in the spring, when the Mezquite bushes are clothed with the delicate green of their fresh feathery foliage and brush-like yellow flowers; when the gigantic blossom-shoot of the yucca is crowned with its hundreds of white bells, fair as the lily of the valley, though as large as a tulip; when the shoots of the fouquiera are adorned with scarlet panicles, and on the ground the large fiery-red blossoms of the mammillaria dazzle the eye; when a dark blue sky, brilliant and clear as no dweller in the north can possibly imagine, expands over the landscape, while the air fills the whole frame with the most exquisite sensations of health and strength, and power for exertion,—then must we render justice to the beauty of this remarkable country.

Such are the general characteristics of the scenery through which my long journeys will take me; and therefore, to avoid repetition, I shall henceforth only refer to the more peculiar features of each district. The Mexicans give the name of "chaparral" to a kind of shrubbery growing freely throughout the greater part of northern Mexico. The word originally indicated a thicket of holm-oaks, from chaparra, a holm-oak. It has, however, received a more general meaning, though not to the extent in which it is used by the North Americans, who call every thicket of shrubs in Mexico, and in the former Mexican countries now belonging to the United States, "chaparral." That the word is corrupted in this process of adoption is a matter of course.[1]

We reached El Paso by noon. The town lies on the west bank of the river, which we forded on horseback. In the evening, however, we returned to the east side, where Franklin and—about two miles lower down the valley—Macgoffinville are situated, both belonging to Texas. These are rising towns, but as yet contain only a few houses. Near Franklin are the mud buildings of a former fort of the

[1] Even Mr. Bartlett always spells it "chapporal."

United States, Fort Franklin, which has been superseded by Fort Bliss, near Macgoffinville. We passed the night in this last town, in an inn kept by a German. The man had more than half forgotten his own language, as also what English he had learned in the United States; French, which he had once spoken well, had also entirely faded from his memory; and of Spanish he had learned only a few imperfect phrases: so that literally he was almost devoid of language. There was a billiard-table in the house, and all needful accommodation for brandy-drinkers. In other respects his resources were very limited, and, but for the life we had led, we should have thought them wretched. Coffee with milk and well-baked bread were, however, great delicacies, and I slept—once again in a bed—so soundly, and awoke so refreshed, that I forgave the slovenliness of our host, who brought me in the morning a dirty tablecloth for a towel.

CHAPTER IX.

El Paso and its Environs — Character of Landscape — Productions — Trees and Silver Ore in the Mountains — Strata of Hills near Franklin — Insecurity of the Country — Pueblo Indians — Col. Langberg's Survey of the Mexican Eastern Frontier — Negotiation with the Custom-House Authorities, and their Treachery — Continuation of Journey — Two Roads — Armed Travellers and Mexican Cavalry — Unsuccessful Military Colonies — Guadalupe — Expedition of the Inhabitants — Topography of the Road: El Cantarecio — Pass over the Sierra de la Ventana — Charcos del Grado — Whirlwind and Pillars of Dust — Cerro de Lucero and Ojo de Lucero — Spring at the top of a Sand Hillock — Efflorescences of Soda — Laguna de Los Patos, and Character of the Plain — Ojo de la Laguna — Carrizal — Former Wealth of the Locality — Ojo Caliente — Fish in Hot Water — Chihuate — Bones of Men and Animals — Great Cattle Hacienda — Herd of Antelopes — Laguna de Encinillas — Arrival at Chihuahua.

El Paso is a small deserted looking town, the population of which,—as is often the case in Spanish America,—first neglected, then retrograding, has ultimately been demoralised by foreign elements. The inhabitants calculate the population at 5000; but the place spreads itself in scattered dwellings among fields and meadows, vineyards and orchards, along the poplar bordered banks of the river, eight or ten miles down its course, and contains an entire population of 14 or 15,000. The name, in its full Spanish form, is El Paso del Norte, *i.e.* the passage over the North river.[1] The market presents a very striking scene to the stranger. On the one side stands the church, a square block with a flat-roofed nave, devoid of all architectural beauty. The tower is built separate. On the other side

[1] The river is called Rio Grande del Norte, or Rio Bravo del Norte, of which three abbreviations are used, namely,—Rio Grande, Rio Bravo, and Rio del Norte.

are one-storied houses, the flat roofs of which project, and are supported by rough columns. Above these tower the bare summits of the adjacent mountain chain. Under this primitive piazza women sit and offer onions, beans, chile, fresh and dried fruits, &c., &c., for sale. All are dear, which seems a strange contrast to the poverty of the place. But every family grows what it needs, and, as a whole day may pass before some traveller or North American trader may appear to purchase the half-dozen eggs or single melon, which have constituted a poor woman's whole stock, the value of her time must be added to that of the goods. But such is the case almost everywhere in Spanish America.

The gardens and fields of El Paso are well irrigated from the river. Nothing could be grown here without this resource; the vineyards even, and orchards, being dependent on this artificial supply. The ground is therefore everywhere intersected by acequias, which spread fertility through and around the town. The exquisite climate, at the level of 3800 feet above the sea, and these environs of cultivated land, contrasting forcibly in their vivid green with the grey alluvial hills and rocky mountain crests, impart to the place a charm peculiar to all the scenery of Northern Mexico, which has something of the Levantic or North African character.

Better dwellings and a safe neighbourhood would make El Paso a delightful abode, although German taste in scenery would find little that was familiar and homelike. For those who prefer verdure, masses of foliage, and that pearly vapour which characterises our northern landscapes, the atmosphere here would be too transparent, the skies too darkly blue and metallic, the beauty of the bleak mountains too severe and plastic, and, above all, the lack of verdure too apparent. I remarked this last circumstance to an intelligent inhabitant of the place, and his reply was remarkable, "We, in Mexico, think that the green colour is more for cows than for men;" and every trader knows that, in Mexico, stuffs and other materials of that colour find no sale.

Some of the garden and field products of El Paso deserve especial notice. Wine is made from their excellent grapes, which only requires better management and an improved process to be first-rate; at present it tastes like a mixture of Malaga and vinegar: but the grapes are mostly used to make brandy. The raisins of El Paso are eaten in the country stewed like dried plums in Europe. Quinces abound in the orchards. Pears are only good for cooking, but then are excellent. Apricots, which are unknown in the United States, grow here, but are small and poor. Peaches are but ordinary, and apples thrive best in the cooler localities of the Sierra Madre; all these fruits, however, might easily be improved. Of vegetables there is a great variety; the onions are remarkable for size and delicacy of flavour, and in these respects surpass even those in California.

Excepting the fruit trees in the gardens and fields, and the poplars and willows by the river, there are no trees near El Paso. The chaparral of the hills is the same I have already described, and is found, with slight variations in character, in corresponding situations as far as, and beyond Chihuahua. But the mountain chain to the north-east of El Paso has pine forests on its eastern declivity, and North American woodcutters have settled there, who saw the planks by hand. Poplar is the sole timber here for building and joiners' work. The mountains on each side of the valley are said to be rich in argentiferous lead-ore. A North American worked a mine in the above-named pine forest; the ore was found on the surface in large lumps, and was smelted and sold without any attempt at separating the lead and silver it contained. Of the results of this crude attempt I am ignorant.

The insecurity of the country and the narrow limits of my time prevented my examining into the geological structure of the surrounding mountains, in which limestone, sandstone, granite, porphyry, and different metamorphic rocks appeared to prevail. The pebbles and fragments in the alluvial masses near Franklin, which I was able to examine close to our camping-place, were very interesting. They consisted of porphyry and granite, with every transition between both; metamorphic masses in which the original limestone or sandstone may still be recognized; while in other cases the original nature of the rock has disappeared in the various grades of transition between the sedimentary, the plutonic, and the volcanic masses. As in the vicinity of Hart's Mill, I saw metamorphic masses among the detached fragments which contained shells and crystals of felspar.

The insecurity of the country is a constant hindrance to the researches of the naturalist. I was by no means timid, but caution was so strongly urged upon me that it would have been folly to have disregarded it. "How are the Indians?" was Mr. M.'s first inquiry on our arrival at El Paso. "Son malisimos ahora"—"worse than ever," was the answer. Only a short time previously they had attacked the farms on the North American side of the stream, and carried off the cattle close to the houses in Franklin and Macgoffinville. They had also attacked several caravans near El Paso. Here I became acquainted with Colonel Langberg, by birth a Dane, but educated in Germany, and then in the service of the Mexican republic, commanding the troops on the frontier; and he advised me in the strongest terms never to leave the road, even for twenty paces, alone. Although we encamped close to the houses at Franklin, it was considered necessary to bring our mules at night into the courtyard of the empty Fort, and to keep guard over them.

These dreaded Indians are chiefly the Apaches, who inhabit the mountain districts of New Mexico, Chihuahua, and West Texas. The christianised Indians of the valley of the Rio Grande, known as the Pueblo Indians, are peaceful cultivators of the soil, and are fully admitted into the rights of citizenship. They possess a village called Sinecú, within the limits of El Paso, and are seen daily in the town, the men with their long braided hair, and the women with their painted faces.[1] Whenever the country around El Paso is unmolested by the Comanches the respite may be attributed to the hostility existing between them and the Apaches. Farther on I shall have to refer to a treaty drawn up by Colonel Langberg, between the State of Chihuahua and the Comanches against the Apaches, which has not been without good results. The above-named officer —in an extensive military survey of the eastern frontier of Mexico, from El Paso to the lower Rio Grande—visited a powerful Comanche tribe in their own dwellings. Colonel Langberg showed me here some beautifully-executed topographical drawings belonging to the survey, by a Polish gentleman serving under him.

Our arrangements at El Paso occupied us from the 3rd to the 9th of November. Of these the negotiations with

[1] The North Americans call these Indians simply Pueblos, incorrectly using the name as that of their tribe. But a Pueblo, according to the old Spanish colonial law, still in effect in Mexico, is a *community* of Indians recognized by the government, and endowed with certain rights and privileges. Pueblo Indians are, therefore, those who belong to the State, and possess civil rights, of whatever tribe they may be.

the custom-house authorities formed the greater part, and I had to translate the detailed invoice of our large mercantile stores into Spanish. This gave me an insight into the manœuvres carried on by each party upon the occasion of any large importation of goods: The custom-house officers take advantage of a very complicated and involved mode of calculation in settling the amount of duty, while the merchant equally profits by their ignorance of the real value of his goods and their taste for bribes. Thus for several days a kind of sham fight is carried on, till at last a sum is agreed upon in the lump, which seldom exceeds a half or a third of the fixed dues. Even thus, we had to pay duty to the amount of 10,000 dollars.

On the 7th and 8th our caravan crossed the river. The water being high, we had to use the ferry. By low water the waggons could have been driven through the stream without difficulty, speed only being necessary on account of the quicksands. On the 9th the goods were examined at the custom-house, which was little more than a form, as the amount of duty had been previously settled. Some goods are entirely prohibited, and made-clothing comes under this category. We had several chests of such things, and Mr. M. having openly declared them, they had been included in the same arrangement as the other goods; but when we arrived at Chihuahua we discovered that they had been denounced as contraband—an act of perfidy which furnished all the custom-house authorities at Chihuahua with a rich and elegant wardrobe, free of cost.

We encamped the night of the 9th–10th three miles beyond the town, at the limit of the valley. On my watch I heard a dull growling, and one of our Mexican drivers said it was a bear.

For the first five or six days' journey from El Paso to

Chihuahua, we had the choice of two roads. The one is considerably shorter, but dangerous and difficult, as it takes a southern direction over the notorious médanos, or quicksand hills; the other avoids these by following the course of the river two days' journey as far as the village Guadalupe, and again joins the high road somewhat to the north of Carrizal. We chose the last, and our caravan proceeded therefore down the valley to Guadalupe.

The road at first passed close along the base of the alluvial terrace, through thickets of mezquite and a shrubby plant of the order of compositæ; then it wound up the terrace, which consists of sand, gravel, and fragments of rocks, overgrown with mezquite, larrea, fouquiera, artemisia, shrubby labiates, cacti, yuccas, &c. &c. In some places the river had formed its channel close to the terrace, forming a perpendicular sand cliff, rendering the road at its very edge in no slight degree dangerous. We met several travellers here, alone and in parties, on foot and on horseback, but all, without exception, armed with guns, pistols, lances, and even bows and arrows. A division of Mexican cavalry passed us armed with carbines, pistols, lances, sabres, and *shields.* Colonel Langberg had been sent with this troop to quell a revolt in the military colony near Guadalupe, to which the poor colonists had been driven by hunger, and which the Colonel met with great forbearance and consideration. The people had driven away their commander, had seized some cattle, satisfied their hunger, and demanded arrears of pay. Some had crossed the river and deserted to Texas.

The Mexican military colonies are villages for married soldiers, who are bound to cultivate the land as well as defend it; but the plan does not appear to answer. Although this colony[1] is only a few miles distant from

[1] I cannot find the name among my notes.

Guadalupe, the Apaches had carried off thirty cows from the immediate neighbourhood of the houses, only the evening before we arrived there. A respectable inhabitant remarked to me that "the soldiers starve, and have neither horses nor clothing; how can they protect us from the Indians?" They are not less afraid of them than the inhabitants of Guadalupe are; and these again fear the soldiers as much as they do the Indians.

We reached Guadalupe the evening of the 12th. Few men were in the village, eighty being in pursuit of the Indians. Such expeditions (campañas) are very frequent throughout Northern Mexico, and it is an error to suppose that the people fail in courage and bravery, although they are seldom successful. The population of this village consists principally of immigrants from New Mexico, who have given up their former homes since the annexation to the United States. These immigrants formed the best portion of the old population of that territory. About six miles lower down the river, a new village—named San Ygnacio—has been founded by the settlement of New Mexican immigrants.

From hence, leaving the Sierra de Cantarecio on the left, and the Sierra de Guadalupe on the right, the road rises gradually to the higher ground south of the Rio Grande. The space between the above-named mountains is a plain rising somewhat to the south, and covered with the common chaparral of these localities. At noon we stopped at Cantarecio, a watering-place, where we found only a little muddy water. In the evening, when dark, we passed—turning to the west, by a slow ascending plain of firm clayey soil, which contracted to a broad mountain pass—the chain of hills, by which the terrace of Cantarecio is separated from that of the Médanos, and encamped for the night on the opposite side, on a grass-covered plain. The mountain peaks near the pass are bare, rocky, and in some places of grotesque form. On the right an opening passes through the rock from one side of the mountain to the other; and one of our Mexican drivers told me that this part of the mountain is named, from this circumstance, Sierra de la Ventana, "Window Mountain." This name, however, did not appear to be generally used, for a gentleman, who had accompanied us from El Paso, called it Sierra de los Médanos, or Sandhill Mountain. Behind this rose, as we approached it from the east, the needles and peaks of the Sierra de la Rancheria, which bears a great resemblance to the Sierra de los Organos. Farther on eastward, appears a similar mountain group named Sierra del Candelario. In the plain at the base of the former are the Charcos del Grado, pools surrounded by mimbre[1] bushes. We reached these during the morning, and found fresh tracks of Indians, showing the need for redoubled caution. In the afternoon we distinguished, as we thought, the smoke of five fires in a southerly direction; but the next day we discovered that they had been columns of dust caused by whirlwinds. I saw similar ones subsequently on a larger scale on the road to California, in the steppes of the state Sonora. The immoveability and duration of these whirlwinds are most curious and deceptive; I have often watched them for hours on one spot. The phenomenon has much similarity with water-spouts. I have never heard whether they are attended with such danger in the North American steppes as was experienced by the French troops on the southern side of the

[1] Mimbre is a beautiful shrub, which in northern Mexico, from Rio Grande to California, flourishes on the banks of intermitting streams. It is a bignoniaceous plant, with pink and white blossoms, and long, pendant, lanceolate leaves—a chilopsis.

Atlas.[1] In the evening we advanced over a level plain towards a mountain chain of perpendicular rocks, among which one, remarkably angular and defined in its form, the Cerro de Lucero, attracts attention. We continued our journey through a portion of the night, and encamped the next morning at Ojo de Lucero, a spring near the Laguna de los Patos. This is a lake on the left of the road. The plain is mostly covered with grass, but near the Cerro de Lucero tracts of clay or sand are covered with an efflorescence apparently of carbonate of soda. Our road, at least, took us over places of this nature; and, from appearances, it seemed probable that, to the right of the road, they existed to a considerable extent. It was over this portion of the plain that we had seen, and now saw more closely, those columns of dust; their recurrence in the same locality may be accounted for by the nature of the soil.

At no great distance from the Ojo de Lucero we met with another spring, Ojo del Coyote, remarkable as rising in the summit of a sandhill about 20 or 30 feet high. This curious circumstance is, however, easily explained, the sandhill being built up by the spring. It is entirely surrounded by the same kind of efflorescence. The Mexicans call this salt—which they collect for soap-boiling —"Tequesquite:" evidently an Aztec word. A few miles farther, at no great distance from the Laguna de los Patos, a warm spring rises in several eddies from the white sand. It forms a clear tepid brook, which flows into a piece of water surrounded by tall reeds, on the side of the road. This place was frequented by numbers of waterfowl—ducks, coots, and a large black web-footed bird, with very long

[1] Among the clever views of southern Abyssinia, in Bernaz's beautiful work, there is one which exactly represents what I saw, only from a greater distance, in Sonora.

legs, long neck, and long bill, called by the Mexicans Gallareda. They flew, when disturbed, in wedge-shaped flocks, with outstretched necks like geese. The spring and the piece of water are called Ojo de la Laguna. The water is slightly alkalic, and a white efflorescence collects at its edge.

On the morning of the 17th we arrived at Carrizal, an important but now ruinous village, formerly a presidio or military post for the protection of the country against the Apaches. These foes of all civilized existence have a Rancheria in one of the neighbouring mountain chains. The locality of their fastness was pointed out to me from the houses in Carrizal, and the robbers can, at all times, from their rocky pinnacles watch the remnant of the numerous herds of cattle which must inevitably become their prey. The inhabitants, as in all North Mexican localities, are literally the shepherds to the Apaches; not indeed willing ones, for every man carried his gun. Such constant warfare has made the inhabitants of Carrizal itself wild and brutal, so that the traveller had better be on his guard against them.

The situation of this place is one of the most beautiful on the North Mexican table-land. An extensive plain, watered by several streams, is surrounded in the distance by a girdle of bare, steep mountains. A clear mountain stream, dispensing fertility to field and meadow in its course, flows through canals between raised banks, for miles through the plain, its course marked by long rows of poplars. Twenty years since, herds of many hundred thousands of cattle grazed upon this plain. Now they have dwindled down to the mere shadow of their former number; and, comparing the present state of this locality with the wealth it was known formerly to possess, the conclusion is irresistible, that of all destructive animals man is the worst.

The place indeed is full of ruins, and lies on a raised platform consisting of hard red clay, with pebbles and fragments of sandstone, evidently changed by the influence of heat, red porphyry, black scoriaceous lava, yellow and green scoriæ, much resembling pumice, and numerous pebbles of chalcedony. The country is bare of trees, with the exception of the poplars along the irrigating canals; so that these are literally the only trees visible throughout the whole journey from the Rio Grande to Chihuahua.

Our lady traveller, having met with a serious accident, was compelled to trust herself to the medical care of some of the women of the place. They prepared a decoction from the branches of a shrub, in which at the same time they boiled the gold ring which their patient usually wore. This circumstance caused the caravan to rest here a day. We encamped close to the houses, but our sleep was disturbed by the howling of a pack of wolves, which, during the whole night, fought with the dogs of the village over the carcase of a mule which had died that evening.

We started again on the afternoon of the 19th, and reached towards evening a warm spring of rather high temperature, named Ojo Caliente, which rises at the base of a group of phonolitic hills. The water, which is clear, and pure in taste, forms a considerable stream; but I am not sure whether it reaches the Laguna de los Patos, or is retained in the plain for purposes of irrigation. I could not ascertain the exact degree of the temperature, from want of the necessary instruments; but the numerous fish which sported in its waters seemed to find it very enjoyable. We remained here a portion of the night.

The next was one of the very few rainy days of our

journey. We travelled nevertheless from morning till evening, between bare mountains, over rocky, treeless, but grass-covered hills, and passed a portion of the night on the broad level pass of Chihuate, a notorious place, where numerous bones of men and animals warned us not to leave hold of our arms. Many parties of travellers have been attacked here by the Indians with much loss of life. The rocks consist of a grey and very hard phonolitic porphyry.

We started at two in the morning, in order to reach the Laguna de Encinillas without a halt. Towards eight o'clock we came to a descent in the road, which, from the name of a hacienda situated on the other side of the mountain, is called the descent of Agua Nueva, and leads to the lower level of the lake. The hacienda of Agua Nueva is one of the few large grazing estates in North Mexico where the herds still exist on the old Mexican scale of cattle keeping; and its owner, Don Estanislao Porras, in Chihuahua, is one of the rare instances in this country of a man possessing wealth acquired by his own exertions. He protects his cattle from the Indians by means of numerous and well armed shepherds, although two of his sons and several of his servants have lost their lives by their attacks. As we descended the hill, the largest herd of antelopes passed that I had ever seen. It must have numbered more than 1000, and extended from one mountain to another, straight across the valley, vanishing as quick almost as thought from our sight.

The plain in which the Lake of Encinillas lies, is surrounded by steep mountains, and is one of the richest and most valuable localities in the world for cattle-grazing, in times past supporting innumerable herds. Now it is almost a desert. I shall have to speak again of this region and of the hacienda of Encinillas,—a possession which occupies almost the whole space between El Paso and Chihuahua, and which, in Europe, would form a dukedom.

We continued our journey along the east shore of the lake. On the 23rd of November I hastened forward, with Mr. and Mrs. M., to Chihuahua. From our last encampment the distance was fifty miles, which we accomplished between four in the morning and one in the afternoon; Mr. and Mrs. M. in a carriage, and I, with a servant, on horseback. The road passes the buildings of the Rancho del Sacramento,—an estate which, during the Mexican war, gave its name to an important battle. Arrived in the town, I was hospitably received by a German merchant, Mr. William Feldman, of Hamburg.

CHAPTER X.

Sojourn at Chihuahua — Situation, Name, ancient Splendour, and present Decay of the Town — Silver Scoria as a Building Material — Aqueduct — Climate and Physiological Influences — Insecurity of the Country — History of the later Indian Fights in North Mexico — Examples of Mexican Bravery — Government Measures — Excursions—Cerro Grande—Rough-riding and Mexican Horses — Hunting Party — Santa Eulalia and its Silver Mines.

The town of Chihuahua—which, from November 1852, till May 1853, was, with few interruptions, my abode—is situated upon a plain surrounded by bare and rocky mountains. Dr. Wislizenus has determined its level above the sea at 4640 feet, about 800 or 900 feet higher than the level of the valley of the Rio Grande at El Paso. In spite of the bleak aspect of the mountains, this region possesses much beauty, not only in the generally grand character of its scenery, but in many of its more peculiar forms and features. Two small mountain-streams, near one of which the town is situated, unite at the distance of about half a mile, and form a small river which falls into the Rio Conchos, or, according to another report, disappears before reaching it. One of these small streams rises in the mountains of Sacramento and Torreon, which lie to the south-west of the Laguna of Encinillas; the other in the rocky defiles of the mountain group to the south-west of the town. United, they flow through a narrow pass between the mountains which bound the plain to the east; and then irrigate the cornfields in the plain of Tavalope, on the other side of this mountain chain. The spot where they unite is called La Junta. A mill with

VIEW IN THE MINING DISTRICT OF SANTA EULALIA, WITH THE RUINS OF THE OLD MINING TOWN OF MAGELLANES.

Book II., Chap. 19

an agave plantation, at the foot of a steep rock—surrounded by old poplars shading hollows filled with crystal clear water—and, lower down, this same stream, foaming through a narrow cleft between the mountains, present a scene of much beauty. This locality is well known to the inhabitants as a resort for parties of pleasure, and it would almost seem as if the word Chihuahua, which means a place or town of pleasure, applies especially to this spot. The word belongs probably to the Tarumare language, in which names of places are indicated by *tchi* or *tchic*, usually added to the end of the word. Smelting works have lately been established here, which prepare the silver ore raised at St. Eulalia either from new mines or from old ones lately reopened. These mines are from twelve to fifteen English miles distant from Chihuahua; and from 1703 to 1833, in spite of this distance, the ore was brought here for smelting. The town of Chihuahua derived its ancient wealth and splendour from the rich mines of Santa Eulalia and the decline of the town has followed that of the mines. The population, which amounted to 76,000 during the prosperity of the mines, has, since their decline, and the separation from Spain, sunk to 12,000; and, with the exception of a few families in which old property has been retained, or gained afresh by an awakening spirit of enterprise, poverty with an accompanying amount of demoralisation has gained ground. The town is more or less unsafe. Going into the courtyard, one evening soon after my arrival, I was surprised by Mr. M.'s advising me to take my pistol; and, upon my remarking that our court was inaccessible on all sides, it was with still greater surprise that I was bid to remark the windows of the adjoining houses which commanded our court. This was in one of the first houses in the best part of the town; and so long as I remained here I never slept without my revolver under my pillow. Among the women prostitution is prevailing; but, notwithstanding its extent, this evil must not be judged too severely. These people have good qualities, and are by no means deficient in better feelings; but the change in the time of a generation from long habits of affluence and luxury, with a natural taste for pleasure, to extreme poverty—exposed to the seductions of unprincipled libertines and rich travelling merchants—the results were almost inevitable. To this may be added the common practice of the Church in Mexico, as well as in most parts of Spanish America, of fixing marriage fees at a price unattainable by the general body of the people, while no civil marriage contract exists; so that it is not to be wondered at that connexions take place opposed to the moral feeling and to the welfare of society. The temporary residents make light of the evil, and have all their concubines pro tempore.

The whole design of the town, with its pleasant streets and many noble edifices, marks the past periods of its splendour; and, even in its present decay, it is far more beautiful as a whole than any town of similar pretension in the United States.

The reader may form some idea of the vast quantities of silver-ore formerly smelted here, when I mention that hundreds of houses, and the walls of all the gardens and fields in the environs, are built of the scoria, in which, according to trustworthy analysis, enough silver remains to make fresh smelting, under better and more scientific management, a profitable undertaking. Forty-three millions of marks of silver have been the produce of these mines in 130 years. Farther on in this chapter, I shall describe the mines of Santa Eulalia more exactly. I will only now remark that, for them and for the town of Chihuahua, there is every prospect of a renewed and lasting period of wealth and splendour, since, sooner or later, there can be no doubt that capital and enterprise will be found, to develop the natural resources of the locality into permanent activity.

The town lies at the foot of the Cerro Grande, an isolated mountain peak of the elevated eastern bank of the southward-tending river. From the low level of its bed its waters are not available for the benefit of the higher ground; but a stone aqueduct, raised for many miles upon magnificent arches, conducts a small mountain stream for the irrigation of the higher gardens and fields, and supplies the streets of the town with an abundance of excellent water. This noble structure, which would do honour to the largest town, was built at the sole cost of a private individual. It has an imposing effect in the landscape, and, by the fertility it spreads over garden and field, adds much to its beauty. For, although wheat and other field-produce are sufficiently watered by the summer rains, yet the gardens would be bare, without irrigation, and even the fields would become green several months later. No rain falls here before the end of May, and only plants of peculiar organization shoot forth before that period. The general characteristics of the climate of Chihuahua are those common to all the higher northern regions of Mexico: a peculiar transparency and dryness of the atmosphere during the longer half of the year, and a remarkably favourable influence upon bodily health and activity. It is assuredly one of the most healthy climates in the world, for, although the people are subject to many illnesses, this may be truly attributed to the miserable state of the poorer classes, who are neither sufficiently fed nor provided with means for warmth and clothing. Some little snow falls occasionally in the winter, and hoar-frosts occur during the night, when some ice forms upon the pools. But the days succeeding these frosty nights are peculiarly beautiful, and tempted me to longer and shorter excursions, as often as my duties allowed.

But the insecurity of the country was a greater barrier to these excursions than my daily duties. No walk could be taken even close to the town without arms. Crosses were erected not many hundred paces from the houses, indicating spots where murders had been committed by the Indians. At no greater distance shepherds carried guns to protect their cattle. The occupation of these men is excessively dangerous, and nothing but resignation or great courage can make it endurable. The larger number of those who yearly fall a sacrifice to Indian barbarity belong to this class; and this fact is statistically so clear, that merchants hesitate to give credit to the most respectable among them, "because at any moment they may be murdered by the Indians."

In their relation to the Indians, it is unjust to attribute cowardice to the Mexicans. The lower classes, on the contrary, exhibit much bravery; and though many throughout North Mexico are killed daily by these savages, the reverse is frequently the case. The masters who, without compunction, expose their shepherds and labourers to such danger, are much more to be blamed, and, above all, the Government,—which is too cowardly and negligent to grant the people sufficient means for their own defence, and yet have neither the strength nor the will to protect them. The inhabitants of a village in the State of Chihuahua—having had their cattle stolen by a band of Apaches, some women and children carried off, and some of their men killed,—called upon their neighbours in another village for help, and undertook an expedition into the mountains against the robbers; but they were censured by the Government for thus helping themselves, and told not to meddle with what belonged to the military power of the State! And, while these Mexican Regents are jealous of any indication of self-reliance in the people, every lower official turns against the higher and demands help and protection. In the "Pronunciamiento" of the garrison of Chihuahua with which, on the 23rd of December, the Revolution of 1852 and '53 broke out, one of the faults attributed to the government of the President Arista was the absence of protection against the Indians in the Frontier States.

Farther details of my narrative will bring to light the fearful condition of those portions of Mexico which are exposed to these Indian marauders; and I will now mention only a few instances of the bravery of these greatly decried Mexicans, with which I became acquainted during my residence in Chihuahua.

Gabriel Guzman, a herdsman on a neighbouring estate, with seven others, in order to protect their master's cattle, resisted a band of sixty-seven Comanches nine hours, instead of seeking their own safety in flight, as they might have done. All eight remained upon the ground, after having killed or mortally wounded a much larger number of the savages. Guzman and a Comanche were found grasping each other's hair, and each with the knife of his adversary in his body. This happened not very long before my arrival.

Another of the same class, Jesus Dominguez, was my companion in several excursions, and was well known for daring as well as courage; I shall have to speak of him again, on my journey to the Sierra Madre. He had often been wounded, and was suffering, when I first saw him, from the effects of an arrow wound near the spine. In order to recover for his master some valuable horses, which had been stolen by the Apaches, he, with several others, followed the thieves close to their haunts in the mountains. As the night approached, they could see the robbers in the distance. Dominguez, who, when a boy, had been for a long time a prisoner among the Apaches, took off his clothes, and assumed the appearance of a Comanche warrior. By a more direct path he got before the Apaches, and, as they approached with the horses, he sprang suddenly from behind a rock raising the Comanche war-hoop, shot down two of the Apaches, and so terrified the whole band, that, in the confusion, he not only succeeded in bringing away the stolen horses but some others also.

For this heroic fulfilment of duty the men of this class often meet with base ingratitude. On another similar occasion Dominguez lost his own horse, it being shot from under him; but it never occurred to his master, a very rich man, to replace it. The miserable and cowardly selfishness of the higher classes, to whom in Mexico almost all the landed property belongs, is the cause of the wretched state into which the localities exposed to the Indians have fallen. There are certainly some few praiseworthy examples of courage and energy among the higher classes, but they are counterbalanced by deplorable examples of the reverse. Don Pedro Zuloaga, belonging to one of the first families in Chihuahua, who, with others, had pursued a body of Indians who had ventured into the immediate neighbourhood of the town, fell, shamefully deserted by his companions, alive into the hands of the Indians, by whom he was hewn in pieces. Portions of his body were found afterwards in a small circuit, attached to the mezquite bushes.

Many distinguished families in Northern Mexico bewail the loss of children stolen from them by the Indians. The following tale was related to me in Chihuahua by a member of the family concerned.

Two sisters, ladies from Durango, lived, each with a child—a boy and a girl—at the Rancho de la Tinaje, two leguas from the town. The neighbourhood was attacked by a band of Comanches, and the ladies, whose husbands were absent, sought refuge with their children in the town, but were seized by the Indians on the road. Just as this happened, one of the husbands approached, and, seeing his wife in the hands of one of these savages, fired both barrels of his gun at him, but missed; and was immediately speared by the Indian. The lady fortunately fainted, and the Indians, who were immediately pursued, fled, leaving her for dead. The other lady also escaped by a lucky chance. The band having ridden rapidly for some distance, came to a river, where they stopped. While the Indians bathed here, the stolen horses took to flight and were followed by those of the horde. The Indians hastened after them, and left the lady. They had now only the two children. The girl was sharp-witted; caressed the old Comanche, who held her before him on his saddle, and coaxed him till he let her go, close to some inhabited place. But the boy, as his friends afterwards heard, resisted, and struck the Indian who carried him in the face. As a punishment they stripped him of his good clothes, and changed them with those of a poor lad who had been carried off with him from the same estate, and who afterwards found his way home again. Thus, little Ramon Lopez remained alone in captivity, and nothing has since been heard of him, although his family promised a reward of 4000 dollars to any one who could effect his recovery. I made known the circumstance and the reward in Texas and other localities bordering on the United States, but with little chance of success, as years had already elapsed. Should the lad still be living, he must have become a savage, and has probably won his first laurels as a robber, if not near his birthplace yet with as much satisfaction as a real Comanche. It is generally asserted that boys captured from a civilized race, and brought up by the Indians, become more dangerous robbers and greater enemies to civilized existence than the Indians themselves.

The government of Chihuahua has put many plans into operation for combating these destructive wild Indians, and for getting rid of the Apaches from their territory. The history of these measures is not uninteresting, and I will relate what I have learned about them.

About fifteen years since, an Irish adventurer, named James Kirker, who had become captain to a band of Shawnee Indians, came, I know not by what inducement, into this neighbourhood, and with his troops entered into the service of the State of Chihuahua under an engagement to carry on a war of extermination against the Apaches; and they quite fulfilled their word, till their own lessened numbers made it impossible for them to cope with the stronger forces of their enemy.

For a similar purpose, in 1850, the Government took into its service a dangerous desperado from Texas, named Glanton, who, with a similar band, had arrived at Chihuahua on his way to California. These wretches, who had been promised a certain sum for every Indian scalp, found it easier to sell to the Government the scalps of its own citizens, whom they shot down whenever it was practicable. With the exception of the shameful part they took in betraying and murdering a whole tribe invited to a peace conference, they did but little injury to the Apaches. They soon became more dangerous to the State of Chihuahua than the Apaches had been, and all rejoiced when they continued their journey to California. On the Colorado, where they took possession of the passage over the river in order to levy a high toll from the passengers, they were killed in a tumult with the Yuma Indians.

In the beginning of 1852, Colonel Langberg, during the before-named survey of the Rio Grande territory in the State of Cohahuila, met with the Seminole chief, "Wild Cat," well known in the history of the Indian wars of Florida, and the equally well known negro, Gover Jones, with the rest of the expatriated Seminoles. The Colonel enlisted the whole party, and brought them to Chihuahua, in order to employ them against the Apaches and other hostile Indian tribes. But the Government of the State—whether from fear of the Seminoles, or from jealousy of Colonel Langberg, or want of money—refused to ratify the treaty; and the two heroes who had gained a classic name in the Florida war, left Chihuahua full of indignation, declaring that there was not one "gentleman" in the whole body of the Government.

Though, in this instance, Colonel Langberg's exertions failed, the treaty which he concluded between the Government of Chihuahua and the Comanches of the Bolson de Mápimi against the Apaches has had important results.

The haunts of these last do not extend to the south of the State of Chihuahua, and when they venture their attacks in that direction they come across their sworn enemies the Comanches. The Government has profited by the enmity of these two nations to oppose the one to the other. The history of these Indian wars, in which the civilized or half-civilized population of the country is involved, is full of interesting episodes, which would furnish rich materials for the pen of a Cooper. When Colonel Langberg visited the Southern Comanches who inhabit the Steppes, known by the name of the Bolson de Mápimi, the tribe was commanded by an old woman, called by the Mexicans "the Generaless of all the Comanches." The eldest son of this Indian princess was known in Mexico by the name "Bajo-el-Sol," or "Under-the-Sun." He had raised himself above the level of his tribe, and had he lived would have been its reformer. He considered his promise to the Government of Chihuahua, to fight the Apaches wherever he met with them, as a sacred pledge. Upon an expedition which—accompanied by some few young warriors of his tribe—he undertook to discover the position of the enemy, he came unawares, in the first dawn of the morning, upon a rancheria of the Apaches, of the tribe of the Espejos. They were not remarked, and the companions of the young hero urged him to retreat. But this was not his intention. "I have given my word to destroy the Apaches," he said, "and Bajo-el-Sol will never break his word." Hereupon he raised the war-cry of his tribe; six of his companions followed him, and like wild beasts they broke into the Apache village, cutting down everything before them, and spreading death and terror around, till they had all fallen themselves. Such events as these are quickly made known throughout Mexico by the captives escaping from these tribes; and the Mexicans themselves are so conscious of their Indian origin that they take pride in all deeds of Indian valour. I have remarked at least that such events are related with much satisfaction. After the death of Bajo-el-Sol, his brother, who became the head of the tribe, considered himself bound to carry on the war with the Apaches. During my stay at Chihuahua he attacked one of their rancherias, and brought away thirty-seven scalps. Subsequently, on my journey from Chihuahua to Texas, I passed the Presidio del Norte (on the Rio Grande, below El Paso), whence the Espejo Apaches had shortly before carried off several young girls. The Norteños, as the inhabitants are called, had sought aid from their allies the Comanches, and with them had concerted an expedition to the Sierra Rica, where the Espejos tribe then dwelt; and, as we had encamped near the Presidio, we were roused in the night by a troop of horsemen who passed us with laughter and song. They were a body of Norteños and Comanches just starting on this expedition. I subsequently heard that they succeeded in driving this Apache tribe from the Sierra Rica into the territory of Texas. On a subsequent journey from Texas to California, at the eastern base of the Limpia Mountains, I met the remainder of this tribe, which, joined to another tribe of Mescalero[1] Apaches, were long the terror of another portion of the State of Chihuahua; they made some demonstration of attacking our caravan.

During my residence at Chihuahua, the Mescaleros, being hard pressed by the Comanches, sent an envoy there to arrange a treaty of peace. A safe conduct is given on such occasions. I was told that these messengers were murdered on their return by order of the government, but I cannot answer for the truth of the statement. Such treachery, however, has in earlier times been recklessly committed, as for instance under Glanton.

---

[1] The Espejos are only a sub-division of the Mescaleros. Perhaps they no longer exist. The name was only the plural form of that of their chief, "Espejo" or "the Mirror." Many small tribes or bands, existing but temporarily, derive their names in a similar manner.

In order to complete my catalogue of the government measures, I must here refer to the military colonies, of which I have already spoken in the previous chapter. I then commented upon their uselessness. A totally different military system—the introduction of a well-armed militia—arming the whole population, with at the same time freedom of movement—in short, the *decentralisation* of all offensive and defensive measures, and the encouragement of every manifestation of individual strength, would soon keep these savages in check, and eventually get rid of them, if only a Mexican government possessed sense and energy enough for such a system.

There is one way, however, in which individual enterprise in this direction has been excited. The government has set a high reward for every Indian either captured or killed. It gives 200 dollars for every adult Indian, alive or dead. In the last case the scalp and ears of the victim must be exhibited in proof of the fact. An Indian woman, alive, is valued at 150 dollars; a living boy at the same sum, while for one dead 100 dollars is given. Captive Indian children are placed by the government in good families to be brought up. I have seen many such quite civilized. The girls become good servants; but the boys, as a rule, run away as soon as they have reached a certain age.

From this digression I return to an account of my excursions. One of the first was to the summit of the Cerro Grande. The steep sides of this isolated mountain, which consist of grey and reddish trachytic porphyry, are covered with grass, interesting varieties of cacti, and other plants peculiar to this region. From the summit you overlook a wide range of bare valleys, plains, and mountains. At the base, to the south-east, a vein of manganese rises to the surface. The ore is *Psilomelan.* A superficial shaft has been driven there, probably in expectation of a more valuable metal.

One can go quite round this mountain, passing over a broad and rather elevated pass behind the town, and returning through the valley of Tavalope, past the Junta. This tour, which describes a circle of about ten miles, I made on horseback with a man whom I shall subsequently have often to mention. Don Guillermo had offered me a horse which not every one would have liked to ride, and which indeed taxed all my skill to control. But though I occasionally nearly lost my seat, our wild gallop over the rough ground, intersected by deep watercourses, and covered with the thorny chaparral, was achieved without accident. We were some distance from the town when we remembered that we were without arms, and that consequently, should we meet any Indians, our safety must depend upon the fleetness and surefootedness of our horses. With such a stimulus the excitement became great, and I shall ever remember this ride for its extreme enjoyment. When we got on to the road of Tavalope, clear from the chaparral, we gave our steeds the rein. And along the deep bed of the stream, between steep rocks, and lighted by the glory of a Mexican full moon, we flew, while Don Guillermo, who took great pleasure in repeating poetry, recited the most beautiful verses of Zorilla's Don Juan Tenorio. Even this was characteristic. It was indeed a genuine Mexican ride, which cannot be imagined without Mexican scenery, Mexican ground, a Mexican sky, Mexican dangers, and above all Mexican horses. The surefootedness and endurance of these horses upon the roughest ground are unequalled. During hunts they will gallop up and down the steep mountain sides, and even take their riders at full speed over the jagged lava remains of a

Malpais.[1] As I am now speaking of the superiority of Mexican horses, I will just mention that Don Guillermo once rode 90 leguas, or 270 English miles, in two days on one horse.

The hunting parties which met almost every Sunday on the plain of Tavalope added much enjoyment to the many pleasant hours I spent in Chihuahua. We generally drove out six or eight miles, and then, leaving carriages and horses under the care of servants, we followed our game, and met again in the evening, each one bringing what he had shot. The river, the irrigation canals, and numerous ponds hidden among the long grass and trees and bushes, harbour innumerable ducks of many kinds. Geese are also found, and hares are abundant among the chaparral. We had all double-barrelled guns, and, for our own defence in case of need, a pair of revolvers; no opportunity, however, occurred for using them. We generally brought home sufficient game to serve two households for a whole week.

Accompanied by a naturalized Frenchman, who is much interested in the mines of the State, I visited Santa Eulalia, a small mountain town, of the celebrated mines near which I have already spoken. From the east side of the Cerro Grande, crossing a plain about ten miles in breadth, you arrive at a steep mountain-chain, in a narrow valley of which lies Santa Eulalia. Its aspect is very remarkable. The lofty mountains are covered with grass, yuccas, cacti, and in places with a thick coating of agaves like magnified turf. The buildings, one-storied mud huts with flat roofs, are going to ruin; but a large portion of the population, amounting to 1500, lives in rocky caves, the entrances to

[1] Malpais (or bad ground), a place covered with blocks and fragments of lava or basalt; in short, an old lava-bed.

which are visible at the foot of the rocks enclosing the valley. Water fails greatly during the dry season, and the smelting operations, for which it is indispensable, cannot be carried on. It was principally on this account that the smelting-works were transferred from hence to Chihuahua, where there is a sufficient amount of water-power. Good drinking-water is also much needed at Santa Eulalia, that of the place being rendered poisonous by metallic particles. I can offer no opinion as to the correctness of this assertion. Two facts are however certain,—first, that gentlemen from Chihuahua, who are obliged to remain there, drink no water but what is fetched from Chihuahua; and second, that I fell ill the day after my arrival, with gastric fever, which my companion attributed to my having incautiously drank some of the water of the locality. The greater number of the inhabitants, however, are too poor to have water fetched twelve miles daily. They have probably other springs nearer in the mountain.

This illness must be my excuse if my remarks upon this interesting place are few and insufficient. I was taken ill the day after my arrival, but during the forenoon visited the Guadalupe mine, which had been shortly before opened high up the mountain. The silver-ore, consisting principally of chloride and bromide of silver,[1] appears in a layer which enters the mountain almost horizontally among caverns and stalactitic formations, between the limestone strata of the mountain. The composition of these ores was as little understood here as at Chihuahua; my previous definition of their chemical nature has, however, since been confirmed by an analysis undertaken by Dr. Genth in Philadelphia. To what period the limestone strata belong

[1] Partly the pure chloride, partly Embolit.

I cannot say. The formation of the ore seems to have depended upon the contact of the limestone with the masses of porphyry, both repeatedly alternating. In smaller proportion the layer contains argentiferous galena, and in larger masses the carbonate of lead, associated with carbonate of iron.

These ores were formerly smelted in the valley, and the silver gained by cupellation. I witnessed the whole process, but have not sufficient technical knowledge to make any remarks upon it interesting to the professional metallurgist. The process is certainly very imperfect. The ore is conveyed from the mine on the backs of mules, and the labour is so hard that many of these animals die in consequence during the year. The scenery is wild and peculiar. From the height I saw the shafts of several disused mines on the opposite mountain, and in the valley the ruins of a place called Magellan.

In the afternoon I explored the mountain on the south side of the valley, and followed a stag up to its summit without being able to get a shot at it. Here also I observed the contact of limestone with porphyry. The latter had, in places, been extensively decomposed, and regenerated; in other places its surface was covered with fibrous radiated quartz as if with a glaze. Near the summit there is a deep ravine, the precipitous sides of which were covered with the gigantic lily-bearing stems of the yucca—an enchanting sight wherever seen. Yuccas, dasyliriums opuntias, and agaves covered the mountain sides, with many thorny shrubs, acacias, köberlinias, berberis trifoliolata, &c., growing among them. It was the last day of March, and all plants which could subsist without the summer rains were in full spring beauty.

Within a space of six English square miles all the mountains around Sta. Eulalia contain silver. More than two hundred mines have been worked here, and more than fifty of these have shafts above six hundred feet in depth. Several of them are so extensive that it takes a whole day to pass through one of them.

When these mines were at the height of their prosperity a tax of two grains of silver upon each mark was levied to build the cathedral of Chihuahua and the church of Santa Eulalia. The first cost 600,000 dollars, the last 150,000, and a surplus of 150,000 remained to the building fund when both were completed. The amount of this tax shows the produce of the mines to have been 14,500,000 marks of silver.[1] I have already stated that from 1703 to 1833, namely 130 years, according to a census taken at the end of this period, a mass of silver amounting to 43 millions of marks was raised from the mines of Santa Eulalia.

Since 1833, when these mines ceased to be regularly worked, up to this period, the inhabitants of the small town have always managed to find enough in them for their maintenance. People who, without knowledge or scientific resources, find their livelihood in the abandoned mines, are called in Mexico, Gambusinos. The whole population of Santa Eulalia is of this class. To give up working a mine is, according to Mexican law, to give up all right to it; and, still more, any one who will declare that he can work a mine more profitably than the person then holding it, may compel him to give it up, upon payment of a rent in proportion to the amount of ore hitherto

[1] According to Wislizenus, the cathedral of Chihuahua was seventy-three years building, and cost 800,000 dollars. The above statement is taken from a more extensive paper respecting the gold and silver mines of the State of Chihuahua, intended for the Mexican Congress, which was communicated to me in the MS., and which, translated into English, I published in the 'New York Tribune,' August, 27, 1853.

raised. Most of the mines of Santa Eulalia, according to this definition, may be considered as without owners, and may be taken by any one, whether a native or a foreigner, who is able to work them. The gentlemen of Chihuahua who, during my residence there, built new smelting-works on the Junta, found it more profitable to buy the ore at Santa Eulalia than to work a mine on their own account.

As regards their composition, the ores of Santa Eulalia are the poorest in the State of Chihuahua, and it has been only by the enormous quantities of the ore that such large results have been obtained. It seldom contains more than three ounces of silver to a carga or 300 lbs. of ore.

The following day I was compelled by the fever to keep my bed, and was obliged to return to Chihuahua in a carriage, being unable to sit my horse.

Some longer journeys which I undertook from Chihuahua will form the subject of the next chapter.

CHAPTER XI.

Western Region of the State of Chihuahua — Jesus Dominguez — "Novedades" — Cañada del Fresno — Different Character of Vegetation — Plastic Beauty of Mexican Scenery — Santa Ysabel — Mexican Country People — Hospitality and Simplicity of Manners — Romance in North Mexican Life — The Table-Land — The Bufa de Cosihuiriáchic and the Sierra Madre — Orological Remarks — Pass and Valley of Coyáchic — Lakes on the Table-Land — The Laguna de Castilla and its Environs — Valley of the Rio de Papigóchic and Watershed to the Pacific Ocean — Villa de la Concepcion and other Places in the Valley — Statistics of the Mines of Jesus Maria — The Tarumare Indians and their Customs — Cretaceous Formation in the Sierra Madre — Diminution and Restoration of the Mexican Population — Episodes of Mexican Life — A Robber Chief — A Mexican Free-thinker — Unnecessary Excitement — Return to Chihuahua.

IN the beginning of February a most welcome opportunity arose for me to visit the almost unknown regions in the extreme west of the State of Chihuahua. A merchant of the town, whom I have already mentioned as Don Guillermo, had to seek the payment of some old debts in that distant region, and invited me to accompany him upon his journey. The request was not quite devoid of self-interest, for the journey was dangerous, and a trustworthy companion desirable. Not only did the road pass through the most notorious haunts of the Apaches, but through districts rendered unsafe by other bands of robbers. Where, in Mexico, the Indians cease, more civilized robbers begin, and some places are exposed to the plundering attacks of both. Don Guillermo's purpose of collecting money was especially adapted to draw upon us the attention of some cavaliers of an older fashion, who were in the habit of performing their heroic deeds in the neighbourhood of the

Villa de la Concepcion, and on the road to the mines of Jesus Maria, perhaps simply to correct the injustice of Dame Fortune at the gaming-table. In proportion, however, to the degree of courage needed for such a journey was the flattering nature of the invitation to me; and, as I had been looking out for a travelling companion who would afford me some security in an excursion to the Sierra Madre, I could return the same compliment to Don Guillermo which he had paid me, and therefore agreed to his proposal. A carriage with two excellent horses formed our means of locomotion. Don Guillermo drove, while in dangerous places I sat next him with my gun on my knees, ready to fire. I had a double-barrelled gun, and he the same, with the addition of a rifle, in the carriage. Each of us, besides these, had a pair of Colt's six-shot revolvers of the largest calibre. A servant, the same Jesus Dominguez of whom I have already made honourable mention in the foregoing chapter, rode before our carriage, and was armed with a rifle and two single-barrelled pistols. Altogether we had thus thirty-two balls always in readiness.

Jesus Dominguez was of as much value to us as an escort of ten common servants. Courageous men prefer in this country a small but trustworthy travelling party to a large caravan. Our servant would have been scalped alive rather than have deserted us; and I would willingly give the reader some description of his character. He was as gentle as a child, and this gave a great charm to his large and powerful frame. His temper was hot, but completely under control, and on this account he would never be tempted to touch spirituous drinks. Withal he was a humourist and a philosopher, and liked to make his remarks upon any phenomena. He was an excellent mimic: he could perfectly imitate the Indians in the different scenes of their savage life, in the tones of their voices, their actions and expression; and enjoyed the fun of frightening an occasional party by such acting, and then laughing at them. He had gained this exact knowledge of the Indian character during his captivity among them as a boy, and through frequent intercourse with them afterwards. His father and brother were murdered by the savages; but he was so fortunate as to please Gomez, who at that time was the most dreaded chief of these savages in northern Mexico. Gomez became attached to the boy, gave him his freedom, and brought him back himself close to the town of Chihuahua, where, in taking leave of him, he gave him the good advice to avoid the Apaches for the future. "When you are on a journey," said the old chief to him, "avoid the road. Find a path a few hundred yards from the road, for there the Apache lies in ambush and will kill you." Jesus Dominguez had, however, evidently Indian blood in his veins. His complexion was dark brown, and his black hair hung straight and stiff about his broad face.

We left Chihuahua on the afternoon of the 3rd of February, and took the road to Santa Ysabel, a small town or village, lying about thirty miles to the south of the capital. Immediately upon quitting the town, the road passed over rocks of porphyry and fragments of basalt, then through the worn and deeply-cut beds of torrents, which, though now dry, bring down floods from the mountains in the rainy season. Even here the traveller must be on his guard, for many a poor unarmed woodcutter has been shot here by some concealed Indian, while harmlessly following his loaded mule. This evening we had accomplished but twelve miles, and bivouacked close to the buildings of the

Rancho del Fresno.[1] A bright fire was soon burning, at which Jesus Dominguez prepared our supper, and round which other travellers soon assembled. The evening passed in cheerful conversation, the principal subject of which was the danger of the road. A man from Rio Conchos, who was driving a small herd of cattle to the town, brought "Novedades"[2] from the south of the State. A number of men from Chihuahua, who were on the road to Durango, had been attacked by a band of Comanches, and several lives had been lost and 3000 dollars in specie. An old man from the Villa de la Concepcion, where we were going, told of much mischief perpetrated by the Apaches quite lately in that locality, and showed the scars of gunshot and arrow wounds which he had received in encounters with the savages. Indeed, I was the only one who had not suffered either directly or indirectly by them.

The next morning we had to pass the Cañada del Fresno, one of the most notoriously dangerous places in the State of Chihuahua. This is a valley of about four miles in length, between hills covered with dwarf oaks, ascending gradually to the higher table-land. In this pass the Apaches have so constantly availed themselves of the advantages of the ground that, without exaggeration, no hundred steps of the whole four miles can be trod, upon which the blood of some unfortunate traveller has not been shed. A governor of Chihuahua, once travelling through

[1] A "Rancho," in this neighbourhood, is the name of an estate, or of the buildings on one, especially devoted to cattle-breeding; while an agricultural estate is called a "Labor." These are smaller estates, though generally extending over several square miles. Large estates are called "Haciendas." Several ranchos and labores may belong to one hacienda.

[2] "Novedades," "news," means generally in this country misfortunes, especially such as are caused by the Indians. "No tiene u. novedades?" "Have you any news?" is the same as "Have you had any ill luck?" or "Are you well?" and is the usual greeting of travellers on the road. "No hay novedades," "There is no news," really means that "the road is safe. We have seen no Indians."

it, found the way so beset with crosses as to resemble a graveyard; and he ordered them to be taken down and burned, saying that the sight of them made men cowards. But since that time the number of these Memento Mori has quite sufficiently increased to make travellers familiar with the thought of death. Fortunately, we reached the higher ground without accident, where herds of cattle were grazing, and from whence we could see the fine buildings of the hacienda de los Charcos. This beautiful and valuable estate belongs to Don Estanislao Porras, whose name I have already mentioned in a foregoing chapter. He was at this time erecting a strong building at the upper end of the Cañada, in which travellers might find shelter and safety from the savages. The building was almost completed as we passed. But four weeks later, when we had returned safe and unmolested to Chihuahua, it was seized in the night by a band of Apaches, who attacked from it, in the early dawn, a passing caravan, and murdered from twelve to fifteen persons. In the savannah above, we saw another evidence of Don E. Porras' enterprising activity. It was a canal he had cut from the mountains to the north-east, as far as the road, a distance of at least eight or ten miles, in order to irrigate the intervening land, which is all his property. But the Apaches had actually made use of this as an intrenchment, in order to reach the road unperceived, and, lying in the hollow, had thence shot down some passing travellers.

Before proceeding farther in my narrative, I must remark that the character of the vegetation in the south-west portion of the State of Chihuahua changes greatly. The chaparral of the steppes of the Rio Grande, which extends north-west down the Gila to the Californian, and south-east to the Mexican gulf, disappears from the moister regions at the eastern base of the mountains which border the table-land to the west. It would be useless here to look for cacti and yuccas, for agaves, dasyliriums, the mezquite bush, and the larrea, the long, thorny rods of the fouquiera, the prickly leafless *koberlinia*, the artemisias, chenopodiaceous shrubs, and the other characteristic plants of the chaparral region. Instead of this strange-looking vegetation, the high plains are covered with a thick carpet of the finest grass, the mountain sides and hilly slopes with groves and woods of evergreen oaks, giving a park-like appearance to the savannah, while the high peaks of the Sierra Madre are clothed with dark masses of pine forest. Steppes and deserts, and barren rocks, with their stiff prickly plants, and grey thorny shrubs, only appear again in the lower region of Sonora, at the western base of the sierra.

The plain above the Cañada del Fresno exhibits one of the characteristic scenes of northern Mexico, which, though seen hundreds of times, can never fail to strike the intelligent traveller with its peculiar beauty. Nature hides none of her charms here, and leaves nothing either to fancy or to feeling wherewith to adorn the sharply-defined, bare reality. No groups of trees—shading the soft, green turf—tempt thought to wander to the happiness of a peaceful home. No stream or brook carries our imagination down the valley to the distant land its waters seek. No cloud floats over our head. The atmosphere here forms no portion of the landscape,—it is only the empty space by which it is bounded; while the distant mountains enclose the picture so harmoniously, and so perfectly, that one forgets to think of what exists beyond them. It is the purely plastic beauty of the scene which affects the feelings so powerfully. A broad, flat plain, surrounded by bare mountains, is spread before us. The contrast between their rugged alpine forms and the smooth plain before them is softened by the intervention of a beautiful curve at their base. No disturbing details of form, no trivial decoration is to be seen. The whole, as an artist would say, has been carried out by nature in the strict purity of the historic style. And truly the whole picture is historic; the plain record of great natural events.

The road through the savannah was as flat as a table. Don Guillermo, jokingly, tried how fast, in case of need, the horses could go, and put them to their full speed. Our carriage flew over the grassy plain with the rapidity of a railway train. The plain was soon behind us, and we found ourselves at the entrance of a mountain pass through which the road descends into the valley of Santa Ysabel, over porphyry, trachyte, diorite, and basalt rocks, with scattered fragments of blue and green chalcedony. Here, by the side of a small stream bordered by poplars and willows, the green wheat-fields showed the value of irrigation, while the catkins of the willows, and the swelling buds of the poplars told of the influence of a February sun. Later in the year, when these trees shade the stream whose transparent waters flow over many-coloured pebbles, —when the cornfields wave and the meadows around the town are decked with flowers,—Santa Ysabel must indeed be a delightful spot. The valley is surrounded by high grotesquely formed mountains. The northern group of these was formerly the haunt of an Apache tribe. When these savages held their feasts at night the hollow sound of the Indian drums could be heard in the town, and hence these rocks are still called the Sierra del Tambor. The place was originally founded as a mission for the Tarumare

Indians, and its position, like all similar places, was admirably chosen.

In the afternoon, while Don Guillermo prosecuted his affairs, I took my gun in order to shoot some wild ducks in the cornfields by the stream. Here, among the poplars and willows, I came suddenly upon a man who looked at me with as great astonishment as I should have felt had I seen a piece of the moon fallen down. "Where does your honour come from?" he asked in a timid tone. "From Europe," I replied jokingly. "Ahora?—ahorita?" "Now?—just now?" he asked again. "A short while since," was my answer. "But where do you come from now? just now?" "From your town." "But how did your honour get there?" "In a carriage." "With whom?" "With Don Guillermo." "Ah! with Don Guillermo of Chihuahua," he said now, apparently satisfied. "I know his honour very well; and since your honour has seen the world, you can perhaps tell me something of a young man, a relation of mine. We sent him to a person in Doñana for four years to learn four trades; and six years have gone by and we have heard nothing of him."

Our next day's journey was short. We left Santa Ysabel at noon, and reached Carretas at four. This village, or small town, lies in a well cultivated valley, the small river in which joins that at Santa Ysabel, whence united they fall into the Rio Conchos. This valley, like other valleys of this region is a deep indentation in the huge alluvial masses which cover this table-land, and is probably 500 to 600 feet lower than their average level. We remained here the whole of the next day, Sunday, and I cannot speak too highly of the hearty hospitality which we received from Don Felipe and his family. Indeed, nothing can exceed the friendliness and unaffected kindness, the good breeding and politeness of the Mexican country people. In almost every respect they are superior to our German peasants, and distinguishing the never ungraceful naïveté of their natural habits from coarse indecency, such as I have witnessed among the former, I must say the Mexican *ranchero*, or farmer, is much the more refined of the two. Puritanical prudery is no rule, but this has nothing in common with the above comparison. Beds were prepared for us the first night at Don Felipe's in the large saloon, and I remarked to Don Guillermo that I was tired, and wished the family would leave us alone that we might betake ourselves to rest. "You may wait then a long time," he replied, "for they stay on purpose to see us undress," and actually we were obliged to go through this ceremony in the presence of the Señoritas, who, with the closest attention, yet with perfect propriety of manner, watched every movement and every article of our dress till we laid ourselves down, when they wished us good night.

On Sunday evening the principal men in the village met in the house of our host, and, as usual, Indian adventures were related. One of these was so remarkably characteristic of the wild romance of North Mexican life that it greatly interested me, and I will repeat it here.

Some years ago an Apache chief, who had received a christian education in the house of a priest in the State Sonora, made himself a terror to this neighbourhood. He made use of his power to read and write as any civilized robber chieftain would have done. He intercepted the post from the mining localities, opened and read the letters, in order to learn when goods and silver were to be conveyed, and thus was able to arrange his plans successfully. At last, with his band, he fell into an ambush laid for him by some Mexican troops, and all were destroyed. This Indian lived with a Mexican girl whom he had stolen from her parents' house. She took part in the fight with these troops just like an Indian woman. Her country people called to her that she was recognised, and that she had nothing to fear if she would surrender. But she rejected the proposition and fell with the last of the band, having previously killed several soldiers with her arrows. On a later journey through the continent, I was told a similar circumstance by an inhabitant of Mesilla (on the Rio Grande) whose niece had been stolen by an Apache band, and now lived willingly with them. This man had met her at Santa Barbara with the chief of the Coppermine Apaches, then at peace with the North Americans, who assured him that there was no obstacle to the girl's return to her friends; but the girl rejected the proposition with disgust, and, when her uncle eagerly persuaded her, refused to speak to him. "Y era muchacha cristiana!" "and that was a christian girl!" adding indignantly as he told me the tale, "pero indiada, apachada!" "but turned Indian, turned Apache!"

We continued our journey the next day. The road up the side of the plateau is very steep. When we reached the plain we saw the village in the midst of its green cornfields far beneath our feet. On the other side of the valley the eye followed the horizontal line of the opposite plateau, above which isolated mountain groups raised their bare rocky peaks against the dark blue sky.

On the plain our road lay in a north-westerly direction, rising higher and higher for ten or twelve miles. The plateau here is a sloping plain. Before us rose two conical mountains like a double island on the horizon. The road follows the depression between them, called the Puerto de Coyáchic (Pass of Coyáchic). At first one does not see why, for the table-land around seems as level as the floor of a room. But nearer the two peaks, the plain is intersected by deep crevices, which are not visible till you are quite close to them. To the left of the twin mountains, a portion of the horizon intervening, rises another isolated mountain. This is the Bufa de Cosihuiriáchic. Dr. Wislizenus was the first who marked the geographical position of this mountain peak; but European geographers err in making it one of the main peaks and vertebræ of the Sierra Madre. The mountain rests upon the plateau, above which it is not much raised, at the edge of a deep ravine, from the bottom of which it may certainly have a considerable altitude. But above, it is entirely surrounded by the plain of the plateau and thus completely separated from the chain bearing the name of Sierra Madre, and from the axis of which it stands considerably to the east. It belongs in fact to the isolated groups occurring between the Sierra Madre and the town of Chihuahua.

As regards this mountain chain and its celebrated name, I shall endeavour farther on, in a general survey of the orology of North America, to rectify the prevailing errors on this head. I will only now remark that in Mexico (including New Mexico and California) there are several mountains called Sierra Madre, not in the slightest degree connected, but which geographers have incorrectly placed in contact, and that the Sierra Madre mentioned at this part of my journey must be defined as a mountain girdle, consisting of thickly set parallel chains, which forms the western orolographical limit and edge of the Mexican table-land, but which, in a hydrographical sense, stands on the slope to the Pacific Ocean; since the rivers passing through this region to the Gulf of California rise on the eastern side of the chain, on the table-land itself, and only reach the western side by forcing their passage through this mountain girdle. This definition agrees strictly with the terms used in the country, according to which the name of Sierra Madre is never extended to the chains and groups of a table-land. Indeed, these can in no respect be looked upon as spurs from that mountain barrier. On the contrary they mostly run parallel to it, rising from the plateau, like islands of an extensive Archipelago rise from the sea.

According to Wislizenus, the Bufa de Cosihuiriáchic has an elevation of 7918 feet above the level of the sea, and 1613 above that of the little town of Cosihuiriáchic. As this is situated in a cleft of the table-land surrounding the mountain, at the depth of at least 700 feet, the summit of the mountain must be about 900 feet above the plateau, and the latter about 7000 feet above the sea. From hence, north-west to Cerro Prieto, the small lake of which lies on the broad watershed between the Mexican and Californian Gulfs, the level gradually rises. At Carretas, on the contrary, it is lower, and at Santa Ysabel still lower. The plain of Chihuahua, as already mentioned, is only about 4600 feet above the sea level, and the Rio Grande, in a neighbouring portion of its course, has a fall, calculated at from 3000 to 4000 feet. Thus it follows that, from the Rio Grande to the eastern base of the Sierra Madre, the general level of the table-land rises gradually for about 3000 or 4000 feet.

To return to our journey. The road upon the slowly ascending plateau was so good that our horses took the eighteen miles to the foot of the pass of Coyáchic in a constant trot. The lofty plain exhibited very remarkable scenery.

The level ground was covered with the finest grass. To the right and to the left were the first slopes of the declivities into the valleys which bordered the plateau on either side. Bushes and groves of gnarled evergreen oaks, about the size of old pear trees, covered these slopes, and, scattered over the plain, gave it the appearance of a park. To the west, nearly parallel with our road, extended a line of mountains —the Sierra de San Borja—covered with dark forest, and separated from us by a deep narrow valley, which at first could not be seen, the mountains on the other side appearing as if standing on the same uninterrupted plain with us. The village or little town of San Borja lies in it, and it is the same valley in the upper portions of which Coyáchic and Cosihuiriachic are built. Wherever we could get a peep at San Borja, the sides of the valley were covered at regular intervals with small oak trees, giving them the appearance of an orchard of many miles in length.

We arrived thus at the foot of the pass of Coyáchic, where the road became more steep and rugged. There was no difficulty, however, in the ascent. Above, the scenery is extremely wild: grotesque rocks of porphyry, covered with grey, green, and yellow lichen, rise on each side in cliff and pinnacle, up to the very summit of the two peaks. Several kinds of oak, and pines with needles half a foot in length, grow on the ledges and in the crevices. The entrances of caves are seen in several places.

As soon as the summit of the pass is reached, one looks suddenly down into a deep valley, or rather upon the other side of it, exhibiting a steep, rugged strangely-shaped cleft in an enormous alluvial mass, or conglomerate. It seems impossible for a carriage to get down into this abyss and to make its way out of it on the other side; but the descent, which is well known to the drivers under the name of Cuesta de Coyáchic, is less difficult than might have been imagined. An enterprising and wealthy man, Padre Gallejo, curate of Coyáchic, has had a road made at his own expense, proving himself at the same time to be a good patriot and a prudent speculator. When we reached the valley he sent a boy to require half a dollar from us as a toll. The appearance of the road down to the village, with its interesting old mission-house, the grotesque rocks and ravines of the plateau, with the mountain rising from it behind us, were altogether most singular.

On the other side of the village we found in the valley a small "conducta" or caravan encamped, to which, as it was going in the same direction with us, we joined ourselves, in order not to encounter the dangerous passage of the Puerto de las Casas Coloradas alone. We started early the next morning with this party. The road ascends through oak woods in the broken ground of these clefts in the table-land. Their sides are so precipitous near the summit that a few steps bring you into what appears another country. From the wood, which ceases with the cleft in a sharp line, one enters upon a broad grassy plain, which branches off in the distance between different mountain chains and groups, and which contains a number of larger and smaller lakes; some of these are not far from the road. Farther on, in a south-westerly direction, the Laguna de los Llanos spreads its extensive surface at the foot of the distant mountains belonging to the Sierra de los Ojos Azules. To the north, at no great distance, yet not visible from the road, lies the Laguna de Castilla, the largest lake in North Mexico, surrounded by the richest pastures which, irrigated by warm springs, remain green winter as well as summer. I was told it was twenty leguas in diameter; which must, however, be an exaggeration. It is, however, remarkable that this lake is not given in any maps, at least not in any which I have been able to see.[1] Persons well acquainted with this lake and its environs told me that in places on its shores the land is hollow and gives way, so that man and horse may be swallowed up. The situation of the lake is geographically interesting, since it occupies the summit of a central part of the table-land. Round it are the sources of brooks and rivers flowing to the four quarters of the world; south and eastwards into the Rio Conchos, and subsequently into the Rio Grande; westwards into the Rio Yaqui, which flows into the Gulf of California; northwards through the Rio del Carmen, the Rio de Santa Maria, the Rio de las Casas Grandes, and other streams, into a succession of lakes—the Laguna de Encinillas, Laguna de los Patos, Laguna del Candelario, Laguna de Santa Maria, and Laguna de Guzman. This region, with all these lakes, is the most unexplored part of Mexico.

We travelled with this conducta in a north-westerly direction over the table-land, approaching a mountain chain which begins in this locality and continues north-north-west till we at last passed it at the Puerto de las Casas Coloradas, the Pass of the Red Houses. We might have gone round the southern extremity of this chain; but our companions, whom we followed, feared the lower region, called Bajio del Chato, notorious through the crimes of the Indian chief. The Pass of the Red Houses is scarcely of less evil repute. In several places we found the remains of waggons which

[1] Mr. Herman Ehrenberg completed his map, which he published at San Francisco, from my sketches and notes, which I have likewise sent to the War Department at Washington. See 'Map of the Gadsden Purchase, Sonora, and portions of New Mexico, Chihuahua, and California, by Herman Ehrenberg, C. E. From his private notes, and those of Major Heintzelman, Captain Sitgreaves, Lieut. Derby, Bartlett, Gray, Julius Froebel, and others. San Francisco, 1854.'

had been plundered and destroyed by the Apaches. On the other side of the pass we came to the plain of Cerro Prieto, which is only a continuation of the table-land extending round the southern base of the mountain. Here, for the first time, we came upon a portion of the real system of the Sierra Madre—a long mountain-ridge covered with thick and lofty pine forests. This joins the plain at Cerro Prieto, and bounds on the south-west a small strip of the table-land, which, enclosed to the north-east by the Sierra de las Casas Coloradas and its offsets, imprisons a small stream belonging to the watershed system of the Pacific Ocean for full sixty miles in a north-westerly direction between these mountains. A small lake, already named as the Laguna de Cerro Prieto, lies on the watershed. The plain surrounding it is a real Alpine prairie, into which the lofty pine-forest of the Sierra Madre descends. The village of Cerro Prieto lies to the south-west of the lake; we left them to the west of our route. The water and its shores were covered with flocks of geese and ducks. We went on in a north-westerly direction along the above-named narrow strip of table-land. This forms at first the base of the valley between these two mountain chains; but gradually, as the bed of the stream washes deeper into the alluvial ground, broad terraces are formed, the surface of which belonged perhaps originally to the declivity towards the Gulf of Mexico, while the worn river bed exhibits the first lowering of the ground towards the Pacific Ocean. The small stream, rapidly augmented in size by the mountain torrents, forms one of the branches of Rio Yaqui of Sonora.

We spent a wretched night of hunger and cold near some inhospitable houses, called los Ranchitos, or the Huts. Passing the buildings of the deserted Rancho del Rosario, the limits of which enclose a very beautiful territory, and through the village of San Antonio—where the valley becomes safer, and we saw the first herds grazing in the meadows—we arrived the following day at the Villa de la Concepcion, the most important place in the western portion of the State of Chihuahua. The Indian name of this small town, Papigóchic, belongs to the Tarumare language, and means "Snipe town." The brook we had passed unites here with a considerable mountain-stream flowing from a lateral valley of the Sierra Madre. Thus augmented and continuing in a north-westerly direction, the Rio de Papigóchic passes the villages of Santo Tomas, Tejológachic, Mátachic, and Temósachic, and, between this last and Yepómera, breaks with a sudden turn to the west, through the Sierra Madre.

This elevated valley forms the richest portion of the state of Chihuahua, and is looked upon as its granary. When there is drought on lower ground, rain never fails here, nor water in the rivers, for irrigation. The scenery is beautiful and the climate perfect. Snow and ice are not unknown in winter, but the cold is never severe; and the heat in summer is not oppressive. The region is celebrated for its excellent apples, which are sent as far as Sonora. A mule's load of this fruit, worth here 3 dollars, would be sold at Guymas for 40. Oranges are purchased in exchange for them. The celebrated mines of Jesus Maria, in the Sierra Madre, close to the frontier of Sonora, lie within a few days' journey from Concepcion, or the Villa, as it is here called, and are supplied with wheat, maize, &c., from hence. These mines, now greatly neglected, made the town of Concepcion formerly an important place, and even now it contains much wealth. The merchants of Chihuahua still consider its inhabitants their best customers, and they have always a good day when a conducta from the villa arrives to make purchases. But here, as elsewhere, the facile but precarious acquirement of wealth by mining exercises an injurious influence on the morals of the place. Its inhabitants are the most determined gamblers in the whole State; and as in other places a man's credit depends upon his good or bad speculations, as far as they may be known, so here it is influenced by the results at the gaming-table. "Will Don N. N. pay me?" asks one man of business, in confidence, of another. "Yes, I think he will; he won 5000 pesos yesterday," is the kind of answer.

I will here state some particulars I learned from good authority respecting the celebrated mines of Jesus Maria.

These mines, which yield auriferous silver ore, lie near the source of the Rio Mayo, in the very heart of the mountains. Some are worked exclusively for gold, as the Mina del Rosario, which occasionally has yielded 10,000 dollars' worth of gold in a week. Still silver is the chief produce, but, on account of its constant admixture with gold, a marc of the silver of Jesus Maria is worth 10 dollars at the mint of the country, while pure silver is worth only 8½. Among the many mines of this locality, that of Santa Ludubigen has been worked since the expulsion of the Spaniards; and in six months, from May to October, 1839, yielded a clear profit of 400,000 dollars. But the principal mine at Jesus Maria is the Santa Juliana. It has not been worked since the expulsion of the Spaniards, and is now full of water. According to competent judges, it would require 200,000 dollars to empty it and resume the works. The ores of this mine have never been found to contain less than 3 marcs, or 24 ounces of silver, in a carga or 300 lbs. of ore, and have even held the unusual quantity of 40 ounces; so that a mule's load of the ore was worth 400 dollars. Even now, although the mines are no longer worked, the town is supported by the results of the unskilled labour of numerous "gambusinos," who, having money advanced to them by capitalists, are bound to sell them the ore they raise, monthly, at a rate of 16 per cent. lower than that of the mint at Chihuahua. One man, who employed 20,000 dollars in this kind of speculation, doubled it in a year. But though the mint at Chihuahua pays 16 per cent. more than the miner gets for his ore, it gives full 20 per cent. less than its real value. It is easy, therefore, to see of what extraordinary results these mines are capable.

We found a most hospitable and friendly reception in the house of one of the first men in the Villa de la Concepcion. Don Rafael, having remarked my desire to learn something of the Tarumare Indians, communicated several facts, which, connected with the results of other inquiries, appear to me worthy of being better known than I have reason to believe they are.

First, I must premise that all civilized Indians in the State of Chihuahua are called Tarumares, although they are not all of the same race. The greater number of them, however, have one origin, and speak a common language, the grammar of which is well known, as a treatise on it, published in Mexico, still exists in print. Whether the language of the so-called Tarumares, who are not of the real tribe, though differing may have some affinity with the real Tarumare language, I cannot say. Here I speak of the genuine Tarumares.

These Indians form a portion of the population of the Villa de la Concepcion, and of all the other communities in the valley; and all these places have the rights of

Indian pueblos, although the majority of their present inhabitants consist of "gente de razon," "reasonable people," as the Spanish Mexicans call themselves, in contradistinction to the Indians. These Tarumares, although retaining their own language, have, however, given up the greater part of their old customs. But remnants of this nation exist in the more remote mountain regions, who, though calling themselves Christians, and standing in some degree of political connexion with the State, have still preserved some portion of their own social system. Their land is held in common, and from time to time is redivided in proportion to the necessities and labour of each family. A certain portion is reserved for the exigencies of the old, the sick, and the helpless; is cultivated by the united labour of the tribe, and the produce stored in a public magazine. These stores, as also those for whom they are collected, are under the care of especial functionaries of both sexes, called tenanches. One tribe of the Tarumares still exists, however, in some of the valleys of the Sierra Madre, near the celebrated mines of Batoseágachic, which retains, unchanged, its old Indian religion and social habits. These people, though not exactly inimical to the Spanish Mexican race, abstain from all intercourse with strangers. If a traveller enter their dwelling, they leave it; if they see him coming, they avoid him; if he speaks to them, they give no answer, even if they understand him; and the largest sum will not tempt them to sell him anything. A traveller might die of hunger in one of their villages unless he appropriated what was absolutely necessary, a proceeding which this singular people permits. The characteristic stubbornness and reserve of the Indian race appear, among these, in their most rugged, though passive form.

I heard much of certain national games of the Tarumares and other Pueblo Indians of the States of Chihuahua and Sonora. Whole tribes or communities have foot-races, continuing from sunrise to sunset, the aim of which is to see who shall hold out longest. Each party rolls a ball before them over hill and valley. I was told that when they sink exhausted, they open the veins of their legs, and that women stand at certain parts of the road ready to pour water over those who faint.

We left our carriages at Concepcion, and continued our journey down the valley on horseback. The first village on the road is Santo Tomas. Its situation is full of geological interest. The eastern sierra rises here to its greatest height, the Cerro de Santo Tomas, at the foot of which the valley is crossed by a bank consisting of layers of a chalky limestone enclosing flints, through a narrow cleft in which, with precipitous sides, the stream has forced a passage. Beyond this singular threshold it passes by the village of Tejológachic into the open valley which bears the same character as mentioned above. We hastened forward without any stoppage, and passed the night in Mátachic. Two days previously the Apaches had stolen 150 head of cattle, and almost the whole male population of the village, joined by that of Tejológachic, Santo Tomas, Temosáchic, and Yepómera, had started on an expedition against the savages. Between Mátachic and Temósachic we stopped at a rancho belonging to a friend of Don Guillermo. We found old Don Blas in a pitiable condition. An Apache had run him through the body the week before with a lance; yet it seemed to me that he would recover from the dangerous wound. Upon our return we slept at the same rancho, and it struck me that, were the Indians to destroy some of its inhabitants, their places would soon be filled by those who remained. "Que muchacheria!" "what a housefull of girls!" exclaimed Dominguez, as upon our arrival we were surrounded by a dozen young women; while the court swarmed with children, of whom these were the mothers. I could not discover a proportionate number of fathers. But be that as it may, large families are common in this country. At Santo Tomas I saw a very young-looking woman who was the mother of eight children.

Temosáchic was the farthest extent of our journey. The river here breaks to the west through such a narrow cleft of the Sierra Madre that the opening is scarcely perceptible, and one wonders to where it goes. The village of Yepómera, a few miles farther north, is the last in this region of the State of Chihuahua. An uninhabited district, with the ruins of buildings destroyed by the Apaches, with wild cattle, the remains of former herds, extends towards Corralitos, Casas Grandes, and Yanos, the most northern limits of the State, whither a rarely-used road leads from hence. There are many springs in the valley, near Temósachic and Yepómera; and some of these are sufficiently warm to promote the growth of the grass in winter, a great advantage for the cattle of these villages.

The course of my narrative affords me an opportunity of showing how the peon system influences the existence of the Mexican people.

A respectable man in Temósachic had from time to time bought goods of Don Guillermo in Chihuahua, who had never hesitated to give him credit for a few hundred dollars, and the debt was always paid at the expiration of the term. The man died, and his son came to Chihuahua with a letter, written apparently by his dying father, in which he requested the merchant to show his son the same kindness he had displayed to him. Don Guillermo willingly granted the request, the young man took goods for a few hundred dollars: three years elapsed, no payment was made, and nothing was heard of the young man, and now his creditor appears suddenly in Temósachic. "Where does Natividad Andrada live?" asked Don Guillermo of the first person we met as we rode into the village. "There is his mother's house," was the answer. We rode on to the open door, at which a respectable-looking old woman appeared. "Is Natividad at home?" "No, Sir." "Is he in the neighbourhood?" "He is in the village." "Let him be called; I must speak to him." In two minutes he came. He was a young man of more than middle height, well formed, and with good regular features, on which an irregular life now began to show its traces. "Natividad," said Don Guillermo to him, "as you have not come to me, I have been obliged to come to you. Why have I never seen you again in Chihuahua?" "I was unable to pay your honour." "Can you pay me now?" "No: I am poor; I have nothing." "Do you know how much you owe me?" "Not exactly." "Three hundred dollars." "It is so, since your honour says so." "Cannot you pay me at least a portion of it?" "I have nothing." "Then you must come with me and work for me." "I am ready; I believe your honour's demand is just." "Then get ready: I cannot wait." "I am ready; I wear all I possess." This consisted of an old straw hat, a coarse cotton shirt, wide unbleached cotton trowsers, sandals, and a gay-coloured ragged woollen blanket, with which the poorest man gracefully covers his rags.

During this conversation, which deeply affected the fate of several persons, we had not got off our horses, and the old woman had not spoken a word. She now burst into tears, and, turning to Don Guillermo, said, "Your honour claims your right; but how miserable am I in my old age! He is my only child. But I have long seen that he would not be the comfort of my latter years: he has not followed his father's example. But will not the gentlemen dismount and enter my poor house?" she added, with the politeness which the lowest of the Spanish race never forget. "Yes," said Don Guillermo, as we entered the small clay hovel, "your husband was a worthy man. How has his son fallen into so miserable a position?" "Ah, Sir! he has gambled away everything." "I should have given him no credit but for the letter of his father: how could he recommend a son whose bad character he must have known?" "Ah, Sir, my husband never wrote that letter; my boy forged it at the instigation of his bad companions." "Then it is right that you should be punished," said Don Guillermo to the young man: "and your Señora," he continued to the mother, "must comfort yourself. As the lad now is, he can never give your honour any help. I will take charge of him. I will teach him to work and to live like a respectable man, and the time may come when he will return to you an estimable character. You will go with me to Texas," he then added, addressing himself to the son. "Wherever your honour pleases;" and after a short stay, during which the old woman regaled us with "tortillas" and "frijoles," and Natividad took leave of a young woman and kissed a child, we left the place, and set out on our return.

It deserves especial notice that this transaction, which did not occupy half an hour, was settled without the intervention of any public authority

A similar transaction, with regard to another debtor of Don Guillermo's, took place on our way back to the Villa de la Concepcion. Guadalupe Vargas was a sly, satirical, but at the same time careless, good tempered fellow. Later, in a confidential hour, when we were sitting together under the shadow of an oak in the Californian mountains, he acknowledged to me that for some time he had been one of a robber band. Don Guillermo was probably not aware of this circumstance, when he trusted him with some hundred dollars' worth of goods to begin business as a hawker. The goods were easily sold, and the money as easily gambled away, and Guadalupe cared little for his debt, till Don Guillermo surprised him as suddenly as he had done Natividad. In a few words, Guadalupe was just as willing as his fellow-debtor to follow his creditor as a peon, though he looked upon his fate rather differently. When he heard that he was to accompany his master to Texas, he asked permission to see his old mother once more, who lived in a neighbouring village. "I wish to have my mother's blessing upon this long and dangerous journey in a strange country," he said, with a mixture of sanctimonious piety and careless banter. Natividad, who, with all his vices, possessed a more serious and affectionate disposition, sighed deeply. "My mother," he said, with real, repentant sorrow, "will not bless me." "What do you sigh for, man?" exclaimed his companion in misfortune; "repentance is of no use. Begin a new life! Does not Don Guillermo, a distinguished cavalier, open the door of the world to you? What have you known of the world as yet? Nothing! Now you will get acquainted with it! You will see the United States! You will be a man! You will pay your debts! and when, after an absence of some years, you go back to your native place, your mother may be dead, but your children will be grown big, and who knows but their father may become Alcalde of Temósachic?" All this is so thoroughly Mexican that I cannot refrain from placing it before the reader as distinctly as I am able. Both these men, with whom I subsequently travelled many thousand miles, and of whom I must therefore speak, are instances of the good and evil qualities of the Mexican character; and, although the first might be clouded by the last, yet I can truly say that later they were both distinguished by their perfect good will, their untiring activity, and irreproachable honesty. Their fate is typical of that of their nation,—a nation which, in the whole history of the Spanish race, has been in the worst possible position for moral development; but which possesses good natural powers, which in the farther history of the New World will not be lost.

But I must return to Temósachic. While we were in the house of our present servant, a young woman came in to inquire for her husband, who had gone to Chihuahua, and had remained longer than he had fixed. The man's name was Don José Jesus de la Luz Miramontes. What harmony of sound—but what empty noise in a name! In another country, the man would have been Dick, or Jack, or Bill. It is a positive misfortune for a people to have too beautiful a language, and the English and the North Americans would assuredly not have developed their energy of character could their language make pretension of being musical.

The appearance of the young woman I have just mentioned struck me very much. She had light hair, blue eyes, and a complexion as delicate and fresh as that of any German blonde. This type is not unfrequent in the "tierra fria," the higher and cooler regions of North

Mexico. I do not venture to assert whether this shows the influence of climate and the power of adaptation in the human constitution, or the reverse,—the immutability of types and races.

When we remounted to leave Temósachic, it was extremely painful to me to see that Natividad was obliged to follow us on foot, and in a quick trot to keep up with our horses. But I could make no alteration, and could only watch with surprise how, like a faithful dog, he trotted on, now before and now behind us, and then again at our side. Vargas joined him at the villa, and, though at first his speed was insufficient, he soon taught his legs to move, when he saw that he must either keep up with our carriage or run the risk of being scalped by some wandering Apache. This treatment of the two men was assuredly cruel; but it is not considered so in Mexico. An extraordinary rapidity and endurance in running is common to all Mexicans of the lower class. In the next chapter I shall bring forward some instances of almost incredible performances in this respect.

On our way back, we stopped a night in the house of the Alcalde of Santo Tomas. We had been told that this man, although the first official in the place, was literally a robber chief. Don Guillermo asked him jokingly at table, if he knew the character imputed to him. "Ah," he replied laughing, "I know all about it. It is a mistake. The Christian name as well as the surname of the chief are the same as mine, and his wife has the same name as mine; but it is another man, and he lives in Cerro Prieto." This was actually the case. It was the band to which our friend Guadalupe, by his own account, had formerly belonged, and about which he, at a later period, gave me many details. "Your honour might have travelled safely there with me," he said; "none of them would have hurt you in my company."

Santo Tomas was originally a Mission of the Jesuits, and all the Patres are buried in the church of the place; among them the founder of the Mission, which must have been established at the beginning of the seventeenth century. The Alcalde showed us the church and took us into the vaults, where Dominguez had preceded us. When we entered, we found our servant standing before the embalmed body of the canonized Padre, which he had taken out of its sarcophagus and placed upright against the wall, talking to it in the following manner: "So you are a saint: well, you can't have had much sense; you have had too small a scull for that." And indeed the scull was remarkably small. The Alcalde laughed. We took care that the sacred remains should be carefully restored to their resting-place, and helped to close the tomb with its stone.

Proceeding farther homewards we came by Cerro Prieto, leaving the small lake near it, this time, to the east. Among others, Don Guillermo visited here the robber chief; and had it been feasible we should have brought him away also as a peon, for he too was one of Don Guillermo's debtors. But great folks cannot be treated like small ones; and, besides being captain of a brave band, the man was one of the first inhabitants of the place. However he received Don Guillermo with the greatest courtesy, and the business was settled with many polite expressions from both parties. Of course there was no payment, and indeed had it been made we should probably have had to relinquish it again on the road.

We now came to Los Llanos, a village by a lake of the same name, which I have already mentioned. Don

Guillermo had here a debtor, whom he would have gladly brought away as a peon; but the man refused to go, and the judge before whom the matter was brought decided in his favour. The whole business, with the judge's decision, was settled in an hour.

In passing the notorious Bajio del Chato, we had a slight alarm. A flock of geese and cranes rising in the distance made us think that they had been disturbed by Apaches. Our infantry, consisting of Natividad and Guadalupe, was quickly armed, and our cavalry, consisting of Dominguez, sent on to reconnoitre. He was at once in his true element. Throwing his hat into the carriage, and binding a red kerchief about his rough hair, he set spurs to his horse, and with his rifle in his hand galloped directly towards the suspicious spot. A depression in the ground hid him from our sight, when sidewards at some little distance we saw a horseman who, with violent gestures, made us all sorts of incomprehensible signs. As, from his position, he could see our servant, we felt sure that he had fallen into the hands of the Indians. We could not desert him. Don Guillermo drove furiously, and our foot soldiers followed breathless, as fast as they could. But, when we reached our man, he was standing quietly near a stranger who had spoken to him on the road. It was this person who had startled the geese and cranes and frightened us. But even such insignificant circumstances as these are characteristic of a North Mexican journey. On the 20th we arrived safe and well at Chihuahua, our journey having occupied seventeen days.

CHAPTER XII.

March of General Trias' Brigade from Chihuahua to El Paso, and the Author's Return by the Sandhills — Cause of this Military Movement — The Mesilla Valley — Accompanying Circumstances of Mexican Politics — Proclamation of the Garrison of Chihuahua — Don Angel Trias — Departure of the Brigade — In what Capacity accompanied by the Author — March, and Camp Scenes — Important Intelligence — Burning Prairies and Insolence of the Indians — El Sause — Sheep herded with Artillery — Hacienda de Encinillas — Ojo de la Laguna — Plan de Alamos — El Carmen — Punta de Agua, Disappearing River — Alamos de Pena and Reappearing River — Carrizal — Forced March of Eighty-four English Miles in Twenty-four Hours — El Paso — Electric Bed — Return — Ojo de Samalayuca — Drive over the Sandhills, and Natural Flower-garden of gigantic proportions.

In April, 1853, while Mexico was disturbed by one of its numerous revolutions, it appeared as if the most trifling frontier question would have sufficed to produce actual hostilities between this republic and the United States. Difficulties arose in a mixed commission of both republics, in settling the boundary line, the result of which was to make the large village of Mesilla, with a portion of the valley to the right of the Rio Grande, the subject of a serious struggle. This small territory has, under the unsuitable name of the Mesilla valley, gained a reputation far beyond its merits. Although its area does not exceed a few English square miles, and does not form a separate valley, still it belongs to the most beautiful and fertile portions of the valley of the Rio Grande. The dispute was, however, subsequently adjusted, by the Republic of Mexico, under the Presidency of Santa Ana, agreeing to sell to the United States a strip of their northern frontier, to which, in addition to a desert of some 300 or 400 miles in length, the

VALLEY OF THE RIO GRANDE, NEAR MESILLA.

Book II, Chap. 12.

beautiful plain of Mesilla, with the village, belonged. Before this agreement, however, some North American speculators had endeavoured to set in motion less peaceful means for obtaining this desired annexation; and the governor of New Mexico was misled to issue a proclamation, in which he threatened to take possession of Mesilla by force.

By this step the hot-headed governor of New Mexico came in contact with the equally hot-headed governor of the State of Chihuahua, then placed in circumstances recommending decisive action.

The revolution, which dislodged the President Arista and for a time placed old Santa Ana at the head, had been preparing during the latter half of the year 1852. The outbreak occurred in October, in Guadalaraja, and the "Pronunciamiento," or revolutionary programme, under the name of the Plan of Jalisco, was rapidly spread over all the States of the Mexican Federation. In January, Arista was compelled to retire from the Presidency, and a few months later Santa Ana assumed the highest authority. During the interval the President's chair was vacant, and there were many perhaps who might have thought themselves able to take possession of it.

As an entire stranger to Mexican affairs, and being but just arrived in the country, my surprise was excessive at learning early one morning in December—it was the day before Christmas-Day—that the government of Chihuahua had been dismissed by a "Pronunciamiento" of the garrison, and that General Trias, hitherto military commandant of the States, had been summoned to act as provisory governor. No one opposed the step, which was accomplished without loss of blood, and though individual enmities might produce some animosity, General Trias was not the man to uphold any unworthy party spirit or persecution, so that this revolution in Chihuahua was the most harmless and amiable one it has ever been my fortune to witness.

Public life was naturally full of excitement, and more interesting to a stranger than under the usual course of events; but the European would err greatly in thinking that such a political change in the less civilized Mexican territory must necessarily assume a harsher form than in Europe, justly proud as she is of her refinement. Chihuahua at least, where the change was deeply felt by all, could have shamed by her example, the party-spirit of many German states under similar circumstances. The controversy was conducted by the press with vigour, but without coarseness. Five newspapers appeared at that time in this small town, and their numbers, with other temporary papers, were always announced daily in the streets. The inhabitants from time to time were roused by the bells tolling in the night, that they might learn some important intelligence, some new success which had attended the principal party. Thus, on January 31, it was told through the town that General Trias had been requested to come from Guadalaraja and take the command of the army of the Pronunciados, then marching towards the capital, and that, in case of success, powerful support for the presidency was promised.

Don Angel Trias is an interesting man, well known both in Mexico and in the United States. At this time I was introduced to him by Colonel Langberg, and spent an evening with him in animated conversation about natural history, literature, and the latest political events in Europe. Referring to the geology of the country, he showed me a well-preserved grinder of a mastodon, which had been lately found on the eastern side of the Sierra

Madre, near the Villa de la Concepcion. General Trias understands German well, and he has Schiller's and Goethe's works in his library. He speaks French and English fluently. I was told some curious anecdotes of his youth, and of the circumstances which led to his having undertaken some extensive journeys; and I will repeat them here, without, however, making myself answerable for their accuracy. A youthful adventure involved results for which his confessor refused him absolution, referring him to the Bishop of Durango. The Bishop of Durango took the same course, and referred him to the Archbishop of Mexico. The Archbishop sent him to the Pope at Rome, who enjoined upon the young Mexican a pilgrimage to Jerusalem, and penance at the Holy Sepulchre, where at last he received absolution. On his return through Turkey, and up the Danube, he visited Germany, and remained for a time in some of its principal towns.

When the intelligence reached Chihuahua that the Governor of New Mexico intended to take possession of Mesilla, General Trias immediately put in motion that portion of the Mexican army under his command, and without waiting to be empowered by the then disorganised central authority, set off, April 7th, with his brigade from Chihuahua to El Paso.

I found an inducement to accompany this expedition in a fixed capacity. For the transport of its stores and ammunition, the detachment had hired of my friends, Mayer and Co., ten of the largest waggons which had formed our caravan from the United States, with about 110 mules, muleteers, drivers, and waggon-master, for the sum of 3000 dollars; and I undertook to represent the firm during the journey, and after its arrival at El Paso. The personal character of the general, and my acquaintance with several officers of the brigade, Colonels Langberg and Justiniani, made this a pleasant task, the fulfilment of which gave me an opportunity of seeing a part of the State which I had not yet visited, for the prevailing drought on the direct road to Carrizal compelled us to go round by El Carmen.

The detachment consisted of 500 infantry, 50 or 60 cavalry, and 6 or 8 guns. The larger number of the soldiers were well dressed, and looked respectable; but there were some of doubtful character and appearance, who resembled more nearly a band of gipsies than any portion of the military power of a state. This rabble, with the crowd of women and children which always hangs on the skirts of a Mexican army, gave our march and camp scenes a most motley and grotesque appearance. Here was one whose whole uniform consisted of a shirt and a straw hat; another who had wrapped his naked body in a gay-striped blanket, and adorned his stiff hair with a regular shako; a third, who having only a pair of trousers, had found even these superfluous, and had rolled one leg up above the knee. Here a woman with one child in her arms, and another at her side, following the long day and night marches without complaint; there another carrying two large gourd-shells full of water, balanced on each hand above her head for miles from the last spring, ready, in spite of weariness, to share her supply with the thirsty. The devotion and endurance of these women are wonderful; for it is solely their desire to be near their husbands, and to assist them on the road as well as in the camp, which induces the desperate resolution of accompanying them upon a march, during the first forenoon of which, many of the soldiers were struck down by sunstroke.

Still, in spite of all the difficulties of the march, our camp was always a scene of merriment and good humour. Three bands assisted in keeping up cheerfulness; and we cooked, and ate, and drank amid talk, and joke, and laughter. The conversation of the Mexicans is witty, and their range of ideas is far from being coarse or low. Two of our teamsters, one of New Mexico the other of Chihuahua, had a conversation full of sarcasm. "In New Mexico," I heard the former say, "the people make good verses—componen buenos versos—and you can't do that." "True," said the one from Chihuahua, "the people of Chihuahua are not so poetical, but they have more knowledge of the world"—"No es tan poeta la gente de Chihuahua, pero sabe mas del mundo." I should like to know on what high road of Germany a couple of waggoners would have chosen such subjects of conversation? One day, going round the camp, I saw a soldier reading a book about the French Revolution. He entered into conversation with me about it, and then passed on to the circumstances in which Mexico was placed, of which he took a gloomy view.

We halted for noon at the Rancho del Sacramento, the scene of a battle little calculated to inspire our soldiers with hopeful feelings. Dinner was spread on the ground near the buildings for me and the mayor domo of our train, and we had just seated ourselves in Turkish fashion, when a pig ran grunting among our dishes. Their contents were scattered about, a cock, quickly perceiving his opportunity, called his dames around him, and before we could turn ourselves about, every trace of our meal had vanished. The next day, however, made amends for this misfortune. The general, with the most precise attention to etiquette, sent an officer to invite me to dine with him in his tent. The party was cheerful and unconstrained, and the conversation quite on a par with that of men of the same class in Europe. I was asked my birthplace in Germany—"Rudolstadt." "Ah, Schwarzburg-Rudolstadt," remarked one of the officers. "There is also a principality Schwarzburg-Sondershausen." I looked surprised. "Do you think we Mexicans are savages, who know nothing of geography?" he added laughingly, as he remarked my surprise. The knowledge of this Mexican, as regards Germany, went so far that he had heard of the old and younger lines of the house of Reuss.

On the 14th we were encamped at Punta del Agua, a very interesting spot, when a Chihuahuan courier arrived with despatches from Mexico, the capital. They contained the intelligence that Santa Ana was president, and that he approved the expedition for the protection of Mesilla. Our camp immediately became a scene of festivity. A band played the whole evening before the General's tent, and the soldiers, though with no relaxation of discipline, were in the highest spirits. Some who, in spite of the prohibition, had ventured to play at cards were severely punished. While the general came to the entrance of his tent, and himself gave some of the soldiers wine in his own silver cup. I cannot take upon myself to say whether the rejoicings at Santa Ana's elevation were sincere or not.

The audacity which the Indians displayed during the march of so large a body of soldiers proves how difficult it is to restrain them. As soon as our encampment for the night was chosen, the cavalry had to ride in all directions in order to clear our neighbourhood from them; but as soon as it became dark, the grass was on fire at some little distance all round us. Almost without exception, we had an illumination every night by the burning of the prairie. Fortunately the grass in this region is neither thick nor long, or we should have been often in danger, and, as it was, we were several times in great anxiety as to the safety of our ammunition. We encamped the first night near the buildings of the Rancho del Sause, which belongs to the hacienda of Encinillas. On the morning of that day the Apaches had murdered a man there. A flock of 6000 sheep were grazing here, under cover of two pieces of artillery, which, one on each side the flock, were driven up and down the plain. A few weeks later, however, as I returned from El Paso, the space before the buildings was covered with dead and dying sheep. Nothing remained of the large flock; and the guns were without horses. The women came out to us weeping and lamenting. A band of Apaches had attacked the flock, killed the shepherds, put to flight the artillerymen, driven the larger portion of the flock into the mountains, and for amusement had speared about 100—a pleasure which these savages never deny themselves on such occasions. A few days afterwards, these savages were in their turn surprised by the inhabitants of the village San Andreas, the stolen sheep retaken, and sixteen or eighteen Apache scalps brought away in triumph to Chihuahua. In May I undertook a journey from Chihuahua to the Presidio del Norte. On the second day we arrived at the Hacienda de Bachimba, where we found its inhabitants in the greatest state of excitement. The Apaches had just murdered on the road, quite near, a party of men, women, and children —in all fourteen—who were returning from the warm baths at Julimas. The bodies of four women were found pierced by lances, stripped, and with their hair tied in a knot; the children had been dashed against the rocks;

the men had been shot with arrows, which probably struck them before they perceived their danger. This was the revenge of the Indians for their defeat by the men of San Andreas, and the continuation of their murderous attack upon Sause.

From this rancho, the route of the brigade diverged from the direct road, which I had already travelled, to Carrizal. Leaving this to the right, we turned towards the principal buildings of the Hacienda de Encinillas, containing an entire village, with a church, and continued our march on the west side of the lake, while the road runs on the east. From the 10th to the 11th we rested near a spring at the north-west limit of the lake, by the ruins of a deserted rancho. The spot is called Ojo de la Laguna—Spring near the Lake. We remained here half the next day, for we had 42 miles before us without water, and these had to be accomplished without stopping, through the night. I took advantage of the opportunity to examine the country. The chaparral in the neighbourhood of the camp was one of the characteristic plants of the North Mexican Steppes, but I had not hitherto seen it so prevalent and so vigorous. It is the tepopote—an Ephedra, whose stiff, green, leafless, broomlike twigs, like those of the Spartium junceum, grow half as tall as a man. Pretty spring flowers blossomed in other places, dwarf asclepias, œnothera, gilia, &c. &c. The lower plain, on a level with the lake, is marshy, and its banks are covered with reeds, among which the ground is covered with soda. It is difficult to reach the water, as you sink in the ground among the reeds, but I managed to secure an avocet and some other water-birds, which I shot here. Ducks, divers, water-hens, strand-snipes, plovers, snipes, bitterns, herons, falcons, and ospreys, flew in such numbers around me, that I literally did not know in what direction to fire. The plain in which this lake lies is surrounded by steep and mostly bare mountains. Pine forests are said to exist in the valleys of the western chain. Altogether this spot is remarkably characteristic of some of the peculiar modifications of North-Mexican nature.

We arrived by dawn the next morning at the Plan de Alamos, a well-watered grassy plain, most grateful to our eyes, surrounded by steep and bare mountains. A brook as clear as crystal, and bordered by yellow mimulus in blossom, flowed through the rich grass. The country round, not yet revived by the summer rains, still looked grey and dead, in the midst of which this watered plain lay like a green island. I followed the brook for about 500 paces, and came to two large circular basins in which the springs bubbled up.

Passing over a dry and dusty plain, on a higher level, we came into a green meadow valley bordered by shady trees, through which a rapid mountain stream flows. The village of El Carmen, near which some silver mines were formerly worked, lies contiguous to it. One of the mills, with its great waterwheel in good preservation, and smelting works, still remain. These mines are said to be by no means exhausted, but they share the fate of so many of the mines in this region. The mountains around are bare, but the sierras to the west appear to be covered with wood. This valley would be a desirable and peaceful abode, were it not for the dangerous vicinity of the Apaches who haunt the adjacent mountains. The river breaks on the north-east, through a narrow cleft from the valley, into a plain in which poplars and willows mark its course till it disappears. The place is called Punta del Agua—end of the water. It was here that we received the intelligence of Santa Ana's elevation to the presidency.

We continued our march through a district without water, covered with withered grass, till—at the foot of a rocky hill—poplars and willows again appeared, among which a small river flowed. It rises not far from this spot, and is said to be, I know not how correctly, only a reappearance of the Rio del Carmen. The place where it again seeks the light is called A amos de Peña. While I stood here to fish, I saw the fresh track of Indians and deer.

From this place we came to Carrizal, where we fell into the usual road between Chihuahua and El Paso. Having already described this locality I shall have but little to say respecting our farther march.

At Carrizal we learned that we should find no water either at the Charcos del Grado or at the Cantarezio, and we were therefore obliged to prepare for a forced march of a very hazardous extent. As a preparation for it, we took a whole day's rest at Ojo de Lucero. At dusk in the evening the brigade commenced its march, which, with two short interruptions, it continued for 24 hours, till we arrived the following evening in the dark at Guadalupe, on the Rio Grande. During this terrible march I saw the foot soldiers, with the women and children, keep up for hours in a trot with the cavalry, the artillery, and the baggage waggons. At the two halting-places it was distressing to see the poor exhausted creatures coming slowly and painfully on. But to lag behind was to die, if not from hunger and thirst, yet by the blood-thirsty Indians who followed us like a pack of wolves. The brigade accomplished 28 leguas, or 84 English miles, in these 24 hours! Water-casks were sent to meet us five or six miles before we reached Guadalupe.

On Sunday, April 24th, the brigade entered El Paso. The gardens and fields around the town were at this season in their fullest beauty. The whole scene was exceedingly picturesque, and would have yielded an artist subjects for numerous pictures.

The first indications of the approaching rainy season appeared during our sojourn in El Paso, towards the end of April. Hitherto the sky had been clear, but now the clouds collected dark and heavy. We had thunder and lightning, but no rain, and the sky again became clear. At night I was completely frightened, by the electric fire which appeared at every movement I made on my couch, in my travelling-carriage. I had two woollen blankets over me, and as I separated these the sparks flew about me, cracking and snapping, and lighting up the whole inside of the carriage. When I took hold of the blanket sparks came from the ends of my fingers, and I felt a slight pricking. After a time this ceased, but it returned again after I had laid still for a while under my blankets: beneath me I had a buffalo's skin.

My commission terminated April 30. I requested of the general an escort of ten soldiers for my journey back, which was immediately granted me. Thus, in some degree tranquillized as to our safety, we set off on the evening of the above-named day. Our waggons were light, and we therefore resolved to take the much shorter road over the Sandhills—los Médanos—as the natives call them. We then began to ascend to the right from the valley, drove through the night, and arrived the next morning in good time at the last watering-place, before our entrance into this American sahara in miniature.

The spring of Samalayuca is a beautiful and delightful spot; a small oasis covered with numerous interesting shrubs spreading round a clear spring. Numberless doves flitted among them; and flocks of quails came to drink at the water's edge.

If the African sahara has been compared to the sea, the little Mexican desert of the Médanos may be likened to a lake. A body of shifting sand lies between limestone hills, bounded like a lake, but with a surface in waves like those of the ocean. Those, however, who have seen the snow-fields extending between the pinnacles of the Alps can form a still better idea of its appearance. The wind which has driven the sand here to form hills of a hundred feet in height, produces the same curves and hollows, and segments, as those which are seen in the snow-drifts of Mont Blanc and Monte Rosa, while the sharp peaks of the Sierra de la Rancheria and the Sierra del Candelario, may be well compared with the pinnacled heights of the Alps.

We left the watering-place in the afternoon and reached the Sandhills at the commencement of night. The road from the spring passes first over limestone, then for a short distance sandstone appeared. Whether the shifting sand of this desert is supplied from this source, or has any other origin, I cannot say. On the border of the sand we left half our waggons, in order to give our whole mule power to the rest. I remained with a portion of our forces to protect these. The day had been hot, the night was bitterly cold, ice formed on our water vessels, and, with my feet deep in the sand, I felt exactly as if I were standing in snow. My feet were quite benumbed, and I feared they would be frost-bitten. We dared not light a fire, lest it should attract the Indians. Even when the mules returned after midnight to fetch us, a five-hours' fatiguing march scarcely restored warmth to my feet. The toil of this road is very great. With the wheels sinking into the sand as far as their axles, the waggons have to pass over the short but steep acclivities and declivities of the ground, with occasional hills apparently 100 feet in height. The pedestrian sinks almost up to his knees in the sand, and, where the ground rises, slips back almost as much as he advances. The shouts of the drivers, the cracking of their whips, the deplorable cries of the mules, the night, the cold, the weariness,—all combined to make it a dismal scene. The next morning, by daybreak, we arrived thoroughly exhausted at the so-named Mezquite Alto, a tree which marks the limit of the Sandhills. Here, in the warmth-imparting rays of the morning sun, we sank down upon the sand into deep sleep. Our mules were afterwards driven back to Samalayuca to be watered.

I have but one more characteristic locality and scene to describe, on our long journey back to Chihuahua.

The road continues from the southern limit of the Sandhills, over the elevated plain, between the Sierra del Candelario and the Sierra de la Rancheria, and from which the view is remarkable. Yucca trees, with their gigantic lily-bearing stems, rose from the hard ground, covered with sharp fragments of porphyry, jaspar, and limestone, while the horizon was studded with mountain groups of every possible shape—horns, combs, peaks, and pinnacles. The scene was like magic, as if awakened out of some former age to the present time,—a flower-garden, in short, for a race of giants.

CHAPTER XIII.

Return to the United States — From Chihuahua to the Presidio del Norte — Magnificent Desert Scenery — The Presidio and its Environs — The Norteños — Leaton's Fort — An Episode of the Middle Ages — Orological Features of the Country from the Presidio to San Antonio de Bexar — Details of the Journey — Watering-places — A Cuguar Lair — El Saucillo — Porphyry Terrace of San Estévan — Ojo del Berendo — Puerto del Paisano, and Ojo del Paisano — Ojo del Leon — Breakfast with a Cuguar — Agua Delgàda, and Road from El Paso — Ojo de Ahuancha — Ojo Escondido — Vegetation at the end of May — The Rio Pecos — Post from El Paso and bearded Nursemaids — Life Oak Creek — Howard Springs — Strayed Buffalo — Trees and Shrubs between Pecos and Devil's River — Valley of this last — Wild Scenery — Indian Brutality — Gloomy Wilderness — The Devil's River again — Old Hut and terrible Recollections — Character of the Country farther to the East — Abundant Game — Military Station — First Settlement on the Road — Return to Civilization — Stay at San Antonio — German Settlement on the Upper Guadalupe — Sudden Rise of Texan Rivers — Dangerous Adventure — Indianola — Return to New York.

The trade in the interior of North Mexico is in such a primitive condition that remittances for goods are almost always made in coin. The time, therefore, arrived, when my friends had to send some cartloads of Mexican dollars to the United States: the consignment was to go *viâ* Texas, and I determined to take this opportunity for returning to the East. Our caravan was headed by Don Guillermo, of whom I have spoken in former chapters. It consisted of seven waggons and about 100 mules, with a proportionate body of men; Don Guillermo considering it advantageous to have a surplus of Mexican servants with the mules, who, on their return to Chihuahua, would become drivers, as it was intended to bring back a fresh transport of goods.

The preparations were soon made. The money was

sewn into wet bullock-hides in parcels containing 3000 pesos (dollars), and packed into two of the waggons; the other five were loaded with maize for the mules, and provisions for ourselves, and on the evening of the 12th of May our caravan took the road to the Presidio del Norte, by the ascent of the Cerro Grande. We were accompanied by friends from the town, till night compelled them to return.

We reached the Presidio on the 20th. The road passed through a desert country on the grandest scale, affording the naturalist a field for the most interesting observations. The Cañon del Ojito, a pass between the plain of Mápula and that of Bachimba, deserves the closest attention of the travelling geologist, as it seems to give the key to the formations of this region. Travelling quickly past, and limited to the road, I could only judge from a distance. Near, there were only alluvial heaps, with dry crevices and ravines, on the precipitous sides of which a white and a red variety of the mimbre (chilopsis) stood in full blossom, and the yellow tufts of the acacia filled the air with its violet perfume.

I have already related the outrages committed by the Apaches at the Hacienda de Bachimba but an hour before our arrival. Seeing the buildings at a distance, I had ridden on before our caravan. When I arrived, I saw the men and women collected on the flat roof of the principal building, apparently much disturbed, the men endeavouring to mount a gun of small calibre, and I immediately learned what had taken place. It was by the merest chance that I escaped the band.

Between Bachimba and the warm baths of Julimas, we passed over a plain covered with yuccas in full bloom, the most enchanting sight which Mexican scenery can display;

their gigantic pannicles, covered with the richest profusion of large white bells, rising from a circle of stiff, radiant leaves, on a stem of ten to twelve feet in height.

The village Julimas is a bathing-place of great repute in Northern Mexico, and we found here a numerous assemblage of our friends from Chihuahua. Among them was the apothecary Jaurrieta, a learned man, according to whose analysis the water of the spring contains a considerable amount of chloride of lime. There are seven different springs, varying in temperature from 31° to 35° of Réaumur. An enormous agave grew on the margin of one; but, not having taken its exact measurement, I fear being disbelieved if I name its apparent size. The warm steam from the adjacent spring was probably the cause of its unusual development.

The Rio Conchos, near which Julimas is situated, is a clear stream, in which soft-shelled turtles are found. One measuring 1½ foot in diameter was caught by one of our servants. It happened that a French gentleman living in this part of Mexico, the Marquis de V——, was then in our camp, and he offered to make us some turtle-soup of superior quality. We possessed the ingredients he required, namely, Bordeaux, Madeira, vinegar, and spices, and, as the Marquis was a skilled gastronome, we had a dish, literally fit for a king; and which was not the less enjoyed from being eaten out of tin plates, and lying on the ground. Our people afterwards, but with considerable trouble, caught a diver, a beautiful podiceps. The bird is unable to fly, and endeavoured to escape its pursuers by diving for long periods.

Beyond Julimas, we had to make two forced marches, both of about ninety English miles, without water. The intervening watering-place, called El Chupadero, was a well, which we were obliged first to clean out, before we could reach the water with a bucket. In order to water our animals, we dug a hole, trod the ground down hard, lined it with stones, and then filled it by buckets from the well. It required more than half-a-day's work before the animals could have a drop of water.

The limestone about this spring contains many fossils. But I had no time to observe them, for, under our circumstances, our horses and mules were of more importance than any question of science. While we encamped here, some Mexicans arrived who had been trading with the Comanches in the neighbouring territory of Texas. They had three boys with them, whom they had ransomed from the savages, and were taking to their families, trusting to reap some advantage on their outlay.

The road from Julimas to this spot presented a succession of the grandest desert scenery. Now over bare plains surrounded by steep mountains of the most grotesque and rugged character; then through rocky defiles; through the dry beds of some wild mountain torrent, or down declivities covered with yuccas and lechuguilla agaves in full blossom. We travelled through the night, and the charm of these mountain scenes by moonlight is beyond description. By daybreak we descended over a limestone hill to the deserted Rancho de la Mula, the bare solid rock of the dark rough mountain-chain frowning upon us through thousands of these giant plants. How little could the boldest fancy realise the beauty of such striking scenes. The most daring imagination of a scene-painter would never have ventured upon such a picture, even for a fairy tale! White nyctagineæ grew by the road-side, shedding the sweetest perfume from their long tubular blossoms.

The country was scarcely less barren or bleak as we approached the Presidio del Norte by the Rio Grande. I never, either then or subsequently, saw an inhabited region which so strongly retained the character of a savage wilderness. The Rio Conchos unites its clear waters here with the muddy stream of the Rio Grande. The junction of these rivers is surrounded by rocks and remnants of the alluvial masses, consisting of clay and sharp broken stones, and forming the lowest terrace of the valley. Afar, the eye rests on nothing but gloomy mountains of the most irregular and varied forms, while near, a high, thick, thorny chaparral obstructs the road and the view, as if guarding a paradise.

It is difficult, in the orological confusion of this region, to designate its general character in a few words. Thus much, however, may be said:—the valley of the Rio Grande is closed at the Presidio del Norte by a mountain rampart, like a bar pushed across, through which a narrow inaccessible chasm gives passage to the river; many falls occur in its course, which is said to be indescribably wild, and I was even told that it burrowed under a mountain. Geographers may expect to find desirable information in the publications of the scientific labours of the Mexican North American Boundary Commission.

The people here are savage, and their habits as rude as the nature around them. The Norteños—as the inhabitants of the Presidio del Norte are called in Mexico—are the allies, spies, powder purveyors, the receivers and buyers of stolen goods, of the Texan Comanches. Necessity may have driven them to this, for, isolated and exposed as they are, they could scarcely otherwise have held their ground between the Comanches and Apaches. Their alliance with the Comanches is in so far advantageous to their Mexican countrymen, as by it they assist in the extermination of the Apaches. I have already spoken of attacks upon these by the united forces of the Norteños and Comanches. This friendly intercourse is maintained with some of these tribes by written correspondence, which the Comanche chiefs carry on by means of their Mexican prisoners. The system of special treaties between individual villages and ranchos and the Indians is universal in Mexico, and neither patriotism nor morality can say much against this fulfilment of the law of self-defence.

We took our loaded waggons over the Rio Grande on a ferry; the empty ones were drawn through the stream by oxen. We encamped on the other side,—in Texas.

Our camp was not far from a large building surrounded by a mud wall, called by the North Americans Leaton's Fort, and by the Mexicans only El Fortin. A North American, not then living, had fixed himself on this spot in defiance of the Indians, in order to oppose their depredations. This man was too remarkable a person to be passed over in silence;—a character for any tale which may be written of the wild frontier life of this region. I should call him a noble Desperado. We had business to transact here with another North American, who only wanted heroism to be a similar character. He called himself "Doctor," but I question whether he was acquainted with any other medicine than gunpowder. In my presence he placed a pistol at the breast of an unfortunate Mexican, merely because he would not agree to the price offered him for a mule. Leaton and the Doctor were foes, and enmity in this country is enmity for life and death. It happened once that Leaton, riding past a thicket, heard the click of a gun which missed fire. Drawing his revolver from his belt, he instantly turned his horse to the spot, and found the Doctor in the act of putting on a fresh cap. "Doctor, let that be," said Leaton with imperturbable coolness, pointing his revolver at him. The Doctor obeyed. "Put down your rifle;" the Doctor obeyed again. "Now come out;" again the Doctor obeyed. "So, so, Doctor," said Leaton, taking hold of his ear, "you wanted to shoot Mr. Leaton, did you? Don't try that again: you are too clumsy for that. But now Doctor come with me; you shall be my guest." Thereupon, with his revolver in his right hand, he led the would-be murderer into his court-yard, where he bound him to a post with a chain, and kept him several days in this position. Every day he brought him his breakfast, dinner, and supper, when he always tormented him with the following kind of sarcastic jokes: "So, so, Doctor, you meant to shoot Mr. Leaton, but your powder was not dry. Mr. Leaton, however, is a good man and regales you with the best. How does his cooking please you?" After mocking him several days in this manner, he let the poor wretch go with a suitable admonition.

During the night we had several alarms in our camp. First, one of the watch fired—more in joke I think than in earnest—upon a human figure which immediately took to flight, and was followed by several others who appeared to rise out of the ground: some other shots were fired; but they proved to be some common Mexican women, who had visited our drivers during the night. A few hours later there was another shot again upon a human figure, but this time a more dangerous one. A regular chace ensued, and wherever a shadow was seen among the bushes it was fired at. I can only hope that no harmless passer-by was injured.

On the 22nd of May we were again in motion. The road we took from hence is known as Connelly's Trail, after a

Dr. Connelly, who a few years since made the first carriage track through the wilderness. This road, at the watering-place Agua Delgada, joins the more frequented one which connects El Paso with San Antonio in Texas.

The bearing towards this place, which we reached on the 29th, is north-easterly. We travelled mostly by nights, and rested by day, so that I could make no connected examination of the country. I can only say, in general terms, that the road from the valley of the Rio Grande, passes over sand and gravelly hills, through deep watercourses and over steep cliffs in the alluvial region, till it reaches the first terraced side of the valley. Farther from the river it ascends to hills of conglomerate, sandstone and limestone, respecting the geological character of which I can say nothing. Passing through valleys shut in by these hills, and over elevated plains, round which rise table-mountains composed of strata of sandstone of different colours, and limestone of various quality, we came to the perpendicular cliff of a terrace of porphyry, the surface of which forms a sloping plateau. Rising over this, we arrived at the base of the Puerto del Paisano, a pass in the porphyritic chain, which forms the direct south-easterly continuation of Sierra del Diablo, in which the Limpia Passes exist, and which in a more general sense belongs to the southern continuation of the Rocky Mountains; for these, in their farthest southerly extension, stand here on the east side of Rio Grande, till by the great curve of the river, they come to take their place on the western bank, towards Cohahuila. From the level of the plateau on the east side of this mountain chain the country descends in terraces towards the centre of Texas, the road passing now over the table-land itself, then through the valleys by which it is intersected, and the sides of which are generally formed by tabular mountains. I will now bring forward what was most remarkable in the details of this journey.

The first watering-place eastwards from the Rio Grande is called Los Alamos. We reached it in the morning after a night's journey, and found a spring surrounded by poplars, and thickly bordered with reeds, among barren hills covered with scanty grass, cacti, yuccas, lechuguilla agaves, dasyliria, and a poor growth of bushes. The journey through the next night brought us into a well-watered valley of considerable extent and ramifications, opening towards the Rio Grande. It is bounded by hills of conglomerate, a few isolated and curiously formed mountains being only seen upon the horizon to the east. Where the road comes upon this spring, the place is called Punta del Agua. The road passes through this valley along a brook bordered with high reeds. The cuguar, called by the Mexicans, leon, abounds here. We passed the haunt of one of these wild beasts disturbed by our vanguard,—the skeletons of several deer lay around. Riding on I saw several snakes among the reeds, probably the Mocassin snake, which is known to be very dangerous. This valley is broad, and fertile enough to make it a desirable place for future settlements. Willows and other shrubs grow along the stream. The hills are barren, and the grass upon them thin, but—like all mountain grass of this country—of good quality. On the horizon, beyond these hills, isolated mountain groups are seen, many of them of singular forms. On our road from the Presidio, to the left, an isolated hill, like a castle rock, was always in sight. It was called the Cerro de Jacinto. A few days' journey farther on we had the Picacho de la Cienaga de Valles before us, a rocky mass resembling a church with towers and cupolas.

One of our next halting-places, where water and grass

were in abundance, was El Saucillo—the Willow Bush. The plain is bounded on the one side by steep tabular hills of sedimentary rocks; while on the other the long perpendicular wall of a terrace of porphyry extends. I climbed one of the hills close to our camp. The lower stratum was a soft green sandstone; then came one of a sandy marl, then a third of hard sandstone, covered by one of a coarse conglomerate formed of pebbles and boulders of porphyry, green vitrified lava, and other plutonic and volcanic masses. We drove through the night over hard smooth ground, and arrived in the early morning at the foot of the porphyry terrace. The place where the road ascends it is called Cuesta de San Estévan. This porphyry is of a light yellow and greenish colour, full of caves and arched vaults. A rising plain lies eastwards on the summit, upon which, at the edge of the precipice, Táscate bushes grow, a species of juniper, bearing red berries.

The Ojo del Berendo, or Antelope Spring, rises in this terrace; a very suitable name, for we saw numerous herds of antelopes all around. In hunting these animals, both Mexicans and Indians disguise themselves with an antelope's head. A Virginian, who had joined our caravan at the Presidio, carried one with him for this purpose, and made the first trial of it here. Although he did not succeed in his attempt, he amused us excessively by his pantomime. While, with the horned head above his own, he endeavoured to act his part correctly, by making the most extraordinary jumps, which he evidently thought were inimitably true to nature, hundreds of antelopes stood, in a large semicircle, watching the actions of this strange mongrel figure, but never lessening a wide distance between themselves and him; so that, in spite of his dramatic talent, our friend did not accomplish his purpose. This watering-place had a good spring, but it was insufficient for our animals. Quite near there was an abundance of standing water, of a coffee-brown colour, in pits in the ground, among which separate bunches of rushes grew. This water was so saturated with soda that it tasted like lye, and made the skin slippery. Notwithstanding this, our animals drank it. The plateau, smooth and sterile, with the rushes and waterpits in the foreground, and the rocky peak of the Picacho de la Cienaga de Valles in the background, formed a most characteristic desert scene.

We reached the Puerto del Paisano, a mountain pass with most interesting scenery, over a plain full of the prairie marmot. The mountain chain through which it passes forms the eastern limit of the plateau, while from the eastern side of this chain the ground sinks into a lower level. The precipices and detached rocks of this pass, with scattered oaks, form a most interesting landscape. Valleys shut in by perpendicular walls, with towering pinnacles, intersect these mountain masses; and single rocks stand isolated like obelisks. We thus reached the Ojo del Paisano,[1] one of the most beautiful and interesting watering-places of this neighbourhood. The valley forms a space surrounded by steep mountains, opening eastwards towards the plain. The mountains are covered with groups of evergreen oaks, and there is no lack of grass, although this year scarcely any rain had fallen to rouse the slumbering vegetation. In spite of this, however, the scarlet blossoms of the Castilleja occurred here and there in the valley.

[1] With reference both to the pass and to the spring, the word paisano means a before-named bird, Geococcyx viaticus, the paisano or correcamino of the Mexicans—the ground cuckoo.

The Lion's Spring—Ojo del Leon—was our next watering-place. This name also proved to be a correct one. The advance of our party drove a cuguar from his breakfast,—a freshly-killed stag, which was yet warm. Our people cooked it for their own meal. The water of this spring forms a clear and plentiful brook, flowing for about a mile between flat hills, after which it disappears.

From hence we came to an abundant supply of water, called Agua Delgada. Bordered by rush and reed, a small stream flows through a succession of singular ponds, the clear but brackish waters of which are from twenty to thirty feet in depth, with precipitous sides in the bog, and contain numerous turtles. The valley on each side is covered with rich grass, intervening spaces occurring which exhibit efflorescences of glauber salt, common salt, soda, &c., and terminate in a reedy marsh; the plain beyond being sterile. The road from the Presidio joins that from El Paso here. The spring of Ahuancha, an Indian name corrupted into Comanche spring, lies about fifteen miles to the north-east. A remarkably long flat mountain, extremely regular in its form, and evidently a remnant of a more elevated plateau, rises here above the low plain. At its base I found some fossils, apparently belonging to the jurassic formation. In the plain, several strong springs, rising in a space of a few hundred feet, form a stream, in the deep and clear waters of which we caught a quantity of cat-fish. This stream probably ceases farther on in the steppe.

Then follows the Ojo Escondido, or Hidden Well, a clear but brackish spring. It forms the Arroyo Escondido, or Hidden Brook, a sluggish streamlet covered with reeds and rushes.

Hitherto we had found but little fresh grass on our road,

and our animals had had only the dry haulm of the previous year; low moist places, and the bottoms immediately round the springs, had been the only exceptions. But now, as we approached the valley of the Pecos, an entire change took place in the scene. On the 31st of May we arrived at a plain covered with grass and flowers, and surrounded by regularly-formed table-mountains. The grass and flowers were so thick and high, that our horses had difficulty in making their way through, and the sweetest perfume, principally of the superb american centaurea, filled the atmosphere. This transition to a more advanced season was not caused by any difference in the level above the sea, but was the result of heavy rains, which had not fallen more to the west. From hence eastwards to Texas the steppe was in its most gorgeous beauty.

We reached the river Pecos on the 1st of June, and continued our journey for three days along its course, athough the road runs occasionally at some distance from it, and is even separated by isolated tabular mountains. The sides of the valley are broken up by parallel and other valleys branching from it. The higher ground consists without exception of flat mountains, which on each side unite, forming a horizontal table-land of limestone. The valley itself is narrow, irregular, full of turns and windings; the stream flows in a deep bed between steep clay banks, so that you may come close to it without perceiving it. For many miles the water is beyond the reach of animals, the banks being so perpendicular that they fall into it and are carried away by the current. Willows, poplars and oaks occur along the stream; but they grow chiefly below the banks, on a level with the water, on narrow strips of ground bordering the river; while their tops, barely rising above the chasm, look like bushes, and scarcely betray the course of the stream. The water is clayey, brackish, and unwholesome.

We crossed the river at a spot where, by a great decline, it becomes shallow. The passage is rather dangerous, requiring care and presence of mind.

The mail from El Paso passed us here. Two carriages, each with four mules; coachmen, guard and passengers all fully armed. One of the passengers was a little girl of three or four years old, who—entrusted to the coachman, and with no other companion—was thus sent the 700 miles from El Paso to San Antonio. The other passengers, however, joined him in taking care of her; and it was touching to see how these rough, bearded men, with their pistols and daggers, supplied the place of a mother's care to the tender little creature. It was a true picture of wild American life, where the highest qualities in human nature are often found, united with the roughest externals.

To the east of the valley, the road ascends again by a lateral branch to the plateau. The stream of this side valley is called the Life Oak Creek; and the valley gave us a pleasant halting place. In a short time we caught sufficient fish to afford an ample meal for the whole caravan.

An enchanting prairie scene surrounded us above. The level plain was covered with fresh young grass, and bushes of cypress-like junipers marked the beginning of the declivity towards the Pecos valley. Farther to the east the ground became more undulating, while scattered shrubs gave it the appearance of a park. We arrived at the Howard Springs, at the base of some limestone hills. On the road we saw several stags, a bear in the distance, and the carcase of a buffalo. A few days previously we had found the head of one of these animals, with the horns attached.

It may be that a stray one is occasionally driven thus far south by the Indians hunting.

On the 6th of June we arrived, after a harassing journey, at the notorious Devil's River. The name is justified by the wildness of the scenery, though more in reference to the difficulties of the traveller than to its artistic effect.

We reached the valley by a steep descent, the sides consisting of rocky, and in many places perpendicular, hills. Here it was like another world. Above, a stony steppe with short grass, different kinds of cactus, dwarf yuccas, and the stiff dasylirium with its giant spikes of flowers; below, plane, oak, and walnut trees, thickets of wild plums, intertwined with vines, and high thick grass, from among which were visible the scarlet ipomopsis, and the blue tradescantia.

But before I proceed with my description of this valley I must speak of the region through which we passed from the Pecos. One peculiarity is the repeated occurrence of dead mezquite trees, of considerable size, with the growth of young ones,—there being no intermediate stage of size or age. This probably has been caused by repeated prairie fires, which destroyed the old trees, and prevented the growth of fresh ones. If this is the case, it must stand in connexion with a periodical peopling of the country. At Chihuahua, a man who had been a great deal in this locality told me that for a long period no Indians had lived there, during which it was covered by a thick mezquite wood. Subsequently certain hordes came here, and with them the prairie fires began. In later times the advance of the whites into Texas has driven back the savages, and restrained their visits; and the prairie fires ceasing, trees and shrubs have again appeared.

It is asserted that this process may be watched throughout West Texas; that the increasing growth of trees and shrubs changes the climate and increases the amount of rain, so that by degrees the steppes will be covered with woods and thickets.

Whether every fact in this chain of sequences is correct I cannot say; but the belief in a change of climate and an increased amount of rain was at that time very general in West Texas. The old Mexican inhabitants ascribed the increased humidity to some mysterious influence of the North Americans, the change having apparently come with them. The subsequent droughts, however, from which Texas suffered so severely, must have shaken this belief. The sudden appearance of a young mezquite vegetation after so long a period of obstruction to its growth, may be explained by its growth from the roots, since the algarobbia sends out very long and deep roots.

We continued our journey four days, partly through the valley of the Devil's River, partly through lateral branches of the same, and over adjoining table-land. This locality is one of the most interesting I have seen in America. The valley, with its branches, is literally a defile through the plateau, and opens into that of the Rio Grande, where this enters the lowland of Texas. At the upper part of the valley our caravan passed over masses of heaped-up blocks and stones, which, in places, covered the ground from one mountain's side to the other. These heaps are terrible indications of the fearful power exercised by the periodical floods. I saw drift wood remaining high up the trees between forked branches, showing to what an incredible height the valley was sometimes filled with water. These floods are however of very short duration. Where we first entered the valley it was quite dry; but farther on, the road having taken us for some hours away from the bed of the river, we found it filled with a crystal, clear, powerful stream. It is said to rise at some distance in the mountains from a single spring. I did not see the spot, which is considered very beautiful; but as such springs are well known in Texas, I have no doubt as to the correctness of the statement.

Lower down, the course of the stream varies, between broad stagnant extensions, and contractions with a rapid current. Shrubs and tall trees line the banks. We passed an old camping place of the Indians, with the remains of their huts, and piles of stones in many places, indicating where murdered travellers had been buried. In one place, where the river falls through a narrow contraction of the valley, the road ascends on its west side to the plateau, which here has a considerable declivity southwards to the Rio Grande. High mountains are seen in the distance to the south-west, probably in the State of Cohahuila.

When we reached a well-known place on the plateau called Palo Blanco, we found an Indian camp, from which they had but just moved. Don Guillermo, who had followed a stag some little distance from the camp, came upon the fresh track of a band of Indians, who must have crossed the road scarcely an hour before us. A most repulsive object met our view upon the very spot where we had intended to encamp. The grave of some traveller had been opened near the road, the half decomposed body thrown out, the head set upon a pole, and some waggon boards which had served for a coffin were placed on the road in a certain form as if indicating something. Whether anything besides insult was meant by this, it is impossible to say; but the night passed undisturbed. We continued our journey in the morning, and reached a depression of the plateau which brought us to the rocky valley of the Painted Cave, called by the Mexicans El Arroyo de la Cueva Pinta. This is a lateral branch of the Devil's River Valley, and one of the most gloomy localities I ever saw; so barren and inhospitable as to produce the most painful impressions. Some excavations in the rocks were filled with water. The thousands of the gigantic flowering spikes of the dasylirium, a plant characteristic of the stony deserts of western Texas, tended to heighten rather than soften the wild character of the locality. Their gigantic proportions are quite overwhelming, and I felt as if I were lost. This dismal valley descends through a deep and narrow cleft between grotesquely shaped rocks, which rise in peaks and pinnacles and contain a number of round openings. These are the entrances into caves, some of which are said to contain numerous Indian paintings on their sides; but I was unable to examine them. The cleft opens into the lower part of the Devil's River Valley, which has much the same gloomy character. The road, after crossing a lateral valley, ascends again to the plateau, and then for the last time rejoins the principal trunk.

Here, where the road again approaches the river, this valley displays the truly classic beauty of a wilderness. The river now a broad crystal stream, flowing over flat, polished, yellowish-white limestone slabs, is here surrounded by noble trees, wreathed by vines, above which the enclosing rocks lift their towering heights. The river-bed is very remarkable, and the transparency of the water such as to make every line and crevice in its marble floor visible. Here and there, where a flaw has occurred, mud has collected, in which high reeds have taken root. The contrasts in these particulars are uncommon, and the harmony in which they are composed is equally rare. Luxuriant vegetation in the valley surmounted by naked rocks, lofty trees shading a brilliant water surface, islands of reeds on the flat bed of a rapid stream, are features seldom united in one picture. A picture truly of wild and brilliant beauty.

The remains of a hut made with branches, and of a fireplace close to it, were visible, where the road passes through the lowest part of the valley. Here, some years since, when this region was less frequented than it is now, some passing travellers—so I was told—once found the roasted remains of a human being. Some runaway negroes from Texas had concealed themselves here, and urged by hunger, had killed one of their companions in his sleep, thus seeking to preserve their own lives. They voluntarily gave themselves up to justice.

A few days' journey eastwards from Devil's River brings you to the settlements in Texas. The table-land, to which you ascend quickly through rocky defiles, gradually slopes from thence, and the landscape assumes more and more the appearance of a park. With increased irrigation game also increases, and continues to do so after the first villages are reached. Our waggon-master in passing, and close to the road, shot in one day three stags. Wild turkeys are nowhere more abundant in America than in the vicinity of the Devil's River, and from thence eastward. We came repeatedly upon the track of the cuguar, and in one of the first houses we met with, the children were playing with three young bears.

Coming from the west, we met the first settlers on this route, in Fort Clarke. This is, or was then, the most remote military station of the United States on this road. In order to give the reader an example of American contrasts I would just state that preserved fruits, anchovies, pickled oysters, and champagne, were to be had at a store adjoining the fort. On the road farther to the east is Fort Inge, which we passed some little distance to the south. The Mexicans call this last military station Fortin de la Leona, and the first one Fortin de la Mora.[1]

Besides these forts, the first settlement we met with was situated where the road crosses the Sabinal River. It was a well-built house, near which another was being built: the position is beautiful, and will undoubtedly give rise to a considerable place. Noble specimens of the Texan cypress, called by the Mexicans sabine, grow by the river: they are the first which occur on this road coming from the west. The Cañon de Uvalde, which has since been bought by Victor Considerant as a second home for himself and his unsuccessful colony, is situated farther up this river.

Dhanis, to the east of the Rio Seco, was the first large collection of houses we met with. It is a village of emigrants from Alsatia and Würtemberg. Before we arrived at it I met a man on the road, to whom I in vain addressed myself in English, and then in Spanish, and who at last made himself known as a German from Alsatia. There is a numerous settlement of Alsatians in this western region of Texas, and I remarked that they all called themselves Germans.

At the Rio Hondo I was made welcome in a house near the road, inhabited by a family from Würtemberg. The mistress and her sister, this last a genuine "Schwabe-mädle," pressed me with much kindness to join them at table, upon which a dish of "spätzle" was smoking. The

[1] The North Americans constantly corrupt this name into Fort Moro, and, by the same corruption, change the name of the Rio de Mora, a stream which falls into the Rio Grande, into "Moro Creek." It is a repetition of the corruption of a similar name in New Mexico. Mora is Spanish for mulberry-tree, and this gives the name to the fort and the river. The name has nothing to do with the word moro, "moor."

husband, an equally genuine Swabian, replied to my question as to how it suited him here, with a favourable picture of his domestic circumstances. "So far it is well enough," he said; "but what is all this if there is no beer and no wine? And it is not all as it should be: I remarked it as soon as we left Würtemberg. Things looked badly when we got to Cologne, and I said then to my wife, the thing looks bad." By Vandenburg, Quihi, and Castroville, all inhabited by Alsatians and Germans, we came to San Antonio, the most considerable town in West Texas, where I once again found myself in civilized life.

The reader will probably have remarked that I have but imperfectly described the latter half of the road from Rio Grande to San Antonio. The length which the Second Book has already attained compels me to keep within limits; but if the reader will kindly accompany me, I shall take him again through a portion of these wildernesses and deserts in the Third Book of this work.

The number and character of the German population in West Texas were almost entirely unknown to me, when, on my arrival at San Antonio, I found myself suddenly in a circle of well-educated countrymen, who received me with every possible mark of kindness and esteem. The surprise was great and most agreeable. I had intended to continue my journey to New York without stopping on the road, but I yielded to these pleasant circumstances; and, having done this, I decided also to visit some friends settled on the Upper Guadalupe. The group of German settlements in this beautiful locality is especially interesting, from the civilization which they have thus brought into the wilderness, and which has struck Anglo-American travellers. Bartlett, and also Olmsted, remarked favourably upon this subject. The ride thither from San Antonio occupies a day. At the end of my journey I had to cross the Guadalupe, a small stream flowing, like all others of this region, in a deep bed, bordered by cypresses and other beautiful trees. The place where it is crossed is full of beauty, like many such spots in this country. The stream, which is usually as clear as crystal, was somewhat higher than usual; and, as on horseback it was more difficult to avoid the roots and stems of the cypresses, I left my horse behind, and waded through it, up to my neck, holding my clothes high in my hand. Continued heavy showers raised the water during the following night at least 20 feet above its usual level, and thus my return to San Antonio was prevented till the stream should subside again. Such sudden floods are common to the rivers of Texas: they are great impediments to all communication, and sources of danger to the imprudent. Drivers who have encamped in the valley of such a stream have been frequently carried away, with their cattle and their waggons, by the unexpected flood. The permanent water of the rivers in this region is clear spring-water, the quantity of which is but little influenced by the atmospheric changes. These rivers, however, are the drains for extensive plains and hilly ground, which in dry weather are quite parched, but during heavy rains receive a superabundance of water. Of this but a small portion penetrates the hard soil, and consequently all the water which runs off a space of many hundred square miles, is collected into a deep and narrow river, which it fills with a rapidity admitting of no escape, to 20 and 30 feet above its natural level. As in the valley of Devil's River, I saw driftwood here on the banks of the Guadalupe, entangled in the highest branches of lofty trees.

As soon as I was able to continue my journey, I took a place in the stage-coach which runs between San Antonio and Indianola. The coach was to start at midnight, and the conductor promised, according to the custom here, to take me up at my friend's house, that of Mr. S., whose guest I was. It was only of one story, and the room in which I slept with my friend had a glass door opening into the court-yard. In order to be ready for the stage-coach, I had lain down dressed, and had left a light burning so that the conductor might the more easily see me, and wake me. The door, as is usual in Texas, was not locked.

I had slept some time when I was roused by a shot in our room, and starting up saw Mr. S. struggling with a man who held a six-shot revolver in his hand. Mr. S. endeavoured to get hold of this weapon; but as I rose the fellow fired at me, but missed me, and we then succeeded in forcing him out of the door, which we could not however lock. We looked in vain for some weapon. S. had none in his bedroom, and I had fired my pistols off during the evening, thinking them unnecessary. Our situation was, therefore, really critical, for the fellow forced his hand through the glass, and sought to aim first at S., and then at me. We were obliged to lie down below the glass portion of the door, partly to protect ourselves, and also to keep the door closed. We could not long have maintained this position, when my friend caught sight of a piece of cord lying near. A noose was quickly made in it, and thrown round the hand of the rascal, who was thus our prisoner. He fired a third shot with no better success. And now he put his head into the room to see his way, and to try and free himself; and at this instant I succeeded in wresting the revolver from him. In the heat of the moment I pointed the barrel against his head, and fired; the shot missed, as also the two remaining barrels. We now threw the cord round the fellow's neck, and drew him into the room through the hole in the glass door. While we were binding him, the police-watch, attracted by the repeated shots, arrived, and they not only took possession of our prisoner, but seized an accomplice in the courtyard, who had probably been keeping watch. The stage-coach arrived just as the two were in safe hands. My friend and I congratulated each other on our escape from injury, and I soon forgot the adventure in the tragi-comic circumstances of a night journey on a road where the carriage every few minutes sank in mud above the axles of the wheels.

I learned later that our assailants were Irishmen, and disbanded soldiers. In November I was again in San Antonio, on my journey to California, and found that they were still in confinement under trial, for which my arrival as a witness had been waited; but I remained in San Antonio two months without its taking place, and I afterwards heard that they were set at liberty without punishment.

The stage-coach journey from San Antonio was most peculiar, and would probably have excited the ill humour of a less-tried traveller; but it only awakened merriment in me and my companions. I paid, if I mistake not, 12½ dollars for my seat, for which price I secured the privilege of walking three-fourths of the distance—about 160 English miles—and was obliged to help to pull the coach out of the mud-holes in which it should stick fast. The reader can scarcely imagine what this necessity amounted to. Without giving the details, I will only say that it was the hardest and dirtiest work I ever undertook. Like all travellers returning from savage to civilized life, I had equipped myself afresh from head to foot, and all my bravery was ruined in this two days' journey. At Indianola I had to throw the whole away, and equip myself again. For miles I had to walk in mud and water, and in extricating myself from an unusually deep place, I lost my pocket-book, containing many valuable notes and letters.

Indianola is well known as a town of German origin.

I was hailed by my name immediately as I went out, and found myself greeted by one of my two companions on my journey from San Juan de Nicaragua to Granada, who had settled here. Mr. S. had my luggage fetched from the hotel, and I remained his guest, enjoying the kindest hospitality.

After a few days I took the steamer which plies regularly from hence to New Orleans. The passage deserves no farther remark, than that I found myself in the society of several officers belonging to the army of the United States, whose refinement of manners was as agreeable as the interest they took in scientific subjects.

I was a stranger to New Orleans, which, in so many respects, is a peculiarly interesting town, and I would gladly have remained some weeks there; but the time of the year was unfavourable. The yellow fever, which committed such ravages in the summer of 1853, had just broken out; every one who could was hastening to leave the town, and I therefore determined to leave it the next day by the river steamer to St. Louis. We had, as might be expected, the fever on board, but, as far as was known, only one death occurred.

I remained two days at St. Louis, which I spent principally with one who had been my playfellow in childhood, and who, like me, had been led into the "far west" regions of America. Both on the Rio Grande and in the State of Chihuahua I had constantly followed the steps of Dr. Wislizenus.

The rest of my journey to New York I accomplished by the railroad, which from St. Louis, south of the great Lakes, runs directly across the country, and then from Albany along the Hudson River. I arrived after an absence of rather more than thirteen months.

Book III.

JOURNEY FROM THE COAST OF TEXAS,

AND

THROUGH THE DISTRICT OF THE GILA AND COLORADO,

TO SAN FRANCISCO;

RESIDENCE THERE, AND RETURN.

CHAPTER I.

From New York to San Antonio — New Orleans — Galveston and Port Lavaca after the Epidemic — Journey to San Antonio — News from the Camp — Sickness among the Mules — Rattlesnake Bites, and a poisonous Caterpillar — A Fight, and American Opinion on it — Neighbourhood of San Antonio — Climate in the Winter — The River and its Sources — Subterranean Water-courses in Western Texas — Changes in the Physical Geography of the Country — Adventures of a young German — Prince Bonaparte — Reminiscences of Texan Desperadoes.

LATE in the summer of 1853, my friends, Messrs. Mayer and Co., had finished their preparations for a new trading expedition to Chihuahua, and at New York they made me the offer of accompanying the caravan a second time. To give a general idea of the management of such a trading business I must observe, that one partner of the firm generally resides as purchaser in New York, whilst the other accompanies the transport through the prairie, and superintends the sale of the goods at Chihuahua. Mr. Kaufmann, who had hitherto been engaged as the New York resident of this nomadic firm, was desirous, in order to learn from personal observation the relative state of the markets, to make the journey on this occasion; and, as he urged my accompanying him, I accepted the invitation.

The expedition was to start this time from Texas, where the remainder of the former equipment was waiting to join us with twenty new waggons. These had been ordered at one of the celebrated manufactories in Pittsburg, sent by the steam-boat down the Ohio and Mississippi to New Orleans, and thence to Port Lavaca, on the coast of Western Texas. To that harbour the goods had been forwarded from New York; and on the 10th of October I went by "The Black Warrior" steamer, in company with Mr. Kaufmann, by way of Havanna to New Orleans, intending to proceed to the above-mentioned port. We reached New Orleans on the morning of the 20th. The yellow fever, which had made terrible ravages that year, had passed away. On the 23rd, we continued our voyage on board the steamer "Mexico," and on the 25th arrived in the harbour of Galveston, where I had time to visit some acquaintances. Three months before, on my journey to New York, I had dined here with ten or eleven young Germans, all of whom, but three or four, had been carried off by the yellow fever, and I was told that, of fifty Germans who had come in the spring, with other emigrants, only three survived. The epidemic had never before been so fatal here. It had also exhibited unusual symptoms, and was asserted to differ essentially from the ordinary yellow fever to which they were accustomed, and which was not so much feared. The first autumnal north wind checked the ravages of the fever, and from that time no new cases appeared; but the change of weather caused the death of most of the patients.

We landed at Indianola, and immediately jumped into the first post-coach going to Port Lavaca. In both places the epidemic had raged fiercely, and had interrupted the whole trade of the country. Ships had been laid fast in port for weeks, for want of men to unload their cargoes; trade was at a stand, and the houses to which cargoes were consigned were closed. We found part of our chests and bales lying on the shore quite unprotected, and their contents much injured.

We travelled to San Antonio by the post-coach. The road was in no better state than on my journey down in July, and similar tragi-comic occurrences happened now as then. The first night I was obliged to run before the carriage for a considerable distance with a stearine candle in my hand, through a deep marsh, in order to find out the road, of which all trace had disappeared in the soft soil: this was near the coast. The road above Victoria was better; but the second night, and not far from San Antonio, the wheels on one side of the waggon, which had got a little off the road, together with one of the horses, sank into a peculiar muddy sand, overgrown with the grass of the prairie. A kind of dangerous quicksand lies under the turf, which I afterwards often observed in this part of Texas. We were obliged to seek help in the neighbourhood; and eight men were hard at work for two hours before the carriage was again in motion. The coolness and equanimity which Americans show in such cases is admirable, and quite shames the European, at least the man from the continent. During the whole affair no loud words were heard; no impatience was exhibited; no unwillingness to assist. Early the next morning (the 30th) we arrived at San Antonio. Here I learned what had befallen, during the three months of my absence, the small caravan with which I had started from Chihuahua. They had encamped in the prairie, a few miles from San Antonio: sickness had broken out among the mules, and carried off nineteen of the best animals; and, afterwards, more died on the road. Several had been bitten by rattlesnakes, and saved with the greatest difficulty. The same thing happened to one of our drivers; but a remarkable accident befel the waggon-master: he had crushed on his hand a little hairy caterpillar, which was crawling on it, and in a few minutes the most alarming symptoms appeared. A shiver ran from the hand through his whole frame, and especially down his back. His abdomen swelled, his tongue was heavy, his consciousness became dimmed, and for a week the man was in imminent danger. I afterwards saw the little caterpillar in a collection of insects at San Antonio, where the patient recognised it. If he was right, it is a little worm covered with long yellowish hairs about a quarter of an inch long: it resembles a caterpillar, but whether it really is one I cannot say. I afterwards heard of other examples of the extraordinary effects caused by this creature. In a garden at Indianola one of them dropped from a tree on to a child's arm, who immediately screamed with pain; the arm swelled, a violent fever came on, and the child's life was in great danger for several days.

On our arrival this camp was immediately broken up, and the waggons sent down to the coast to join the new ones from Pittsburg, and to receive the cargo. The route lay through the town, where a quarrel ensued between the waggon-master and a Mexican muleteer. The latter had drunk a little too much, and stood holding a bottle of spirits, when the former attempted to knock it out of his hand. The Mexican defended himself, and the waggon-master gave him several sharp cuts with his whip; then the former snatched up a stone and threw it at the waggon-master's head, which it laid open. The view taken of this affair by the Americans present is characteristic of the views of morality current in the United States: at first they shouted to the waggon-master to shoot the Mexican; but the former, a German by birth, though hot-tempered was a humane man, and such an act was foreign to his nature, although he carried a revolver in his belt and was an excellent shot: I have seen him shoot a hare with a pistol while riding, in California. When the Americans saw how coolly he bore the injury, with the blood streaming down his face, they turned from him contemptuously, and sided with the Mexican, shouting, "The coward! stone him! kill him!"

It would be wrong, however, to imagine that a love of shedding blood actuated this judgment. Not so. But in the United States men who get into a rage, and quarrel and beat one another, are despised, unless it be a regular boxing-match, as in England, which is begun and carried out with coolness, and where the spectators form a silent circle round the combatants, without taking any part in the contest. In the United States to kill a man at a blow is thought less of than a noisy and brawling fight. Public morals are based on this sentiment; that a punctilious etiquette should always be observed, such as Sovereigns show to one another, though certainly of quite a different kind to what passes for courtesy in France or Germany; and an intentional disregard of these manners is considered a declaration of war. Public opinion will generally justify a death-blow, if the other party was the first who threatened to strike; but a blow which one man gives another is here generally revenged with the death of the aggressor: of course this remark does not include the relations of master and slave. Our waggon-master, who used his whip pretty freely to enforce respect from the Mexican drivers and muleteers, would assuredly have long been killed had he only raised his arm threateningly against a North-American. This practice has one advantage, that it obviates the brawls in America, which I have so often witnessed in Europe. Screaming, scolding, quarrelling, threatening, beating, very rarely occur in the United States, and in the few cases I have noticed the row invariably proceeded from Irish, French, or Germans. The next day I spoke with the Mexican, who, although one of our most useful and trusty servants, was in consequence of this conduct dismissed. He dissected the whole affair very quietly to me, and I perceived that his three months' residence in Texas had given the fellow notions of equal rights and dignity, although the native element of Mexican submission still remained in his character. "I had a knife in my belt," said he, "and could have killed the waggon-master, but I would not do so, as he was my superior." Such an idea never enters the head of a North-American, excepting, of course, in the army and navy.

The country around San Antonio is not remarkable for any beautiful or grand scenery, but it is of an agreeable character, and has many charms which contribute greatly to the pleasantness of a residence here. Where it is not cultivated there is a variety of prairie, trees, and bushes, boasting a peculiar and gorgeous flora. The *Sophora speciosa* and *Unguadia speciosa* are here among the commonest shrubs. You are continually reminded of the scenery on the higher terrace, at whose southern foot this town lies, by the numerous mezquite bushes, single barren strips of prairie, and other characteristic marks of the vegetation of the more elevated regions.

The climate of this spot is celebrated for its beauty and healthiness, the epidemics of the coast not extending so far. Travellers, it is true, have often brought the fever with them, but it has never been known to spread. This healthy character of the interior of Western Texas begins much further down the country: in fact, in a climatical point of view, only a narrow strip of the coast is dangerous; and when a railway shall hurry the traveller over this belt of land, he will have little cause to fear. I had, above all, an opportunity of admiring the beauty of winter here. It certainly cannot be said that a Texan norther is pleasant, but I shall soon have to speak of this more particularly. These violent and icy gales, however,—but for which this region would have almost a tropical climate,—prevail only a few times every winter, and seldom last more than three days. They must be looked upon as an exceptional phenomenon, and to these probably it is owing that no miasmata collect, which would in this part of the country be highly dangerous. The salutary effect of these northers upon the healthiness of the climate extends as far as Yucatan and the coast of Honduras. I have spent several months at San Antonio, from the end of October to the middle of January, and in my daily walks I have found the climate in winter as splendid as it is beneficial to health. A brilliant and warm day usually succeeded a light night-frost.

The river forms one of the principal beauties of San Antonio. Its sources are only a few miles distant, and gush forth from the rock, amidst wood and shrubs, just like the river,—a deep, rapid stream, clear as crystal. These springs are probably as copious as any on the face of the globe. I have already mentioned that the permanent water of the Devil's River is said to gush forth from the rock in a similar manner. These phenomena are very common in Western Texas, although on a smaller scale, and enforce the opinion that the almost horizontal strata of limestone, on the southern declivity of which San Antonio is situated, cover a vast number of subterranean water-courses, many of which never find an outlet to the surface. Sudden as well as gradual changes appear to take place in these water-courses, the water in one spot removing an obstruction, and in another creating some new one. Mr. P., an engineer of San Antonio, told me the following fact:—The Rio Verde, a river now entirely dependent on the atmosphere for its supply of water, and which falls into the Rio Hondo, was formerly a permanent, clear, and broad stream, several feet deep; people settled on its bank; when, it all at once disappeared, nor did it appear again. A deep well, dug near it, at first yielded some water, but afterwards became dry. Suddenly, one night, a regular torrent broke forth from it with a tremendous noise, but it flowed only for a few hours; in the morning the well was again empty. At noon the torrent gushed forth anew. This continued for several hours, since which time it supplies very little permanent water. Of course I cannot vouch for the accuracy of these statements.

From numerous intelligent friends at San Antonio I learned many interesting facts relative to the nature and features of this country, with which—being differently engaged—I should not otherwise have become acquainted. One of my friends had been recently to the Atascoso, a small river about fifty miles S.S.W. of San Antonio, and had made some observations which complete my former remarks on the changes of the vegetation and climate in Texas. The Atascoso flows into the Rio Frio, a tributary of the Nueces. The country there is—or was at that time—quite wild and uncultivated, mostly covered with wood, consisting of scattered very old trees and a thick growth of young ones. The soil is formed of an upper stratum of sand, beneath which is a layer of black humus.

My friend added the following observations:—This country was once covered with forest, which was destroyed by fires in the prairie, with the exception of those trees which had already reached a very considerable size, and therefore resisted the effects of the fire. Thus, the driftsands of the adjacent sandy regions had free access, and overflowed the humus on the surface. The woodlands were changed into a sandy desert, with some old scattered trees. The prairie-fires have ceased, since the increasing white population has driven back and partly exterminated the Indians, and a new growth of young wood has been formed, in addition to the old trees that remained after the fire. I learned, at the same time, that thick trunks of old trees are found everywhere in the large sandy Cactus region, between the Nueces and the Rio Grande; that there, likewise, a strip of humus is found under the sand layer on the surface, and that latterly there, too, a young vegetation of trees has begun to spring up,—phenomena which are explained in the same manner.

I made several excursions in the neighbourhood with a young architect, whose wanderings during the space of four or five years border on the incredible. Mr. K. was a pupil of the Berlin Industrial School (Gewerbeschule), when the events of 1848 broke in upon his studies. He took part in several events at Berlin, left Prussia, passed through Austria to Hungary, and by way of Turkey to Rome. On his flight thence he went to Sicily, and thence to Tunis. He then crossed to Spain, travelled on foot through the Pyrenæan peninsula and to France, embarked at Havre to Hamburgh, but deeming it not the most prudent course to remain there, he sailed for America. He landed at New York, took part in the expedition of General Lopez to Cuba, fled to Texas, and there joined the expedition of the Mexican revolutionist Caravajal. When I made the acquaintance of this young man at San Antonio, he was settling down to a more quiet life, and a more promising career as architect. I could not but regret that such elasticity of mind, combined with many other good qualities, could not be employed with more advantage to the world.

I was present at San Antonio at an elegant ball, given to celebrate the wedding of a couple from New Orleans. Among the numerous guests a young officer of the United States interested me particularly; a tall man, of a serious, pleasing expression of countenance, and simple manners. This was Prince Bonaparte, a grandson of Jerome, by his marriage with Miss Patterson, of Baltimore. He had been recently quartered in one of the Texan frontier forts, and was now on his way to visit his cousin, the Emperor of France. Among the ladies of the party was the widow of a man who has left behind in Texas the character of a reckless desperado. His widow, a Mexican by birth, is universally respected; and the unhesitating manner in which she defended the door when the officers were in pursuit of her wicked husband, after a murder he had committed in the open street, and the very centre of the town, was looked upon by the population as a meritorious act, rather than a reproach. I have mentioned the name of Glanton, in connexion with some measures against the Indians on the part of the government of Chihuahua. Before this man went to Chihuahua, and thence to the Californian Colorado, he resided in Texas, and was one of the most reckless and wicked of a band of murderers and gamblers, who for many years made San Antonio one of the most dangerous places. He shot men for sport on the high road. Once, when after an act of this kind he was on the point of being arrested, he was rescued by an armed band of gamblers, and the intimidated or partial jury returned a verdict of "Not Guilty." Nearly all the new territories of the United States have been obliged to pass through such a period, until the reign of terror has grown intolerable, and the quiet and peaceable part of the population have expelled or hanged the culprits. This happened soon after in Texas.

Whilst Glanton usually attacked or murdered weak and defenceless men, another of the Texan desperadoes distinguished himself by a certain noble generosity. Whenever he fell into a quarrel and drew the revolver, he would ask his adversary, "Are you armed?" And whenever the answer was in the negative, Bill Hardy desisted from any violence. After numerous murders, he was taken prisoner in one of the small towns on the Texan shore of the Rio Grande, brought to trial, and sentenced to death. His friends succeeded in conveying to him a loaded revolver, and when about to be removed from the prison, he with this weapon put the guard, and others present, to flight, and was thus free. But instead of escaping across the river into Mexico, he returned slowly and calmly into his prison, and hanged himself. He is said to have uttered these words:—"The world is so full of cowardly rabble that it is not worth while to live." Even if no one heard this expression, it characterizes, at least, the reputation in which the man was held.

CHAPTER II.

The Author returns to the Coast — Money-transport on the Matagorda Bay — "A Norther," and an Opportunity of getting warm in it — Starting of the Caravan from Port Lavaca — Fragment of the Author's Diary, characterizing a Texan Journey by Freight-waggons — Arrival of the Caravan at San Antonio.

Business affairs connected with the loading of our waggons at Port Lavaca, obliged me early in December to return to the coast from San Antonio. The disorder caused by the yellow fever in the stores of our agent, the damage done by the weather to the contents of chests and bales which had lain unprotected, and other circumstances, occasioned a very vexatious loss of time. I was directed to hasten as much as possible the departure of the caravan from the coast, and on the 5th arrived at Lavaca.

The following day I was obliged to hire a boat, and in spite of a "Norther" setting in, to cross the Bay of Matagorda, to convey a transport of Mexican dollars to the steam-boat "Perseverance" lying at Indianola. This business was accompanied with various unpleasant circumstances. The boatman asked me, when we were in the middle of the bay, how I could have ventured to trust myself with so much money to strangers like him and his men; adding, that he would advise me not to try the same with just any boatmen on the Texan coast. The money was, in the Mexican fashion, sown into bags of undrest ox-hides, which, when dry, are as hard as bone, and thus form an extremely solid package. But the mice had nibbled the skins, so that the bright dollars were visible, of which three thousand were stowed in each bag. Any one might have easily enlarged the holes with his fingers, and filled his pockets. I had to be very watchful, and keep my eye on the bags; and I felt no little anxiety in thinking how the money was to reach in safety its destination at New Orleans. I afterwards heard that not a dollar was missing: a fact which will interest those who, in matters of property, consider American morals worse than European. No person would have been answerable for losses caused by bad packing. The violent wind also kept me in constant fear for the money; for the boat rocked about so, that I was afraid the money-bags standing on the deck might slide into the sea. The deck had no railing, but the boatmen thought my fears unfounded. At the same time the violence and cold of the norther were so great, that, with the little protection afforded by the boat, I should not have lived through the night on the water. On landing, I was so frozen as hardly to be able to walk. I went to a German inn, warmed myself with some tea, and went to bed. But scarcely had I fallen asleep, when I was awakened by a bright glare, and saw just before my windows a whole group of houses in flames. I was quickly in the road, where the norther blew so violently that my back was icy cold, whilst the skin of my face was scorched by the fire of the burning houses.

On the 10th, the first attempt was made to put to our animals,—a task which occupied the whole day, without even stirring the waggons. The following day the caravan was at last put into motion; but how this was effected will be seen from the following extract from my Diary, which I subjoin, to give an idea of the toils of such a journey. I beg the reader not to consider this unworthy his perusal, though it leads him into the low details of a waggoner's life; and if, whilst reading it, he should be enjoying the comforts of civilized and refined life, may he realize the contrast of his situation with mine at that time, and convince himself that, in Europe, the knowledge of man's physical, and, in many respects, his moral powers also, is attained in exceptional cases only. It is true the soldier during a campaign has to suffer similar hardships, sometimes still more severe: but he does not undergo these of his free will, not even when he has entered the army as a volunteer; and consequently he has seldom to give, for any length of time, the whole strength of his will. Not one of our party was bound; for the laws of the United States would have afforded us no coercive remedy if suddenly all our people had left us in the midst of our difficulties. Some of our people—Europeans by birth—actually did this. The following is the extract from my Diary:—

December 11*th*.—Men and beasts were obliged to fast from early yesterday until this morning. All worked without ceasing. I have been crippled this morning by rheumatism. In spite of every exertion we have not advanced more than a thousand paces during the day. In the evening half the waggons remained scattered in the road. Two drivers, disheartened by the toils at the outset, have left their horses and waggons in the road, and disappeared.

12*th*.—The caravan has been with difficulty put, and kept, in motion. It begins to rain. Half the waggons proceed about five English miles from the town, and there encamp; the others remain scattered on the road.

13*th*.—The waggons which remained behind are fetched, and in the evening all are formed into a camp. Torrents of rain. It is out of the question to think of proceeding.

The camp is quickly under water. It is impossible to make a fire, and our people yesterday ate for breakfast our last cooked food. All business in the camp is transacted upon the knees in water and mud.

14*th.*—Two of the axletrees, which snapped two days ago, could not be repaired till to-day. From time to time torrents of rain. The water rises in the camp.

15*th.*—Impossible to get out of this hole full of water and mud. We live on raw ham and ships' biscuits, and drink the muddy water in which we and our animals wade about. We have ordered a hunded yoke of oxen to help in extricating our waggons, but the promised aid does not come.

16*th.*—The rain continues. We must get away at all hazards, and a desperate effort must be made. Doubling the teams, we get half the waggons as far as Prairie Cottage, —a small isolated dwelling in the prairie. I mount guard during the night, with two Mexican lads, beside the waggons.

17*th.*—The rest of the waggons are brought up, and this labour continues till two o'clock P.M. No advance to-day.

18*th.*—This morning the ground covered with hoar-frost. By dint of great effort, the caravan proceeds to-day three miles.

19*th.*—The mules are in danger of perishing for want of provender. The grass of the prairies, ordinarily dead and without nourishment, begins to rot. I ride on to Victoria to purchase a few waggon-loads of maize for the animals, and to hire some hundred yoke of draught-oxen.

20*th.*—The road to Victoria almost impassable. I make some acquaintances in the hotel, to find out how and where I can obtain what I want; and at table I fall in with some "old Texans." I give here a specimen of their jokes and tales. "To be worse than I am," said one to another, "is what I call perfectly ridiculous. I am sometimes ashamed of myself; and to be so I must be bad indeed; but Bill is still worse, and this I call ridiculous." This man called out to another, during the conversation, "Don't be afraid, fool! I never killed a man half as white as you are." The conversations of these bravos drew my attention to a female character of the Texan frontier life, and, on inquiry, I heard the following particulars. They were speaking of a North American amazon, a perfect female desperado, who from inclination has chosen for her residence the wild border-country on the Rio Grande. She can handle a revolver and bowie-knife like the most reckless and skilful man; she appears at dances (*fandangos*) thus armed, and has even shot several men at merry-makings. She carries on the trade of a cattle-dealer, and common carrier. She drives wild horses from the prairie to market, and takes her oxen-waggon, alone, through the ill-reputed country between Corpus Christi and the Rio Grande.

21*st.*—I rode in vain to all the farms in the neighbourhood: the folks would not let out their draught-oxen, fearing to lose them on the bad roads.

22*nd.*—Return to the waggons without having succeeded, and find them encamped beside a small deep brook, in the prairie called the Zorillo. On their arrival, the mules had been unyoked during a violent norther; and in consequence of the sudden chill several of them died in less than half an hour. Fortunately maize has arrived for the animals. Our Mexicans are merry in the midst of toils and privations: this evening I hear them singing till late at night. "Are we not brave fellows?" exclaims one:

"we sing, whether it be cold or warm, whether we be wet or dry, and whether we have food or not."

23*rd*.—It has rained all night. In the morning the clouds break. We remain encamped, and feed our mules on maize.

24*th*.—The night very cold, with a violent north-wind. We still remain here for the animals to rest. An unpleasant Christmas-eve in the barren prairie.

25*th*.—We start in the morning at eight o'clock, with half the waggons and double teams, and proceed to within three English miles of Victoria, when the other waggons are fetched up. A farmer of the neighbourhood, with his wife, comes in a coach to visit our camp, and brings us a few bottles of egg-punch.

26*th*.—Pass through Victoria to the Guadalupe. From Lavaca to this place the distance is about thirty English miles,—a journey which we performed in sixteen days.

27*th*.—The waggons are ferried across the Guadalupe, which occupies the day. Meanwhile ten of our men are at work mending the road on the other side of the river.

28*th*.—The mules are ferried across in the forenoon. The rainy weather is over. A splendid clear sky, warm sun, and mild air. Seven waggons are taken on to the prairie from the lower land.

29*th*.—Cold night, beautiful morning. The other waggons are brought up. The soil on the banks of the Guadalupe is a stiff black clay, which in bad weather is almost impassable.

30*th*.—Continue our journey, and in the evening cross the Coleto.

31*st*.—From the Coleto to the Manahuia. The waggons sink deep into the wet sand of the prairie, as soon as they at all leave the beaten road.

January 1st, 1854.—Night very cold,—day warm. Cross the Manahuia; a bed of quicksand, like that of the Coleto. Encamp for the night near Goliad.

2nd.—Frost during the night. Proceed from Goliad to "Water Holes," where there is standing water in the prairie.

3rd.—Warm night. The mild temperature has brought a few rattlesnakes out of their holes in the earth.

4th.—Continued warm weather. We proceed nearly as far as Helena, a small new town on the river San Antonio.

5th.—A very warm night. The mosquitoes disturb our rest. Old Lopez is stung (?) in the face by a poisonous creature—scorpion or millipede. The place is somewhat inflamed and swollen. The man turns giddy, falls down, cannot rise again, and his tongue is speechless. The universal remedy, brandy, is resorted to; but we have only half a pint left. The day is very close. Towards evening the most fearful storm suddenly comes on from the north that I have ever seen in Texas. From a temperature like that of a pleasant summer-day (certainly not under 75° to 80° Fahrenheit), the air falls in less than ten minutes to freezing point; or, more correctly, ice is formed upon the wet surfaces which are exposed to the wind. I was on horseback, without coat or neckcloth, when I saw a thick mist approaching us, whilst the air began to show currents of unequal temperature. I had scarcely time to put on my coat, and tie a kerchief round my neck, when the icy storm burst on us with great violence. We happily succeeded in reaching the valley of the Cibulo, but after unharnessing several mules again perished with cold.

6th.—Stopped by the violent storm. Sleet (*candelilla*)

begins to fall. One of our Mexicans, an old man, who had suffered for a week from dysentery, sent for me last night with a message that he was dying. I went to him, when he declared that he was at the point of death—not however from illness, but from want of food ("*por falta de alimento*"). I had forbidden his eating dried beans (*frijoles*). "I must have my little beans" ("*mes frijolitos*"), said he, in a mournful tone which I could not resist. I allowed him to eat as many beans as he pleased, a permission of which he availed himself fully: from that moment he got better.

7th.—Continued storm from the north, with sleet, still prevent our travelling. Several mules are missing, which have run away from the drove to seek shelter from the inclement weather. Several of our people are gone out in quest of other animals, which from the same cause ran away some days ago. We have no men and saddle animals left to send in search of the draught cattle.

8th.—The north wind has passed; the storm has ceased. The night has been calm, and the country was covered this morning with ice and hoar-frost. We start, and travel without intermission the whole day until we come to a halt near a group of dwellings, belonging to some Mexican Texans, about a thousand paces from the Rio de San Antonio. In the vicinity is a lagoon, covered with thousands of wild-geese, and on the shore of which are large flocks of cranes. Last night I had a violent attack of fever, but to-day I am quite well again, and we are sitting this evening round a large camp-fire, in the best spirits possible. Don Guillermo has shot two wild turkeys, which, cooked with rice, make an excellent meal.

9th.—A pleasant and quiet night, although in the morning the ground was thickly covered with hoar-frost.

We ride over hills of tertiary sandstone and conglomerate, with oaks scattered here and there. Several deep hollowed watercourses impede our journey to-day. We get as far as the Arroyo de Calaveras.

10th.—It takes us six hours to cross this little river. On the prairie are several small lagoons, with innumerable water-fowl. We halt near one of them.

11th.—In the night, again the north-wind, but not so violent. We proceed to the Salado, were we remain, not to take our animals through the cold water in the evening.

12th.—We cross the river, and encamp on the other side.

13th.—Reach San Antonio, and proceeded three miles beyond.

I beg the Reader's excuses for these details, which, though in themselves of small interest, are the only means of giving a lively and general idea of a Texan waggon-journey in the winter.

It took us thirty-three days to travel a distance of at most a hundred and sixty miles, so that we did not even proceed five miles a day. During this time we suffered almost daily hunger, cold, and wet, and often to an intolerable degree. Violent attacks of illness seized several persons in our caravan; but in every instance the patient recovered, although in the open air, exposed to wind and rain, hoar-frost and cold, on a hard bed, and with coarse food. Sleeping in wet clothes, which I was often obliged to do, gave me severe rheumatism, which however passed as quickly as the attacks were violent, leaving no unpleasant consequences.

These last remarks I have added to encourage those of my readers who may desire to make a similar journey of pleasure.

WATERING-PLACE, CALLED THE DEAD MAN'S HOLE.

Book III., Chap 3

CHAPTER III.

Journey from San Antonio to El Paso — Appearance of Trap in the Limestone — A suspicious-looking Hermit — A Tanko Indian — A warm 'Norther' — Fossil Fish — Geese and Pelicans — Turkeys, Eagles, and Beavers — Meeting with Friends on the Pecos — Human Skeletons — Road to El Paso — Fire in the Prairie — Warm Wind, Dust, and Electric Sparks — Electrical Phenomena — Snow Storm — Valleys and Defiles of the Limpias — Limpia Porphyry — Harmony in the Physiognomy of Nature — Meeting with Apaches — Alamos de San Juan — A Human Corpse — Scenery on the Summit of the Plateau — Hardships of travelling — The Dead Man's Hole — Metalliferous Veins — Eagle Mountains and Eagle Spring — Yucca-wood — The Rio Grande — A rocky Defile — Gypsum Formation in the Alluvial Masses — Arrival at the Settlements — San Eleazario — Socorro, Ysleta, and El Paso.

WE were detained at San Antonio by various affairs until the 19th of January, when the camp at the Alazan broke up, and the caravan proceeded on their journey.

As far as the watering-place Agua Delgada, mentioned in a former chapter, we followed the road by which I had travelled in the spring from Chihuahua. I will make only a few remarks on this portion of the journey.

We travelled the distance to that place in thirty-five days. As far as the Rio Frio, the most considerable tributary of the Nueces, nothing of importance occurred. But the spot where the road crosses this river deserves mention. Like most of the streams in this part of the country, the Rio Frio is successively deep and shallow, in one part appearing a considerable stream, in another a small brook. At the point where the road crosses it, a plain stretches out at the foot of a perpendicular hill. On the opposite flat shore grew oaks and nut-trees, and the whole spot presents a very interesting landscape, especially to the geologist. From the Sabinal, eruptions of trap are seen on the road. Here, on the Rio Frio, a distinctly separated eruptive mass branches out like veins into the adjacent stratified rock. This latter has undergone a change from contact with the trap, and appears as a cellular weather-worn, frequently green, breccia-like mass. The trap, on the contrary, is in parts blue, with fibrous filaments, like Arragonite, Cœlestine, or Serpentine Asbestos, running through it like a net. At Fort Inge, another eruptive mass is visible in the limestone, forming a conical hill of a grey kind of porphyritic trap with feldspar and augit; and similar eruptions of trap are seen between Elm Creek and Fort Clark.

In climbing about the trap rock on the Rio Frio, I seemed to have struck upon a kind of path, which I conjectured to be the track of a bear; I followed it with eager attention, till it led me to the edge of a perpendicular precipice. At the base, the wall receded so much that it was not visible, and appeared, from the place on which I was standing, overhung with the rock; over which, during rains, the water rushes down. To the right and left of this spot the rock rises from the deep water of the river, while here a small flat beach lies between it and the wall. The locality, as may be imagined, is almost inaccessible, being approachable only by swimming across the river, or climbing down the wall. Great was my surprise, therefore, when I perceived that this isolated spot was inhabited by a man. A path led from the overhanging rock to the water, on the banks of which lay some poles, which appeared to belong to some fisherman. Among the bushes I discerned the leafy roof of a hut, and once I fancied that I heard below a human voice. I recalled to mind the hut of the runaway negroes on Devil's

River, and the roasted human flesh, and I felt no desire to make any further search after the inhabitant of this retreat.

At Fort Inge our camp was visited by an old Tanko Indian (Tancoway), who met several of our people in rather ill humour, and did not meet, therefore, with a very friendly reception. On his giving the usual assurances of amity, one of our men replied, "You talk now of friendship, but if one of us fell into your power you would cut his throat." The man understood that our friend wanted to cut *his* throat, and looked enquiringly around the circle, to learn whether he had to expect this fate from *all* those present. When his eyes met mine my look probably assured him that I at least did not desire his blood; he stretched out his hand to me, and embraced me, exclaiming repeatedly, and in an expressive manner, "*Manito!*" no doubt a corruption of the Spanish "*Hermanito*," i. e. "dear brother." He appeared now to be quieted, but he soon quitted our inhospitable camp. On our arrival the next day at a village of the Tankos, on the Nueces, we found it deserted. The fires were still burning, and it was evident that our appearance had driven the inhabitants away. Whether the unfriendly treatment and misunderstanding of the old man had occasioned their flight, or the jokes of some of our people that they would visit the Tanko ladies, I know not.

On our way from the Nueces to Turkey Creek we encountered a violent north wind of a remarkably warm temperature. A warm norther seems a contradiction; but the fact is easily explained by the supposition that the wind had made a circle, either in a vertical or in a horizontal direction, and that what met us as a wind from the north, had originally come from the south.

In a quarry on the road near Fort Clark, I found, among other indistinct petrifactions, the traces of small fishes, the structure of the fins and skin being still discernible: the latter was not scaled, but granulated like a shark's. The rock consists of alternate strata of dense limestone and thin slaty sand-marl.

At Soquete Creek, a brook which is probably connected with Maverick's Creek, I saw some wild geese of a species quite new to me, and of an extraordinary size. We put up three still larger birds, which we at first took for swans, but were more probably pelicans: they were white, with black wings, and made a loud piercing scream.

San Felipe is the name of a clear and rapid spring, which rises from limestone strata, and forms a charming little prairie river, running rapidly through the grass with frequent little cascades. In one deep hole I caught with a rod and line a cat-fish of considerable size. The family of the Silurides is numerously represented in all the rivers and brooks in this part by a variety of species. I described the vicinity of Devil's River at the end of the last Book, and will only observe here, that at this season (February) the valley contains large numbers of wild turkeys. Eagles, with white bodies and black wings, and of an extraordinary size, are seen hovering over the bushes in which the turkeys lie. Some of our best shots tried in vain to bring down one of these monarchs of the air; the nearest shot carried off one of the large wing feathers. Our table was, however, well supplied with game during our journey over this tract. The wild turkey is a bird of the size and beauty of which the domestic one gives a very faint idea. Several stags were also shot by our sportsmen. I observed the marks of beavers' teeth on the trees upon the banks of the river; a large sycamore-tree had been thrown down by these animals, and the bark was stript from many of its branches. Since we passed this way in the spring, a great number of Indians must have resided here.[1] In several places we found groups of deserted huts, which had not been there on our previous visit.

We travelled without stopping from hence to Howard Springs, a distance of forty-five miles, from eight o'clock in the morning till two o'clock the following morning. I had been on guard from four to six o'clock in the morning before starting, and, on our arrival at the next encampment, my turn to mount guard was from two to four o'clock in the morning. I had therefore at that time been on active duty quite twenty-four hours. Four hours' sleep however sufficed to banish all my fatigue.

On the Pecos we fell in with an encounter which agreeably broke the monotony of the journey. A caravan came up, in which we recognised some friends, who had come from the point to which we were travelling, and we had, consequently, occasion to interchange much important information.

On the Ojo de Ahuancha (Comanche Spring) we found four human skeletons, and at a little distance a fifth. We were afterwards informed that, since our journey in the spring, several men, on their route from California, had been killed by the Comanches. The Indians offered for sale, at the Presidio del Norte, some of the articles they had stolen from travellers, and boasted of the exploit.

I must here explain the name of the watering-place where the road to the Presidio separates from that to El Paso. I have before called this place Agua Delgada, and

---

[1] In 1857 this valley was again the scene of bloody battles with the Indians, in which the troops of the United States even suffered considerable loss.

I retain that name. The North-American and Texan maps call it Lion Springs, whilst the Mexicans apply this name—in its Spanish form, Ojo del Leon—to the first watering-place on the road from hence to the Presidio; and they call the spot at which the road divides Agua Delgada. I imagine the older and more correct name has been retained by Mexican travellers.

At this encampment we narrowly escaped a great peril. Our waggons had halted in the long and dry grass, in which there were occasional barren spots; on these we made our fires. Mr. K. feared that the grass might catch fire, and I was growing quite impatient at his continual expressions of fear, when suddenly my eye fell on a spot where the grass had just caught the flames. I ran to extinguish them, but could not master them, in spite of buffetting them till I was quite exhausted: no sooner had I smothered the fire before me, than it rose up behind. The hot air which I inhaled burnt my mouth and throat, and I nearly lost my consciousness: my hair and beard were burnt, and I should have been compelled to abandon the field to the devouring element, had not twenty or thirty men hastened up with blankets, who succeeded, at least, in arresting the flames on the side of the waggons, though unable to stop their course on the other side. The mules were driven to shelter in time, and we had now nothing more to fear. Had the assistance come a minute later, our waggons would most probably all have been burnt, and the lives of the whole caravan been in danger. How much further the fire may have spread I know not.

I must relate our journey to El Paso more in detail, as it leads me upon new ground: it occupied twenty-eight days.

From the watering-place, we first proceeded to a desolate plateau, covered with grey bushes and scanty grass, where we saw large herds of antelopes. In a few hours we reached a level tract, upon the bare clay soil of which grew, here and there, an *Opuntia arborescens.* In the distance rose the Limpia Mountains, to which our road lay. At their foot we observed some columns of smoke—Indian signals, as we ascertained some days later. During the journey the sky was overcast with dark clouds, which, with a sultry air, seemed to indicate the approach of a thunderstorm. Some large drops of rain fell: a violent gale filled the air with such clouds of dust that we were almost stifled, and our caravan was quite darkened. Later, when night came on, our clothes and the harness emitted electric sparks when stirred: every lash of the whip on the animals' backs was a small streak of fire. I have often witnessed similar electrical phenomena in the interior of North America, and have before spoken of them; but have never seen them exhibited in so striking a manner as on this day (February 24th) on the plain of the eastern foot of the Limpia Mountains: sparks from my fingers were at times quite perceptible when I touched any part of my clothes. I may here observe that, coinciding with these electrical phenomena, I repeatedly felt a sudden rheumatic affection, which all at once paralyzed, temporarily, my left leg, and gave me a violent headache. The former attack, happily, never lasted above one or two hours.

We continued our route till about two o'clock in the morning, during which time the warm air was succeeded by an icy north wind, accompanied by a snow-storm, which obliged us to halt for twenty-four hours. Our animals had all this time no water, but they appeared to suffer little from this want, either from the dampness of the atmosphere, or that they allayed their thirst with snow-water. The next day the weather was again mild, the snow was melted, and we continued our journey.

As I was riding in advance of the caravan, I saw three mountain-sheep, one of which I might have killed if I had ventured to follow them; but, at a distance, I mistook the animals for bears, and confess that I had no desire to encounter three of these beasts alone. When I discovered my error they were too high up between the rocks.

We had now entered the Limpia Mountains, from which the Limpia Valley opens upon the plain. The Mexicans call a series of springs and pools of water along a line of valleys and defiles "Las Limpias;" through them our route now lay for several days: the word may, perhaps, be best translated "the clear waters." This mountain forms part of the porphyritic range, over which, in a southern section, the road leads to the Presidio del Norte, through the pass I have before described, under the name of the Puerto del Paisano. The Guadalupe Mountains, across which, further north, another route passes from Texas to the Rio Grande, are connected with this chain. Another part of it bears the name of Sierra del Diablo—"the Devil's Mountain," a designation which would not be inappropriate to the entire range. The long rocky passage through which the El Paso road crosses the mountains, or, perhaps a certain part of it, is called by the North Americans the "Wild Rose Pass." It probably more especially designates the pass over a certain yoke of mountains, called by the Mexicans the Cuesta de las Limpias. This, however, is not the central pass over the chain: it only cuts off a bend and an impassable part of the valley.

In this the traveller proceeds through a series of long defiles and narrow clefts, till he unawares reaches the western side of the range, and the actual summit of the plateau on this side of the Rio Grande.

From the western foot of the chain the water of the rainy season runs through this succession of valleys and defiles to the plain at its eastern foot, where it loses itself. In the dry season, on the contrary, the traveller is dependent on some insignificant springs and accidental pools of water, and the consequence of wandering from the route might very probably be death from thirst.

At the point where we entered the mountains from the plain, a lofty mountain rose on our right, at the east foot of which horizontal strata of limestone bordered on the porphyry. Whether they belong to the cretaceous or the jurassic formation, both of which are represented here, I do not know; but the porphyry of the Limpia Mountains is certainly older than these limestone strata, which I noticed in many places covered with pieces of flint.

On our left commenced a range of porphyritic rocks, which, seen from a height, looked like a vault cleft longitudinally, and, consequently, like a double row of rocks, with a deep fissure between.

In several places there are evident indications that the masses of porphyry, of which this whole system is formed, have originally spread in horizontal sheets over the underlying rocks, and that similar casts of melted matter have occurred repeatedly one over the other. The highest, or, at least, the most imposing mountain in this part—Whiting's Peak—with others of a similar altitude near it, are capped by sheets of porphyry in their original horizontal position; and below we find successive terraces of the same rock in a similar horizontal position. On the north side of Whiting's Peak, and between it and another similar mountain in its neighbourhood, the whole system of these repeated casts of melted matter has sunk in, and a valley has been formed towards the centre, of which the sheets of porphyry are inclined from both sides at the same angle.

This simple arrangement is visible, however, only from a little distance. When near, it is hidden in a chaos of the most astonishing forms of separation, which may be compared to basaltic columns, but exhibit an extraordinary variety of shape. The perpendicular walls are divided into an infinity of columns, pinnacles, cones, towers, spindles, shafts, oval and rhomboidal portions: a mountain scenery of the strangest character. In general, the Limpia passes are among the most interesting things in nature I have ever seen.

I was struck by the wonderful harmony and unity of the physiognomic elements which compose the landscape. Nature appears here, more than anywhere else I have seen, like a landscape-painter, composing a picture with the most simple yet refined taste. For instance, on the pinnacles and turrets of the brown rock is found a species of juniper, which, in its growth, seems to imitate the strange forms of the mineral masses. In other parts of this remarkable region, where the Gothic style of the masses of rock passes into the antique—their rocky walls resembling gigantic steps with broad grass-grown mountain-terraces—the character of the vegetation likewise changes in a corresponding manner. The pointed juniper-tree is succeeded by the oak, with its spreading, umbrageous crown, decorating the sunny turf in small groups among the rocks.

I shall now return to our entrance into the valley of the

Limpias, after the snow-storm. The first watering-place to be looked for, a little spring among the rocks on its northern side, known to the Mexicans by the name of Agua Escondida, or Los Barriles, was still about two English miles distant, and our animals had not tasted a drop of water for two days. On a sudden our progress was stopped by a band of eighty to a hundred Apaches, all well-armed. They rode directly across our road, and stuck a lance into the ground, as a sign that we were not allowed to proceed. Hitherto we had only had to contend with natural obstacles, but it appeared now that we should have to cut our way by force of arms. The meeting presented a very exciting scene. As soon as the advanced party of our caravan perceived the Indians descending a hill in regular file, and carrying a banner before them, the foremost waggons at once began to form into a corral, as the cry of "Los Indios!" ran quickly through our train, from the van to the rear, where I happened to be. I had dismounted, intending to proceed a little way on foot, and had left my fire-arms in the waggon. On a sudden this cry reached my ears, and I saw all our waggons driving off at full gallop. The teams of mules, with the bell-mares and loose animals, dashed past me. The entire caravan hurried to the spot where the corral was being formed, and I saw myself left behind alone and unarmed, whilst the Indians began to advance from their centre, a wing right and left, to surround us in a wide circle. With the utmost exertion and difficulty I just succeeded in reaching the corral before being cut off.

Matters, however, had meanwhile taken a more peaceable turn than we had at first anticipated. Our movements had been made with great rapidity and order; and although some of our Mexicans had behaved in a cowardly manner—doing nothing, at the most critical moment, but rub flour over their faces, probably that the Indians might take them for whites—still we numbered thirty good shots, planted behind our waggons, all armed with guns; and the savages would have come off badly had they ventured to attack us. They might, perhaps, have calculated all this beforehand, and determined to try, at least, to frighten us, and thus to induce us to make them liberal presents.

This band of Indians had two chiefs—the brothers Marcos and Soldadito—notorious names. They belonged to the Mescaleros, and had formerly lived on the shores of the Rio Grande, near the Presidio del Norte, where, for a long time, they were the terror of the country around, until they were driven into the wilderness of Texas by the Norteños, and their allies the Comanches. I afterwards heard that the remnant of the band of the notorious Espejo had joined them, against whom, nine months before, the war-party of Norteños and Comanches, whom we had met near the Presidio, were marching.

As soon as I had a little recovered from my fatigue, I went up to the group, where the two chiefs were in treaty with my companions. There I saw the lance which had been stuck into the ground: the long blond hair of a white woman they had murdered was fluttering from it in the wind; the end was formed of an old sword-blade, bearing the inscription, "Por el Rey Carlos III." A Mexican prisoner acted as interpreter at this conference, and through his mediation Marcos harangued Don Guillermo, who had undertaken to act the part of "Captain." "You are a rich man," said the Apache: "your waggons roll over the country like thunder. We have seen you from our mountains crossing the plains. You sit by your fires and smoke much tobacco. We are poor and peaceable: we also like smoking tobacco. We are your friends." A liberal present of tobacco then sealed our terms of peace and friendship. Old Soldadito took great pains to make me understand that we had no longer anything to fear from them. He laid his head in his hand, with his eyes shut, whilst pronouncing the word "Seguro!" in order to give me to understand that we might sleep in safety. "Don't you think," he added, through the interpreter, "that we could have plundered you and killed many of you? We have watched you for many days, and have been in your neighbourhood. But we are not ill-disposed to you: you can travel on without fear; you will not see us any more." At first the whole troop—which had been considerably increased by the women and boys who had come up, and who were as well armed as the men—wanted to accompany us to the watering-place; but, on our objecting to this, the chiefs at once yielded to our wishes. One of them said a few words to his people, and immediately the whole troop dispersed, singly or in couples, to all sides; and, in fact, we did not see them again. Before and behind us they have robbed and murdered, but from us they have not taken a single mule.

After the excitement of the day, and our previous sufferings from the weather, we passed a tranquil night at our watering-place, which refreshed and rested both man and beast. For four days we continued our journey through the Limpia defiles, until we came out on to the plateau west of the mountain-chain on the 3rd of March. The topographical details of this journey would tire the reader too much, and I have already given a general description of the natural features of this remarkable country.

One great evil, from which we had suffered sufficiently

in the valleys, was increased when we reached the plateau. Over a wide tract, on mountain, valley, and plain, the grass had been burnt, so that our animals suffered greatly from want. Here and there only were some remains of the old grass, and in a few of the most favoured spots the young grass was springing up. The burnt-up tract extended over hundreds of square miles; and where this desolation terminated, the ravages of the prairie-marmots commenced, and spread over an equal extent of ground.

The want of water increased greatly as we proceeded. Several caravans with waggons drawn by oxen, and large droves of cattle, on their route to California, had at this time lost hundreds, nay thousands of their beasts in these very parts, and the road was strewn with their bones.

The last watering-place of the Limpia range (on the plateau to the west of the defiles) is called by the North Americans "Head of the Limpias." I am not sure whether this is not the same spot to which the Mexicans have given the name of Alamos de San Juan. At all events the two spots, if not the same, are situated close to one another. We halted at the Alamos, where—in a depression of the plateau, at the foot of rocky hills with interesting detached masses of porphyry, enclosed by a grove of old poplars and surrounded by evergreen oaks—we came to a copious spring. Some of our people rambled over the hills, where they found among the rocks the naked corpse of a white man, which appeared to have been lying there for several days. The place bore traces of a desperate fight, but we had no time to search into the matter further. As the corpse was not scalped, it seems that the murderer was no Indian.

Proceeding hence, we came to a barren, high plain, with single mountains and isolated rocks, mostly of rounded forms. Masses of white quartz-rock, bordering on the brown porphyry, produced a strange effect in the landscape. Unfortunately we travelled over this part in the night, and I regretted missing the view of the grand scenery of which the moonlight gave me a faint idea. Some of the views which we saw by day were of a truly classical beauty in outlines and grouping, notwithstanding the absence of trees and shrubs. The same monotonous grass steppe extended over hill and valley, over plain and mountain, day after day, as far as the eye could reach.

A difficult route led us uphill and downhill over the rocky spurs of a mountain range, until we at length came to a lower terrace of the plateau. In a state of exhaustion we reached a dried-up brook at midnight, where we had fully reckoned upon finding water. There we spent the following day, in digging wells and watering our animals. It is impossible to give an idea of the difficulty of this task: each single animal had to be caught with the lazo, led down to the deep and rocky bed of the brook, and there to drink out of the bucket; and we had about three hundred and twenty animals! Before the turn of the last one came, the first were thirsty again. The two divisions of the droves,—those which had already drunken, and those which were still to be watered,—had to be kept separate,—an almost impossible task! whilst all the while a strong armed guard had to be placed over them. No man could give a moment for repose; and even the hands needed to prepare the food could hardly be spared.

We had confounded this spot with the next watering-place, which bears the ominous name of "The Dead-Man's Hole,"—in Spanish, "El Muerto." The water at this last place seemed not to be much more abundant or accessible. A small valley extended for some miles between the terraces of piled-up and columnar porphyry, the steps of which are covered with groups and groves of evergreen oaks. In narrow hollows the traveller is surprised by a remarkable shrub, a species of Arbutus, with smooth copper-red bark. Here, in a corner between the rocks and among the bushes, we discovered a spring trickling over the stones, filling some holes with a few pailsful of water. Fortunately one of our people found a larger spring in another valley, a few miles distant, which gave us a sufficient supply of water for our cattle. The animals had to be driven several hundred feet up on the side of a precipice, as the water was lost immediately on reaching the foot of the mountain. However we succeeded, and, to give our parched animals time to drink, we halted here for the day. The spot was remarkably wild and desolate. Here and there a steep cliff, upon which we placed our sentinels, rose isolated out of the grassy plain at the foot of the mountains. The valley in which we first sought for water had all the interest of which the wildernesses of this region are capable.

A march of thirty-six miles over a barren and dusty plain brought us to Van Horn's Wells, where the cattle of a caravan which had preceded us had exhausted all the water; we were therefore obliged to continue our journey without watering our animals. All around cattle left behind by preceding caravans lay dying with thirst. It was indeed a melancholy spectacle. Many of the poor beasts, still alive, had their eyes dried up and their tongues hanging out of their mouth: we shot several of them, in passing, out of mere compassion.

We had still twenty-two miles to journey to the "Eagle Springs." The road led over a mountain ridge, where, between nearly horizontal limestone strata on one side and porphyritic masses on the other, a system of metamorphic strata appears, consisting of micaceous slate, choritic slate, hornblende slate, and stratified serpentine, and covers the summit of the pass. In these strata are found masses of copper pyrites, malachite, and octahedric loadstone, and I believe a search for veins of ore might be well rewarded.

At the point where the road descends to the lower plain, behind which the "Eagle Mountains" rise, the declivities of the hills are covered with a scattered forest of yucca-trees, which imparts a singular and interesting character to the landscape. The "Eagle Springs" lie not far from the road, at the foot of the mountains. A thin forest of very old yuccas grows around them, looking almost like a forest of palm-trees. I have nowhere seen larger or more numerous yucca-trees; but this species is not remarkable for the size of its flower-stalks. At sunset, when the thick old stems and their radiating crowns were surrounded with a net of light, they formed a wonderful scene. A black pointed mountain stood out clearly among the foliage against the bright horizon.

The "Eagle Springs" yield a sufficient quantity of water to satisfy the wants of several caravans, succeeding one another, even in the dry season; but it is necessary always to husband carefully the supply of water. The locality is only a few miles distant from the Rio Grande, but the river appears to be inaccessible, the road running for thirty-three miles over a desert without water, until at length it reaches the shore of the river. Along this road we again passed hundreds of oxen perishing from thirst, which had been left behind by caravans and transports that had preceded us. Many died in sight of the river, which they were unable to reach; and others in its waters, or in the quick-sands in its bed.

On the road porphyry again succeeds the limestone of the Eagle Mountains. A narrow and winding defile, in which first limestone and then a species of porphyry and a slaty hornstone are seen, leads to the alluvial terrace of the valley, where an extensive formation of gypsum occurs. The defile is only three miles long, but the road through it is so difficult for large waggons with long teams, that it took us ten hours to pass through it. At about midway, by the road-side, is a rounded rock covered with Indian hieroglyphics. The gypsum in the valley appears as a loose earthy mass of red, yellow, white, and greenish colour, containing innumerable crystals of selenite in laminæ, scales, and fibrous aggregates. The gypseous clay is destitute of vegetation, whilst the adjacent alluvial soil is covered with rich grass. Here, and in the defile, I frequently observed the chino-grass (*Sacate chino*) which is celebrated in Mexico, and is prized far more than the gramma-grass, and as much as oats: it grows only a few inches high.

By the river we lost several mules, which drank so much water that they dropped, and could not rise again.

We now found ourselves once more in the vicinity of human settlements, and despatched people to San Ygnacio, to purchase some waggon-loads of maize for our animals. Without this supply we should hardly have been able to reach El Paso, as they were so exhausted that almost hourly one or another of the animals dropped down before the waggon, and was with difficulty got on its legs again.

On the 20th of March we encamped opposite to the above-mentioned Mexican village. The inhabitants came over the river to bring us poultry, eggs, and milk for sale.

Our condition, as well as the surrounding country,

began to assume a more cheerful aspect. The poplars by the water side were nearly in leaf. Crossing an arm of the river we reached the island, which contains three considerable villages,—San Eleazario, Socorro, and Ysleta. Peach and pear trees were here in blossom. No one who has not spent months in travelling across an inhospitable wilderness can understand the feelings with which I beheld once more the indications of civilization and friendly intercourse. The island is in some measure protected from Indian attacks, and is in part well cultivated. A great part, however, consists of sandy tracts, which lie too high to admit of irrigation, and are overgrown with saline vegetation and chaparral.

With Mr. K., I drove on in advance of the caravan to El Paso, where we arrived March 23rd.

CHAPTER IV.

New Custom-house Regulations on the Mexican Frontier — Continuation of the Journey to California — Mexican Passport System — Commencement of Spring Vegetation in the Sand — Crossing the Rio Grande — Valley of Mesilla — Geological Features — A Murderer joins our Party — Smallpox effects a Life Insurance — Rio de los Mimbres — Ojo de Inez — Long March without Water — Dry Lagoon — Natural Wells — A beautiful Spring and Indian Beastliness — Guadalupe Pass — San Bernardino — Origin of the Rio Yaqui — Monument with Indian Hieroglyphics — Springs of the Rio de San Pedro — Apaches — Charming Valleys — Strata of Conglomerate — Impassable Mountain Pass — Santa Cruz.

THE measures which the President Santa Ana had adopted since our last expedition had so injuriously affected the importation of merchandize across the Mexican frontier, that we could not think of passing our goods through the custom-house of El Paso. These measures, although they were terminated by the fall of Santa Ana, merit a brief explanation.

The tariff of the Mexican Customs was in general so high, as to be almost a prohibition on all importation;—but it was never enforced. The merchants who appeared on the frontier with their transports of goods, made their special bargains with the custom-house authorities, and never paid more than a half, often only a fourth or fifth, of the tariff impost. This practice benefitted both the merchant and the custom-house officers, as well as the purchasers, and ultimately the public; but the exchequer was the loser, together with the high authorities. Santa Ana, in consequence, bent all his efforts to effect a reform, which afforded him an opportunity of keeping up a show of morality and improved state economy. He reduced the duties, and, at the same time, threatened the officers of the customs with capital punishment should they connive in defrauding the public revenue by excusing any part of the custom-house dues. The result was singular: the tolls were considerably lowered, and yet the merchants declared that, under these circumstances, they were unable to import their goods. For example, under this reduced tariff, we should have had to pay seventy to eighty thousand dollars nett, whereas, under the old tariff, we should have passed our merchandize for fifteen or twenty thousand.

The Dictator of Mexico, occupied with extensive schemes, whose insatiable avarice is explained by his intention of amassing the means of founding a Mexican empire, left one door open by which the country could be supplied with cheap goods: he held out the inducement of a reduction of the imposts to all those merchants who should come voluntarily to the capital, and state their business personally to the President. By this measure he effected at the same time several objects: he diverted the bribes—which these merchants had been accustomed to pay—into his own pocket, and restricted the Mexican import trade to large undertakings, which made it worth their while to obtain a hearing from him, even at a considerable cost. At the same time he promoted the maritime commerce, which is chiefly European, at the expense of the inland trade, which is principally carried on with the United States. Thus, whilst the imposts were almost prohibitory for the land-transport, the interior of Mexico was inundated with cheap European goods from the seaports. Under these circumstances, no course remained to my friends but to leave the goods with which our waggons were loaded, on the Texan side of the Rio Grande, and to await some change in the affairs of Mexico—in short the fall of Santa Ana. Several merchants from the United States, who had arrived there before us, were similarly situated. In the few buildings at Franklin and Macgoffinville, there were probably lying merchandize to the value of about half a million dollars, destined for Chihuahua, which could not be imported.

The reader may imagine the unpleasantness of a merchant's position, who, after having embarked his capital in an enterprise, finds it suddenly locked up in this manner. My friends viewed the matter coolly, and then took a sudden resolution: the goods were left at Franklin, under the care of Mr. M. whilst Mr. K. undertook to proceed with the mules and empty waggons to California, where good prices for them might be expected to realize the capital embarked; this was estimated at about 40,000 dollars. For my own part, the misfortune of my friends facilitated the accomplishment of my wish, of travelling across the rest of the continent; and I did not hesitate a moment to accompany Mr. K. to California.

Before, however, inviting my readers to accompany me across the steppes of Northern Sonora, the deserts of the Gila and Colorado, and the mountain passes of Los Angeles, to the shores of the Pacific, I must make a few observations relative to my stay at El Paso, from March 23rd to June 4th.

Our object in making this long stay was twofold: first, our animals had arrived so exhausted, that they needed a long rest before they were able to undergo fresh toil and privations; we had, likewise, to await the commencement of the summer rains in the steppes west of the Rio Grande, and the ripening of the mezquite pods in the deserts of the

Gila and Colorado, where this fruit, for hundreds of miles, is the only food for the cattle. I could almost have made a journey to Chihuahua in this time; and indeed I did set out, but only accomplished half the distance. The person there with whom I had business met me accidentally half way. I had at the same time an opportunity of learning by experience the Mexican passport system, much improved by Santa Ana, which has since been quite changed; at that time it was unique in the New World. Pleasant recollections of long-forgotten advantages of European life were awakened in my mind. I was obliged to appear at the "Jefatura," where my description was taken down, and my weapons and those of my servants were entered. A guarantee had also to be given. But when all this was done, the passport was not ready, and I was told to come again in two hours. "Es muchisimo trabajo!" (It is a great labour), said the Jefe Politico, or Prefect of El Paso, as he eyed his slowly-writing secretary. Doña Concha, the wife of one of my companions, who was attached to the "conducta" going to Chihuahua, was excepted from these police regulations. "De las Señoras no dice nada la ley" (the law says nothing about the ladies), said the "Jefe Politico," with Spanish gallantry.

If the United States have outdone the English system of governing as little as possible, Mexico has surpassed the system of the European continental states of governing as much as possible. Both American neighbour republics go to the extreme; but with this difference, that the United States owe their greatness to their "governing too little," whilst Mexico and other Spanish American republics owe in part their decline to the system of "governing too much."

About the time of our arrival at the Rio Grande, two scientific expeditions passed through this part of the country, both commissioned to discover an advantageous line for a railroad to the Pacific. One, under the command of Lieutenant Park, sent by the Government of Washington, had begun their works at San Diego, on the coast of California; and had progressed eastwards as far as the Rio Grande. The other expedition, under Colonel Gray, was in the service of a company of New York, and penetrated from El Paso westward. Not long before our arrival at Franklin this latter expedition had made a vain attempt to reach the little-known Laguna de Guzman, the upper end of which, as was afterwards discovered by a second more successful expedition, lies sixty-two miles south, 50° west from El Paso, in the steppe. The first attempt nearly met with an unfortunate termination: the party wandered about in the steppe, unable to find the lake, and want of water forced them to return to the Rio Grande, leaving behind a waggon, and all the baggage in it. Several persons had gone mad from thirst, but they soon recovered. The day after our arrival, I saw these courageous men start afresh; and a fortnight later a messenger brought to the United States Consul at El Paso the tidings that the expedition had found the lake. In this corps was a young German, Mr. Schuchart, from Hesse-Cassel, whom I afterwards met again in the south of California, where he had joined an expedition to explore and work some silver, gold, and copper mines on the river Gila,—a task still more dangerous than that of Colonel Gray.

Before leaving the Rio Grande, I may remark that this year the poplars were in leaf at the end of March and the beginning of April; that in the second week of April the algarobbiæ were green; and that in the third week the various species of acacia came into leaf, which form part of the underwood on the sandy banks of the river. The different species of cactus had flowered from the beginning of the month.

I must not pass unnoticed a phenomenon I observed here repeatedly, which will interest those who study the physiology of plants. It had not rained for many months; the loose sand was dry, and was daily heated by the sun; in spite of which I observed seeds germinating in this very sand. This phenomenon is connected with the general question, by what natural means vegetation is maintained in a country without water, with an exceedingly dry atmosphere, and with a periodical absence of all rain for six months.

Early in June we started for California, following, with a few slight deviations, the road through the basin of the Gila, known by the name of Cook's Route. At Fort Fillmore our waggons were conveyed across the river on a flat boat. The mules were obliged to swim over, which was not easily effected, and many of them were carried down the stream; others returned back to the shore when half way across, and others still stuck fast in a quicksand. We thought ourselves fortunate that the whole drove was brought over without loss. A German, who had joined our caravan on this occasion, sank up to his waist in a quicksand, and had to be pulled out with cords. I have said above that these sandbanks render the Rio Grande exceedingly dangerous.

On the other side of the river we found ourselves in the valley of Mesilla. The political interest connected with it has been mentioned in a former chapter. This village has great advantages of soil, being fertile and easily irrigated. The beautiful appearance of large tracts of the valley deceived and disappointed us, looking as if covered with rich grass, which proved to be only a plant of the family of

Compositæ, with green, pointed, leafless stalks, and small white flowers; it grows luxuriantly over many square miles, but quite unfit for fodder.

To the west, this green bottom-land is bordered by a lateral terrace with a steep declivity, which, forming a kind of plateau, has given its name to the place. Mesilla is the diminutive of *Mesa*, or table—a word by which the Mexicans designate a plateau. On the 12th we began to ascend to this terrace: the road presenting interesting geological features, disclosed in a rocky fissure near the road. Masses of porphyry lie here, over nearly horizontal strata of limestone, containing fossil shells, and which have been much changed by the influence of heat in contact with the plutonic or volcanic rock. Higher up the road led us through the deep ravines of an extensive and interesting formation of gypsum, where the inhabitants of New Mexico fetch isinglass for window-panes.

Viewed from this height, the valley of Mesilla, with its green bottom, the river seen here and there through a thick grove of poplars, and the opposite range of the Sierra de los Organos, presents an aspect of truly imposing grandeur.

We passed the night on this elevation, and our animals were driven back into the valley for grass and water. Whilst encamped here, a North American—Mr. W., from Virginia—joined us. He had been living in New Mexico, where he had committed a murder, and, to escape the consequences of this deed, he begged permission to travel with us to California. Such company cannot be avoided in these countries. I have observed this man for months during the journey, and found him to be very good-natured and to have many good qualities; but he could not resist drinking spirits, and when drunk he was like a wild beast. During the journey he had no opportunity of yielding to this weakness, as we resolutely refused to let him have a drop of the dangerous fluid. As soon, however, as we reached the first Californian settlement, he freed himself from this control. Having got drunk, he insisted on my drinking with him; and on my refusal he flew into such a rage, that I thought myself fortunate to escape without serious injury. People of this kind are met with very frequently in North America; and this, amongst other things, should be taken into consideration, in giving just credit to the efforts of the Temperance party.

Mr. W., who had lived in Santa Barbara, had often come in contact with the Copper-mine Apaches, who at that time lived on a good understanding with the North Americans, and were frequently seen in the settlements. He brought us the unpleasant tidings that a misunderstanding had recently broken out between them and the whites. A son of the old chief, who went by the name of Ponce, had been ill with small-pox, and the commander of the neighbouring fort, it was said, would not allow the army surgeon to visit the patient, who afterwards died. The old man hereupon removed with his tribe, threatening that in future travellers should not find him so friendly as hitherto; and, in fact, a few days after, we became aware that this threat was made in earnest. In our party were some North Americans, with their Mexican wives, who were in the habit of journeying in advance of our caravan, partly in a travelling-carriage and partly on horseback. When we approached within a few miles of Cook's Spring a Mexican servant of these people suddenly returned in the greatest haste, telling us that his master and mistress had suddenly been surprised by a band of Apaches at the watering-place, and were murdered. Accompanied by Messrs. W. and C., I hastened to the spot as fast as our horses could carry us; but before we reached the place these people came to meet us: an accident had saved them. One of the travellers was suffering from small-pox, and his face was greatly disfigured. When the Indians surrounded the carriage, and looked into it in search of booty, they saw this patient; and such terror seized them, that the whole band immediately ran off. Their leader was a Mexican renegade of ill repute, called Delgadito, from whom these travellers might have expected the worst treatment.

On this occasion I heard several anecdotes characteristic of old Ponce. He had taken prisoner a man from Mesilla, and the savages made all the preparations to burn him alive. Everything was ready for the ceremony, and the men of the tribe were busy getting drunk, to heighten their enjoyment of the scene; when, at nightfall, one of the wives of the chief came to the prisoner, cut his cords, and aided him to escape. Ponce loves spirits above everything. When his son died of small-pox, he sold his finest mule to procure a large quantity of whisky, observing that his heart was heavy, and he must lighten it. To his younger son he made a present on this occasion of a whole cask-full: "The boy," he said, "takes his brother's death so much to heart, that I must cheer him up."

The water at Cook's Spring is of a good taste, clear, and cool; but the spring lies in a black peaty soil, and the footsteps of any animals speedily transform the water into mud. This is a difficulty that often happens at the watering-places. The next spring we came to, Ojo de Vaca, was of the same kind.

If the Sierra de los Mimbres, a chain of mountains said to connect the Rocky Mountains and the great Sierra Madre, really existed anywhere except on maps and in geographies; our road must have led over it. Between Cook's Spring and the Rio de los Mimbres we twice crossed some heights, but these belonged only to the lower spurs or advanced groups of mountains more north; and the road might have passed round them further south over a plain, if its course had not to be determined by the watering-places. In these spurs are found the sources of the Rio de los Mimbres, a small and beautiful river of the steppe, flowing through a wide plain southward, and reaching, in the wet season, the Laguna de Santa Maria. This prairie-lake is not separated by any mountain from the Rio Grande. During the dry season the river dries up in the steppe. At the part where we crossed, it was surrounded by green meadows, and bordered by a thick underwood of Mimbre (*Chilopsis*); it looked one of the pleasantest spots I have seen on our long journey. In the neighbourhood game is abundant.

We found, on our way through this part of the country, in several places, limestone and sandstone; the latter overlying the former, and both bordering on porphyry and trachyte. Sometimes the sandstone formed crenelated walls. But, on the whole, the landscape was an undulating steppe, overgrown with grass, bordered, here and there, with isolated mountains and mountain-groups. On the other side of the Ojo de Vaca, where the road leads over the advanced spurs of a group of mountains which we left to the north, and the highest peak of which the North-Americans call Ben Moore, a spring is said to rise in the hollow of a rock, which owes its name—Ojo de Inez—to a romantic event, the deliverance of a

Mexican girl, carried off by the Apaches, by the North-American boundary commissioner.[1]

I was tempted to penetrate several miles alone into the mountains, whilst our caravan was passing the mouth of this hollow. My adventurous ride, on a beaten Indian trail, trusting to the swiftness of my horse and my excellent arms, led me into a mountain-scene of great interest and beauty, shut out from the world. The rocks, consisting of a bluish, yellowish, and greenish grey pearl-stone, presented twisted and elongated stripes, similar to half-melted glass. Here and there I started a herd of stags, but did not venture to fire, for fear of betraying my presence to the Indians in the vicinity.

In this part of the country the road makes a bend due south, and crossing the most north-eastern spur of the Great Sierra Madre, in the Guadalupe Pass, famous for its difficulty, it leads through Santa Cruz, San Xavier del Bac, Tubac, and Tucson, the three latter places of which have since then been incorporated in the territory of the United States, with the so-called "Gadsden Purchase." But a man of the name of Leroux had tried successfully a much shorter line, which, cutting off the whole bend, leads straight to Tucson, and which since has come into use under the name of Leroux's Route. It had been our intention to take this shorter road, on which as yet, however, there were no waggon-tracks. At El Paso we made the acquaintance of a man with a large drove of cattle, on his way to California, and who had obtained all the necessary particulars relating to the route. This man (and I mention the circumstance as characteristic of the state of

[1] The account of Inez Gonzales, which is only one of a thousand similar stories that happen in the north of Mexico, may be seen in Bartlett's 'Personal Narrative,' in Chapters XIII., XVII., and XVIII. of Vol. II.

things in America) was a physician, a man of education, who had studied at Paris, possessed a considerable fortune, but was not deterred from spending part of it in purchasing cattle in Texas, and speculating in this article; he was obliged therefore, to make the journey himself, and, like a patriarch of old, to travel with his herds over this portion of the globe. We depended on his knowledge of the road, and, as he had preceded us a few days, we intended to follow in his tracks.

On regaining the plain we observed that the traces of some waggons, and the footsteps of cattle, in our line of march, suddenly deviated on one side, and disappeared in the grass of the prairie. I was convinced that this was the spot where Dr. E. had quitted the beaten road, and proceeded direct west; and perhaps my opinion would have been adopted by the commander of our caravan, had not a musket, found lying in the road, and the devious course of the waggon-tracks in the grass, countenanced the other supposition, that the Doctor might have met with an accident, and the deviation from the road at this spot have been a compulsory one. In this uncertainty, I undertook, accompanied by Mr. C., to reconnoitre the prairie, and see whether we might not, further on, find clearer traces of the Doctor's waggons and animals. We rode unsuccessfully for several miles over a grassy plain, intersected by small rocky hollows, until the sun, near setting, reminded us that it was time to turn back, and hasten to rejoin our caravan. The latter had meanwhile continued in a direct southerly course, and I had no doubt it had already passed the point where the new route was said to diverge; and this was really the case. We continued our journey on the old road, and did not reach the point where the former rejoins the latter until after four weeks. Here, at San Xavier del Bac, we met Doctor E. with his heads of cattle, who had arrived there a fortnight before us. Our having missed the shorter way, caused us a loss of some weeks, and a cost of at least a thousand dollars.

This disagreeable fact, however, was not credited by all our party for many days. The first inconvenience was that we hunted in vain to discover on the old road the watering-places of the new one, of which we had a list. I was not deceived about it, but I could not make the others adopt my view.

The very first night we were obliged to pass without water, after our long journey from Ojo de Vaca. Our animals were very thirsty at starting in the morning, with a prospect of travelling thirty-five miles without meeting with any water. In the evening of this day both men and beasts were utterly exhausted, and a general depression seized the whole caravan. On a sudden a smooth and bright surface appeared at a distance in the prairie, which our people took to be a lake. A general joy burst forth at this sight; which, however, I did not share, well knowing where the next watering-place would be. My objections were not listened to, and those of our party on horseback hastened towards the supposed lake. The refraction of the light increased the apparent surface of the water, and it had quite the appearance of a large lake filled with yellowish water, and with small green islands from which rose the tops of single yucca-trees. Meanwhile the caravan was gradually approaching, and saw themselves at last on the edge of a level and dry plain, on the opposite side of which rose a chain of high mountains. It was at the foot of these that we had to look for our next watering-place. The dry lake is laid down on the map as the "Dry Lagoon;" the Spanish name is "Las Playas." There are, however, in this part of the country, two similar localities. We found the bed covered with a smooth layer of gypsum, which is dissolved by a periodical overflow: it solidifies again, after the drying up of the waters, and crystalizes in parts. The road passes over this. The gypsum was so hard that the wheels made little impression, and in many places the surface shone like a mirror. I cannot tell whether this space is annually covered with water, or only at longer intervals and under unusual circumstances—I suspect the latter is the case: at all events the bed never fills above a few inches with water, as the vegetation on the banks and on the small islands shows clearly.

It was high time that we reached some water on the other side. The store in our casks was quite exhausted. In a hot atmosphere, our animals had not tasted drink for the last forty-eight hours, while the men too were tormented with thirst. For the first time I felt the tantalizing effect of the Fata Morgana, which led us to imagine the presence of water. I had read much of this phenomenon, and had, during my travels, seen it a hundred times, but never when suffering from extreme drought. This country exhibits many enigmatical phenomena. On the other side of the Dry Lagoon, we came to a luxuriant grassy plain, with a large number of deep round holes, filled with water as clear as crystal. The level of the water is considerably higher than the Dry Lagoon, and yet no brook flows in the direction of it. The water-holes are in parts so large and deep, that some mules, which tried to drink on the edge, and fell in, disappeared for a time under water; on coming to the surface again, we were obliged to drag them out with cords. At the edge is a perpendicular slope of turf, which goes down to the lowest depth. The watering-place is known by the name of "Natural Wells." The view, in looking back, extends over one of the most peculiar and grand landscapes I have ever seen; to which the varied forms of the opposite mountains contribute, as well as the palm-like trees of a species of yucca, of peculiarly pleasing shape, standing in rows along the edge of the barren plain.

Our road now led over a mountain, on the western side of which we found a spring, by the side of a torrent, which periodically gushes out of a rocky defile. Its bed was now dry. The plains extending before us were overgrown with grass, in which were single large agaves, with gigantic flower-stalks,—the latter just in that state of development when the stalk is filled with a sweet sap, affording a welcome refreshment. Along the dry bed of the brook grow plantains, which appeared to me to be a different species to the North American sycamore (*Platanus occidentalis*), as well as to the plantain of the Old World. This species, which has drooping branches, a deeply serrated leaf, and a bright green colour of the bark, is found in the mountainous defiles of North America, and usually on the edge of beds of intermitting torrents, filled with detached masses of rock, as far as California. By Mexicans it is called Aliso.

In the evening a thunderstorm came on, which lasted the whole night. Our animals, which were at the same time watered and washed by it, appeared the next morning greatly refreshed. As we proceeded, columns of smoke arose in different places in the neighbouring mountains; and during the next night we saw fires very near our camp. In consequence of this suspicious circumstance, one half of our men had to mount guard over our animals in the pasture.

We next came to a group of natural wells, similar to those described above, in a wide basin covered with grass, and surrounded by barren mountains. The whole landscape was in fact treeless. A great number of large and deep holes in the turf were filled with a milk-white water, but of a good taste. Our mules, falling one after another into these holes, gave us great trouble; and before we proceeded, all the wells had to be examined, to make sure that we had not left any mule behind. Concealed below the edge of one of these holes, a beast of prey, probably a panther, had its lair. Scattered about lay the remains of a number of stags and antelopes, which had been killed when coming here to drink. The place looked like a slaughter-house; and a quantity of antelope's hair was mixed with the water. Half a day's journey brought us to a spring, which forms a charming brook running through the meadows. Not far from this we saw a group of deserted Indian huts, whose inhabitants had evidently decamped at our approach. Probably from revengeful feelings at this disturbance, or to express their hatred to us, they had soiled the spring with their excrements. In the night we saw fires near our camp, and again kept up a careful watch. Whilst in advance of our caravan, the next day, I saw in the dust along the road the prints of a small female foot, with light shoes, amidst the footsteps of a band of Indians; these savages had doubtless carried off some female captive.

We had now the dreaded Guadalupe Pass before us. The road ascends gradually for the last five miles, until we suddenly find ourselves on the edge of deep precipices. Higher mountains rise in the vicinity, but the road leads nowhere over a ridge. From the edge of the plateau we looked down into a chaos of defiles, rocks and ridges, overgrown with juniper-bushes, dwarf oaks, yuccas, dasyliriums, cacti, and agaves. To the inexperienced man it is incomprehensible how large baggage-waggons can be brought down. This operation was attended with such difficulties, that it took two entire days to proceed a few miles. Every waggon was obliged to have two wheels locked, and to be kept up with cords, whilst several drivers had to lead each couple of every team through the underwood and blocks of stone lying about. We had to drive the herd back from the place where we spent the night to the spring we had last passed; and it was taken at night to pasture on the mountain-sides, along which I had to grope my way on hands and feet, gun in hand, while on guard. From these heights the road sunk into a labyrinth of defiles, in which it was difficult to trace any connexion. Huge masses of débris—from which rise mighty blocks and towers of solid rock—showed different colours, like masses of clay which, containing various oxides, had been exposed to fire; had the road passed through the large open crater of a volcano the scene could not have been more wild and chaotic.

At length we came to a more regularly formed valley, which led out of the mountains into open country. Along the road we saw horizontal layers of limestone resting on the eruptive masses of the mountains, and therefore, of course, more recent than the latter. In a narrow cleft amongst the limestone strata copious springs gush forth, forming a beautiful clear brook, and, following its rapid course, we came at last to a large circular plain, surrounded on all sides by hills and distant mountains, and covered with green meadows, with numerous springs and watercourses overgrown with reeds. Here, upon a dry acclivity, on which grows the brushwood, common to the hills of débris in this country, stand the ruins of extensive buildings. These, together with a large tract of land, which is amongst the most valuable in Northern Sonora, form the deserted Hacienda of San Bernardino.

These springs, with others in the neighbourhood, are the sources of the Rio Yaqui, the principal river in Sonora, and the largest that empties into the Californian Gulf. In crossing the Guadalupe Pass we had left the table-lands that descend toward the Rio Grande, and had reached that declivity of the continent which inclines towards the Pacific. Perhaps the reader may remember that my excursion from Chihuahua to the Sierra Madre brought me to the sources of the Rio de Papigochic, which also empties into the Yaqui. Thus I had visited the two chief branches of the river.

After travelling two days further, we came to the sources of the Rio de San Pedro, a tributary of the Gila. Leaving the plain of San Bernardino, we drove up an acclivity, the first hills of which consisted of basalt. Higher up we found limestone, and further on porphyry, spreading out in a large mass of mountains. Here we spent the night without water. The next day we came to a plain, where we searched in vain for water; nor could we possibly find the watering-places stated to be further westward. A thunderstorm, however, accompanied by torrents of rain, deluged the country, and gave us an abundant supply.

Continuing our route to the Rio San Pedro, we had to journey round the broad base of a lofty mountain, with a pyramidal peak. We left it on our right. All around rose other high mountains, separated from one another by large plateaus. In this neighbourhood I saw close to our road a stone covered with Indian hieroglyphics: this was undoubtedly brought hither intentionally and for a special purpose, as some memorial or boundary-stone. I saw no similar one near.

In this district there are seen many wild horses, of which I could only catch a sight from a great distance. Wild cattle also are frequently met with.

From these heights we descended into a valley containing copious springs. A small stream runs from each, and these all unite like veins, forming together the commencement of the Rio de San Pedro. On the banks of this river, —still a small rivulet—I saw for the first time wild clover, which further on, and especially in California, becomes so prominent in the natural pastures of the country. One branch of the road follows the river, which receives water from all sides, and soon becomes a considerable stream. We crossed its upper part, and then directed our course again toward the heights. Viewed from above, this territory presents a grand and remarkable landscape; great mountains, with oak woods at their base and pines on their summits, surround a large plain, now horizontal, now sloping gently, or precipitously, in long straight lines.

In flat trough-like basins of this tract rise the numerous springs which may be traced for many miles by the green colour of the grass, the reeds and rushes. Altogether this district occupies at least a hundred English square miles, but by means of artesian wells, which promise here quite as certain a success as in the valley of San José in California, it may be extended to three or four times its size; and at the same time the mass of water in the river may be tripled or quadrupled. According to the provisions of the Gadsden Treaty, the frontier between Mexico and the United States passes through the upper part of the valley in which the sources lie; numerous settlements will soon be formed on both sides of the frontier. The neighbouring mountains, as in nearly all this part of the country, are rich in minerals, especially copper-ore; and, as wood and water-power are sufficiently abundant, advantageous prospects are opening on this privileged country. The valley of the river further down excites the admiration of all who have seen it. In short everything combines to attract hither, ere long, a numerous and active population.

In passing through the valley, we saw at the distance of about a mile and a half, on a height, two Indians, who approached us slowly. When within about half a mile, they hoisted a white flag: we did the same. They came nearer: one of our party rode on to meet them, and a conversation commenced. Gradually twenty to thirty persons joined the group; they were Apaches, whose physiognomy differed much from that of others of the same tribe I had seen before, whilst it at the same time exhibited a marked character, and a great uniformity of the national type. Here was no trace of those flat mongrel forms which I have observed in the Texan Apaches and Lipans: the profile of their faces was more Grecian; the brow, nose, eyes, and mouth were well formed, and the Indian was seen only in the high cheek-bones, and the sinister expression of the features. They wore a hat of leather and scarlet cloth, shaped like a helmet, ornamented with feathers and, round the crown, with a piece of yellow cloth cut in points like a coronet. The plumes, of an antique shape, consisted of the tail-feathers of the wild turkey, and at the side hung the feathered skins of various little birds of bright plumage. A leather strap fastened this head-dress under the chin, and the whole presented an extremely warlike appearance both in man and boy. From some drawings I have seen, this costume is found among the Navajos, in New Mexico.

These Apaches had with them some stolen Mexican boys, one of whom they offered us for sale. We should have gladly purchased the boy's freedom, but could not agree about the bargain, as the Apaches demanded powder and shot, which they might afterwards have used against ourselves. To decline this demand in the least offensive way, I told the chieftain that we had no great store of those articles. But Mr. K. interrupted me, exclaiming in a violent tone, "We have plenty of powder and shot, not for, but against the Apaches!" Hereupon the chieftain, without noticing anything that had passed, declared that he would fetch the prisoner, in the hope of making some other bargain; but, as soon as he returned to his people, the whole troop rode hastily off. We afterwards heard that this chief was a man well known by the name of Miguel, one of the greatest savages among the whole tribe of the Apaches.

Among these people was an old man who spoke Spanish

tolerably well, and had a certain dignified demeanour. On my expressing, in conversation with him, a certain mistrust of his assurances of friendship, he raised his hands and eyes towards the sun, and said, "Do you not believe that God—this Sun—(*que Dios, este sol*)—sees what we do, and punishes us when it is evil." The expression interested me much; and yet I should not willingly have trusted my life to the sanctity of the oath. This troop was known in the villages of Sonora by the name of the Biscainos, which means, "from the State of Chihuahua," as this latter was formerly known by the name of New Biscay.

The continuation of the journey led us through a charming little valley, with rocks on each side, and with a clear rivulet running through it. Shady oaks grew at the foot of the rocks, and a few old poplars on the edge of the brook. The higher mountains in the background consist of porphyry, rising in pointed forms. But between these eruptive formations, strata of a coarse conglomerate are found in the valley, in their original horizontal position, and apparently belonging to the causes of the great number and peculiar arrangement of springs in this region. This formation appears to be very extensive, spreading far into Sonora; but only filling up valleys between eruptive masses, and perhaps itself an accessory product of the eruption, especially of the granite found here likewise.

The main road, from which we nowhere saw any other route branch off, led us straight toward a steep mountain, and into a defile full of clefts, which reminded us of the Guadalupe Pass. The ground was covered with oak-wood. The road became more and more difficult, and at last impassable; nothing remained but to return to the plain.

We were not far from Santa Cruz, the first inhabited

place since leaving the valley of the Rio Grande. The North American travellers who accompanied us had preceded us to this little town, following the road to the mountains. They had succeeded in penetrating through them, and reaching Santa Cruz, and had had the good sense to send to meet us a native, to whom the road was known. This man conducted us round the mountain, and we came into a beautiful valley, shaded by splendid ash-trees, walnuts, poplars and plantains. Behind the grassy hills in the vicinity, with here and there a few oaks, arose lofty and steep mountains, their summits crowned with pine forests. The whole country looked cleared and orderly as if it had been cultivated for a century. But a heap of the remains of burned waggons reminded us that we were still in a wilderness, where the Apaches still practise their ill deeds with impunity. We spent the night in this fine valley; and, as our people shot two wild oxen, there was plenty both for man and beast. Crossing some flat grassy heights, with groups of gigantic agaves, we arrived the next day in the valley of Santa Cruz, one of the most beautiful parts of northern Sonora.

CHAPTER V.

River and Valley of Santa Cruz — Landscape Scenery — Hacienda de la Calabasa and its German Inhabitants — Fights with the Apaches — The old Mission of Tumacácori — Travelling Companions — Saguarro, or the Giant Cactus — San Xavier del Bac — Old Acquaintances — Christian Pimas — European Adventurers in the Service of a Sonora private Gentleman — Tubac — Tucson — A Desert of Dust and Clay — Isolated Pyramid of Rock — Scenes in the Desert — Gila Lagoon—Heathen Pimas — The Mezquite Bean — Idyllic Scenes, and Character of the Pimas.

THE valley of Santa Cruz, a few miles below the town, makes a great bend; and the small stream through it, which in the upper part runs south, takes in the lower part a north-west and north course. To judge from this direction, it appears inclined to unite with the Gila; but, before reaching this river, it is lost in the desert a few miles below Tucson.

The town of Santa Cruz, a small dilapidated place, with a population who cultivate their cornfields at the risk of their lives, lies in this valley, just at the western foot of that wild and rugged mountain which obliged us to retrace our steps. It is said to be the highest inhabited place in Sonora: at all events it belongs to the "*tierra fria*" (the cold region) of Mexican climatology. Snow falls here in winter: the summer rains come on at the end of June or the middle of July, and with them begins the second growth of vegetation, and the summer grass-crop, unless where springs or an artificial irrigation renders the soil able to dispense with rain. In October there is frost again. The climate is, to a northerner, unquestionably one of the most beautiful, as it is one of the healthiest in the world; and is peculiarly adapted for the cultivation of wheat and different kinds of fruit. All the numerous and deserted estates in this country have still their orchards (although in a wild state), in which apples, pears, peaches, apricots, and further into the country also grapes, figs, and pomegranates, grow wild. Nothing but security is wanting to make this valley the abode of a thriving population: dread of the Apaches prevents the timid inhabitants of this country enjoying the advantages which nature offers. In the large bend of the valley lie some large buildings of a hacienda, which, like so many others in these parts, has been abandoned on the same account. Only a few days ago the savages had stolen several horses close to the town of Santa Cruz, and a division of Mexican cavalry from Tucson made their appearance during our stay at the former place, in pursuit of the robbers. Since then the country may have become more secure; for, although Santa Cruz, in the new frontier regulation, has remained on the Mexican side, yet the establishment of a United States fort, at San Xavier del Bac, has no doubt exercised a salutary influence over the whole neighbourhood. The frontier line now runs past Santa Cruz, at a small distance on the north, and cuts through the valley in two places; now in the southern, and again in the northern course of the river. The upper and lower parts of the valley, belonging to the United States, are thus separated inconveniently by an intervening tract of Mexican territory.

The valley at its head, where only flat heights surround it, is treeless, and loses itself in the adjacent steppes of the table-land; but at Santa Cruz, and further down, the banks of the river, and the valley itself, are covered with poplars and willows, ash-trees and plantains, oaks and walnut-trees. On the lower part of the mountain declivities, which are mostly clothed with turf, oaks grow scattered; whilst the higher mountains, rising in peaks of grotesque alpine forms, are clothed with pine forests. Some portions of this valley are of such grand, rich, and simple beauty, as for instance Tumacácori and San Xavier del Bac, that they would be remarkable in any part of the world. In some parts the green turf was enlivened by the yellow Mimulus: in other parts, remarkable *Cucurbitaceæ*, with deeply serrated leaves, run in long tendrils over the hard soil; and, as if reared by the gardener according to the rules of his art, rise the circular masses of a magnificent *Convolvulacea* with shining leaves, and large crimson flowers. A plant, not unlike a *Martynia*, with orange velvet-like flowers, filled the air with a perfume of musk and violets combined.

As we passed the Hacienda de la Calabasa, the first inhabited spot below Santa Cruz, I was invited by a Mexican servant into the building. In the courtyard I was greeted by two Germans, who inhabited this place, with their numerous retinue of Mexicans, Pima Indians, and "tame" Apaches. One of these gentlemen, M. de H., had been implicated in the so-called Francfort *attentat* of 1832, and been obliged to leave Germany. Since that time he had lived in various parts of the world, and had at last come to Sonora from California. Here he had made the acquaintance of one of the most distinguished men of Mexico, Don Manuel Gándara, who owned this hacienda; and they had joined in making an attempt to establish here a civilized population, in spite of the Apaches, and to introduce the breeding of sheep on a large scale, for which the country is peculiarly fitted. M. de H. had been so fortunate as to meet with another German who resolved to share this bold enterprise with him. Gándara, to make a beginning, had transferred to them five thousand sheep; they had brought together the necessary number of shepherds and labourers, male and female: and in this situation I now met my two countrymen, who welcomed me kindly, and treated me with a glass of Mezcal, or Agave spirits, the only refreshment they had to offer. One of our drivers, an educated young man from Weimar, was so much pleased that he resolved to remain here. I fear that the numerous Indian girls, collected in the courtyard of the building, and amongst whom were seen some very pretty faces, and many perfect figures, had a great share in this resolution: I hope that he will not have had cause to repent it. Life in these parts of the country is a dangerous existence. The two gentlemen told me that, soon after they had established themselves in this *Hacienda*, they were surprised by a band of Apaches, and how some fortunate circumstance had befriended them. The Indians, who had in their *rancheria* talked over their predatory expedition, were so imprudent as to betray their project to a Mexican prisoner, who, on the departure of the band, escaped, and reached Tucson in safety. The Commandant of the Mexican garrison in that place, when informed of this fact, ordered his men to mount instantly, and go to the succour of the threatened hacienda, Just as the Apaches were descending the hill on one side, the Mexican troops appeared on the other; and, in the battle that ensued,—in which, as I afterwards heard, Mr. H. killed three Indians with his own hand,—the savages learnt such a lesson that they have ever since left the hacienda unmolested.

Below Calabasas the valley shows an interesting formation. The mountains on both sides recede somewhat, and the wide valley is filled with granite-hills, and horizontal layers of a conglomerate similar to that of San Pedro.

The river makes its way through these rocks. Below this opening the valley widens again, and large poplars, willows, and walnut-trees, grow along the bank of the river, while the hills are covered with mezquite, holm-oaks, and juniper-trees. The mountains in this part are said to be rich in gold and silver, the working of which is only obstructed by the Indians.

The following day we reached the Mission of Tumacácori, situated in the valley, and consisting of an imposing stone church, with other considerable buildings. Three Germans and a Frenchman have settled here, and claimed to be the lawful owners of the Mission, and the property attached to it. The situation is very interesting: high mountains of columnar porphyry rise behind the buildings, in front of which runs the river, bordered with a shady thicket; the bottom of the valley stretches out on both sides, and the new-settled colonists have still the fruits of the old garden of the Mission. A second travelling companion, Mr. C.,—a German likewise, and an educated man,—left us here, and joined the inhabitants of Tumacácori.

I have already spoken of the various appearance of the Mezquite or Algarobbia; and I am here reminded in passing through a little wood of mezquite trees, to refer to this subject again. This remarkable plant appears in different forms on the coast of Texas, on the high plateau of the Pecos, on the Rio Grande, in the south of Chihuahua, and lastly, here in Sonora, on the Gila and Colorado. In these latter places it is an elegant little tree, but its feathery foliage yields little shade. One evening we were driving through a wood of these trees, one-half of the sky was illumined by the full moon, and in the other a storm was coming up. The uncertain light shining through the delicate foliage upon our dark road, lighted up occasionally by a flash of lightning, was an interesting scene.

In the lower part of the valley of Santa Cruz, the gigantic columnar cactus (*Cereus giganteus*) is first seen upon the road. The inhabitants of the country call it Saguarro; but various authors, and recently Bartlett, have applied the name of Pitaya (Pita-haya) to this remarkable plant. This name, however, belongs to another species of cactus, of a similar but much lower growth. The latter also appears not to be found so far north, but occurs frequently further down in Sonora. I have obtained my information respecting the difference of these two species of cactus from a good authority—the chief of the Pimas—who told me decidedly that the cactus-shafts in that part were not Pitayas, but Saguarros.

The Saguarro presents a thick fluted column, the size of a man's body, and thirty, forty, and even fifty, feet high, with sometimes three or four branches at its top, the whole looking like a gigantic candelabrum. The fig-shaped edible fruit grows at the edge on the top of the columns; and from the great height of the latter it would be difficult to get at them, did not this remarkable plant itself afford the means of reaching it. The old stems, when decayed, split into a number of thin poles, standing in a circle, the height of the entire column enveloped in a loose net-work; and by the aid of these the traveller is enabled to knock down the fruit. I have been told that these poles form an article of export from the port of Guaymas, and in Europe are made into walking-sticks, and sold under the name of "Spanish canes." I cannot, however, vouch for the correctness of this account. The Pimas at the old Mission of San Xavier del Bac had a large store of Saguarro fruit, which is used as food in various ways. It is eaten fresh;

the sap is boiled to a syrup, known throughout Sonora by the name of "Miel de Saguarro;" and a flour is prepared of the cleaned and dried seeds, which have some resemblance in appearance and taste to poppy-seeds, and are contained in the fruit in great quantities. This flour is made partly into bread and partly into a chocolate-like drink, called Atole.

The fruit of the Pitaya is said to be far better than that of the Saguarro. Both are of great importance to the population of Sonora. In some bad harvests, occasioned by the want of rain, shortly before my journey through this state, a large portion of the inhabitants were obliged to live on these and other wild cactus fruits.

I can scarcely recal any surprise greater than I experienced at the sight of the buildings of the old and celebrated mission of San Xavier del Bac, standing in a region of sublime and simple grandeur, a monument of the wonderful activity and energy of the old Catholic missionaries. A broad plain, mostly in a wild state of nature, covered with grass, bushes, and groves of algarobbia, is encompassed by imposing mountains and masses of rock. The fields of wheat, regularly divided, are the property of the Christian Pimas who were formerly settled here. Grand natural features are here united with important conditions of civilization. From its situation, the place is destined to become the capital of this central region,—a region of charming oases, and rich mineral wealth.

The stately church is in good preservation, and is considered one of the most beautiful in the State of Sonora: in it, by the side of tasteless carvings and barbarous decorations, is an altar richly overlaid with gold. Near this edifice stand the low mud huts of the few Pimas still residing here. They are proud of being Christians, and speak of the heathen part of their tribe—"los Gentiles"—with great contempt. They have, however, long been without any spiritual or other instruction, and have retained many of their heathen usages: for instance, the destruction of the property of a dead person,—a custom which renders all improvement in their material condition impossible. They are a good-natured, quiet, honest, and inoffensive people, maintaining a strict discipline, which they may have acquired from a mixture of Jesuit discipline and the remains of old Indian customs. They understand Spanish tolerably well, but they refused to speak it with us. We had a difficulty in making any purchases from them, partly from their having little to offer for sale, and partly from their being apparently quite devoid of any speculative spirit. There was an unmistakeable obtuseness in them, apparently peculiar to the Christianized Indians—a downcast retiring manner, which I have noticed among this class of people in other parts. They made frequent visits to our camp, but they sat there for hours, mute and motionless: their children entertained us by exhibiting their skill in shooting with the bow. Their arrows were pointed with flint, which was covered with a dark substance, which they said consisted of the poison taken from a serpent; but this seems to me very improbable.

The position of these people and the condition of the spot, must have altered entirely since that time. San Xavier del Bac is now a military station of the United States, which is the certain commencement of a town.

We remained here several days, during which time we received and returned visits with other caravans which happened to be in the neighbourhood. In these I found several persons whom I had met before accidentally. One of these was Mr. H., from Brunswick, with whom I had slept in the same tent, and under the same blanket, in New Mexico. I met him again in Chihuahua, at El Paso, in the Steppe on the Rio de los Mimbros, and later on at Los Angeles and San Francisco. A Mr. M., from Texas, whom I had last seen at El Paso, was also at this time at San Xavier with his cattle: this man met with a remarkable adventure in his journey to California. A partner in his enterprise had, it appeared, plotted to put him out of the way during the march, and to take sole possession of the herds. To accomplish this project, he headed a mutiny of the hired cattle-drovers. They openly refused to obey Mr. M., who found himself in a very unpleasant situation, when the Apaches murdered the two ringleaders of the mutiny. This circumstance led the rest to believe that it was an infliction of Divine vengeance, and they returned to their duty. It, however, occasioned Mr. M. the loss of part of his herds: another part perished from want of water, and the rest were taken by the Indians; so that he arrived at California with the loss of his whole property, where I heard this account of his adventures from himself.

I visited the Pimas in their dwellings. At first they were shy; but, at length, I succeeded in gaining the confidence of an old man, with whom I carried on an animated conversation. The women then regaled me with peas-porridge and cakes made of wheaten flour. They also cultivate beans, gourds, and melons, and grow the cotton for their own use. I saw them busy weaving, which they do in a very primitive manner. The threads are stretched horizontally the length of the intended piece of cloth, and the woof is then worked in by the hand. The coloured belts, with which the girls fasten a piece of cloth round their waist, to serve as a kind of petticoat, are woven very artistically. They are tasty, and the figures woven into them are of the old Mexican style. The blue colour of the figures is said to be their own indigo dyeing, and the red colour is produced by threads of such red stuff as they meet with in trade, and which they unravel. It would be erroneous, however, to imagine that these arts have been promoted by their conversion to Christianity: on the contrary, they are found in greater perfection among the pagan Pimas.

Near this spot rises a conical hill, consisting of an eruption of *Hypersthen-rock*. Several similar hills rise in the plain, and some steep hills, which border this plain on the west like towers or walls, appear to have the same petrographic character. The brown rocks, with the Saguarro columns, give a peculiarly sober and severe aspect to the landscape.

During our stay at San Xavier, Mr. Cubillas, one of the prominent politicians of the State of Sonora, and a man of great wealth, arrived, accompanied by a numerous retinue. He was on his way to inspect his extensive estates, which, being situated in a perfect wilderness, had hitherto been valueless; he had now the prospect of their becoming of great value, in consequence of the transfer of the territory to the United States. I was surprised at observing that the retinue of this gentleman consisted of men of various nations—a German, an Hungarian, a Dane, two Irishmen, and a North-American,—all, doubtless, adventurers by profession, who had met by accident in these remote parts. The Dane had successively settled in China, in East India, and in Peru; the rest had come from the United States.

Not far below San Xavier, upon a height in the valley,

close to the river and surrounded by a thick mezquite-wood, lies the little place of Tubac, the population of which are mostly Indians, amongst whom are many "tame" Apaches. The women and girls of this people sat by the road-side, staring at us with their broad, fat, mongol, expressionless faces.

The last inhabited place in the valley is Tucson. At that time it was the most northern of the Mexican military posts: having now, together with Tubac and San Xavier, been transferred to the United States, Santa Cruz has probably taken its place. We encamped a few miles above the town, in a pleasant part of the valley. A rapid brook, clear as crystal, and full of aquatic plants, fish, and tortoises of various kinds, flowed through a small meadow covered with shrubs. The meadow itself was situated at the foot of a steep rocky hill, with a watch-tower on the top, where the Mexican garrison used to keep a guard stationed to watch the Indians. The sides of the hill were so covered with cactus-columns that it might have been called a Saguarro-forest, could the term have been applied to a spot overgrown with bare trunks, without any crown whatever. Here I saw for the first time a small tree resembling a Genista, Spartium, or Retama. It has a green stem, green branches, and green twigs delicately subdivided, with only a few slight rudiments of leaves. It bears yellow blossoms, and pods with a single seed. This tree, which we often met with afterwards, and which belongs to the plants characteristic of the rocky deserts on the Gila, was called *Corchi* by the Mexicans; they suck the acid gum which oozes from its bark to allay thirst.[1]

[1] I have no doubt this tree has already been described, and my account of it above is of course not intended for botanists, but for those who take an interest in the general physiognomy of landscapes.

We had hitherto been following the course of the river of Santa Cruz, which, although its channel was found dry in several places, constantly re-appeared. But below Tucson it loses itself in the desert, through which our road now lay.

In the evening of July 16th we broke up our camp and and entered upon this desert, extending as far as the Gila, and in which, according to the latest intelligence, we had not to expect to find any water for the distance of eighty or ninety miles.

At the beginning our road led through a thicket of mezquite, but gradually all vegetation ceased. Darkness had set in, and our waggons toiled through dust ankle-deep, the thick clouds of which were, from time to time, illumined by the lightning of a thunderstorm over the mountains of Tubac and Tumacácori. After several hours' toil, we reached a plain covered with hard clay, and breathed a purer and cooler air. We continued our march in silence through the night. When morning dawned, the clayey desert, hard and perfectly barren, stretched before us to the foot of the *Picacho*, a bold pyramidal rock, rising abruptly from the plain. I rode on in advance of our caravan. On approaching the mountain the road began to be moist: here and there mud had collected. At length there was the gleam of water: a small pool! a second! a third! I jumped off my horse, and led it from one to the other until it had relieved its thirst; then I laid down flat on the ground, and drank with avidity the yellow clayey fluid. Rain had fallen during the night, but insufficient for our caravan, which therefore continued its route without stopping.

We halted nearer to the foot of the mountain, by the

side of some pools of water, the slimy contents of which swarmed with the larvæ of insects and gigantic toads, and of which our beasts drank with great repugnance. The scene around our encampment was very peculiar: the surface of the desert ascends towards the mountain, forming a flat elevation, from which the black gigantic mass of rocks lifts its pointed summit. With the elevation of the ground at the foot of the mountain begins the vegetation characteristic of the rocky desert of this part of the country, such as I have already described: small trees and mezquite bushes, various kinds of acacias, and leafless but yet green corchi, columns and candelabra of the saguarro. For the first time our beasts, fed exclusively on the pods of the algarobbia or mezquite-beans, this region being absolutely devoid of grass. Other rocks rise from the plain at various distances, and, to judge from their colour and form, belong to different eruptive mineral substances: in some places black masses, as if just sprung out of the ground, rise straight up. On continuing our journey, in the evening at sunset, such a rock stood exactly in the centre of the ocean of light which illumined the western horizon, and golden beams were playing through an opening in the dark wall. The scene produced an almost theatrical effect.

Again we travelled throughout the night, and halted in the morning near some pools of water, with the same disgusting appearance of larvæ and toads. We continued our route in view of a long and steep ridge of rock, apparently consisting of piled-up blocks of syenite, or diorite, and arrived towards noon at the Gila-Lagoon, a deep, brown, brackish water of small extent, and surrounded by tall algarobbiæ and a tolerable grass. Here we found a party of Pima Indians, who were busy in gathering the algarobbia-pods. They belonged to the heathen remains of that nation who dwell on the Gila, while its greater part, under the name of the Pápagos, live in the State of Sonora, forming an essential portion of its civilized and Christian population. This party consisted of men, women, boys, and girls, who were at once on friendly terms with us.

The Pimas[1] have been mentioned favourably by various travellers, and they produce, indeed, a pleasing impression. The dwelling-places of the tribe, the so-called Pima-villages on the Gila, are known to geographers, and marked down on all maps. The small party near us on the Laguna was merely temporarily here. When the pods of the algarobbia are ripe, this tribe disperses in the thickets near the river to gather in this important article of food, which I have nowhere else found in similar perfection. This year it was to them especially important: the river had little water, and only a few fields could be cultivated, as their productive power entirely depends on irrigation from the river.

The pod of the algarobbia, or so-called mezquite-bean, has also been described by travellers, and their importance to the inhabitants of the Gila and Colorado districts, as well as to the herds of cattle which pass this way on their route to California, is well known. I will therefore only make a few observations in order to present the reader with an illustration of the subject I speak of. Let him imagine a small tree with thorny branches and a feathery foliage, full of green or yellowish pods, which do not dry on the branch, but fall off as soon as they are in a certain state of maturity. At these times the ground of the mezquite woods is often covered with them inch-deep. In this state

[1] Not "Pimos," as many North Americans write.

the substance of the pod which surrounds the beans is more or less dry, pithy, and of a sweet taste. The half-ripe pods fall on shaking the tree. In an earlier stage of maturity the covering substance has a pleasant acid taste, similar to that of a good summer apple. But these pods are quite uneatable, they can only be chewed and sucked, and they thus proved a pleasant refreshment. I have been told that the dry ripe pods are ground in Mexico, and that bread is made of the flour, but I did not hear whether the beans are used for the same purpose, nor whether the Pimas understand this culinary process. These people offered us an acid drink, extracted from the pods, which are soaked in water until fermentation begins; they seemed to be fond of it. The fruit constitutes here the chief provender for horses and mules, grass growing but scantily. When these animals have once tasted it, they conceive such a passion for it, that it is difficult to keep them in order when the road leads through a mezquite country. The abundance of this product in many places of the Gila and Colorado is incredible.

We and our Indian friends were soon engaged in an animated barter. We received from them some green ears of maize, which are excellent roasted over a coal-fire, and proved a perfect luxury to us travellers, tired as we were of our caravan diet. I exchanged, with a pleasing looking girl, one of the most elementary articles of my dress for the whole of her national wardrobe, consisting of a home-woven, thick, cotton blanket, which she wore wrapt round her body, reaching down to the knees, and of one of those pretty figured belts, which serve to fasten it. The latter was a production of her own industry, and she seemed to part with it reluctantly. It is due to her to observe, that her change of dress was not performed in my presence, and that in this bargain I had considerably the advantage of her. The modest demeanour, bright eye, and pleasing manner, which I noticed in our intercourse with these people—features so peculiar to them—produce a most agreeable impression, and they often presented genuine scenes of idyllic life. Here and there, under the shade of an old algarobbia or of one of our waggons, might be seen sitting or standing a merry, innocent group: old men stretched out upon the ground; women and children sitting by their side; boys standing near in pairs, one with his arm round the other's neck, and the latter leaning on his bow; pretty girls, in their semi-paradisic costume, walking quietly and naïvely among our drivers and muleteers, who never ventured any rude gallantry—all this formed such a pleasing scene as quite to call forth every gentle feeling in us, who were accustomed to meet the Indian only armed for attack or defence. To complete the picture of this Indian tribe, I must add that it unites such decided courage with his peaceful and amiable qualities, as to inspire even the savage Apaches with respect. I believe that the character of the aboriginal Americans can be seen to such advantage among none of the remaining tribes.

SAGUARRO TREES.

[Book III. Chap. 9.]

CHAPTER VI.

Journey down the Gila — Casas Blancas — Campo Grande — Hydro-geological Remarks — The Cocomaricopas — Ethnological Remarks from the Narrative of their Chief — Hair and singular Head-dresses — Robbers and Murderers in our Camp — Insecurity of the Gila and Colorado Region — Revolutionary Movement in Sonora — Valley Pass and rocky Desert — Heat of the Gila Valley — The Chief of the Pimas and indescribable Music — Hickey's Hollow — Annual Grasses — Lava Terraces of the Gila Valley — Indian Hieroglyphics — Opinion as to their Meaning — Footpath worn in the Rocks of a Mountain Summit — Conjectures as to the Age of the Hieroglyphics — A Party of Cocopás in our Camp — View from Summit of Mountain — Arrival at the Colorado — Camp Yuma — The Yuma Indians — Colorado City — Passage of Steamer — Crossing the Colorado.

AFTER passing the lagoon we travelled through the night, and rested the following day in a grove of algarobbias, on the bank of the Gila, near a group of temporary huts of the Pimas. The river, which I had pictured to myself as a large stream, was here only a small brook, flowing over a sandy bed. Poplars, willows, and various kinds of shrubs, grow on its banks; the rest of the bottom land is covered with algarobbias, while barren alluvial terraces rise on each side, covered with the usual desert growth of these regions. At noon the water of the stream, which is clear, and has a considerable fall, was so warm that our animals would not drink.

We travelled again through the night, and passed some Pima villages in the dark, so that I lost the opportunity of seeing the domestic life of this interesting race. At Tucson we had engaged some muleteers, who had been often along the Gila; and they told me that in one of the villages was a "Casa blanca de Montezuma"—a white house of Montezuma. This is the expression used by the

Mexicans of Tucson, as well as by the Indians along the Gila, when they could command so much Spanish, for the ruins in this region. By others they are called "Casas grandes de Montezuma." Bartlett is right in considering that the addition "de Montezuma" is not Indian, but a repetition from the Spaniards. On the other hand, M. Garcia, the commander at Tucson, maintained that the Pimas had old traditions extending beyond the conquest of Mexico, when they belonged to the empire of the Aztecs. This, however, I doubt. The assertion of our muleteers from Tucson, that an old Indian ruin existed in one of the Pima villages may be incorrect, for I find no mention of one, in any of the accounts of this region with which I am acquainted. But I regret still on this account that we did not travel by day, and that I could not require our people to show me the supposed "white house of Montezuma." Bartlett visited and has described[1] the ruins near the Salinas, as also those higher up, near the Gila; and although, like many others, he passed through the Pima villages, he mentions nothing corroborative of what these Tucson muleteers asserted. According to his description of the "casas grandes" which are found beyond the Gila lagoon, near the river, the Commander of Tucson is also in this respect wrong, for he told me that I should see these ruins from the road. With this object in view, I several times stood up on my horse in order to gain what height I could, and was afterwards convinced, from Bartlett's account of them, that I made this experiment uselessly.

After a prolonged march through the night and part of the next morning, we reached an extensive space in the

[1] Bartlett's Personal Narrative, vol. ii., chaps. xxxi. and xxxii.

valley, covered with grass, and containing many springs. The Cocomaricopas and the Pimas who visited us here called the place "el Campo Grande"—the Great Camp. Below this spot the valley becomes contracted by rocky mountains, and, leaving the bottom, the road had to ascend to the left among the rocks of a gloomy desert, from which a hot wind met us. We therefore encamped upon the grass to rest, before commencing this laborious march. The ground among the grass is covered in places with an efflorescence of salt. The numerous springs are similar in their quality to the "natural wells" near the dry Lagoon, which region indeed this resembles. Conditional upon certain geological causes, the springs throughout an extensive region are all of the same character, while from similar reasons they differ in others. Strong, clear, rocky springs rise in the Texan chalk formation, while in the region between the Rio Grande and the Gila, where we now were, the prevalent form of springs is a deep hole in the grassy bottom of a valley, several being grouped together.

While we remained here we had numerous visits from the surrounding Indians. The Cocomaricopas, whose villages were close to our camp, came as well as the Pimas. A man of the former nation, who spoke Spanish tolerably, explained to me that the Pimas and the Cocomaricopas had agreed with two other tribes, the Cocopá and the Quejuen, to maintain themselves by agriculture; and that five other tribes, less peacefully disposed, the Apaches, Macjave, Simojueves, Comedás, and Cuchian, were their confederate enemies. He did not name the Yumas, although they belonged to the enemies of the Pimas and their allies; but they may have been included in these names. This man told me farther, that some years previously, these had all assembled by the Colorado, and had sent a messenger to challenge the four tribes to war. They took the field, and, after a march of ten days, came upon their enemy. A battle, which lasted two days, ensued, in which they were the victors. The account appears true; and one of our guides, who had been farther down the Colorado, stated that even now numerous skeletons remain at a place where the Indians once fought a great battle.

An old Cocomaricopa, who we were told was one of their chiefs, came to our camp, asked for our leader, and made Mr. K. very politely a present of green maize. We gave in return some tobacco, upon which he asked for a shirt, and, having received one, came and sat down by us. There was a certain etiquette in the whole transaction, which probably we did not understand or sufficiently acknowledge.

The Cocomaricopas appeared to me less amiable than the Pimas; neither could we praise their honesty, for several things were stolen from our camp. A young lad, with his face painted blue, took a loaf of bread, ran to the nearest water, where he washed himself, and then mixed with others of his tribe, convinced that we should not recognise him. Another very old man sat close by me the whole day, and smoked segars which I gave him. He then shared our meal; but after it, when I asked him for some words of the Maricopa language, he at first pretended not to understand me, and then refused unless I gave him a shirt. "We are very poor," he said; "if you want me to tell you something, you must give me something for it." I had made an exchange with a young man for a flute, which was interesting to me not only as an instrument, but on account of the original carving with which it was adorned. Repenting his bargain, he brought me back what I had given him, and required the flute again. Upon my refusal, he became insolent; and when I told him that I would complain to the chief, he laughed, and said that the latter was his uncle. He then supported his claim by remarking that, as I could not play upon it, I ought not to have it. However, since I have learnt from Bartlett's work that the young men of the Cocomaricopas serenade the maidens at night on their flutes, I have not felt surprised that he regretted exchanging his instrument for an article of old clothing.

These Indians are especially remarkable from their hair, and the way in which they dress it: the quantity, thickness, and length of it are almost incredible. They plait and wind it round their heads in many ways: one of the most general, forms a turban, which they smear with wet earth, so that when dry it forms a hard crust; the scorching heat of the sun in these regions has probably led to this custom. I speak here only of the men, as I saw no woman in the tribe.

In this respect their conduct entirely differed from that of the Pimas: with them their women came principally into our camp, where they conducted themselves with perfect ease, but at the same time with entire decorum and modesty. The Cocomaricopas, on the contrary, seemed to mistrust their women, keeping them quite apart from us, and evidently not relishing a proposal made by some of our people, to visit their village.

From hence and lower down the valley we met some suspicious and dangerous characters, who, as we afterwards learned in California, belonged to an extensive band of robbers, or were upon the point of forming themselves into one. Five North Americans came first to our camp, of whom one related that he was the last of a party who were journeying from the interior of Sonora, by El Altar, to the Gila river, and of whom four had perished on the road from want of water. He had himself been several days without food and water, and had but yesterday met with four other travellers from California. It was possible that the man had originally belonged to Walker's expedition against Sonora, which not long before our journey through the Gila territory, had come to a tragical end; but the good looks and the slight hunger of the man were suspicious, as being inconsistent with his statements. The remarks of an old Indian also were singular, and I regretted not being able to understand them fully. What I believed he said was, that a few miles off in the desert, a dying man was lying near the road, who belonged to this party, and to whom they had promised help, which they purposely avoided giving. Farther down the river, a few days later, we met three more adventurers. They also told us that a fourth belonging to their party had been killed on the road, and that we should probably find his body. He had been missed by them, and when found was dead and covered with blood. It struck me that some murder was at the bottom of all these tales, probably committed upon one of their fellow travellers. After the last-mentioned three had been entertained by us, and assisted from our stores, they repaid our hospitality by getting possession of one of our best mules at the rear of our caravan, by a falsehood. Riding past the muleteers they said that they were to choose a mule, having bought one of Mr. K., and having selected one they took it away. Our people recognised one of these three men: he was a notorious character from Texas, who had joined Walker's expedition against Sonora, and he even boasted to one of our men that, with some others, he had taken a small town in Sonora, and forced a contribution of 12,000 dollars from its inhabitants. Subsequently, when I was staying in California, this fellow was named in the public papers as the leader of a robber band, which spread itself from the gold mines to the valley of Santa Cruz in Upper Sonora, and later still I saw the following notice in a Californian paper:—"Many will remember M. Staudt, of San Francisco, who went two years since to Sonora, and who on his journey back to California was robbed and murdered by his two travelling companions. Major Emory, of the Boundary Commission, met with the latter on the road from El Paso to Chihuahua, where they sold him two of Staudt's mules. The one is a Dane or a North German, a desperado, of the first class, and known under the name of Dutch Charley; the other is a Texan, called Ned Hines." This was the name of the man whom we received in our camp on the Gila.

After the unsuccessful expedition of Walker the American, and of Count Raousset de Boulbon, the Frenchman, the State of Sonora continued to be the scene of action, and the object of numerous adventurers of every description, who attached themselves to the leaders of the different native parties. I have already mentioned a circumstance illustrative of this state of things. Goldseekers, and men engaged in wild speculations in mines and land, immigrants into the territory lately ceded to the United States by Mexico—all these, including highwaymen and criminals escaped from California,—men of every shade of character from the best to the worst, appeared to hold themselves in readiness for an outbreak, by which the State of Sonora and the peninsula of California would be separated from Mexico. Casual remarks which reached me from different people in widely different places, and lastly, from fugitives who had reached California from Sonora, convinced me of the fact. It is well known even in Europe that an attempt tending in that direction, and ending still more unfortunately than the two previous ones, has been made after the time of my passing through the country.

We broke up our camp in the evening; but, in spite of the late hour, the wind met us hot from the rocky desert through which we had to pass. We had suffered from the heat all along the Gila. I had no thermometer with me, but it is well known that the summer heat of these regions ranges from 100° to 120° Fahrenheit in the shade. But the effect of this high temperature upon the body must be estimated by the dryness and the rocky character of the soil, rather than by the scale of degrees. The ground was so hot that if our mules stood still for a minute or two, they twitched up their feet in evident pain, and even after midnight I could not sit down on the rock with comfort. Our Mexican drivers during this journey would sit the greater part of the night, naked upon their mules, and yet were bathed in perspiration. Towards morning alone, was the slightest degree of coolness to be perceived. The shade, during the day, brought no refreshment, and wind increased the scorching heat, by adding fresh supplies, instead of lessening them. I was obliged one day, lower down the valley, to go about a mile in the river, in search of some missing mules; and the water was as hot as that of a very warm foot-bath. Whenever I came upon a dry sand bank, I found it too hot to bear more than a few steps upon it; indeed I am sure that 100 steps would have blistered my feet.

The old chief of the Pimas, whose authority is recognized by the Cocomaricopas, and whose name, whether, according to some travellers, it may be Cola Azul, or, according to others, Culo Azul, has an equally inexpressible meaning, wished to escort us for a short distance with a small body of young men, in order, as he frankly said, to have the pleasure of riding in a carriage. I placed myself with him in one of our empty baggage-waggons, and was greatly amused by observing how his Indian Highness enjoyed the shaking and jolting of this horrible road. During a portion of it, which was smooth, our mules quickened their pace, and the escort of my noble companion trotted after us, expressing their satisfaction in a sort of chant, in short broken sounds, which I can compare to nothing, except perhaps the regular bark of at least twenty dogs.

The journey of this night took us through a gloomy granite desert, over the bare rocks of which our waggons jolted and tumbled as if the wheels must have gone to pieces. At break of day the scene was wild and grand in the extreme; but, wearied and exhausted, we all, men and animals, crept down the road towards the river; the mountain pass by which we descended, opening into the clayey desert below. Masses of granite rose on either hand, bare from their base to their summit, with the exception of a few *Saguarro* shafts, cacti covered with long white thorns, acacias, and some small *Corchi* trees. Towards noon we reached the river, having accomplished forty-five miles in seventeen hours without stopping.

We rested during the day, and journeyed on again through the night. In the morning we reached a camping place called Hickey's Hollow. This is a narrow strip of land about one hundred paces wide and several miles long, lying two or three feet lower than the general level of the flat region near the river. This hollow remains moist and receives a sufficient quantity of alluvial soil, from an extensive region of basaltic or doleritic lava, to form quite an oasis in the desert. It is shaded by mezquite-trees, and we found it covered with fresh grass just sprung up from the seed. Most of the grasses in this region, as also in the desert of the Colorado and in many parts of California, appear to be annuals: excepting the seed, not a trace remains of the growth of the former year; but this, washed by the first summer rains, together with the soil, into the hollows around, shoots up in thick masses forming little meadows. After a few months, this in its turn dies off, leaving the seed to flourish again the next summer. This appears to me an important indication as to the possibility of cultivating certain portions of these deserts.

A broad terrace of doleritic lava with perpendicular sections towards the valley, extends from hence far down the Gila. Our road brought us over a rough tract of rocks of the above-named character, where I saw some desert plants unknown to me and of very remarkable appearance, but I was not able to examine them more closely. Reaching the bottom of the valley, we found it to be covered with loose sand, either bare and drifted by the wind, or covered with an impervious thicket of several varieties of ashy-coloured chenopodiaceous shrubs, in which thousands of the Californian quail found shelter. A variety of these shrubs, called by the Mexicans, Chamisso, yields a serviceable food for cattle. Our mules and horses, however, would not touch it. The road continued bad down the valley. Then through the deep sand which the wind had heaped up on the lava terraces, our waggons had again to be dragged up to their upper level. The shouts and oaths, the cracking of whips, the whining of the mules, —the Mexican drivers themselves call it *llorar*,—the jolting of the waggons over the blocks of lava, the black, heated masses of rock, looking doubly black in the dark night,—a few ghostly *Saguarro* shafts,—all combined to produce a weirdlike scene unequalled by the gloomiest imagination.

The flat rocks and blocks of stone on the precipitous sides of these terraces are, for considerable distances, covered with Indian characters, cut upon them. The traveller who would study and collect these strange and, as yet, unexplained carvings, would find occupation for many weeks.

I will venture here to make some remarks upon this subject. Mr. Bartlett[1] is of opinion that these so-called Indian hieroglyphics have no historical meaning, but are simply the production of an imaginative fancy; and the number of drawings he has given in his book appear to

[1] 'Personal Narrative,' vol. II. p. 195.

have been chosen in support of this theory. I here give some delineations which may serve to uphold a contrary view of the subject.

Among the many hundreds of these carvings which I saw along the Gila and elsewhere, two distinctive kinds are very evident. The one contains representations of distinct objects, such as men and animals. Probably even these possess a more general meaning by their combination with each other and with the less explicable characters. But—be that as it may—I am convinced that the second class of characters must have some general meaning, and were intended as a communication of ideas.

I have frequently asked Indians for an explanation; but either they could not, or would not give me any. This last was evidently the case with the Chief of the Yumas, who took much trouble to convince me that the figures on the rocks near the Lower Ferry over the Colorado had no meaning. They were, he said, nothing but children's play, and done by knocking one stone upon another; and he took up a stone in his hand and showed me how it was effected. But I have reason to believe that he did not speak the truth. It is possible, and even probable, that a modern, and in this respect ignorant generation, should amuse themselves by imitating the already existing figures; and thoughtless imitations may have thus produced unmeaning results. The original intention of these representations may have been only known to the chiefs and principal men of the Indian tribes, as among civilized nations not all can read. But many circumstances tend to disprove, that these characters were *originally* nothing but the results of an early attempt at art. In the first place, the similarity of the style, in localities a thousand miles apart, and its extreme peculiarity, preclude every idea of an accidental similarity. One cannot imagine how the same recurring figures should have been used over and over again, unless they had a conventional character, and were intended to express something. The localities also in which they are found are such as to give them importance. For instance on the Gila, figures and characters are cut on rocks, which cannot be climbed

without difficulty; also on precipitous sides of rocks, which could not be reached without mechanical contrivance.

It is scarcely to be imagined that men would take the trouble to get at such places, and there to carry out a difficult and laborious work, unless they had some important end in view; and the more so, since rocks and masses of stone abound close by, where the operation might have been effected easily, had it been undertaken merely for amusement. I saw at the summit of a lofty and steep mountain near the Gila, below the region of the lava terraces, to which I have above referred, the rocks covered with these characters. Old footpaths, in places trodden into the rock, occur in great numbers along the side of the mountains, all tending to the summit. In my opinion these footpaths could only have been formed during many centuries of constant use; and it is impossible not to draw the conclusion that some important object was connected with them, and with the characters carved on those rocks. The locality gave me the impression, that only a religious motive could have induced such repeated and long-continued pilgrimages. I also remarked these characters in places where the footpath passed a rock, as if such a prominent spot had been chosen, to impart information to the passers-by. They were also engraven upon isolated stones near the road, of one of which I have given a drawing in a former chapter of this Book, it having been evidently placed near the road to attract attention. This road, as a carriage road, is certainly of late construction and by the white man; but the roads now used by civilized travellers mostly follow Indian paths, the direction of which has been determined by the few watering-places of the country. I have given here an accurate copy of some of the carvings which more especially struck me, that the reader may form a general idea of their character, and of the opinions I have brought forward. One of the carvings by the Gila is particularly interesting as occurring on a rock on the precipitous side of the lava terraces, the present position of which, half covered by another mass, hiding part of the carving, proves that the changed position of the rocks, through some natural phenomenon, is of later date than the figures.

Other engravings, also taken from the lava walls along the Gila, have more the character of an inscription, or of the communication of connected thoughts, than any others that I saw.

A desert covered with pebbles and fragments of granite, porphyry, syenite, greenstone, jasper, &c., &c., extends above the lava terraces, on each side of the Gila. At the foot of the wall the ground is so saturated with salts, produced by the action of the atmosphere upon the volcanic

rocks, that the damp of the night changed the soil into mud two inches in depth. Lower down I found it dry.

In this neighbourhood we met one evening some twenty Indians of the Cocopá tribe. These people were engaged on a diplomatic mission to the Pimas, in order to arrange an expedition with them against the Yumas. They told us this, and the eager questions which the Yumas addressed to us respecting it when we reached the Colorado, proved that the latter had been aware of these proceedings. The Cocopás, who appeared friendly, and conducted themselves perfectly well in our camp, used English words to make themselves understood; all other Indians whom we had met, had only understood Spanish besides their native tongue. They were evidently influenced by the vicinity of California, for they are too remote from intercourse with the military station of Camp Yuma. The way in which the chief of this little band addressed me was very comical. "You Captain, me Captain," he said. "You give plenty flour, plenty beans. Cocopá not hungry—good friends.—Not hungry—plenty to eat—no stealing, no *hay* steal;" some Spanish getting mixed with their English. These people were darker in colour than the Cocomaricopas and the Pimas.

Our camp was fixed one day upon the high bank of the river, at the base of a steep mountain peak terminating a rocky mountain chain. I climbed its summit, from whence I overlooked the desert to the north of the river—a grey plain, bordered by precipitous hills of a similar colour. This mountain is formed of a puddingstone, consisting of large masses of granite imbedded in a cement of diorite. As I contemplated the scene, I suddenly saw flames rise in the valley near our camp. Hastening down with the utmost speed, I found that our waggons fortunately were in a safe place; and, our mules having been removed from the danger, we watched the burning of the high and dry plants in the valley with the interest which so striking a scene affords.

We had now reached the lower course of the river, where the bottom land is covered with shrubs and trees, and enclosed by the perpendicular embankments of higher alluvial masses. The shrubs are principally acacias, many of them the same as in similar localities on the Rio Grande. On these embankments I remarked what is interesting as explanatory of facts in the vegetation of this region. The roots of the algarobbia were laid bare, and it was evident that they sought the necessary humidity at a depth quite extraordinary in comparison with the proportions of the shrub or tree. It is thus clear how the mezquite becomes green and blossoms in the spring, before the advent of the summer rains. At the same place I saw, for the first time, a remarkable and very beautiful tree or shrub, which somewhat resembles the above-mentioned Corchi. It seems rare, for I found it two or three times only. The stem, branches, twigs and small thorns are of a greyish green; it is without leaves, but the twigs are so finely divided, that from a distance it appears covered with delicate foliage; twigs and thorns are covered with small red glands, containing a resin or oil, which is strongly scented, like a mixture of carraway, aniseed, and violets. The seeds, which were just ripe, were in pods, each containing one small bean: the pods are more thickly covered with the same red glands, and the scent is still stronger of aniseed than on the twigs. The ground was covered almost an inch thick with the dry flowers, of a dark violet, with the richest perfume. When in blossom, the little tree must be remarkably beautiful; its appearance altogether is exceedingly delicate and remarkable. The flower is papillonaceous.

We now reached the plain through a rocky pass in the valley, forced open by the Gila. Here this stream unites with the Colorado, and we were now not far from Camp Yuma, a military station of the United States at the junction of the two rivers. The bare, steep, and rocky hills of this pass are a kind of syenite, consisting of finely-grained dark-green amphibole, some mica, with quartz and felspar, partly white and partly rose-coloured, both minerals in separate masses included as in a porphyry. The rock appears rough, split and cracked, intersected in all directions with quartz veins of small dimensions. Different kinds of cactus grew upon it; among them a delicate little opuntia, quite *en miniature*, and a beautiful small echinocactus, with straight white, and crooked black thorns. We proceeded during the night as far as the junction of the two streams, where we encamped on the southern bank. The fort, Camp Yuma, was opposite to us.

Soon after day-break the next morning we saw numbers of the Yuma Indians coming to visit us on horseback and on foot, over the hills, and swimming through the river. Men, women and children, a sprightly and sociable race; the girls pretty and full of roguery, with long, loose hair, clothed with a single petticoat, consisting only of cords and tassels, and strips of soft dyed bark, but arranged with the coquetry of a corps de ballet. And indeed I could only compare it to a scene in a ballet, as these nymphs wandered about among our rough and bearded men.

But these Indians, with all their sprightliness and sociability, can still not be trusted. They are excitable, passionate, and very jealous of their independence: they have already, several times, murdered the whites who have settled in this neighbourhood, when their numbers were small. The passionate temper of these people displayed itself, upon our asking some of the girls who frequented our camp, to collect the mezquite-beans for us, for a certain amount of payment, as we wished to take some waggon-loads of them with us on our journey through the Colorado desert. They brought us some, but demanded quite a disproportionate payment; then appealed to our gallantry, and not finding their wishes gratified they became violently angry, and some of them threw what they had collected into the river. In conduct these girls were less exemplary than those of the Indian tribes we had met on the Gila; but whether this arose from any original difference in character, or was to be attributed to the vicinity of the fort and its garrison, I cannot say. A town, Colorado City, is rising opposite to the fort, some houses being built and others in the course of erection. It cannot fail to become of considerable importance; for it must be the emporium of all the trade of the Gila and Colorado basins, including also the neighbouring oases of Sonora, and eventually of the great Salt Lake district, or at least of part of it. Already steamers ascend the Colorado as far as the fort, by which means the troops are supplied with necessaries. While we were there, a project was discussed for navigating it farther up with steamers, and it was asserted that this was possible for several hundred miles. I do not know the result, as, even in the United States, intelligence from these distant regions is of difficult and rare attainment.

It was the Yumas who murdered the notorious Glanton when he monopolized the ferry over the Colorado, and levied a heavy contribution from all travellers. The passage over the river is dear enough now, or at least, was so at the time of our journey; for we had to pay three hundred dollars for the passage of our caravan, though it occupied but three men for a day. And yet at this time there were two ferries, and consequently competition: one close to the junction of the Gila, the other twelve English miles lower down, at a spot called Pilot Knob, where some houses also have been built. We chose the latter, where we crossed August 5th, and encamped on the north side of the river.

Our intercourse with the Yumas continued here. As a characteristic circumstance I must relate that I sent a Yuma boy from hence with a letter to one of the officers at the fort, and that he brought me back an answer in less than three hours. He had thus accomplished in this time, twenty-four English miles; but I had to pay him one dollar and a half for his service,—for less than that he would not move. He had run there, but had swum down the stream in returning, having fastened the letter in answer, to keep it dry, in his thick hair. These Indians will undertake long journeys, swimming down stream, with the help of a piece of wood; and I saw repeatedly whole troops of men, women, and children floating down the river, which is very rapid and has muddy reddish water.

CHAPTER VII.

From the Colorado to Los Angeles — The Desert — Old Sea-shore — Discharge of Water from the Colorado into the Desert — Different Qualities of the Soil — Toads and Frogs in the Desert — The Little Lagoon — Dead Fish — Mountain Chains — Rain Water — The Stony Desert and the Gypsum Desert — Bones of destroyed Herds of Cattle — Mineralogical Ants — General Character of the Country from hence to Los Angeles — Extent of the North American Steppes — Region of Annual Grasses and Plants — Wild Cerealia — The original Cause of the Absence of Trees is of a Geological Nature — Vallecito — A half-starved Man — San Felipe — Rocky Pass — Camphor Scent of the Plants — Warner's Rancho — Hot Sulphur Springs — Californian Indians — Large Herds of Cattle — Grass and Clover Seed as natural Fodder for Cattle — Santa Ana — One Meteorological Region encroaching upon another — Colonel Williams's Rancho — An expensive Shepherd — We share the Flesh of thirty Pigs with the Vultures — Extensive use of Strychnine — Tertiary Group of Hills — Asphalt Springs — Los Angeles — Return to Civilization.

The preparations for the continuation of our journey left me no time to visit Fort Yuma, or to make myself acquainted with the nature of the Colorado and the land around it. The notorious Colorado desert lay before us, extending northwards from the river to the foot of the Californian Mountains. Corresponding to this on the south, lies a similar waterless waste, through which the road passes to El Altar, by the so-called Tinaje Alta, a dreaded route upon which travellers every year die from want of water. It took us five days after we left the Colorado to reach the first Californian watering-place. There are a few scanty wells on this road, of natural origin, but improved by the hand of travellers. They contain, however, too little water for the necessities of so large a caravan as ours; we therefore divided into three companies, which were to start at intervals of one day, and it fell to me to head the first party, consisting of seven waggons and about one hundred mules.

On the 6th of August, at seven in the evening, we left the dusty shores of the Colorado, in a west and north-west direction towards the Sandhills, bordering the higher portion of the desert on the side of the valley. These Sandhills form a kind of girdle before this higher portion, and denote, according to American geologists, an old sea-shore. A desert covered with dust lies below, the level of which is somewhat lower than that of the Colorado, and even than that of the Gulf of California. One of the channels of this river flows in a north-westerly direction into the desert, and ceases in some lagoons, which, in certain seasons, become dry by evaporation. A plain of hard argillaceous earth extends above, and, rising gradually to the Californian Mountains, passes into a stony desert, from which, descending through the first valley defile, an extensive formation of gypsum is reached.

Along the road from the Colorado to the first Californian watering-place, therefore, a desert of dust, of sand, of clay, of stone, and of gypsum, are following each other.

After the first night's journey we arrived, at sunrise the next morning, at the first watering-place, named Cook's Well. This well is a hole dug in the bed of a dry arm of the Colorado, lying about twenty feet lower than the general level of the ground hereabouts. I do not know whether it is the so-called New River itself, or only a branch of it. The watering of our animals was a troublesome operation: we were obliged to draw the water in buckets. It was soon exhausted, and we were obliged to wait some hours, until it had collected again. However, as we rested here the whole day, we were able to give our animals twice to drink. Water rises in this well in a clayey bed of alluvial soil. In the evening we started again, and journeyed throughout the night. We now first came to the drift-sand hills, which mark the limit of the higher desert plateau. In the bright moonlight we crossed a tract of sandy downs, on which there was no sign of any road visible. After we had proceeded several miles, I perceived by the stars, that our caravan was unawares taking a circular route, and was actually journeying back in the direction of the Colorado. Not much ground, however, had been lost, and ere long we discovered again the traces of a beaten road.

In this neighbourhood I perceived a smell of sulphuretted hydrogen, which, I was informed, proceeded from a mud-volcano, lying at a considerable distance on the northern side of the Colorado, and the vapours of which were often carried by the wind far across the desert. By daybreak the next-morning we arrived at the next watering-place, called Alamo Mocho: it is a much deeper well than the former one, and is prevented from falling in by boards. Together with the water we drew up innumerable large toads and frogs. At this place we met the postman of San Diego, a young man of education, from Virginia, who, for 100 dollars a month, performs the journey weekly to and from San Diego and Camp Yuma. The well itself is below the edge of the higher region of the desert upon which the road runs. The edge is about fifty feet high, and exhibits various alluvial strata, one of which consists of a fine hard clay, its *fracture* shining with a kind of pearly lustre. This clay seems to correspond to the slippery mud occurring in the Colorado, as well as in the first brooks met with at the foot of the Californian mountains, and which is so soft that, on putting your hand into it, you appear to feel nothing. Above and below this stratum of clay lie sand and loam.

We contrived to divide our drove so that each animal was led down the height singly to drink. In spite of all our efforts to keep back the animals above, thirst made them so unruly, that one after another they tumbled over the edge of the declivity. When the first fell I thought it was irretrievably lost, but to my surprise they all arrived below safe and sound.

We travelled on during the night on an excellent road, over a hard argillaceous soil, almost entirely barren, and only dotted here and there with some wretched stunted bushes. We arrived at the Little Lagoon by two o'clock the next morning—a stagnant sheet of water, which only appears periodically: at times it does not appear at all for ten years together, and then lasts for months, or even years. I have already spoken of its rise from the Rio Colorado. Not far distant is another temporary lake, called the Great Lagoon, which is at times united with the smaller one. The country around is a kind of oasis, bare of grass, but overgrown with a beautiful grove of algarobbia-trees, whose fruit yielded a plentiful repast for our animals. In the midst of the Little Lagoon stand mezquite-trees, which have died off in the water. Judging from their size they must have attained a growth of full fifteen or twenty years, and this without being prevented by water; consequently, at no distant period of time, the lagoon must have been continuously dry for that number of years. It must, however, have been in existence before that period, as the soil contains a collection of the mud of centuries. Round the water lay a circle of thousands of dead fishes; the water, therefore, cannot long have receded from out of the river, the fishes having been killed by a gradual and partial drying up of the water. This had happened about two months before, at which time travellers had found some alive, but the whole neighbourhood was infected with the smell of the dead fish. The water was then undrinkable; but it had now no longer any bad organic taste, and was only somewhat brackish: I drank of it without inconvenience.

It appears to me that the alternate filling and drying up of these lagoons is only to be explained by supposing an alternate rising and falling of the ground; the accidental overflowing of the river appears to be an insufficient explanation.

We had now approached near to the Californian mountains: they rose in the west like a high wall, over which, when we raised our camp in the evening, hung black clouds. There is another steep, though not very lofty, mountain-chain in the north-east of the road. This is the north-western continuation of the rocky range of mountains which begins below Camp Yuma on the Colorado, and to which corresponds a similar chain running in a south-easterly direction on the other side of the river. The Colorado Desert is simply a bay running in between the eastern and western mountains, and forming the extreme north-west corner of the lowlands, which formerly belonged to the bed of the Californian Gulf.

The Little Lagoon lies in the State of California, the frontier of which we now crossed. Towards evening we proceeded further, and pursued our way across an entirely barren, hard, and level plain of sandy clay, which was covered with little snail-houses like grains of rice. On this journey we had an opportunity of learning, by experience, that the Colorado Desert—of which it had been asserted to me that it never rained in it—is sometimes entirely inundated by a torrent of rain. Towards midnight we reached a spot where the water stood several inches deep on the ground: the storm, which we had seen at a distance, had discharged itself here, and the sandy clay had prevented the waters sinking into the ground. We unyoked our animals, and let them drink. At day-break we passed Sackett's Wells, a spring lying at a short distance from the road: it would not itself have yielded water enough for our beasts, but, thanks to the timely fall of the rains, we had enough, and to spare for any travellers who might come after us.

The ground of the desert begins here to be rocky, and takes at every step a wilder character—detached boulders, and fragments of stone of every kind, consisting of granite, syenite, feldspar, crystallized masses of quartz, petrified wood, jasper, mica shining like silver, common sedimentary and white saline limestone, numerous shells and other substances, lie scattered about. At length the road descended from the height which it had gradually attained, into a narrow ravine of gypsum. The desert, in its north-western part, forms a flat *contrefort*, from which the road descends instead of rising, towards the mountains. The wild scene is the more surprising, as the traveller might have expected the very reverse. From the flat plain the traveller is suddenly transported into a chaos of furrows, precipices, horizontal and slanting slabs, ridges, pyramids, and every kind of formation of the ground; and high, naked, rocky mountains rise behind them. The ravines are cut in yellow and green clay, in which are seen glittering everywhere slabs and fibrous masses of gypsum. The whole presents an aspect of indescribable sterility, though even in this region of death a few shrubs appear, such as a cactus, a few leafless bushes, especially an ephedra, and a few miniature annuals. The storm of the preceding day had filled a brook running through these ravines of gypsum, with copious water, by which we rested for a few hours. I do not know whether this brook is permanent or temporary, or whether or no it belongs to the Carrizo Creek. Throughout this whole region—from the edge of the desert plateau through the gypsum ravines, as far as Carrizo Creek—the ground is strewn with the bones and skeletons of thousands of sheep, cattle, mules, and horses. The reader may form an idea of this scene, from the fact, that of a single flock of sheep proceeding the year before from Northern Mexico to California, six thousand lay dead on this spot. Many of the dying animals appear to have crept in the pains of death into holes and corners among the wildest rocks. I found in these places numbers of skeletons wedged into almost inaccessible corners and narrow fissures.

I have heard various opinions respecting the extraordinary mortality among animals driven from the Colorado across the desert, especially on the Carrizo Creek,—a watering-place against the dangers of which we were strongly cautioned. Some asserted the waters to be poisonous; others thought the circumstance of drinking too freely after a long thirst, offered sufficient explanation of the fatal effects; while others attributed them to certain plants growing in this neighbourhood, which are only eaten by animals when suffering extreme hunger. The plant pointed out to me as poisonous, was a small euphorbia covered with a grey film, which might justify this supposition. Another opinion appeared quite natural, that on approaching the termination of the desert the strength of the animals, exerted to the utmost by toil, hunger, and thirst, should at last give way. Probably the truth may be that these different causes combine to produce the result.

The origin of the extensive gypsum formation in these parts, is in many places distinctly traceable to carbonate of lime. It is enclosed by limestone forming banks composed of large quantities of loose or slightly attached shells. I may here mention that I found a specimen of gypsum containing grains of gold in a collection of minerals at Los Angeles. The grains were rounded, and in all probability originally belonged to an alluvial deposit of detached fragments of carbonate of lime, which had been converted into gypsum by sulphuric acid. The gypsum with the alluvial gold may therefore be called a metamorphic alluvial formation. That with the alluvial gold was found on the Tejon Pass.

Before continuing the account of our journey I must offer a remark here, connected with an observation I made in the desert. When traversing certain parts of the North American steppes and deserts I have frequently observed ant-hills, formed exclusively of small stones of the same mineral species, as for instance, small grains of quartz. In one part of the Colorado Desert the hills of these mineralogical ants consisted of heaps of small shining fragments of crystallized feldspar, chosen by these little animals from the various components of the coarse sand of these parts. The last time I was at El Paso, a North-American driver came to me and inquired the value of a small bag of garnets he possessed. On my asking in what place they had been found, I heard that these stones—imperfect crystals of red transparent garnets—were the material of which the ants build their hills in the country of the Navajo Indians, in New Mexico, and that he knew a place where any quantity of them might be collected. These remarks may perhaps not be uninteresting in connection with the question relating to the gold-seeking ants of Herodotus.

The Carrizo Creek is a brook rising in the mountains, running eastward through the defiles of the desert, and finally losing itself there. Here we entered on quite a different country. Our way led us over the barren, treeless, steep, and rocky heights of the southern part of the Californian mountains, where springs, surrounded by grass and a few poplars, exist only at great distances in some valleys. They have no permanent watercourses, but in the rainy season wild torrents sweep through them.

During our first day's journey, from Carrizo Creek to Vallecito, we saw once more the vegetation of the Steppe in all its peculiarities. The sterile heights were almost exclusively overgrown with agaves and cactus,—a flora which I have nowhere seen so characteristic as in this locality. It is the species of agave called Mezcal by the Mexicans, and the sweet root of which is collected by the Indians, baked and laid up for store. But the nearer we approached the coast of the Pacific, travelling west, the more humid grew the air, and accompanying this change in the climate a striking change appears in the flora which clothes the mountains. The heights are covered with evergreen shrubs, but here my botanic knowledge was altogether at fault. Here and there some evergreen oaks stood in the valleys, whilst the highest summits and ridges were for the first time covered with gigantic pine trees (Taxodiums), for which California is remarkable. The growth of trees, however, is even here an exception, and this continued the character of the country down to the shores of the Pacific. It may be asserted therefore, that with trifling interruptions the Steppe, beginning on the Missouri, extends on the one side through the territory of the Rio Grande as far as the Gulf of Mexico, and on the other to the shores of the Pacific. The reader will have seen, from my description of the scenery, that the vegetation, apart from the general absence of trees, is of a greatly varied character. As we approached the slope of the continent toward the Pacific, the annual growth of grasses and herbs is an important feature in the vegetation; but as soon as we cross the principal range of the Californian mountains—which seems to form a complete line of demarcation in reference to the meteorological character of the country—wild oats and wild clover cover hills and valleys almost exclusively for many hundred miles. The clover too—at least some species—is of annual growth, and its seed, which covers large extents of ground, forms for months almost the exclusive food of herds of cattle, which are numbered by thousands. The wild oats I saw in the south of California, and especially those on the hills behind Los Angeles, was as thick, as tall, and with as heavy ears as the finest cultivated oats in Europe. I found wild barley in the neighbourhood of "Warner's Rancho," far from the road or any human habitation, in a perfect wilderness. And lastly, I saw a sample of wild wheat at an agricultural exhibition at San Francisco, which was wonderfully fine; but I could learn nothing more than that it came from the Sierra Nevada. I am thus tempted to call the climate of these parts, from the Gila, where the annual grasses begin, a normal climate for cereals, exclusive of maize, for which California appears to be less adapted; barley takes its place here, at least as fodder for horses and mules.

The absence of trees in a large part of the North American continent is an interesting point for inquiry to the botanist, climatologist and geologist. Throughout California the opinion prevails, that no trees can be grown in those places where none are now growing. There exists, however, positive proof to refute such an opinion. In the farthest settlements of the prairies on the Missouri I have seen planted Robiniæ grow as vigorously as in any spot in the United States. No trees grew formerly in the place on the Texan coast where the town of Galveston now stands, and yet at the present time there is no scarcity of them in the streets and the gardens of the town (mostly Ailanthus), all exhibiting a healthy and vigorous growth. The elevation above the sea has nothing to do with the cause of this phenomenon as considered under a general point of view, since the treeless regions extend from the sea-coast on the one side, across the highest summits of the table-lands of the central countries down to the sea-coast on the other side. The few exceptions from this general character of the vegetation are seen at the bottom of valleys, cut into the plateau, and upon the highest summit of the mountains rising above them. From this fact the conclusion might be drawn, that deficiency of moisture is one of the many causes that produce the phenomenon, although it cannot be the chief cause, for the prairies of lower Texas are as little deficient in moisture as the Californian coast. Without entering further into this subject, I wish merely to offer here an opinion, suggested by my personal observation, that the main cause of the deficiency of trees must be looked for in the geological history of these regions, viz., in the nature of those circumstances which have clothed these regions with any vegetation, and of those which later on befel them. I have no doubt that in the course of time a great part of the present treeless regions of the continent will be clothed with trees.

Vallecito is a small green oasis, surrounded on all sides by barren mountains. The vegetation of the valleys consists partly of grass, partly of mimbre and other bushes of the Rio Grande districts reappearing in this region. Here we saw the first Californian settlement, a single house, which was, of course, a shop: provisions, ready-made clothes, and other requirements for passing travellers were sold at incredibly high prices. The stock of our provisions was unfortunately so low, that I was obliged to make large and dear purchases for the part of our caravan entrusted to me. I conversed here with a sick man, who, a few weeks before, having lost his way in the desert of the Colorado, had been plundered by some Yuma Indians of all he possessed, and had passed several days, naked and without food, until he met some travellers, who took care of him. He was very weak, and had a sore, nearly three inches across and half an inch deep, in his back.

Our road now led us through a succession of settlements. First came San Felipe, a group of houses or huts, inhabited by civilized Indians. The road from Vallecito to this place passes through a defile, with the worst road on the whole extent from the Guadalupe Pass down to Lower California. In several places the cleft was so narrow that the wheels grazed the rocks on either side. The flora of this wild mountain spot was very peculiar: a small agave, with yellow flowers and a sweet smell, a delicate opuntia, a juniper with red berries, and various labiatæ, with a strong scent of camphor, attracted my notice. This scent in some places quite filled the air. I had before remarked on the Gila various herbs with a strong smell of camphor.

We spent the night in the valley, our animals finding the necessary food, and the following morning, over a pass, —called Warner's Pass by the North Americans, and Puerto de San Felipe by the Mexicans,—we reached

Warner's Rancho, a locality known by the name of Agua Caliente to the old Californians. The road over this pass is not difficult, and on the summit we had an interesting view of mountain scenery. Oaks and plantains grow on the elevation, the neighbouring declivities are clothed with evergreen shrubs of various species, and the distant peaks are crowned with a forest of tall pines. Warner's Rancho is a piece of land several square miles in extent, claimed by a Mr. Warner, but which was one of the many disputed land-claims at that time in the State. It is the most beautiful and valuable spot in the whole mountain district, through which our road led. Well watered by numerous springs, provided with excellent grass and all the natural conditions for agriculture and the industry of man, this locality could maintain a considerable town and several villages: a German colony, intending to settle in California, could scarcely select a more advantageous spot. The hills and mountains are overgrown with underwood, intermingled with scattered oaks, in part with regular woods, presenting numerous sites of peculiar beauty. The climate is salubrious: the heat of the Colorada region does not exist here; copious rains fall during the winter, while snow covers the mountains. During the summer, vegetation is sustained by heavy dews, such as fell every night, much to our inconvenience: they constitute one of the characteristic features of the climate of the country from here to the coast; and every morning, during my journey to Los Angeles, I found my blanket, my hair, and beard covered with heavy dewdrops. I can assure timid people, who are afraid of exposing themselves to the night-air, that it does not kill, even when it covers us, in our sleep, with dewdrops, as it covers the leaves and blossoms of the fields.

Several habitations have been erected on the territory of Warner's Rancho since the arrival of the North Americans; but the old place, Agua Caliente, a group of houses built in the Mexican style, lies about two miles distant from the road, near a hot sulphur spring, which forms a brook running through the neighbourhood. One has to go some distance from the source to find a temperature which permits to take a bath. I rode over, in order to see the place, the spring, and neighbouring country; but, when I arrived at the brook, I found great difficulty in inducing my horse to cross it. Every time it came near the water, felt the high temperature and was inhaling the smell of the sulphuretted hydrogen, it turned round. Gradually, however, it became accustomed to this smell; but, before entering the water, it carefully touched it with his foot to convince itself of the temperature. I found the buildings of this place inhabited exclusively by Indians, who, when I asked them for their name, called themselves the Aguas Calientes. This name being only taken from the locality, I questioned the chieftain further as to the original Indian name of the tribe as well as the neighbouring tribes. I found it, however, very difficult to attain my purpose. At last he said, as if he suddenly understood what I meant —"Ah, you wish to know our heathen names" (los nombres de gentiles), and upon my answering in the affirmative, he gave me a list of the names of all the Indian tribes in California in genuine Indian words, so difficult to catch that I made him repeat them several times before I could write them down. This list I have unfortunately lost, together with some other interesting notes. The chieftain showed me the certificates of some American officers, of his being a man of good character, who had in no way participated in the great revolt of the

Indians that broke out in this part of the country soon after the North Americans had conquered California. Nothing less had at that time been intended than an extermination of all North Americans. Some Mexicans and a North American desperado—using the Indians as tools for other purposes—had helped giving the impulse. The revolt was soon suppressed, and the ringleaders were taken prisoners and hanged at San Diego. The Indians at Agua Caliente, who had played a chief part in this affair, seemed to have retained a deep impression of its issue; for several persons, with whom I spoke, referred again and again to the subject, and at every opportunity took care to express their disapproval of this revolt on the part of their brethren.

I engaged two Indian girls, whom I met at the hot springs, to wash a bundle of linen for me, and the next day I rode back to Agua Caliente to fetch it; but in vain I sought for the two girls, and at last heard that they lived a long way off in the mountains. I had no alternative but to go in search of them. This business led me to one of the most romantic spots I have ever seen. Small enclosed vineyards and fields of maize were interspersed among wild rocks of granite, eovered with groups of evergreen oaks. I found the girls with their parents, who received me most hospitably; entertained me with green ears of maize, roasted, and with baked roots of mezcal. I conversed with the old man on the change in their position from the transfer of their country to the North Americans. He was satisfied with the change, and observed that it was a good thing they were no longer obliged to work for anyone. He regretted one result of the change—that they were not allowed to drink spirits. The girls wore dresses of good cotton print, elegantly made in the Mexican fashion. They let their long hair hang down, and had wound round their foreheads a yellow China silk handkerchief. The men were naked, with the exception of a cloth fastened round their thighs.

Warner's Rancho was the place where the three divisions of our caravan were to assemble again. On the third day after our arrival the last division came up, and, to our great joy, not a single animal was missing, nor had any misfortune befallen us during that dreaded march. An ox was purchased and killed, and the whole party joyfully celebrated the termination of our toils and privations in the long journey across the steppes and deserts of the continent.

We had not yet, however, entered the pale of civilization, and had still several mountain passes to cross before arriving on the plain of Los Angeles. The first of these passes was called the Puerto de Ahuanca, after a small Indian village. On its western side we found ourselves between two parallel mountain-chains, on a small plain on which was a salt-water lake. At this advanced season there was not a green blade of grass to be seen far and wide, and our animals fed on the grass and clover seed which lay an inch deep on the ground. The mountain-chain farther west, through which our road now lay, was rather high and steep; and the part we traversed consisted of greenstone porphyry passing over into a dioritic slate. Vegetation here must be very luxuriant in the spring. On every side withered tendrils of passifloras, and a pretty climbing asclepias, still in blossom, entwined themselves among the bushes. After crossing a mountain-chain still farther west, we at length reached the Rio de Santa Ana, where we saw the plains covered with cattle. This ground is part of the Hacienda de Santa Ana, the property of an ancient Californian family, whose estates here number 20,000 head of cattle.[1]

Owing to a sudden rise of the river, occasioned by the heavy rains during the last few days, we were obliged to remain here nearly two days, and await the subsidence of the waters before we could cross over. Such rains at that time of the year were an unusual occurrence, and such as had not happened within the memory of man.

The winter is the rainy season in California, but in the Colorado districts, on the other side of the mountains, it is the summer; and the hard rains we encountered here, on the Santa Ana River, were an exceptional transgression of the eastern climate upon the western side of the mountain-chain. The influence of such irregularities is very unfavourable to vegetation, causing the seeds of the annuals—clover, grasses, and oats—to germinate prematurely, and infallibly perish. A few such rains, therefore, may cause the destruction of thousands of cattle, no artificial means for feeding the cattle existing here.

The hills and plains in this country, over which our route passed, were actually covered with immense herds. Leaving the property of the Yorbas family, we came to the estate of Colonel Williams, which has the name of Santa Ana del Chino, and on which are 10,000 cows. We encamped near the dwelling of the Colonel, who is well known for his kindness to travellers. The distance hence to Los Angeles, to which place Mr. K. journeyed on before, to endeavour to dispose there at once of his waggons and mules, was thirty miles. Many of our drivers—in

[1] I learn from the Californian newspapers that a German colony has recently settled on the territory of the Hacienda de Santa Ana, the members of which turn their attention to the cultivation of the vine. A more favourable situation cannot be imagined.

fact all the North Americans—who had either hired themselves in order to travel to California free of expense, or who, on our arrival in the gold country, demanded too high wages, were dismissed. The Mexican muleteers were sent with the herds to the hills for pasture, and I, with a few others, remained to guard the camp until further arrangements were concluded. Four or five days passed thus, which I partly spent with the Colonel, a native of the United States, who had been married to a daughter of one of the oldest and most prominent Mexican families in California, and was a resident in the country long before its annexation. We had much conversation on the past and present condition of the country. His estates cover eight square leagues—about seventy English square miles—in one of the most beautiful plains in the State of California. Lofty mountains rise all around; some, as the Cerro de San Antonio, so high that they are covered with snow the greater part of the year. The Colonel settled here in 1840; and, before this country was transferred to the United States, and the Mexican peon-law abolished, he had had 1200 Indian peons in his service. But since that change took place, and the Indians acquired freedom to go where they please, they have retired to the neighbouring mountains, and it is difficult to get any of them to work, even for wages. The labour of free whites is paid exceedingly high; for instance, the Colonel has to pay a shepherd five dollars a-day—a rate of wages which, with roast-lamb gratis to boot, will appear rather high to a European landowner. But, apart from these obstacles, the estate had suffered greatly in the Californian war: the buildings were dilapidated, and 10,000 vines, with 4000 fruit-trees, had been destroyed. By the robberies of the Tulare Indians the estate had since lost horses to the value of about 13,000 dollars. Scarcely anything was left of the 13,000 acres of cultivated land, and the orchards and vineyards. The Colonel's possessions now consist only of his land, with 10,000 head of cattle, and a few thousand sheep feeding on it. The breeding of sheep of the better breeds has been recently introduced, and promises great results in every way. The Colonel regards pigs as noxious animals: he sent me word one day to our camp that he had killed thirty pigs, and, if we liked pork, we were welcome to help ourselves—the rest would feed the vultures.

One day I rode to the hills, on which our mules were grazing. A pasture like this is indeed known in scarcely any other part of the world: our animals were knee-deep in wild oats, fields of which stretched over hill and valley. The season was unfavourable, as there was now only the stubble standing: the seed, however, covered the ground among the stubble, and the mules fed on this. In this ride I also passed through a part of the cattle belonging to the estate, which covered the hills for miles. In these herds, many are killed by the wild beasts—wolves, bears, and cuguars. The proprietors use great quantities of strychnine to destroy these, the effect of which I witnessed. As I was riding out one day, I met one of the people of the estate throwing about poisoned meat; and, on my return a few hours later, there already lay a dead wolf in the road. In the same manner the Colonel has tried to destroy the earth-squirrels, which, together with owls and rattlesnakes, live in holes in the ground, and are here the greatest enemies to the farmer. The Colonel strews corn, poisoned with strychnine, before the holes of these little animals.

The hills of which I have spoken form a tertiary group in the space between the high plutonic mountain-chains, and they stretch thence to the coast below Los Angeles. They consist of bituminous sandstone, limestone, marl, and clay, and are remarkable for the numerous asphalt springs found in them. I inspected some of the latter, and was particularly struck at finding several of them on the ridge of a hill, so that they flow down on both sides. The asphalt oozes slowly out of the ground in a thick mass, with a little water. In its course it quickly stiffens, rising like a thick-setting porridge. The inhabitants of this part use this production in various ways. Mr. Williams uses it as fuel; and throughout this part of California flat roofs are covered with it, to render them impervious to water.

On the 6th of September, Mr. K. returned to the camp from Los Angeles, with a purchaser for his waggons and mules. The latter were inspected, and the bargain concluded. We drove to the town in an elegant carriage, with a pair of spirited horses, and thus terminated my travels over the wilderness of North America. At Los Angeles, Mr. Francis Mellus, a wealthy and influential man, and a member of the Legislature of the State of California, offered me the hospitality of his house. I slept on a gilded bedstead with silk curtains, and under a silk counterpane. The furniture of the splendid saloon I occupied consisted of Chinese works of art, with costly carving; and for a time I was surrounded with all the luxury of civilized society. Such contrasts are only to be found in America.

CHAPTER VIII.

Physical Geography of the North American Continent — Retrospect of its Orologic Relations — Southern Termination of the Rocky Mountains on the Upper Rio Grande — Their Southern Equivalents — Sierra Madre — Frequency of the name — The Great Sierra Madre of Cinaloa and Sonora — Its Northern Equivalent in the Californian Mountain-system — Interior longitudinal Basin of the Western Half of the Continent — Depression of the Plateau between the middle Rio Grande and the middle Gila.

BEFORE I offer to my readers my observations and experience during my residence in California, this will be the proper place to take a retrospect of a few of the great physico-geographical relations of the North American continent, respecting which I have been led to differ in some points from the prevalent opinions. In this I refer to the general arrangement of the mountains from the system of the Rocky Mountains west to the shores of the Pacific. I published a little treatise on the subject in a San Francisco journal during my residence at that place, which has been reprinted in the annual scientific report of the Smithsonian Institute. A meritorious American geologist has since propounded opinions on the orology of America which differ from those I have expressed. This led me to reconsider the subject, but I still think I am correct in the following remarks.

It is well known, that the erroneous idea that mountain-chains must necessarily be watersheds, and watersheds must be mountain-chains, has long prevailed among geographers, and especially map-makers, from their imperfect actual knowledge of the earth's surface. Accurate topographical surveys, however, have not only corrected such mistakes on the map of Europe, but have rectified the theories of geographers. Yet in their manner of representing other parts of the world, into which hypothetical opinions must still enter largely, the effects of erroneous theories are not wholly removed; and this, among others, is the case with North America, to the orological system of which country I here allude. Here a connexion of the great system of the Rocky Mountains with that of the Sierra Madre of the Western Mexico is still credited, to have the eastern and western slopes of the continent separated by a great mountain-chain coinciding with the watershed. But the actual nature of things contradicts this opinion.

It would be far more correct to speak of a general connexion between all the mountain-chains and table-lands which occupy the whole western side of the New World, from Tierra del Fuego to the North Arctic Ocean. Conceived as a great system and contrasted with the extensive lowlands to the east of it, the western portion of the continent really forms a natural division, with subdivisions which, of course, are in some connexion with each other. But this fact is quite irrelevant to the question whether two secondary links in this system—the Rocky Mountains and the Sierra Madre—have any direct connexion, or whether, on correct principles, they can be regarded as orological equivalents in the construction of the whole. I shall endeavour to show that this is not the case.

I.—The great chain of the Rocky Mountains is divided, near the sources of the Rio Grande, into two ranges, one of which follows the western, the other the eastern side of the river; the latter as far as the latitude of Santa Fé.

The reader who has followed me in my journey from Missouri to New Mexico, may perhaps remember that the road down into the valley of the Rio Grande leads, on almost level ground, through a narrow passage in the rocks. Supposing that the sandstone ridge through which this pass runs is to be considered a part of the Rocky Mountains, this ridge will in that case lie on the eastern side not only of the Rio Grande but of the Rio Pecos, its southern continuation terminating in the plateau of Western Texas. But between the Upper Pecos and the Rio Grande, the Santa Fé road is bounded on its north side by high Alpine mountains, covered with snow during the greater part of the year. Southwards continues a range of isolated mountain groups, to which belong the Placer, Sandilla, and Manzana mountains. The road runs round the extreme southern promontories of the higher chain over table-lands six to seven thousand feet above the level of the sea, which terminate abruptly towards the valley of the Rio Grande, and the declivities and detached portions of which present here a system of mountains quite of a different geological character to that of the isolated groups rising above the edge of the plateau,—the rocks of which are of a plutonic and metamorphic nature. Regarding these mountain groups and table-lands as the southern continuation of the Rocky Mountains, these are also on the eastern side of the Rio Grande, and likewise terminate in the Texan plateau. In one point of view, it is correct to recognize in these mountains really a continuation of the Rocky Mountains; but it must be clearly understood that it agrees better with the general orological system of this country to connect them with that range which commences on the western side of the Upper Rio Grande, and the subordinate branches of which successively cross the river in the space between Santa Fé and the bend of the river near Santa Barbara.

II.—Whoever has travelled from El Paso down the Gila to California is aware that the old road, known by the name of Cook's Route, in the great southern bend, leading to Santa Cruz, crosses several heights, all of which might be avoided, were the traveller not dependent on the few watering-places in these regions. The road would run round the heights near the Rio Grande, if it kept more to the south; and round those farther west between the Guadalupe Pass and the valley of Santa Cruz, if it kept more to the north. In the first case, it would pass round the last spurs of a mountain-system lying farther north; in the latter case, it would avoid the extreme promontories of the chains situated farther south. But even the former of these two systems, that farther to the north, including the Coppermine Mountains and the Sierra Blanca, with their secondary groups—independently of the fact that, between it and the mountains of the Guadalupe Pass, a broad depression of the table-land exists—cannot well be regarded as belonging to the Rocky Mountains. It forms a group separated from the last chains of that system by another depression occupying the space between the Little Colorado and the Rio Grande, and containing the sources of the Gila. Nor would it affect the principal question if we should find reasons for supposing the mountains near Socorro, which rise in picturesque forms on the west side of the Rio Grande, to belong to the system of the Rocky Mountains, as the heights which extend between Valverde and Santa Barbara on that side find their continuation east of the river, forming that series of narrows which oblige the traveller to leave the valley, and pass through the ill-reputed Jornada del Muerto, or Dead Man's Journey, in which, in the dry season, not a drop of water is met with for ninety miles.

III.—A mountain-chain, called the Sierra de los Nimbres, has been laid down as the connecting link between the Rocky Mountains and the Sierra Madre; but the traveller in vain seeks it at the designated spot. I have before spoken of this circumstance in relating my travels through that territory, and stated that the Rio de los Nimbres, which has its rise in the southern spurs of the Coppermine Mountains, flows in the rainy season over extensive plains as far as the Laguna de Santa Maria. There is, consequently, on the eastern side of this small river no space for any link of connexion between the Rocky Mountains and the Sierra Madre; whilst, on the western side, if it existed, Leroux's Route must pass over it. I do not know this route from personal experience, but I have been assured by all those of my acquaintance who have travelled on it, that they passed over *no* mountain-chain, nor any considerable height.

IV.—Having thus shown that the Rocky Mountains, as a connected range, extend, on the western side of the Rio Grande, no further south than the narrow valleys below Valverde, I will now trace the detached groups and chains of mountains, which form, on the eastern side of the river, the southern continuation, or at least the southern equivalent, of this system. The traveller journeying from San Antonio, in Texas, to El Paso, or the Presidio del Norte, must cross mountains which, west of the Pecos, mark a step of the ground over which the highest region of the plateau of western Texas is reached. The route across this range of mountains to El Paso leads over the Puerto de las Limpias, or "Wild Rose Pass;" and that to the Presidio del Norte, over the Puerto del Paisano. I have before described these interesting defiles and their picturesque scenery, and I have observed that the mountain-chains of the Sierra de Guadalupe and Sierra del Diablo belong to the same chain. South of the Presidio del Norte, in the vicinity of San Carlos, the latter meets again the Rio Grande, and crosses it from its eastern to its western side, the river making here a great bend to the east in a long and narrow defile, with a series of falls. This is the point at which the Rio Grande descends from the middle section of its course which still belongs to the table-land, into the lower plains of the Mexican Gulf. This range, however, forming the eastern boundary of the Bolson de Mapimi, extends farther south, through the Mexican States of Cohahuila, Nuevo Leon, San Luis Potosi, and Vera Cruz, where it forms the eastern edge of the plateau of Anahuac.

V.—I pass on to the Sierra Madre—a name which has led to many geographical errors. The appellation is, strictly speaking, no proper name, but signifies in general the principal mountain-range of a country—literally, the "Mother-mountain," just as the Mexicans call the principal canal in a system of irrigation the Acequia Madre, or "Mother-canal." The name is thus found in various places, and the geographer would be in error to infer that the different chains of the same name belonged to one and the same system. If there exists a mountain-chain under the name of Sierra Madre, belonging to the above-described range of the southern continuation or southern equivalent of the Rocky Mountains, as laid down on the maps *to the east* of Durango, this is quite independent of the great Sierra Madre, which marks the western border of the Mexican plateau towards the lower country of Mechoacan, Jalisco, Cinaloa, and Sonora, and across which, *to the west* of Durango, passes the road from this town to Mazatlan. A third Sierra Madre is mentioned in New

Mexico on the western side of the Rio Grande, and the Mexican Californians give the same name to that chain of mountains which extends north of the plain of Los Angeles, from the Cerro de San Bernardino as far as the coast of the Pacific, and whose highest summit is the Cerro de San Antonio.

With respect, however, to the great Sierra Madre, the western border of the Mexican plateau,—of which alone I am here speaking,—its structure possesses a peculiarity, which, although it cannot be called a rare orographic phenomenon, least of all in mountains extending along the edge of a plateau, yet has caused frequent errors in maps. Almost all the more important rivers which fall into the Californian Gulf take their rise on the high plains of the inner plateau, consequently upon the *eastern side* of the Sierra Madre. They force their way through the border-mountains in narrow fissures or gullies, and enter the coast-land at their lower western foot. I have already enlarged upon this fact with reference to the Rio de Papigochic, one of the two sources of the Rio Yaqui, when describing in a previous chapter my journey from Chihuahua to the Sierra Madre. The river flows for about sixty miles along the eastern foot of the mountain-chain, until it suddenly makes a right angle, rushes into a deep gully, and along this forces its way through the border-mountains. The road from Chihuahua to the rich mining-town of Batosegachic leads through a similar cross fissure, along one of the sources of the Rio del Fuerte. Geographers do not seem to know that the western border-mountains of the Mexican plateau do not form the watershed, but lie *before* the latter to the west, and, from attachment to an exploded theory, they have placed it further to the east; thus bringing it nearer to the most western part of the Rocky Mountains than it is in reality, and the hypothesis of a connexion has gained in probability and confirmed the error.

VI.—The last north-western spurs of the Sierra-Madre system are crossed by Cook's Road, south of the river Gila, in the tract between the Guadalupe Pass and Fort Yuma. Near this fort, and consequently near the confluence of the Gila and Colorado, the chain of mountains which extends along the coast of Sonora and Cinaloa, and forms the western foot of the Sierra Madre system, a system consisting throughout of parallel chains, has its north-western termination; but on the other side of the Gila and Colorado it is continued by a mountain range, which the traveller has on his right, at some distance on his road through the desert. In a pointed angle it advances toward the chain extending from the peninsula of California, until they unite. Persons who have visited this part of the country inform me, that the peak of San Bernardino is the central point of their junction. The extreme north-western continuation of the Sierra Madre system thus unites with the mountain range which Californian geologists call the San Bernardino range, but which was known to the old Mexican Californians, as I have before said, under the *same* name of the Sierra Madre. If therefore the Sierra Madre of Cinaloa and Sonora has a northern equivalent, we must look for it not in the Rocky Mountains, but in the Californian system. The real character of the orographic structure of this region, however, only becomes clear when we consider it as belonging to the general configuration of the western half of the continent.

VII.—The centre of this western half, following the direction of the coast of the Pacific, from the isthmus of Tehuantepec to the Arctic Ocean, is occupied throughout its length by a space, which is enclosed by a partly connected partly interrupted system of mountains in the east, and by a similar one in the west.

The greater part of the surface of this space has an elevation above the level of the sea, which bears the character of a table-land,—that is, the two mountain systems form the eastern and western border of it, separate it from an eastern and western lateral terrace, and single unconnected chains and groups rise scattered upon the inner space itself. It is these latter which may confuse the geographer with respect to the main character of the orographic structure of this part of the world, since they form what may seem to be links of connexion between the western and eastern border mountains. In California and Oregon, Utah and New Mexico, and in the countries farther north, the two border-chains are marked pretty distinctly by nature. We have here the Rocky Mountains to the east, the Sierra Nevada, the Cascade Mountains, and their more northern continuations to the west. In Mexico the western border consists of the Sierra Madre, and is likewise remarkably defined by nature, but the eastern one is greatly broken, and consists of that line of detached and irregular groups and mountain ranges, which the Rio Grande crosses in the defiles and falls of San Carlos. Here the great connexion of the component parts can easily be missed. Nevertheless I repeat, that if the Rocky Mountains have a southern equivalent, it must be looked for in the mountains of West Texas, Cohahuila, Nuevo Leon, San Luis Potosi, and Vera Cruz; and if the Sierra Madre has a northern equivalent, this must be found in the Sierra Nevadá, the Cascade Mountains, and its northern continuations: because the first line forms the eastern, the second the western border of the large inner longitudinal basin of the western half of the continent.

VIII.—Although this great longitudinal basin may be called a plateau or table-land, from its predominating elevation above the level of the sea, yet there are considerable variations in its height, and three large declivities—not to mention similar smaller outlets—open through its borders, and form transitions from its inner and more elevated to the outer and lower land: the slope of the Rio Grande, that of the Colorado and Gila, and that of the Columbia.

Between the central part of the Rio Grande valley and the central part of the Gila valley, the plateau is less high than to the north and south of this line. The Laguna de Guzman, as Mr. Schuchart, the companion of Colonel Gray, communicated to me, lies even lower than the surface of the Rio Grande, near El Paso. The Laguna de Santa Maria has the same level. Into this latter lake, as I have already mentioned, the Rio Mimbres pours its waters coming from the north, whilst from the south the Rio de Santa Maria, flowing down the central plateau of Chihuahua with a rapid fall, empties itself into the same lake. A line drawn from these two lakes toward the Dry Lagoon on Cook's Road, which I have before described, forms a north-western continuation of this depression of the table-land; and from this latter point the central part of the Gila can be reached without having to cross any considerable height.

From the mouth of the Rio Grande, therefore, up this river, crossing from its central course over to the central Gila, and down this river as far as the mouth of the Colorado, we can follow a depression of the continent from one ocean to the other; which depression, quite apart from the above explained general relations, separates the system of the Rocky Mountains, together with the whole of the

Coppermine Mountains, the group at the source of the Gila and the Sierra Blanca, from the system of the great Sierra Madre in the most defined manner.

IX.—From the above it is evident that, to connect the Rocky Mountains with the Great Sierra Madre is a complete misconception of the orographic basis of the whole physical geography of the North American Continent. This erroneous conception makes the western border of the southern half a continuation of the eastern border of the northern half of the great longitudinal basin on the western side of the continent. In this manner the analogous elements of its physical geography are separated, heterogeneous ones are brought together, and the great foundations of climatology are put into confusion as well as those of the distribution of vegetable and animal life.

CHAPTER IX.

Los Angeles and the South of California — Situation of the Town and Climate — Orchards and Vineyards — Exportation of Fruit and Grapes — Production of Wine — Other Resources of the Country — No Gold Mines in this Part of the State — Indians and Mexicans — Criminals and Desperadoes from the North withdrawing hither — Murders — Departure for San Francisco — Mist on the Coast — Monterey — Aspect of the Country — A Whale — Fisheries of Monterey — The Golden Gate and Bay of San Francisco — Situation of the Town.

LOS ANGELES, or, with its Spanish name complete, Pueblo de los Angeles, "the abode of the angels," is justly celebrated for the beauty of its situation. I should not desire a more beautiful residence for myself and my best friends than such a one as educated and intelligent people might form on this spot. Nature holds here that just balance in its products and phenomena—the happy medium between poverty and excess—which has entered so largely into the conditions of that glorious civilization which the early history of our race has developed in the classical countries of the Old World; and, indeed, for points of comparison with Los Angeles and other parts in Southern California, we must turn our view to the Levant: nothing of a similar character is to be found in the rest of the United States.

The most beautiful view of Los Angeles is obtained from the road which leads to the coast. Seen thence, the little town stands cleanly and elegantly at the foot of a hilly plateau, which abruptly terminates here, and, after the winter rain, is covered with grass and a rich flora of splendid flowers. A clear mountain-stream gushes forth from a gully which opens in the hills behind the town. It has its rise in a majestic chain of mountains, forming the background of the picture, and its waters irrigate the gardens and vineyards, which constitute the wealth and the chief attraction of the place. These gardens are shut out from view by impenetrable hedges, but within is seen a vegetation of extraordinary vigour, produced by the water of the little river, which is distributed in channels over the whole territory of these plantations. In general the environs of Los Angeles are without trees; but these gardens are veritable groves of fig, orange, and other fruit-trees, among which even the date is found, although not abundantly: almonds and olives flourish in the greatest perfection. We can thus form a distinct idea of the character of this climate which, besides its mildness, is remarkable by its pure and invigorating air. Those who imagine that slavery is necessary in southern California from climatic reasons, meet with a complete refutation of their theory; for here we have a climate warm enough for the growth of sugar and cotton, in which the whites not only can work, but really do work with pleasure. The gardens of Los Angeles must be seen in autumn: then the golden lemons and oranges hang heavy amidst the dark foliage, the vines are laden with juicy grapes, industrious and well-dressed people sit in the shade, filling carefully thousands of tidy chests with the delicious fruit, spreading a sheet of fine blotting-paper between every two layers. This elegant carefulness is so thoroughly North American, and yet the whole scene is so foreign to the United States, that I hardly knew whither I had been transplanted. The few date-trees and the Levantine fruit remind us of the East, and yet the manner in which they are prepared for the trade belongs so much to the farthest West, that in this scene the extreme contrasts of the history of civilization meet in a manner only possible in California.

At the time of my presence, Los Angeles had, close to the town and in its environs, one hundred and twenty-five vineyards, yielding an average yearly produce of nine millions pounds of grapes. One half of this quantity was made into wine and brandy: about one hundred thousand gallons of wine were produced, of which the gallon was worth on the average two dollars. Fifty thousand dollars were paid that autumn to the proprietors for grapes shipped to San Francisco.

The grape grown at Los Angeles is the Malaga-grape, of which either white or red wine is made; but experience has shown that the climate of this region, as that of the State of California in general, is favourable to the growth of all the superior sorts of grape. There is a choice of situations answering every possible demand, from its northern to its southern frontier, as from the foot of the Sierra Nevada to the sea-coast. The unsuccessful attempts which have been made in the Atlantic States of the Union to cultivate the grape do not apply to California, since the climatic conditions on the coast of the Pacific are more analogous to those on the western side of the Old World. At all events, the sudden and extreme changes of the temperature, which render the climate of the Atlantic States so disagreeable and unfavourable for many branches of cultivation, are unknown in California. The country about Los Angeles will doubtless remain the chief place for the production of wine and fruit on the American coast of the Pacific.

The manner in which the old Mexican inhabitants have carried on the culture and preparation of the wine is so imperfect, that a really good produce could not be obtained; but connoisseurs agree that a proper treatment would produce a very superior article, which would be of repute in trade. Some Germans settled at Los Angeles seem desirous of giving their special attention to this subject.

In the old Mission-gardens in the vicinity are still seen plantations of almond, olive, and date-trees, and new orchards of this kind have been planted lately. Of the fruits of these trees, olives and almonds are seen on all Californian dinner-tables,—the former pickled, the latter as dessert; but I have not seen dates grown in California, although the tree exhibits a vigorous growth in these southern parts of the country. Probably only the planting of both sexes of the tree sufficiently near to one another is required for the production of dates, as the climate is favourable to the culture of all other Levantine fruits. The ornamental trees and shrubs of Italy and the Levant would also do well here. Laurels, with trunks of an extraordinary thickness, are found among the evergreen trees growing in the defiles of the mountains on the Californian coast. This species is poisonous, and its exhalations are dangerous; but the classical laurel of the Old World might undoubtedly be planted in its stead, and the hedges round the gardens of Los Angeles, which now chiefly consist of willows, might quite as well be formed of myrtles, oleander, or pomegranate bushes, whilst the Italian pine and cypress would greatly increase the beauty of the landscape.

The mineral treasures, which have given to California its chief importance, appear to abound less in the south than in the central and northern parts of the country. I cannot, however, assert more than that this *appears* to be the case. The want of water, so general in the southern half of the State, renders gold-washings either impossible in many points where, perhaps, auriferous alluvial masses may exist, or limits this possibility to a short time of the year. Since all attempts are thus rendered difficult, and there is little inducement to make any, much less attention has been devoted to this part of the country. Colonel Williams showed me some gold-dust which had been found on his own property (Colonel Williams's Rancho, or Santa Ana del Chino), and told me that he knew an auriferous quartz vein on the Cerro de San Antonio, which rises above the plain on which his estate is situated, and can be seen from Los Angeles. Gold had been found here even before Sutter made his important discovery in the central part of the State. I have already mentioned the auriferous gypsum, which, I saw in a collection of minerals at Los Angeles, and I will only add here that this, likewise, was found in a southern locality—the Tejon Pass. During my visit to the State, the report that rich deposits of gold-sand had been discovered at various distances from Los Angeles spread at different times, and produced great excitement. But the result invariably was that gold did indeed exist, but in such small proportions as, according to Californian calculations, not to pay the labour of procuring it, and that all the adventurers coming in flocks, attracted by the discovery, were fleeced by those who spread and fostered the excitement, and who quickly set up shops in the places which had obtained this artificial celebrity. And, as in such cases the assertions of the discovery were suspected, the opinions against it were no less so; and it has often been quite impossible to ascertain the real truth, except by personal inspection and experience in the operation of gold-washing. I am not sure whether the southern part of the State does not contain silver ore, it being well known that this is found in the adjacent part of the peninsula.

Among the mineral resources of California belongs common salt, which is found abundantly in both forms, solid as well as fluid. Until very recently this article had been imported, among other localities, from the peninsula, on the coast of which exist layers of rock-salt. During my stay at Los Angeles I was asked to inspect a salt-spring on the coast, where the attempt had been made to establish salt-works. The space between the town and the sea consists of hills of the most recent formation, and is completely without trees; in this respect the country exhibits the character of the prairies. Nevertheless, wherever the ground can be watered, it is adapted to agriculture. The salt-spring fills a small lake with saturated brine, so that the smallest evaporation causes crystallization. A spring of fresh water is on the edge of this salt-lake, and the whole is separated from the sea-shore by some sand-hills a few hundred paces wide, without however coming into contact with the water of the sea. With this situation, and the purity, concentration, and abundant quantity of the material, salt-works might have been carried on here most advantageously, in spite of the deficiency of fuel in the vicinity, had not, in this very part of the country, rich layers of rock-salt been afterwards discovered, which yielded the article even more cheaply.

I have, in the preceding chapter, touched upon the important subject of the breeding of cattle in the country behind Los Angeles. This section of the State comprises a large number of estates, each of which measures the extent of its area by square miles, and calculates the number of its cattle by thousands. On the whole, the Los Angeles county contained at that time about 100,000 head of cattle, and 50,000 sheep. The breeding of the latter was a new thing, and the wealthy proprietors were beginning to expend a considerable capital upon the breeding of a superior race. Large cattle for slaughter was fetching thirty dollars a-head. The breeding of cattle was carried on completely in the Mexican style, and even the new proprietors employed in preference old Californian herdsmen, of Mexican race, who perform their duties on horseback, and whose chief business it is, once a year, to collect together the branded cattle of the estate, to brand the calves with the mark of the proprietor, and to count over the whole of the herds and flocks.

Hitherto the southern part of the State has been influenced only indirectly by the relations produced by the gold-washings and gold-mines of the northern half. Those who have advocated a partition of the present State of California have argued from this difference in its conditions and interests. The wish to introduce slavery in the south is the chief motive, but the motive is by no means merely the wish to extend the political influence and increase the number of the Slave States. The real wants of this part of the country, whom the vicinity of the gold-mines, and the consequent very high wages deprive of all capability of prosecuting agriculture and the breeding of cattle, enter greatly into the question. This state of things is a severe punishment of the injustice and overbearing with which the Anglo-Americans here, as everywhere, treat the Hispano-American and Indian population, from whom alone could have been derived the labour sufficient for the wants of this part of the country. I believe, however, that the slavery-propagandists will succeed as little in their projects with California as in those with Mexico and Central-America. It will be easier and more advantageous, by a wiser system,—not such a one in which an abstract philanthropy and impracticable doctrine of equality is combined with the most brutal insolence of race—again to collect a population of Mexican and Indian labourers, whose natural position is that of a reasonable dependence to the large proprietors of the soil. It is at least my conviction, that undeniable wants and unchangeable conditions will produce in California classes of population with *unequal* political rights, without therefore leaving space to slavery, so that the course of the historical development in the United States will lead to *three* different forms of social organization. Under all circumstances Los Angeles, with respect to commerce and intercourse, must one day acquire an importance independent of San Francisco, as it is the natural *entrepôt* for the intercourse with the extended regions of the interior.

At the time of my stay at Los Angeles, insecurity of life and bad morals prevailed to an extent by which the beauty of situation and climate, and other advantages of the place were counterbalanced, and quite a number of murders occurred in the short space of my sojourn. The fact of Indians being found dead in the streets at morning was scarcely thought of sufficient importance to constitute a case for a serious investigation. Those of the Indian tribes of California who have passed through the discipline of the ancient missions, and had acquired a certain civilization by this school, have sunk very deep in almost every respect since they have been left to themselves. In the streets of Los Angeles they could be seen gambling, intoxicated, quarrelling among each other, and often in the most disgusting situations. There were, however, other classes of the population not much above these wretches, under a moral point of view. Almost every night pistols were fired in the street under my windows, in consequence of disputes originating in gambling-houses and other places of ill repute. Los Angeles, in this respect, was far below San Francisco, where—through almost a year—I have passed the streets at any hour of the night without ever meeting with an accident or witnessing any suspicious proceedings. But it has just been the good police of the capital, the summary executions of Lynch law in the mines, and in general the greater civil order in the northern section of the State, by which the most dangerous elements of the Californian population were driven south, especially to Los Angeles—the place of exit from the State in the direction of the wild and adventurous regions of the Colorado, the Gila, the State of Sonora and the Rio Grande.

On the 30th of September I left Los Angeles for San Francisco.

San Pedro, the port of Los Angeles, is but an open roadstead, and at the time of my embarkation on board of one of the Californian coasting steamers, only one building existed here, containing the offices and store-rooms of the principal forwarding and commission house of Los Angeles, together with some accommodation for travellers.

The dense fogs, which during a great portion of the year are prevailing on the coast of California, deprived me of the opportunity of seeing the maritime scenery, which is said to be very interesting, the greater part of the coast being of a bold and varied character. The atmosphere, however, was clear when we came to Monterey. Here the coast is covered with a forest of pine-trees reaching down to the rocky beach. At some places it is interrupted by tracts of moveable sand, and we passed a line of cliffs covered with different species of seals. The rocks on the coast at Monterey are granite, quite alive, where they are under water, with flower-shaped mollusca fixed on them. Delicate sea-weeds of exquisite beauty of form and colour are strewed over the beach. A whale, caught not long before our arrival, lay close to the shore, and two others had been caught here a few weeks since. A whaling company exists here, exclusively fishing on this coast; and another company has been established at this place for the purpose of fishing and salting sardines in the bay. Some Portuguese, I was told, have introduced this branch of industry in California. Herrings are caught and salted on the Californian coast more to the north; and the same is the case with the salmon fisheries, and the salting of caviar, introduced in California by a native of Hamburg.

On the morning of October 3rd, we entered the *Golden Gate*. Much had I heard of the grand scenery of the Bay of San Francisco, and I can only state that reality surpassed my expectations. Steep mountains, covered with evergreen shrubs, and reminding much of the character of Alpine scenery, in the region below the snow-line, but above the limit of trees, rise abruptly from the water on both sides, so as to impart something of the character of a mountain-lake to the bay, while hills of moveable sand, occupying some tracts of considerable extent, appear in strange contrast with this general tone of the landscape. From the water's edge the city rises on the side of several hills up to their top, and descends into the little valleys between them. Whatever splendid sites of cities other parts of the world may have to boast of, in North America the palm will never be disputed to San Francisco; and in future times, when architecture will have come up to the grand style of nature and the wealth of California, the Queen of the Pacific will undoubtedly be mentioned among the localities of first reputation for their magnificent appearance.

CHAPTER X.

San Francisco — Elements and Character of Society — The Romance of Utilitarianism — A List of Crime and Bloodshed — Points of Comparison — Californian Life distinguished by extraordinary Acuteness of Intellect and Energy of Action — Strange Remedies for strange Evils — Satisfactory Result of a social Experiment — Natural Character of the Environs of San Francisco — The Climate and its moral Influence — Excursions in the Vicinity — The Redwoods — Scenery of the Coast Range — San José — Artesian Wells — Quicksilver Mines of New Almaden.

SAN FRANCISCO may be considered as representing the combined elements of Californian society. All classes of the population of the State,—all nations from which individuals were drawn thither by the attractive power of gold,—all grades of human civilization,—every development of character which can take place under the conflicting circumstances of a period of fermentation like the present, when the noblest and the basest qualities rise into prominence;—all these fill the thoroughfares of the city. Every European, many Asiatic, and some American languages, meet the ear while you are walking in the streets. This apparent chaos of heterogeneous elements has been brought together, and is kept in motion, under the great form and system of Americanism, with its restless labour, its ever-active spirit of speculation, and its devotion to utilitarian purposes. Here, however, the realism of American life has become so complete that it may be said to have reached the zenith, where, like any other moral principle, it takes the character of its opposite, assuming a tinge of poetry and fiction. It is the romance of utilitarianism, which has its heroes just as well as a more ideal system of social interests—its heroes, its sufferings, and its great and glorious achievements. The trader's business in itself may be eminently prosaic; but when you see the stores of precious bars piled up in the banking-houses of San Francisco, while in the street before the windows are lounging about the bearded and weather-beaten men who brought the gold to daylight, you must confess that you are looking on a picture of wonderful fortunes and incidents, of adventurous life, of remarkable human character, and of extraordinary exhibitions of energy, in comparison with which the fictions of a Eugène Sue are dull and trivial. And how wonderfully are all the figures in this grand composition, various as their forms may be, united into one harmonious whole by the influence of the prevailing tone! The gentleman and lady in most fashionable attire, in splendid vehicle or on high-bred horses; the simple man of business, with his acute and worldly-wise physiognomy; the intelligent mechanic with the expression of independence and security in his trade, and with the consciousness of his dignity as a man and a citizen; the European merchant, who has become a cosmopolitan during a previous residence in China, East India, Australia, Chili, Peru, or Mexico; the smart Yankee, never without a scheme for making a fortune; the slippery lawyer and the unscrupulous politician and demagogue, hand-in-hand with the speculator and land-claimant; the scientific physician, who has received his education in the best schools of the United States and Europe, who has studied in Germany or at Paris; the quack, who had been a barber in his native country, and is now transformed into a great doctor in this distant land of gold; the man of scientific pursuits, with some specimens of newly-discovered plants, fishes, or insects; the projector of great enterprises in mining, metallurgy, and other branches of scientific research; the miner, in rude and often wild attire—here what in other countries is the farmer, the fundamental cultivator of the land; the stage-actor and the clergyman of this or that sect and denomination; the gambler and the musician; the German turner and singer; the Mexican and the South American; the corpulent Chinese merchant and the lank Cooley; the prosperous Chinese courtezan and the low Chinese prostitute; the Tartar and the Malay; the Kanaka and the Society Islander; the free Negro and Mulatto; and, finally, the Californian Indian, formerly the lord of this rich land, and now the poorest and last of all its occupants:—it is truly miraculous that all these elements can coexist and be held together, while the law and government impose the least possible restraint upon the movement of every individual!—Can it be a cause for surprise and indignation that in such a mixed society, extending through the whole State, even to regions were public authority exists only in name, crimes should be constantly perpetrated—that offences should be committed by the community as well as against it—that quarrels should sometimes occur between the different races? The European who speaks with abhorrence of a state of society such as that of California, only exposes his own poverty of experience and thought. Californian life, on the contrary, displays more encouraging phenomena to the philosopher in search of evidences of the innate good qualities and future excellence of our race than any that can be discovered anywhere else. The most enlightened European community, according to my full and most conscientious conviction, could not exist upon a foundation so absolutely democratic, and with so little public authority, without social evils of a far more serious nature.

He who lives in an old and well-disciplined society, no doubt, has a right to say that he disregards the question whether men in Europe, under similar conditions of personal equality and individual independence, would prove worse or better than in California. He has a right to declare that he does not like those conditions, however they may explain and excuse what he disapproves. This, in many respects is a matter of individual taste, in which I have no intention to interfere. My task here is merely to describe and explain.

During my stay at San Francisco I collected from the newspapers of the whole State of California a list of the crime and bloodshed of a single week. Californian life, no doubt, has improved decidedly since that time; but I repeat the enumeration here to show, by a statement of facts, the condition of society which then existed. The list runs as follows:—Suicide of Barrett.—At Sutter Creek shots are fired at a crowd, and a man is killed.—At San Gabriel, Americans, Mexicans, and Indians fire at each other, and several persons are mortally wounded.—Escobar and Sebado are executed.—At Bear Valley the Mexican inhabitants of the village make an attack upon several travellers: one of the latter is shot from his horse and stabbed to death.—The corpse of a Frenchman is found in the neighbourhood of the same village.—Two parties of Mexicans and Chilians fight about a woman, and two persons are killed.—A Mexican of Bear Valley, accused of being one of the murderers in the case abovementioned, is arrested; and, as he offers resistance, is killed.—Several Indians are hanged at Yreka.—Two white men are murdered at Scott's River.—Two muleteers are murdered on the road to Yreka.—In Sacramento City several persons are attacked in the streets.—At Shasta one Mexican kills another with a knife.—An unknown individual commits suicide at Bear Valley.

Such a list of casualties may not be thought an attractive advertisement to draw Europeans to California; yet, if crime and personal danger were as carefully published in Europe as they are in California, and in the United States in general, I think it would appear that certain European capitals are not more enticing, under a moral point of view. Comparisons of this nature, however, are not very gratifying.

Be this as it may,—at any rate I must say that according to my observations, there is as much humanity and benevolence to be found in the mixture of Californian population as exists in the most cultivated European communities. But, in California, even charity is managed in that proud style of American generosity which attributes no meekness to the needy and expects no thanks from them. In the Californian wilds a man may perish from want,—in Californian society not. That society is too proud to bear the existence of poverty in the land of superabundance.

Whatever may be the moral estimate of the social elements congregated from all parts of the world to form a new society in California—and many of the best and of the worst have contributed to the result, from the conscious man of business to the most reckless adventurer, from the scientific philosopher to the impudent charlatan, from the puritan missionary or moral reformer down to the highwayman and the incendiary—however disproportioned may be their moral worth, two important traits of character were common to them: an extraordinary acuteness of practical intellect, and an unusual energy of will and action. Men without these qualities could not easily have found their way to that distant and adventurous region, or, if brought there by accident, could never have continued to keep pace with its general tone of life. Something approaching to these circumstances may exist in the gold regions of Australia, and more lately in those of British Columbia; but even a society composed of similar elements must be placed under the conditions of a self-government as absolute as that of California, to develop those eminent qualities to their full power. It is not without some foundation that Californians, more or less, assume the lofty pretensions of forming an *élite*, a society of men superior to others;—a superiority, it is true, which may be characterized by bad as well as by good qualities. But if Californian life, accordingly, has had its extraordinary evils, it has found corresponding remedies to meet them; and the improving energy on the one side has fully equalled the mischievous tendencies on the other. The insufficient wisdom of official legislators has been aided by the private laws and customs of the miners, strictly observed and enforced in their different districts; and the insufficient integrity of judges, at a period when the bench was frequently occupied by unworthy characters, has been remedied by the direct interference of the citizens. Nobody doubts that innocent persons may have occasionally suffered supreme injustice from the irregular proceedings of excited masses; but these proceedings, from the first turbulent crowd by which a poor fellow, guilty or innocent, was hanged to the next tree, up to the second "Vigilance Committee," by whom some old and incorrigible offenders were banished from the country and others executed, have cleared the State of a large proportion of its worst elements; and after it had once become more profitable to observe than to defy the laws of a decent and honest life, many a man who had been an enemy to social order became its zealous defender. In short, the whole process of development through which the social life of California has passed in a few years, is a striking and most instructive instance of the origin, organization, and improvement of human society from motives of advantage and necessity; while the result bears a strong testimony in favour of the political and social forms and usages of the North Americans, without which the Californian experiment could never have succeeded. No European nation would have had sufficient experience and skill in self-government to answer the wants of a situation such as that of Californian society in its nascent state.

Should the reader have expected to be entertained, instead of these general remarks, by a narrative of personal adventures, or by sketches of the extravagances and oddities of Californian life, I regret that I am unable to gratify my own wish to oblige him. While I have no space left for particulars of that kind, other writers have enlarged upon the subject and have printed it in true and lively colours. Besides, the classical epoch of Californian abnormities had passed before I arrived. During my visit, tacks and nails were no longer paid for with an equal weight of gold,—an opera-box was to be had for considerably less than one hundred and fifty pounds sterling per month,—a fiddler had little chance of earning ten pounds in an evening for playing in a gambling-house; and John Kelly, the Irishman, dressed in a green velvet coat with diamond buttons, carry- the big drum suspended from a heavy golden chain, in a public procession, was no more to be seen. The period of the great conflagrations, by which the whole town had been twice consumed, was likewise over. The first "Vigilance Committee," after it had ordered several executions, lived only, like a dismal shadow that had passed over the town, in the memory of those who had not been members of it; those who had, were bound by oath to keep their secrets. The time of the second Committee had not yet arrived. Nevertheless, some strange things happened during my stay at San Francisco, but the more remarkable of them were related at the time in American and European newspapers, and to repeat them here would be superfluous and out of place.

The environs of San Francisco are of a highly interesting character. The scarcity of trees, which is general over a large portion of the State, is more calculated to heighten than to diminish the grandeur of the scenery, which is altogether of that higher order to which supplemental ornaments are not essential. The outlines, borrowed from the North Mexican style of landscape, are bold, and endowed with a remarkable degree of plastic harmony, on which luxuriant vegetation produces no change. The hills and mountains around the bay are overgrown with shrubs and herbs, grass, wild oats, and an extraordinary variety of splendid flowers. The shrubs, for the greater part, are evergreens, of the growth of the myrtle and the laurel; and, as the winter is mild and moist, the hills and mountains around the city appear more fresh and green in that time of the year than during the summer, when the savanas and oat-fields are dry.

The climate of California, in general one of the finest in the temperate zone, varies materially in different sections of the country. San Francisco, in this respect, suffers from local inconveniences produced by the break in the coast range at the entrance of the bay. The fogs which, during the summer, pass over the city every afternoon with monotonous regularity, are cold and unpleasant. They do not extend, however, beyond a few miles towards the interior, and never occur during the winter, which, in many respects, is the finer season at San Francisco. I have seen days of this period when, after a shower of rain, the sky was as bright as on the table-land of Mexico, the air as balmy as on a morning in Nicaragua, and nature had all the freshness of a lovely May in Germany. Whoever has enjoyed such a day, walking along the hills in the rear of San Francisco, with the view over the bay and the mountains around it, will never forget its charms. Snow may occasionally fall in January, or a light frost occur during the night; but I saw roses, pelargoniums, fuchsias, and calceolarias flowering in the gardens of San Francisco at Christmas.

It is an important feature of the climate of California in general, that it has a most favourable influence upon the energy of the mind as well as of the muscular system: the climate excites to activity. In this character it corresponds to that of the Mexican table-land and the interior of western Texas, but nowhere have I observed it extending, in its full and undiminished influence, down to the sea-coast, except in California, even in the southern district. There—in a region where the orange, the olive, the fig, and the date grow—men feel as active and energetic as in the central and northern sections of Europe. This feature of the Californian climate cannot remain without an essential influence upon the future destiny of this favoured region.

A footpath leads along the shore of the bay in a northerly and westerly direction from the city towards the Golden Gate, now passing over the beach where the zoologist can find a rich harvest of shells, of medusæ and other mollusca,—now over rocks of serpentine, worthy of the attention of the geological explorer—now over a wilderness of sandhills, here overgrown with a variety of shrubs, there extending bare and barren like a little patch of the Sahara, or presenting a scanty but interesting flora of various herbs and flowers, highly attractive to the botanist.

If the rambler continues his walks over the higher portion of the hills, in the direction towards the ocean, he will find himself at last on the brow of a perpendicular precipice, with the waves of the Pacific breaking below his feet. Here, sitting on the very edge of the rock, he may look down upon the feats and gambols of different species of seals, slowly ascending, with the aid of the successive waves of a violent surf, the pointed cliffs that rise in the midst of its roar and foam; till, on a sudden, the whole crowd, from the largest to the smallest, taking advantage of some mighty wave to carry them away from the cliffs, plunge down into the boiling sea, whence their round heads soon reappear in all directions, as they swim about to begin their pranks and frolics anew.

Fifty or sixty miles to the south of San Francisco, on the eastern side of the coast range, is a region called the *Redwoods*. It derives its name from having been covered with a forest of the redwood pine, a sort of *Taxodium* very similar in growth and appearance to that other Californian species which has become famous by its gigantic dimensions, and which different botanists have called *Taxodium giganteum*, *Washingtonia gigantea*, and *Wellingtonia gigantea*. Speculation has long since taken possession of that region, and the greater number of the redwood trees of the locality have been brought to the ground by the axe, and transformed into boards and lumber of every kind by numerous saw-mills. The trade in lumber at that spot has given rise to a town called *Redwood City*. The mountains and hills of this region had been observed to contain numerous small and irregular seams of tertiary coal, by which a company of citizens of San Francisco had been induced to make investigations and trials as to the occurrence of this kind of fuel in a sufficient quantity, and under circumstances favourable enough to warrant the working of a coal-mine. The Company invited me to visit the locality; and the little excursion, which was made about the middle of January, afforded an opportunity of seeing some very attractive spots on the eastern slope of the coast range. This ridge of mountains, with the strata of tertiary rocks inclined towards the interior of the country, is generally bare and rugged on its western, and wooded on its eastern side. Its little valleys, in that direction, are fresh and green, and of a wild and romantic character. While the more open portions of the country, towards the bay, are almost without trees, these secluded localities are overgrown with the most beautiful evergreens. Here the royal laurel, and the stately arbutus, reminding us of the classical countries round the Mediterranean, grow in company with the gigantic redwood pine, which made my thoughts recur to the dark valleys of the Black Forest, and the Thuringian mountains; while the evergreen oak, forming little groves in the dale, or scattered over a grassy slope, carries the mind to the Sierra Madre of Sonora and Chihuahua. A little colony of Hungarian gentlemen have taken possession of some of the finest situations of that part of this region which I passed through on my way back to San Francisco. Commodious though small country-houses, surrounded by gardens and pleasure grounds, had sprung up in a wilderness still frequented by the lynx, the puma, and the grizzly bear.

In the month of August, I made a trip to the little

town of San José, and the quicksilver mines of New Almaden.

San José is situated in a longitudinal valley between two parallel ridges of the coast mountains. This is a prolongation of the space occupied by the southern branch of the bay, in a south-easterly direction. The water of the bay is very shallow on its extremity, and expands into swamps covered, during the winter time, by numberless geese and ducks. A steam-boat brings the traveller to the upper end of the navigation, whence he may take a place in an omnibus to San José. The road passes through a plain covered with fine fields of wheat, and bordered, on both sides, by steep mountains. Two little rivers, recognizable from the distance by the long line of trees following their respective courses, run along the base of the mountains, each on one side of the plain, and empty themselves separately into the bay, leaving the middle region of the valley completely without water, except by artesian wells, of which the most extensive use, and with the most satisfactory result, is made in the valley of San José. The town itself is abundantly provided with water by these artificial springs—every garden and almost every house having one of its own. This abundant supply for irrigation in a climate naturally dry, and almost absolutely without rain during the summer, produces an extraordinary fertility and luxuriance in the gardens and fields of San José. I visited the establishment of a French horticulturist, who had dedicated a ground of many acres to the exclusive cultivation of roses, for which, as for other flowers, San Francisco has a rather extravagant taste, and is a very profitable market. In this garden, an artesian well gave origin to a brook sufficiently copious to be distributed in numerous branches over the whole ground, and to irrigate all the different plantations of this extensive establishment, where, amongst other articles of a nursery, I saw a considerable number of young date-trees.

From San José to New Almaden is a distance of fourteen miles. Several omnibuses pass daily to and fro between the two places. New Almaden, even in a country where civilization and the enjoyments of a more refined life are so recent, has already become a point of attraction for pleasure-parties from San Francisco. There is no want of good hotels at that little mining place, situated in a narrow valley between the steep hills of the coast range; and so much are the Mexican miners, who are exclusively employed there, accustomed to the visits of travellers and excursionists, that as soon as you arrive, and without much reference to your wishes or intentions, you are invited to take place on a sort of hand-waggon, moving on rails, and away you are driven into the bowels of the earth.

The road from San José to New Almaden passes over the continuation of the beautiful plain in which the former place is situated, in a southerly direction. As you proceed the aspect of the country becomes more and more interesting by the park-like character which the plain assumes, and the proximity of the mountains. Near San José the principal wild trees are willows and poplars, growing along the banks of the little river. Higher up large sycamores take their place, and begin to be scattered over the plain. By-and-bye several species of evergreen oaks appear amongst them; until, at last, the whole extent resembles an immense orchard. Occasionally you encounter a small habitation and a tract of cultivated land, with wheat, maize, beans, squashes, onions, tomatoes, melons, and other vegetable productions. The *Rancho de los Capitancillos*, then occupied by a Frenchman—who supplied us with an excellent breakfast of coffee, tea, chocolate, ham, eggs, roasted chickens, and other delicacies which no European would have expected in such a locality—is the finest site in this region. It forms an estate of one square league in extent, bordering directly upon the lands of the mining company of New Almaden.

This little mining city, with its fine hotels, the neat houses of the inhabitants, who are all more or less connected with the principal occupation of the locality, the excellent condition of the road in the valley, and of the single street along which the buildings are erected, leaves a favourable impression on the visitor, and the whole establishment, almost elegant in its appearance, is highly creditable to the company to which it belongs; the buildings, without exception, being their exclusive property. On the opposite side of the brook, which runs through the valley, is a mineral spring containing much carbonic acid with a certain proportion of iron, and it is not impossible that New Almaden will become in time a fashionable watering-place for the San Franciscans.

The mine is situated at a considerable elevation above the valley. We left our hotel at five o'clock in the morning to ascend the hill. The road by which the quicksilver ore is brought down on waggons rises slowly along the mountain side, overgrown with a dense vegetation of shrubs. It took us three quarters of an hour to walk up. We found the miners, who are all Mexicans, just ready to begin their day's work. We were struck by the decent and comely appearance of these men, who were all well clothed and fed, and some of them had quite an intelligent expression. They receive very high wages, at least the directors and owners of European mines will think so. According to their skill and application they are paid (or were *then* paid) from four to eight dollars a day, and thus, even in California, could well afford to look respectable. The mine itself, though but of a recent date, has a number of shafts and tunnels extending to a considerable distance into the interior of the mountain. How I attended the morning prayer of the miners in a subterranean chapel in the interior of the mine, before an altar of the Virgin cut out of the solid rock, I have described in an early part of this work.

According to the remarks of Mr. C. Heusch, a German geologist and mining engineer, published in the *Monterey Sentinel*, the cinnabar, here as in other localities of this region, occurs in the veins of a quartzous conglomerate either in the porphyry or on the line of contact between eruptive and sedimentary rocks.

When I returned to San José, I was astonished to see a stream of water rush through one of the streets, which had not existed two days before. The operation of boring an artesian well for the public use of the town had been successfully terminated in the mean time, and had produced the rivulet.

CHAPTER XI.

Eastward Bound — Filibusters on board — William Walker — Return to NewYork.

On the 20th of November, 1855, I embarked in the beautiful steam-ship *Cortéz*, destined to San Juan del Sur.

Besides a numerous company of cabin passengers of Californian gentlemen and ladies, there were about one hundred armed men on board, proceeding to join the army of William Walker, in Nicaragua. With some of them I was personally acquainted, and I can say that, though reckless fellows, they had many good qualities, and were seriously convinced that they had engaged in a glorious and praiseworthy undertaking.

The course of our steamer lay close to the coast of Mexico and Central America. The summits of the gigantic cones of Guatemala, appearing above a stratum of clouds represented a picture of sublime grandeur. As we passed along the coast of San Salvador we could see, at three different localities, the action of volcanoes. At one place, violent emissions of smoke followed each other in regular intervals of time, each producing a globular cloud, which, after having been ejected abruptly as if by an explosion, rose slowly into the air.

We arrived in the port of San Juan del Sur on the 3rd of October. Here William Walker had his head-quarters at that time. The men who had come from California in the *Cortéz* joined him there.

I have nothing to add to my former remarks on San-

Juan del Sur, and on Nicaragua in general. I crossed the isthmus without delay. On the 5th I was at San Juan del Norte, where the boat from the river brought us directly alongside the steam-ship *Northern Light*, ready for sailing to New York.

On the 13th I arrived at the latter place.

THE END.

CPSIA information can be obtained
at www.ICGtesting.com
Printed in the USA
LVHW102115101022
730381LV00001B/140

9 783375 120085